Nor'west by North

The Tenth Carlisle & Holbrooke Naval Adventure

Chris Durbin

Chris Durbin

Dedicated with the deepest respect to the memory of

François Thurot

of

Nuits, France

Privateer, and commander of the French expedition to the north of Britain 1759-1760

Nor'west by North

Copyright © 2021 by Chris Durbin. All Rights Reserved.

Chris Durbin has asserted his rights under the Copyright, Design and Patents Act, 1988, to be identified as the author of this work.

No part of this book may be reproduced in any form or by any electronic or mechanical means including information storage and retrieval systems, without permission in writing from the author. The only exception is by a reviewer, who may quote short excerpts in a review.

Editor: Lucia Durbin

Cover Artwork: Bob Payne

Cover Design: Book Beaver

This book is a work of historical fiction. Characters, places, and incidents either are products of the author's imagination or are used fictitiously. For further information on actual historical events, see the bibliography at the end of the book.

First Edition: August 2021

Chris Durbin

CONTENTS

	Nautical Terms	vii
	Principal Characters	viii
	Charts	x
	Introduction	1
Prologue	King Louis' Commission	3
Chapter 1	Skagerrak	8
Chapter 2	The Hunter, Hunted	18
Chapter 3	Night Engagement	26
Chapter 4	Breakthrough	33
Chapter 5	Harwich	43
Chapter 6	A Revelation	54
Chapter 7	Sophie Featherstone	64
Chapter 8	A Change of Direction	70
Chapter 9	Nor'west by North	82
Chapter 10	A Meeting	93
Chapter 11	The Snare	104
Chapter 12	A Running Fight	114
Chapter 13	The Challenge	127
Chapter 14	The Hunt	136
Chapter 15	Fool's Errand	147
Chapter 16	News of the French	157

Chapter 17	A Missed Opportunity	164
Chapter 18	Line of Battle	175
Chapter 19	General Chase	187
Chapter 20	Captures	196
Chapter 21	Housekeeping	205
Chapter 22	Prizes Galore	218
Chapter 23	The Port Admiral	225
Chapter 24	Carriage for Hire	228
Chapter 25	Perilous Politics	239
Chapter 26	Local Boy	249
Chapter 27	Sea-Change	258
Chapter 28	Unfinished Business	269
Chapter 29	Fatal Errors	281
Chapter 30	A Bitter Failure	291
	Historical Epilogue	299
	Fact Meets Fiction	301
	Other Books	304
	Bibliography	313
	The Author	315
	Feedback	317

//Chris Durbin

LIST OF CHARTS

The British Isles and the North   x

Approaches to Gothenburg   xi

The North of Ireland   xii

Isle of Man   xiii

Lundy   xiv

NAUTICAL TERMS

Throughout the centuries, sailors have created their own language to describe the highly technical equipment and processes that they use to live and work at sea. This holds true in the twenty-first century.

While counting the number of nautical terms that I've used in this series of novels, it became evident that a printed book wasn't the best place for them. I've therefore created a glossary of nautical terms on my website:

https://chris-durbin.com/glossary/

My nautical glossary is limited to those terms that I've mentioned in this series of novels as they were used in the middle of the eighteenth century. It's intended as a work of reference to accompany the Carlisle & Holbrooke series of naval adventure novels.

Some of the usages of these terms have changed over the years, so this glossary should be used with caution when referring to periods before 1740 or after 1780.

The glossary isn't exhaustive; Falconer's Universal Dictionary of the Marine, first published in 1769, contains a more comprehensive list. I haven't counted the number of terms that Falconer has defined, but he fills 328 pages with English language terms, followed by an additional eighty-three pages of French translations. It's a monumental work.

There is an online version of the 1780 edition of The Universal Dictionary (which unfortunately does not include all the excellent diagrams that are in the print version) at this website:

https://archive.org/details/universaldiction00falc/

PRINCIPAL CHARACTERS

Fictional

Captain John Chester: Commanding Officer, *Pegasus*

Captain Julian Coulson: Commanding Officer, *Fortune*

Captain George Holbrooke: Commanding Officer, *Argonaut*

Captain Edward Carlisle: Commanding Officer, *Dartmouth*

Brigadier Pierre Fouquet: Commander of the French expeditionary land force

Captain Philippe Batiste: Commander of the French expeditionary naval force

Lieutenant Carter Shorrock: First Lieutenant, *Argonaut*

Ann Holbrooke: Captain Holbrooke's Wife

Lady Chiara Angelini: Captain Carlisle's wife

Josiah Fairview: Sailing Master, *Argonaut*

David Chalmers: Chaplain, *Argonaut*

Sophie Featherstone: Ann's stepmother

Historical

Vice Admiral Francis Holburne: Port Admiral, Portsmouth

Commodore William Boys: Commander-in-Chief, the Downs

Chris Durbin

The British Isles and the North

Nor'west by North

Approaches to Gothenburg

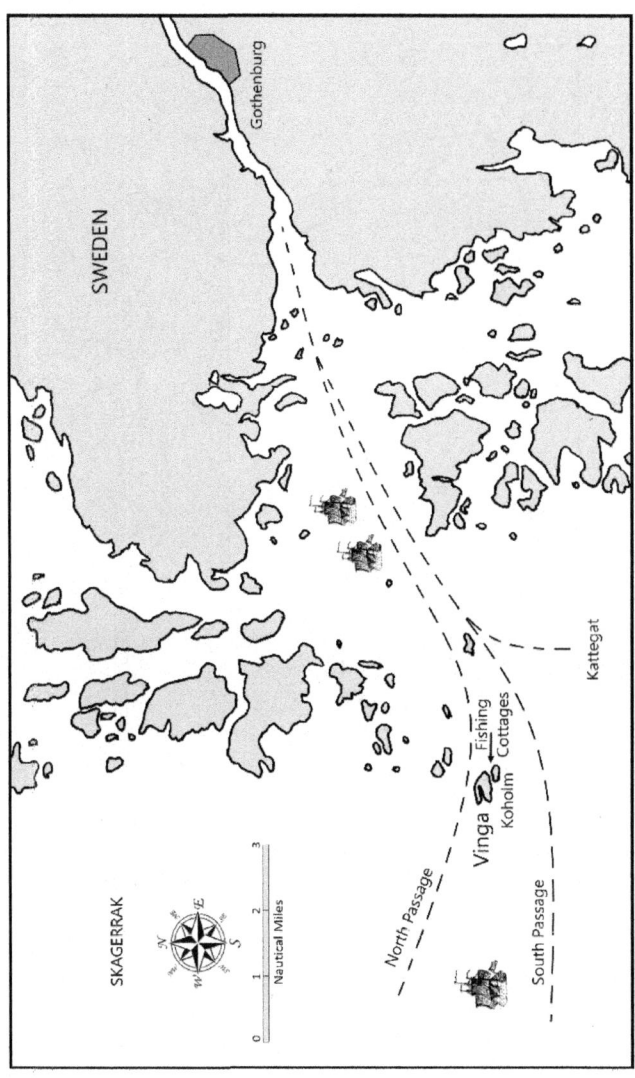

Chris Durbin

The North of Ireland

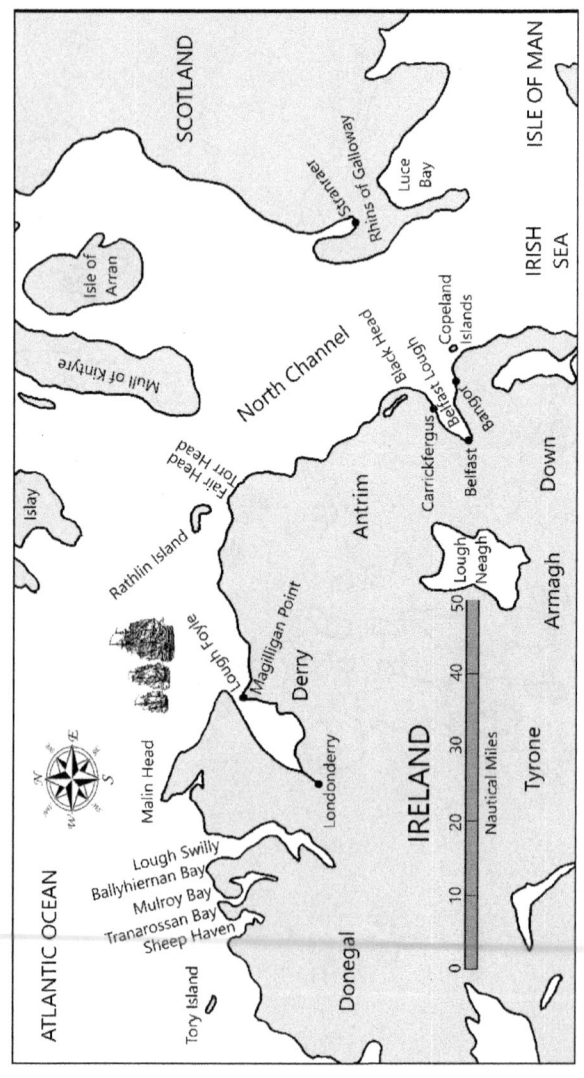

The Isle of Man

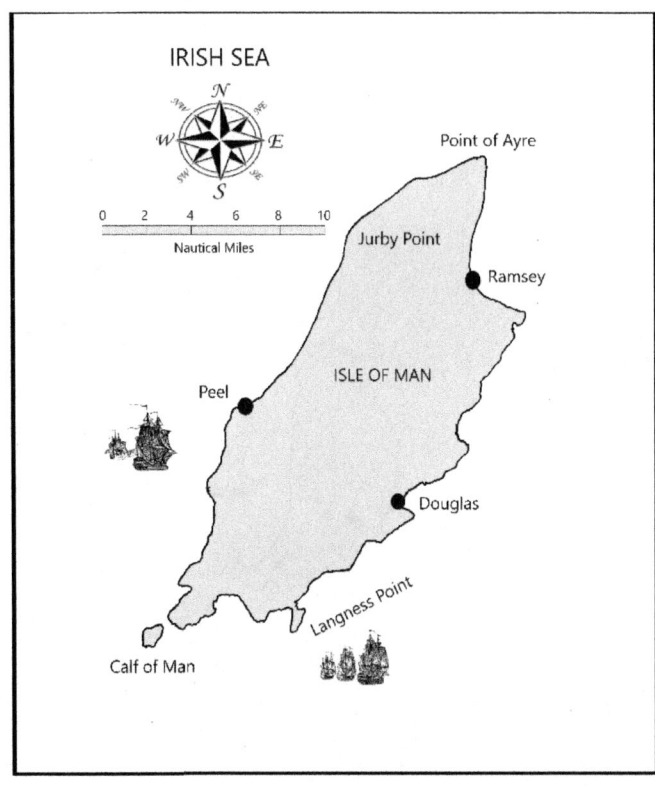

Lundy

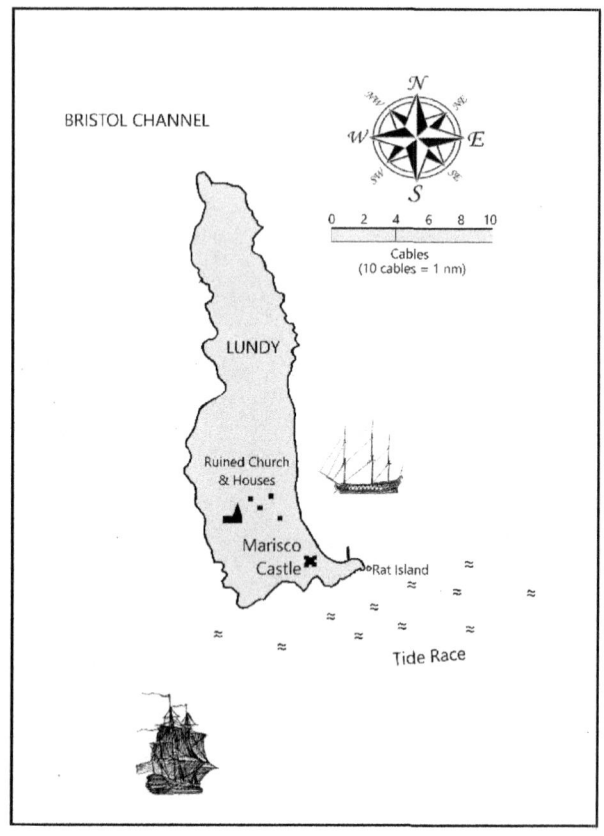

'Full fathom five thy father lies;
Of his bones are coral made;
Those are pearls that were his eyes:
Nothing of him that doth fade,
But doth suffer a sea-change
Into something rich and strange:
Sea-nymphs hourly ring his knell.'
Ding-dong! Hark! now I hear them,
Ding-dong, bell!

William Shakespeare
The Tempest, Act 1 Scene 2

Chris Durbin

INTRODUCTION

The Seven Years War at the end of 1759

The end of 1759 was the turning point for Britain's fortunes in the war. In Europe, the allied forces had won at Minden, and Frederick of Prussia had turned the defeat at Kunersdorf into a strategic victory, as the Austrian and Prussian armies failed to follow up and withdrew to preserve their lines of communication.

In America, the three-pronged attack on New France was nearing its crushing finale, with Quebec and Fort Niagara in British hands and Montreal poised to fall in the following year. In India, the French had failed to take Pondicherry and Madras, and it looked like they had lost their last chance of securing the continent. In the West Indies, the French had lost Guadeloupe and were just about holding onto the remainder of their sugar islands, but at sea their fleet had been soundly beaten at Lagos Bay and Quiberon Bay. The British navy was the master of the world's trade routes.

It was the year of victories, a second *Annus Mirabilis,* and the church bells were worn thin with ringing. It was commemorated in song by David Garrick when he penned the lyrics to *Hearts of Oak*, and such was the mood of national confidence that the massive keel of a first rate ship-of-the-line was laid down in Chatham's No. 2 dock. The building of a first rate was a monumental undertaking in the eighteenth century, and a year later she would be named *Victory* in commemoration of the *Annus Mirabilis*. HMS *Victory* is now the oldest commissioned ship in the world. It can be visited in Portsmouth, UK, preserved from the breaker's yard by a near-miraculous series of interventions.

Carlisle and Holbrooke

George Holbrooke spent the year of 1759 in the Americas. He was without a ship and seconded to the British Army for the expedition against Fort Niagara, as told in the eighth book in the series, *Niagara Squadron*. He organised the vast fleet of boats to carry the army up rivers and across lakes and in a series of brilliant strokes, dealt with the French brigs and schooners that dominated Lake Ontario and threatened to prevent the army from arriving before the fort's walls. Holbrooke returned to England to be advanced in rank to post-captain and given command of the new twenty-eight-gun sixth rate frigate *Argonaut*. His promotion broke down the last barrier that his sweetheart Ann's father had built against their relationship, and the end of 1759 saw them together at last.

Edward Carlisle spent most of the year of 1759 at the siege of Quebec (told in the seventh book, *Rocks and Shoals*). His frigate *Medina* was so severely damaged by French shore batteries on the Saint Lawrence River that it was sent home for repair, and Carlisle was given command of *Dartmouth,* a fifty-gun fourth rate ship-of-the-line. When Quebec fell, he returned to home waters in time to join Admiral Hawke's squadron at the Battle of Quiberon Bay, where the menace of a French invasion was laid to rest in one of the most daring fleet actions in naval history.

PROLOGUE

King Louis' Commission

Thursday, Twentieth of November 1759.
Dunkirk, France.

Captain Philippe Batiste braced himself against the fresh southerly gale and stared at the grey sea and sky. It had been blowing since the previous evening and now the corner of the southern North Sea that lay before him was a waste of choppy waves. Dirty-white spume trailed away to where the sea and sky merged into a vague, disputed zone that was neither one element nor the other. There was no horizon and Batiste knew there would be none until the gale had blown through and the cold, clear air from the north replaced it. His keen eyes scanned from the left to the right, from the straits that separated France from England to the desolate leagues of the open sea that stretched away to the north.

'As I thought, they've been blown off station. They'll be sheltering under the North Foreland until this has blown out.'

He rubbed his hands together and smiled grimly at his companion.

Brigadier Fouquet was not so enthusiastic. Certainly they had to get out of Dunkirk, and it would have been foolhardy to attempt it when the British blockading squadron was in sight, but he didn't care for the sea at the best of times and now in this hard, angry mood, it looked even less inviting than normal. He didn't favour his colleague with so much as a glance but continued staring gloomily at the waves as they beat violently against the breakwater.

'How long will this gale last, Captain Batiste?'

'Long enough to take us clear of the narrow seas, at least,' Batiste replied, giving Fouquet a pitying glance. 'Once we're out into the wider North Sea they'll never find us.'

Pierre Fouquet looked dissatisfied. Not for the first time this unruly privateer captain had wilfully misunderstood him and now he was close to being patronising. Fouquet wanted the gale to stop so that they could have a safe and calm passage – he dreaded the week of sickness that he knew from past experience would be his fate – while Batiste wished it to last to keep the British squadron off their track.

'Then you recommend that we should sail today, Captain?'

Batiste looked at him sideways. Was he jesting? There wouldn't be a better chance perhaps for weeks or months and their mission was urgent. Far away to the south and east of the *Isle D'Ouessant* – what the English insisted on calling *Ushant* – the Comte de Conflans was gathering the Brest and Toulon squadrons together to smash his way through the British navy and escort an army across the channel to bring King George to his senses. The brigadier's fifteen hundred soldiers were intended to be landed in the north of England, or in Ireland, to draw the best of the British army away from the south coast. It was a feint, but a vital one and part of an intricate plan. Batiste was receiving daily messengers from Versailles, demanding to know when he intended to sail.

'Certainly today, Monsieur,' he replied brusquely.

There was no value in explaining his reasoning to this soldier; he had learned that they just didn't have a shared perspective. While Fouquet was a brigadier-general and an established member of both the French aristocracy and the army, Batiste was nothing more than a privateer captain – albeit a notably successful one – and his commission from the French minister of marine was temporary and certain to be revoked if he didn't make a success of this expedition. His whole future depended on getting to sea and carrying out his orders whereas Fouquet's career would continue regardless of the outcome. He turned away to hide his anger and frustration at having to share the command of the expedition with this privileged amateur.

'When will the wind abate?' Fouquet asked. 'Surely it's

dangerous to put to sea in these conditions.'

Batiste stifled a sigh.

'When this gale ends the wind will come from the north or northwest and then the British will be back on their station before we can warp out of the canal. These are the perfect conditions for us to sail. This southerly wind will serve the dual purpose of keeping the enemy at their anchorage and carrying us north. It may be a little uncomfortable but not dangerous. Monsieur, I am sure we have discussed this before, many times.'

Fouquet detected the note of disdain in Batiste's voice. His brief nod could be taken as acquiescence or merely an acknowledgement that he'd heard the privateer. Without another word he turned on his heels and started walking back towards the town, followed by his staff officers. He felt sick already and he could feel a cold sweat breaking out on his brow.

***

It was afternoon before the squadron was underway and the meagre light was fading as the last of the transports left the shelter of the breakwater. Batiste and his sailing master had been watching the weather intently, looking for any sign of a change, but the wind was fixed in the south and the grey blanket of torn clouds hurried overhead much as it had done all day.

'Tomorrow,' the sailing master declared with confidence, 'no earlier, but by tomorrow evening this will have blown through, and the wind will veer into the nor'west or north.'

Batiste grunted and stared at the wild sea. His squadron was clear of Dunkirk's harbour, that was the first step, and now he must decide when to leave the security of the road and steer north. He wanted to be away before the wind changed; he wanted to lose himself in the wastes of the North Sea, leaving the British to guess where he was heading. Batiste looked again at his squadron, backing and filling while they waited for orders. If he sailed now, by the morning this blessed southerly wind would take him far past the British blockading squadron's rendezvous under the North Foreland. He'd have fulfilled the first part of his orders and brought his ships safely past the enemy encirclement, and he knew how valuable that was to Versailles, even if the main landing failed. London's insurance rates would climb, and then many merchants would keep their ships in port rather than risk sailing. Britain's war effort was funded by its commerce, and the navy and the merchants had a mutually supportive relationship. With its overseas trade diminished, Britain would be no match for France.

He scanned the other six ships under his command. Even from here he could see that their decks were in disarray. The soldiers had embarked hurriedly, dismayed to be torn from their comfortable billets ashore in such terrible weather, and now their gear was impeding the handling of the sails. If he sailed now, with only an hour of light left, he ran the distinct risk of losing a ship or two in the night. They wouldn't founder or run aground, but there would be a great temptation to turn back to Dunkirk with the excuse that they would try again when the army's gear was properly stowed. He would have stamped in frustration if he didn't know that half a dozen soldiers – Fouquet's staff officers – were watching his every move. The brigadier himself was nowhere to be seen. He'd excused himself the minute they had nosed out of the canal and was probably puking his heart out in the seclusion of his cabin.

'You are sure of this wind?'

'Certainly, sir. Such a blow is always followed by clear, chilly weather and a veering wind. Tomorrow evening at the latest.'

The sailing master didn't add that the British would be making the same calculations and would surely weigh anchor at the first sign of the change. He'd learned that Captain Batiste – now Commodore Batiste as he insisted on being called – didn't encourage commentary.

'We will anchor at the eastern end of the road,' Batiste declared, 'and we will sail at dawn. Make the signal if you please.'

Batiste was not constrained by the French navy's embryonic signalling system, and he had devised his own for this expedition. A single blue flag hoisted at the maintop told the other captains that the flagship was preparing to anchor and that they should follow his lead. The weather was too wild for boat work otherwise he would have sent orders to each ship to be ready to weigh anchor at dawn, but they would know that without being told. He had used those long months in the basin at Dunkirk to good effect and he was confident that his captains would know what was on his mind, even if they may not always obey him. After all, they were privateers too, for the main part.

By dawn – he hoped – his squadron would be better prepared for the voyage. At the least the decks would be clear to allow the sailors to work the ships and man the guns. He had spent much of the past few months gathering intelligence on his immediate opponent, and what he had discovered had persuaded him that he needed to escape from these narrow seas as soon as possible. Commodore Boys had commanded the squadron that covered the Straights, the Downs and the approaches to the Thames since the beginning of the year. His ships had become a familiar sight as they maintained their tight blockade of the French coast from Dunkirk west and south towards the Bay of the Seine. It was only in southerly gales that his ships couldn't hold their stations, and then they withdrew to the shelter of the North Foreland. Batiste was lucky that not even a cutter had managed to keep the sea off Dunkirk, but even so there were enough fishermen and smugglers to send word that his squadron was at sea. Tomorrow, God willing, they'd be underway and then let the British search for them!

***

CHAPTER ONE

Skagerrak

Monday, Fourth of February 1760.
Argonaut, at Sea. Off Gothenburg, Sweden.

'No bottom! No bottom on this line!'

Captain George Holbrooke of His Britannic Majesty's frigate *Argonaut* stared impassively ahead into the blackness, making no acknowledgement to the report. He had heard it, of course, but his mind was busy with a hundred different calculations and the fact that they were in water deeper than twenty fathoms was just one of the countless fragments of information that he was processing. He was engaged in that most perilous of occupations, navigating his ship on an unfamiliar lee shore – a bold lee shore where the seabed rose from thirty fathoms to the wave-washed rocks in less than a mile – and he was doing it at night. Some part of his mind registered the actions of the seaman in the windward main chains. He saw the lead swing underhand: once, twice, thrice, then a deft shift of the wrist brought it in a whirring arc over the seaman's head. He released the line at its zenith and the nine-pound weight carried it far ahead to drop unseen and unheard into the water. There was a pause as the line ran through the leadsman's fingers until, for a brief moment, it hung suspended vertically.

'No bottom on this line, sir.'

Was there a hint of sulkiness in the leadsman's voice? Holbrooke could hardly blame him; the air temperature was near-freezing and the wind and the constant wetting from the lead line must have been uncomfortable, to say the least. He just hoped that the man had been given a leather apron to prevent his chest and lower torso being soaked, but of course the bosun would have seen to that.

'What's your course now, Master?'

The quartermaster stood aside to allow Josiah Fairview

to peer at the steering compass by the light of the binnacle lantern.

'Nor' by east, half east, sir,' he looked quickly up at the tops'ls, 'full and by.'

Holbrooke nodded but said nothing. If Fairview's calculations were correct, they were being set to the south by the last gasp of the North Sea's tidal influence before it petered into triviality in the Kattegat and then to nothing in the true Baltic Sea. *Argonaut* was being drawn southwards at the rate of two knots and the last cast of the log showed that the frigate was making three knots through the water. Since then, the main and foresail had been clewed up and the frigate's speed had noticeably decreased. *Argonaut* would be moving crabwise across the tidal stream, making barely any way to the north but easing slowly eastwards, down towards the unseen shore. Her tops'ls, jib and mizzen were balanced to a nicety and her movement through the black water was smooth and easy. The only jarring note came from the clewed-up main and foresail where the loose bunts of sailcloth flapped and fretted in their confinement. It was an un-seamanlike practice to sail thus but, in this case, it had the double advantage of keeping the big courses ready for immediate use and avoiding calling the watch below to furl the sails.

He heard the bell from the fo'c'sle – three double strokes and a single – seven bells in the last dog watch. The sun had set two hours before and the waxing gibbous moon wouldn't rise for another hour and a half. For all they could see beyond the gunwales it might have been midnight. The stocky figure of the mate of the watch loomed out of the darkness.

'Two knots and a tenth, sir, if you please,' he said, holding his hat across his chest.

'Thank you, Mister Petersen.'

The mate had an appropriate name for this part of the world, Holbrooke reflected, and he offered another point of data to add to his calculations. Wind, tide, course, speed:

they were all factors to be considered in determining a reckoned position. His last good fix – a compass bearing and estimated distance of the nearest of the islands that lay off the Gothenburg River – had been taken as the last rays of the setting sun glanced off its rocky shore. It was over two hours old and of decreasing value as time passed. Yet Holbrooke was confident. Even the inability to find the bottom with a twenty-fathom line added to his stock of information: it told him that he must be at least a mile from the nearest land.

'What's the name of that island, Mister Fairview?'

'Vinga, sir.'

'Ah, thank you, it had slipped my mind.'

Vinga, the furthest west of the islands that guarded the approaches to Gothenburg. It was a good place to lie in wait for traffic coming down the river. There were two passages through the archipelago and Vinga lay between them. Anything larger than a fishing boat must certainly choose one or the other, and he was betting that his quarry would select the northern, the nearest to their escape route into the wider ocean beyond the Skagerrak. He looked at the sails and at the compass. Yes, the French could just make the northern passage with this wind, if it didn't back further south.

'Deck there. Light to leeward.'

That was the lookout at the masthead. There was just a hint of thickness in the air, not enough to be called mist and certainly not fog, but the lookout was above it, in the clearer, colder air aloft. Holbrooke took the speaking trumpet from its bracket and angled his face upwards.

'Masthead. What do you make of it?' he called.

'I don't think it's a ship, sir, nor even a boat. It could be some houses on the shore. It's four points off the bow sir.'

'Send a midshipman up to have a look, Mister Fairview.'

'There are a few fishermen's houses on Vinga, sir. It could be one of them. It's likely that we would see a lamp a mile or two off on a night like this.'

Nor'west by North

Holbrooke was lucky to have Fairview as his sailing master. Not only had they served together previously, in his old sloop *Kestrel*, but for the whole of the year of 1759, while Holbrooke had been campaigning on the North America frontier – he still had nightmares that involved Iroquois scalping-knives – Fairview had sailed as a master in the timber trade between the east coast ports and Sweden. He knew these waters of the Skagerrak as well as any Englishman and he'd taken his merchant brig up the Gothenburg River on half a dozen occasions. Not for the first time, Holbrooke wondered what malign forces in the Admiralty or Trinity House prevented Fairview being given a ship-of-the-line, but that was a puzzle for another day. In the here-and-now it was only Fairview's presence that made tonight's endeavour possible. Normally he'd have taken a local pilot to navigate these waters, but the political situation was just too sensitive with Sweden clinging onto neutrality at sea while openly favouring King Louis on land. Without Fairview's local knowledge he would never have dared to sail so close to an unknown shore at night.

'What makes you believe it's Vinga and not one of the other islands, Mister Fairview?'

'Vinga's the only inhabited one,' he replied. 'Nobody would care to live out here in the winter, but the fishing is so good that a handful of boats shelter at the southern side of the island in a little gap between Vinga and Koholm. They get the best prices in the fish market in Gothenburg if they're first home, but it's a hard living. They'll be playing cards and drinking for a few hours yet and they'll put to sea with the first light tomorrow and beat the rest of the fleet by a good two hours. We must be drifting south a little to have a glimpse of the houses.'

Holbrooke shivered at the thought of fishing in these conditions. It was cold enough on the deck of a frigate and he could only guess at the hardship involved in hauling nets or long-lines on a fragile, open fishing boat. Like casting a lead-line for an entire day without relief, perhaps. Yet

Fairview's explanation sounded plausible, and it agreed with the navigational information. He had a mental image of the frigate's track. The fishing settlement – he doubted whether it could be called a village – was sheltered under the southern side of the island and would be hidden when they were holding their position with the island abeam. If the frigate were to drift to the south of its station, then the houses would be visible. The tide must be stronger than he'd expected.

'Shake out the courses, Mister Fairview. I think we'll set the fore topmast stays'l as well.'

The master had been expecting that order and so had the bosun. The fore and main courses could be shaken out by the watch on deck but the addition of the stays'l required all hands. It was only fifteen minutes to eight bells but the bosun's call cheated the watch below of that half-glass and brought them rushing on deck to set the sails. There was still some confusion among the landsmen, many of whom had never been in deeper water than their village duckpond before volunteering for the navy, but there was a good leavening of able seamen, mostly taken up by the press. In a short time the sails were set and drawing.

'A cast of the log if you please Mister Fairview.'

It was a strange feeling, navigating blind with no fixed marks to guide him. The lights of Vinga had been seen only by the lookout and the midshipman who had been sent aloft to verify the sighting. Neither Holbrooke nor Fairview had made the climb to the main topmast head to see for themselves. In other circumstances he may have done so but tonight it was all too likely that an emergency would demand his instant decision and he needed to be on the quarterdeck, at the focus of all the information.

'By the mark, twenty.'

Twenty fathoms exactly. The leadsman must have just felt the seabed as the lead line reached the vertical before it was swept astern by the frigate's forward motion.

'Then we're a mile off Vinga,' said Fairview in a decisive

tone. 'The bottom shelves fairly regularly here, except for a few deeper holes. You can be certain of your distance off the shore when the twenty-fathom line strikes soundings.'

That was an important cast of the lead. Holbrooke knew the ship's course and the relative bearing of the fishermen's lights, so the centre of the island must bear between nor'-east-by-east and east-nor'-east. Now he had a fair idea that the frigate was a mile to the sou'-west of the island. That was about the distance that he'd expect to see a lamp from the masthead on this clear, frigid day. He was out of station. He wanted to be further north to cover the two passages through the archipelago, for he had a good feeling about tonight. His prey, a squadron of French men-o'-war and transports, had spent the last two months sheltering in Gothenburg but soon they must come out. Earlier that day, *Argonaut* had spoken to a British brig on passage back to Hull, the very same timber brig that Fairview had commanded, and her master had reported that the French were preparing for sea. They must know that they were being hunted. A dozen sources would have reported the presence of a British frigate in the Skagerrak and where there was a frigate there could be a squadron lying in wait, perhaps in the broader waters past the Skagen point, or out in the North Sea. Either way, the Frenchman commanding that squadron would want to avoid being seen, and most certainly he'd avoid an action against another squadron that could leave a ship crippled and force him to turn back.

'The lights have gone now, sir,' shouted the midshipman from the main topmast head. 'Nothing to see at all to leeward.'

Holbrooke had felt the greater speed of the frigate for the past fifteen minutes, and now it was confirmed by the lights abruptly disappearing. They were creeping slowly north and still edging closer to the land.

'Tide will turn around midnight, sir.'

Fairview had all the data at his fingertips, just as Holbrooke remembered from their time together in *Kestrel*.

He also remembered that the master's one sin was his overconfidence. Sailing masters, as a class of people, tended towards pessimism and caution, which was a good counter to the typical commissioned officer's thirst for action. Most masters could be relied upon to dampen down the enthusiasm of a young captain, but not Fairview. It was something that Holbrooke had to bear in mind.

'They'll wait until the moon is up, I reckon, sir. Even with pilots they won't fancy either of the passages on a black night like this.'

Holbrooke nodded again. Fairview inclined to loquaciousness, and he didn't want to encourage him; he wanted time to think. He knew where the French were, he knew their strength and he knew what their original mission had been. They were part of the grand scheme that envisioned the Brest and Toulon fleets joining forces to carry an invading army to the south of England. The French secretary of state for war, the Maréchal de Belle-Isle, had commissioned a successful privateer, Captain Philippe Batiste, to carry a small French army to the north of Britain to draw forces away from the south. News of the disaster at Quiberon Bay had reached Versailles but had not been passed on to Dunkirk before the squadron sailed. Batiste and the commander of the embarked land forces, Brigadier General Fouquet, had no idea when they left France that they were on a futile mission. They had spent the past two months sheltering from the worst of the winter weather in Gothenburg where they *may* have heard that the main invasion had been abandoned. Now, apparently, they were ready to sail, but where would they go? They wouldn't head into the Baltic – there was no employment for a French army in that landlocked sea – which was why Holbrooke was guarding the northern passage, the most direct route to the North Sea.

They wouldn't turn south into the Kattegat, that was as certain as any intelligent deduction could be. But the urgent question was what they would do when they cleared the

Skagerrak. Would they turn south for home and hope to make their way back to Dunkirk unmolested? That was perhaps the obvious course of action, the prudent course. But Holbrooke could guess something of the character of Batiste, and he doubted whether the cautious policy was the most likely. The whole of England had heard of Batiste; he was the most successful French privateer of the war and he carried out his raids on British shipping on a grand scale, more like a King's officer than a private commerce raider. That was why he had been commissioned for this desperate endeavour, Holbrooke guessed. And now he would want to make a name for himself as a commander of a regular naval expedition. He would want to do something with the fifteen hundred soldiers that his seven ships carried rather than steer tamely for home. Whether it was Scotland or Ireland or the north of England, Holbrooke was certain that the troops would be landed somewhere on British soil. They could destroy shipping in a port, they could ransom a city and be away before a force could be sent to eject them and they could pillage the land around for supplies. And what Holbrooke knew, and Batiste presumably didn't, was that there was no British squadron waiting for them in the North Sea. Commodore Boys was far to the south, guarding the British convoys that gathered at the Nore and the Downs against the very real threat of French privateers engaged in their more accustomed activities. If the French should come out, his task was to shadow them until he knew where they were going, then to speed south to alert the commodore.

Holbrooke paced the weather side of his quarterdeck as he watched the wind, heard the reports of depth and speed, and waited for the moon to rise.

***

'Coffee, sir?'

The question came from below Holbrooke's line of sight, closer to his waist than his head. A mop of unruly red hair sat atop an adolescent face that only a mother could love. This was the least – literally the tiniest – of all his allocation of servants, the thirteen-year-old third son of a country tailor and dressmaker. Holbrooke knew that he shouldn't have taken him. The captain of a twenty-eight-gun sixth rate was allowed only twenty servants, and after engaging the necessary cabin staff – the genuine servants – it only left fourteen or so places that he could use for his own personal patronage. He had naval friends who were clamouring for places on the quarterdecks of King's ships for their sons and nephews, and he knew that he had to nurture his standing in his home of Wickham in Hampshire by distributing his meagre patronage among the great and good of that small market town. The tailor was most certainly not one of the great and good. Yet Ann, his new wife, had pleaded the boy's case. She had known the tailor and his wife ever since her father had bought the corn merchant's business in Wickham, and lately her wedding attire had been ordered from them. The tailor was a member of that awkwardly placed class in English society, one of the middling sort – the *lower* middling sort – and his third son couldn't possibly inherit his business. He would hope for something better for their child than the life of a common seaman or a farm hand, but he couldn't ordinarily wield enough influence to secure a place on the quarterdeck. His wife's friendship with Ann Featherstone – now Ann Holbrooke – had come as a godsend and through his own wife he'd pressed his case vigorously.

Holbrooke eagerly took the cup and drained it while the boy stood there. It would have done no good to put the cup down. Holbrooke knew that he would forget about it as soon as something else demanded his attention and within half a glass it would be nothing more than shards of glazed pottery in the scuppers. Joseph, that was it, Joseph Stitch. Holbrooke had to suppress a smile at the recollection of the Wickham tailor's surname. The sexton – the keeper of the graveyard – of St. Nichols' church where he had been married gloried in the name of Francis Body and the proprietor of the King's Head inn had the wonderfully appropriate name of John Beer; it was that kind of place. Well, Joseph Stitch, rated captain's servant, would have to prove himself before he gained the privilege of walking the quarterdeck without the excuse of the captain's coffee cup in hand. One day he may even be rated midshipman, but that prospect was far in the future.

***

CHAPTER TWO

The Hunter, Hunted

Monday, Fourth of February 1760.
Argonaut, at Sea. Off Gothenburg, Sweden.

Two bells in the first watch and as far as Holbrooke could tell *Argonaut* was still holding her position a mile off Vinga. The leadsman intermittently reported no bottom or twenty fathoms or occasionally a little less and the lights on the southern face of the island hadn't re-appeared. The night had been as black as the inside of a pitch-tub, but now the eastern sky was just starting to show the promise of a risen moon.

'Good evening, Mister Shorrock. How are the broadsides?'

Holbrooke had seen the first lieutenant walking from gun to gun, studying each of the nine-pounders with a shaded lantern. He'd ordered them to be ready for action at a moment's notice, so that when the hands were sent to their quarters, there would be no delay in readying the main armament.

'All ready, sir, but when we can spare number seven gun, I want Chips to have a look at the carriage bed. It seems a little soft to me, like there's a rot setting in. Perhaps it's nothing, but I wouldn't want it to give way if we have a hot action.'

Shorrock was unknown to Holbrooke before he'd been appointed to *Argonaut* little more than a month ago. It was irritating that their Lordships had given him a first lieutenant without any kind of consultation, and Holbrooke knew very well that if he had greater seniority or more influential friends, he would never have been treated in such a cavalier fashion. However, he couldn't really complain because so far Shorrock had proved himself a diligent and skilful second-in-command. He had far more sea-time than

Holbrooke, having been commissioned in the last war and not enjoying the good fortune to be promoted in this one. It would have been easy for Shorrock to patronise Holbrooke but, so far, he'd shown no sign of flaunting his greater experience. Holbrooke's only concern was that Shorrock was a drinker. It may not be known at the Admiralty – it almost certainly was not known because that wasn't the sort of thing that captains mentioned unless it had become a serious problem – but it was very well known throughout the ship. He could detect the sickly-sweet smell of rum on Shorrock's breath now. He must have a private supply because rum was only embarked in the West Indies. It was perfectly legal and none of the captain's business unless it affected the first lieutenant's performance of his duties.

'The gunner is happy with it?'

'He is, sir, but I'd still like Chips to have a look.'

'Well, I'm not planning to use the guns tonight. Our job is to observe and report to the commodore. If they come out through the northern passage, I'll follow them until I know which way they turn, then it's off to the Nore, or wherever Mister Boys may be, as fast as we can sail.'

***

'If you please, sir, I can just see the outline of the island to leeward now.'

Petersen had good eyes. He was only a couple of years younger than his captain, but Holbrooke could see nothing except an almost imperceptible lightening of the gloom to the east.

'Deck ho! Lights on the starboard beam, sir, just to the left of the island that's starting to show.'

Then the masthead lookout could see the island too, but it was the lights that interested him. Holbrooke stared over the starboard gunwale but still could see nothing.

'Masthead. Are the lights on the shore or at sea?'

'At sea, sir, I'm almost certain. They're dim but they look like a line of ships coming past the island. A point forrard of the starboard beam, I would say, sir.'

Fairview was squinting at the suggested bearing and comparing it with his chart.

'The north passage,' he declared. 'They'd have to be right on the quarter to be coming down the southern passage.'

Holbrooke forced himself to stand still when he desperately wanted to pace the quarterdeck. He knew that his people were aware of his every idiosyncrasy, and he was self-conscious enough to supress his instincts when he felt it made him look foolish. *Argonaut* had only been in commission a month and he was still setting the tone. Nevertheless, it was a cursed inconvenience to be unable to make the dozen strides to the taffrail and back, to clear his thoughts.

He stared out across the beam into the blackness. His plan was working, perhaps. He touched the wood of the binnacle for luck, but it did appear that the French were coming out through the channel that gave them the swiftest access to the North Sea. That ruled out the Baltic, although it was always a highly unlikely destination for the squadron. Yet it still left a host of options. When they were clear of the Skagerrak they would have to turn north or south. North meant that they planned a landing somewhere in northern England or Scotland or Ireland. They certainly wouldn't want to make a circuit of the British Isles to return to France without some compelling purpose. Even after almost two hundred years had passed, the fate of King Philip of Spain's armada haunted every would-be invader of Britain. The fearful coastlines of western Scotland and Ireland were no less dangerous now than they were in Queen Bess' time. If it was north, then Holbrooke would have to abandon them and hurry to find his commodore to the south, leaving Batiste free to carry out whatever plan he had in mind, until a few ships could be scraped together too chase him. If it was south, then he must still find the commodore and attempt to bring the Nore squadron into action before Batiste could reach Dunkirk. In that case he must hasten past the French and rely on his greater speed. Either way, until they left the Skagerrak, he must stay in contact.

'Call the men to quarters, Mister Shorrock, but no drum and no pipes, if you please. Send the master-at-arms around the ship to check that we're not showing a light.'

It was a strange, unearthly feeling to see the patterns of urgent movement unfold in silence as the crew of *Argonaut* rushed to their quarters with no more than a muted shout here and there. Really, there was little chance of the Frenchmen hearing a drum or a bosun's call at this range, but stranger things had happened, and sound had a way of carrying surprising distances in cold, clear air.

'No more bells, Mister Petersen,' he added.

Argonaut held her position, balancing the trim of her sails against what they knew of the tidal stream. Holbrooke could see the island now; its rounded top was a black, silver-fringed silhouette against the still-invisible rising moon.

'I can see the lights, sir,' said Fairview. 'Two points forrard of the starboard beam. It looks like four or five ships.'

Holbrooke could see them for himself now. He counted five ships, no more. That was curious. There were seven ships in the enemy squadron, the timber-brig had confirmed that. Perhaps they weren't all showing lights or two of the captains were shielding them against detection. That begged the question why they weren't all covering their lights. It was normal practice in the British navy to show a light only in the stern arcs when sailing in company at night. From where he was standing, perhaps four points on the Frenchman's larboard bow, he shouldn't be able to see anything at all. The hairs on the back of his neck started to prickle.

'The ship's at quarters, sir. Both batteries loaded with ball and run out.'

That smell of rum again. Was the first lieutenant capable of carrying out his duties?

'Very well, Mister Shorrock.'

'Masthead, what do you see on the starboard quarter?'

Every officer on the quarterdeck swivelled round. It was the master who first guessed what was in the captain's mind.

'Do you think he's split his force, sir?'

'Quite possibly, Mister Fairview, quite possibly.'

'Then we'll be caught in the pincers,' said Shorrock, not quite to himself.

'Deck there! I can't see any lights on the starboard quarter. Can't see anything at all, it's pitch-black, sir.'

Holbrooke tapped his foot and thought for a moment. The lookout's report meant nothing. If he, George Holbrooke, were setting this trap, then the southerly group would be in complete darkness, and being so far from the track of the rising moon they would be invisible until they were much closer.

'The French are clear of the channel now,' said Fairview, giving voice to their presumed nationality. 'They'll surely tack to the north soon.'

Holbrooke studied the lights that were now plainly visible on his starboard bow. If there were seven ships there, then two of them were in darkness. Of course, two of the ships may have remained in Gothenburg, or they could have become separated. Perhaps Batiste had decided that he needed a pilot for every ship in these dangerous waters, and it could be that Gothenburg was short of pilots. That didn't seem likely, and it didn't fit the character of the French privateer as he understood it.

Holbrooke looked away to rest his eyes then again turned to study the line of ships. They were still just a group of lights, the rising moon hadn't yet illuminated them, so it was impossible to be certain whether he was looking at only five ships or seven, with two of them darkened. He bit his lower lip. This was the first time *Argonaut* had been in contact with the enemy. He'd been present at her launching at Moody Janverin's yard on the Hamble on the twenty-first of October. That was an auspicious date being the second anniversary of the battle of Cape François, where he had been in temporary command of another frigate, *Medina*. He

Nor'west by North

had stood on *Argonaut's* bare quarterdeck – a mere passenger as the frigate had not yet been handed over to the navy – as she'd been towed around to Portsmouth. After a hectic two months of fitting out and rigging, *Argonaut* was commissioned as the newest of King George's ships. Anson's desperate need for frigates meant that he had only a week for sea trials and then he'd joined the Nore squadron and almost immediately been sent off to watch Gothenburg. He remembered with a gulp that he'd been married somewhere in amongst those frenetic few months, and he'd left his new wife after just eight weeks of marriage. *Argonaut* was un-blooded and worse still, with the exception of Fairview and Jackson, the bosun, he had a complement of officers of whom he knew almost nothing. Well, he just hoped that he didn't embarrass himself in this first important mission.

'They're tacking, turning north,' said Fairview.

Holbrooke relaxed slightly, that was exactly what was expected. He should stop fretting about the two missing ships, most probably they were tucked in at the stern of the group. In fact, the ship bringing up the rear had no cause to be showing a light at all, that would leave only one that he couldn't see. He was worrying about nothing. All he had to do now was keep them in sight until they entered the North Sea and revealed their intentions.

'Brail up the main and foresail, Master. We'll let them get clear of the channel.'

'Aye, aye, sir. I don't expect they'll have seen us yet.'

Fairview turned to give his orders at the same moment as the blackness on the larboard quarter erupted into flames of bright red and orange. Half a second later the sound of the cannons beat against their ears and there was a solid crash as a round shot slammed into the frigate's stern.

Holbrooke grabbed the binnacle to keep his balance. Larboard quarter: that was where the flashes had come from. He'd been duped. There *were* only five ships in the northerly passage, the other two had crept out of the wider southerly passage and had positioned themselves so that the British frigate would be visible as the moon rose in the east. They had manoeuvred around to the west in the darkness and were now in a good position to trap *Argonaut* against the Swedish coast.

Holbrooke rapidly assessed the situation. There was one chance, a decent chance, but it must be grasped immediately.

'Bring the ship about, Mister Fairview,' he said in as calm tones as he could muster. 'First Lieutenant, stand by the larboard battery.'

'Larboard battery ready, sir.'

Drink or no drink, Shorrock was brisk in his actions.

There was a bustle as the hands that had moved towards the brails were pushed to the tacks and sheets. He heard Fairview order the helm put down, he heard the orders for tacking, but his gaze was astern, hoping to catch a sight of the enemy that had sprung the trap. There were two of them, he was sure, and he was also convinced that only one of them had fired so far. Nothing; the blackness to the south was still impenetrable. Those Frenchmen were using the rising moon to their advantage and *Argonaut* must be in sight to them while they lay hidden within their cloak of invisibility.

'How much water do we have to the west, Mister Fairview?'

'Ten leagues, sir, and then we'll run up against Denmark.'

'Then set a course to the sou'west if she'll take it.'

They'd converge with the two Frenchmen, but it couldn't be helped. He must at all costs avoid being squeezed against Vinga Island to the east.

Argonaut's manoeuvre had been well executed. A change of orders from brailing to tacking at night in a newly commissioned ship could so easily have ended in disaster. Holbrooke privately blessed the port admiral at Portsmouth who had given him a fair number of experienced able seamen, some fresh from the press and some turned over from ships de-commissioning. No more than a third of his crew were volunteer landsmen. He blessed also the hours and hours of sail and gun drills that Shorrock had inflicted upon the men. How he found time to drink was a mystery.

Argonaut had just started to sheet in on the starboard tack when the veil of the night was again rent asunder.

'Further east than the first one, I fancy,' said Shorrock calmly.

Holbrooke nodded. That was something, at least. The snare was as neat as could be and could only have been improved by the French frigates moving further west before springing the trap. Every direction that he could steer was hazardous, but by choosing to engage the southerly group and making for the Danish shore he at least was setting himself in the right place to continue his mission – if his ship should survive the next hour.

Crash! Another broadside from the ship that had fired first. Another hit, somewhere on the larboard side.

'I saw him this time, sir, in the flash from his own broadside. A frigate: perhaps a little smaller than we are.'

'Very well, hold your fire Mister Shorrock. Wait until we have a good target.'

Holbrooke fingered the silver whistle that he used to order the guns to open fire and cease firing.

'Pass the word for the carpenter. I want a damage report immediately.'

***

CHAPTER THREE

Night Engagement

Monday, Fourth of February 1760.
Argonaut, at Sea. Off Gothenburg, Sweden.

As *Argonaut* gathered way towards the southwest, Holbrooke could imagine what the French were doing. The group to the north, probably led by Batiste, would be turning south now to complete the trap. The two frigates on his larboard side – Batiste would certainly have detached men-o'-war for that task – would be paralleling his course to prevent him escaping to the south. Even if he could sail slightly faster than the French frigates, in six hours or less he'd be trapped against the Danish coast, ringed about by enemies. That would never do.

'I can see them clearly now, sir,' said Shorrock. 'Two frigates on the same course as us. They're half a mile to leeward.'

Holbrooke stared to larboard. He had time to notice that his first lieutenant was quite composed in this crisis; he didn't appear to easily give way to panic.

Yes, he could see them now, two frigates. He knew that Batiste had four frigates and three transports, so there were two frigates and three transports to the north. The germ of a plan started to seed itself. But he must first survive the next few broadsides.

'Stand by the larboard battery, Mister Shorrock.'

With the two frigates to leeward now in sight and the lights of the northerly group showing clear, Holbrooke could at last start to take the initiative. These frigates, he knew, had sailed from Dunkirk in October. Their bottoms would be foul, unless they'd docked at Gothenburg, which seemed like a breach of neutrality too far, even for the Swedes. In any case, they were built as commerce raiders and neither of them alone could stand up against *Argonaut*.

Nor'west by North

He had an opportunity to engage them in detail, and he could use the night – that great equaliser – to his advantage.

'Bear away two points, Mister Fairview, I want to close the furthest west of those two.'

'Aye-aye sir.'

Fairview turned to give the orders to the quartermaster and Holbrooke could sense that the bosun was preparing to ease the sheets as the frigate turned off the wind. He cast a glance at Shorrock who removed his cap and bowed with a broad grin.

Crash! Another broadside from the south. A scream from forward told Holbrooke that he had his first casualty. He was pleased to see that the injured man was hurried below without taking men from the guns. He sensed rather than saw the bear-like figure of the carpenter looming out of the darkness carrying a lantern so well shielded that only a small pool of light escaped to cast a feeble glow on the deck.

'Now don't 'ee worry, zur,' the carpenter said in his soft Devon accent. 'There's nothing but a bit of planking splintered and wrenched and there's no shot holes below the gunports. It can all wait until the morning…'

The carpenter appeared startled as he looked up and saw the French frigates, now quite clearly visible and about four cables on the larboard beam, but he smiled grimly.

'… so long as those gentlemen don't make any better practice.'

The carpenter was the oldest of the ship's warrant officers and by rights should have been superannuated years ago. However, he had no family and had told Holbrooke frankly that he didn't relish the thought of a lonely cottage; he'd rather be at sea. Holbrooke had no view on his abilities as a carpenter, but he was getting used to the man's avuncular manner.

'Thank you, Chips. I'll try to preserve your old timbers.'

The carpenter faded away into the gloom, back to his station below decks where his softwood wedges, his iron dogs and his oak baulks were stacked waiting to repair more severe damage.

***

All along the upper deck the ugly cast-iron nine-pounders were being edged around to follow the French frigate. He could see the effort that it took to lever the carriages around using the eight-foot-long handspikes, and the delicacy of touch that was needed for the minute adjustments. There was a dark lantern at each gun but so far not the faintest glimmer was escaping from the tin shutters. The moon provided the only illumination and it picked out the hard edges of the gunwales in a faint silvery light. An artist could capture the heroic scene in charcoals, Holbrooke thought, but there was no artist on board that he knew of.

'Stand by Mister Shorrock,' Holbrooke shouted and raised his whistle to his chest level.

The first lieutenant was standing at the quarterdeck rail where he could best see his guns. He raised his hat in reply and grinned savagely. The leading French ship was only three cables away, right on *Argonaut's* beam. He could see nothing more than her outline, but he could imagine the wild activity on her deck as the gunners reloaded ready for another broadside. We'll, they would have to receive before they could again give.

Holbrooke raised the whistle to his lips and blew a single blast. There was a pause. That was good, the crews had been drilled to wait for the first lieutenant's order rather than fire at the captain's whistle.

'Fire!'

Argonaut staggered as the fourteen guns fired almost simultaneously. There was no hope of seeing the effect of the broadside on the French ship as Holbrooke's night vision was destroyed by the flash. He'd seen how well the guns were pointed and he expected at least half a dozen hits at that range. What he hoped – what he almost expected – was that the sharp shock of that well-aimed broadside would unnerve the essentially privateering crew of the frigate. They weren't man-o'-war's men, they were used to firing without receiving any determined resistance, and he hoped that they would take longer to recover than a regular naval frigate would.

'Bring her about, Mister Fairview. Come far enough off the wind to bring the second frigate into arcs.'

The larboard gun crews were feverishly reloading, the worms, sponges and rammers describing elegant arcs in the moonlight as the crews went through their drills. As yet they had suffered only the single casualty – Holbrooke had no idea how badly the man had been injured – but the real test would come when men were falling among the guns. How well would this new crew perform when sharp oak splinters scythed across the deck and the planks were slippery with blood?

The bows came through the wind and the yards were braced across. Holbrooke could see there was some confusion among the men who had to be taken from the guns to help with the sail trimming. It was to be expected but still he would discuss it with the first lieutenant when he had the chance. It was essential that the men detailed as sail trimmers should be confident in running from the guns to the halyards, sheets, tacks and braces. It was also essential that the remaining members of the gun crews should be able to carry on working their guns, at least for a broadside or two, without the rate of fire deteriorating.

'Full and by, sir, I'll come another three points off with your permission.'

'Thank you, Mister Fairview. Just far enough to allow the starboard guns to see the second frigate.'

The details were becoming more distinct as the moon rose higher above the low hills of Sweden. He could see that he'd taken the enemy by surprise. They had likely been expecting him to stand on for the Danish coast instead of apparently putting his head further into the noose. But Holbrooke had learned from a master. Edward Carlisle, his captain in the frigates *Fury* and *Medina*, always preached the necessity of looking beyond the next broadside, of thinking through the tactics while still fighting the ship. Like a bridge player that always led with his trumps, the safest immediate course of action – a race to the west – would leave the solution to the problem no closer. He'd still be trapped between two forces in the ten-league-wide straight between Denmark and Sweden.

'You may fire when the starboard battery bears, Mister Shorrock.'

He had to shout over the sounds of the larboard battery reloading and the sail trimmers hauling on sheets and tacks, but he could see that the first lieutenant had heard him. It was extraordinary how quickly one could assess a man in action. He felt that he knew Shorrock better after the last fifteen minutes than he did in the previous month or so that they had served together.

Shorrock balanced easily on the rolling deck as *Argonaut* presented her beam to the northerly swell that steepened and became more confused as it funnelled from the Skagerrak into the Kattegat. He was watching the relative bearing of the French frigate while waiting for the moment when the deck was most level.

'Starboard battery, fire!'

The night was ripped apart as the French and the British frigates fired simultaneously. *Argonaut* was shaken like a rat in a terrier's jaws by the impact of four or five French balls and the shock of the recoil of the starboard battery. This time the British frigate wasn't so fortunate. Number seven gun – the one with the suspect bed – was over. Holbrooke was glad of the dark because he could see that at least one man was trapped underneath but the gory details were hidden from him. The rest of the crew had recovered quickly, and he could see a pair of hand spikes being used as massive levers to lift the gun. Two men were standing like twin statues of Hercules, pushing up on the massive lengths of oak while two more dragged their trapped mate free.

'Bring her hard onto the wind, Mister Fairview. As close as she'll go.'

The wind had been steadily rising and now the frigate heeled hard over to starboard. The first capful of spray burst over the larboard bow, wetting the men on the forward guns.

'Mister Peterson! Come here if you please.'

The master's mate hurried across the quarterdeck and staggered to a halt in front of his captain as the stern rose to let a wave pass underneath.

'I need you to watch the French astern, Mister Petersen. I expect that they'll follow us, but I need to know their exact movements. I'm sure Mister Fairview can spare you, so station yourself at the taffrail and let me know of any movement. Ah, there goes the leader, he's decided that we really are planning to head north, and he's tacked to follow. I want to know when the second one does so.'

'Aye-aye, sir,' Petersen said, replacing his hat and clutching the railing to prevent an undignified exit.

'Mister Shorrock. A moment of your time if you please.'

Holbrooke could see that the gunner had come on deck to attend to the number seven gun. The unfortunate man who had been crushed had been removed below. Dead or alive, Holbrooke couldn't tell, but badly maimed, certainly. He'd be lucky if he survived to see the new hospital at Haslar and even more fortunate if he lived to be a pensioner at Greenwich.

'You see the situation, Mister Shorrock?'

The first lieutenant looked around as though observing the outside world for the first time. He'd been so preoccupied in commanding his guns that he'd had no time for the tactical situation. It was the absolute best illustration of the need for the captain to have good subordinates. The principal two, the first lieutenant and the sailing master, managed the guns and the ship between them, leaving Holbrooke clear to think through his means of defeating the enemy.

'The two smaller frigates are hot on our tail now, disappointed that we are not rushing westward as was no doubt their plan. The larger two frigates and the transports – you see that one of them is a brig? – have turned south to enclose us. All three of those transports will have a decent armament of three and six-pounders and of course they'll be stuffed with soldiers. They're to the north of the frigates now. The transports are the weak spot, they don't sail as fast and they're not so weatherly. I'm planning to sail right at them and ignore the frigates if they get in the way. When we're amongst them the frigates will find it hard to engage us, although they'll no doubt give us a broadside or two in passing. We'll return the compliment, but I won't be delayed. I want to get up to windward and then we can lead them out into the North Sea.'

Shorrock nodded slowly. He was thinking of his guns not of how to fulfil the mission.

'Chain shot, sir, to slow them down?'

'I don't think so, Mister Shorrock. We can sail three miles to every two that the convoy can make. I'd rather blunt their appetite for a fight. Round shot if you please and be ready to repel boarders. The men are all detailed off with their arms at their stations?'

'Yes, sir. I'll tell them to be ready.'

Shorrock turned to return to his guns.

'And Mister Shorrock. If I should fall, you must follow the French until you know whether they are heading north or south, as we discussed yesterday, then fly like the wind to Commodore Boys at the Nore or in the Channel. Remember, this Frenchman Philippe Batiste has fooled us once already. Let's not let it happen again.'

***

CHAPTER FOUR

Breakthrough

Monday, Fourth of February 1760.
Argonaut, at Sea. Off Gothenburg, Sweden.

Fifteen minutes. That was how long Holbrooke estimated he had before he came up with the transports. Fifteen minutes in which to outthink the privateer Batiste. What would he do now? The moon was high enough so that the Frenchman would be able to see what was happening to the south of him. He'd be disappointed that his two frigates hadn't been able to pin *Argonaut* until his heavier ship and her consort could come down to finish the job. His fallback – presumably involving a chase to the west and a sharp action against the Danish coast – had also fallen through. Now he was faced with a clearly determined British frigate – fast, agile and powerful – that was coming up hard on the wind and evidently planning to break through to the north.

If I were in command of Batiste's ship, Holbrooke thought, I'd do what the other two frigates failed to do and put myself alongside the enemy. A long-range engagement would achieve nothing but a few shot holes before *Argonaut* passed through to carry the news of the French sailing from Gothenburg. Was that how privateers thought? Was Batiste even thinking like a privateer, or had he metamorphosed into a King's officer? It was said that his commission was temporary, for this expedition only, and that he would be a private person again when it was over. It was also said that he yearned for the recognition, the assured future and the step-up in social status that came with a permanent commission. A privateer would preserve his ship at all costs – it was his stock-in-trade after all – but an officer aspiring to hold King Louis' permanent commission would hazard his ship to stop the enemy frigate carrying news of the squadron's sailing. Yes, that was what Batiste would most likely do. The wind was fresh but not so strong that a hard boarding would damage them both.

The range was even closer now and as Holbrooke watched he saw Batiste's ship put her stern through the wind to parallel *Argonaut's* course. The fourth frigate was staying close to Vinga; he could forget any thoughts he may have had of escaping into the archipelago, but it also meant one less to worry about.

The slower transports were only now starting to wear around, which meant that they'd be tangled up with the flagship by the time *Argonaut* arrived. So much the better.

'Mister Fairview, come two points off the wind and pass between the two transports furthest east. You see how the frigate is to the west? We'll make him shift to cover his right wing.'

'The two to the south are hard on the wind now, sir.'

Petersen pointed towards the taffrail, but Holbrooke could see nothing in the darkness.

'They're dropping astern, maybe nearly a mile now. They're following true to our wake, not attempting to get around our flank.'

Petersen had an earnest, thoughtful air about him. He may have none of the first lieutenant's sea-time, but at this moment he appeared to be more intelligent, cleverly anticipating his captain's questions. The man had some promise.

'Pass the word for the bosun.'

Jackson came hurrying aft, smiling broadly. He had been Holbrooke's bosun since *Kestrel* was commissioned in Port Royal. He had followed Holbrooke to the expedition against Fort Niagara in the North American wilderness and he had naturally joined him in this, his first rated ship. Jackson was a true follower of Holbrooke and had no intention of serving with any other captain if he could avoid it. He had even willingly foregone a few months' salary to wait until *Argonaut* was commissioned; there was no pay without a ship for warrant officers.

'Mister Jackson. That frigate will likely try to board us in ten minutes,' he pointed across the larboard bow. 'I see the boarding nets are in place; be so kind as to rig them now and then have your crew ready with boarding axes to cut away any grapnels.'

Jackson had been watching the enemy ship since the rising moon had first revealed its presence. Bigger than *Argonaut* and almost certainly with more crew, soldiers even. He looked astern at the two frigates beating up from the south.

'Aye, sir. We'll not want to waste any time with those two following. I'll take some men from the guns, with your permission, then I can have axe-men in the tops as well as on deck.'

Holbrooke glanced up at the maintop. Jackson was right. Although there was no space to swing a grapnel from the Frenchman's fighting tops, a daring man may climb out onto a yardarm and hook onto any part of *Argonaut's* rigging. Well, he could do something about that.

'Mister Shorrock! Pass the word to the swivel-guns in the tops. They are to ignore the enemy decks and clear away any Frenchmen in their own tops or on the yardarms.'

The first lieutenant waved in reply and spoke to a midshipman who ran up the main shrouds like a monkey.

'Your men are ready, Mister Murray?'

'Aye, sir, they know what to do. Pick off the boarders then meet them with the bayonet. My marines won't let you down.'

Stuart Murray was a Scotsman, a North Briton as the King and government insisted in their continual attempt to integrate the constituent parts of the Kingdom. It had been difficult to get to know Murray; he kept himself to himself and viewed his marines as a separate unit only loosely integrated into the life of the frigate. He jealously protected his men from the everyday workings of the ship and drilled them mercilessly. Holbrooke missed his last marine lieutenant, but Colin Treganoc was dead, killed by a French musket more than a year before in the debacle of the withdrawal from Saint-Cast.

Holbrooke looked again at the enemy. He was shocked to see how close they were, how far his ship had moved in the few minutes that he'd been speaking to Jackson and Murray. Fairview was steering for the narrowing gap between the two easterly transports. They were doing what transports and merchant ships always did when threatened, closing up for mutual protection. Normally that would be a good tactic but today it played into Holbrooke's hands. He wanted to leave no space for Batiste's ship to manoeuvre.

'It'll be a merry little crowd when we meet,' said Fairview, eyeing the frigate on their larboard bow across the compass on the binnacle. 'His bearing's steady and our courses will intersect right where the transports are bunching up. He can haul his wind or bear away, either way he risks us slipping past him.'

Holbrooke barely heard the master; he was busy making his own calculations. What would Batiste do now? If he tried to intercept *Argonaut* before he reached the transports, his chance of a successful boarding was slim, and he'd have to rely upon some lucky shots disabling his enemy. If he were any slower than *Argonaut* – which was likely after nearly three months away from his home port – then he'd end up in a hopeless stern chase. Neither option would be attractive. Set aside any thoughts of prize money and reputation from capturing a British frigate, Batiste's main concern must be to prevent his sailing being reported to Commodore Boys, and more importantly to hide his intentions which must become evident once he was seen to turn north or south in the North Sea. Holbrooke thumped his fist into the palm of his hand. It really didn't matter what course of action Batiste chose. His duty was to escape from this well-laid trap, and he could only do that by breaking through the ships ahead of him. Then he'd be clear to windward, and he could watch and report at his leisure.

'There's not much gap between those transports now,

sir,' said Fairview.

'Can you get through?'

'I think not. I can't come any further to windward. We must bear away or tack.'

Bear away! God, no. That will allow Batiste to trap us against the islands to the east where the fourth frigate waited. The noose was closing, and Holbrooke was running out of ideas. A quick look astern showed him nothing, but he had to assume that the two frigates to the south were still hurrying northwards in his wake.

'Stand by to bring her about, Mister Fairview.'

That made the master stare. The frigate ahead of them would only have to bear away to run them alongside, or he could wear ship and shepherd *Argonaut* to the west until they came to the Danish shore. By that time, the other three frigates would have joined him and then it would be a desperately unequal contest.

'Tacks and sheets,' shouted Fairview, 'stand by to come about.'

'Starboard battery, Mister Shorrock. Stand by!'

Holbrooke stood feet wide apart on the sloping deck. The wind had unquestionably increased and it looked as though it had veered a little. There was no question of outflanking the French to the east so the west it must be. His mind was clear now; he knew what must be done, dangerous though it was.

He could see a group of uniformed figures on the enemy frigate's quarterdeck. He couldn't tell whether they were sea officers or soldiers in this moonlight, but that must be Batiste, standing a little apart and turning occasionally to give helm orders to the steersman. The Frenchman was watching for *Argonaut* to tack. He must have seen the preparations. The men on the fo'c'sle standing by to shift the tack of the foresail would be perfectly visible to him and their actions would be evidence of his intentions. An inexperienced man might have already started to run down to meet the British frigate, but Batiste, he knew, had been a successful privateer through two wars and would know that he could wait.

'You may bring the ship about now, Mister Fairview.'

A volley of orders, the rattle of sails protesting at the loss of a clean wind, then the sharp crack as the courses and tops'ls filled on the starboard tack.

'He's bearing away, sir,' said Fairview. 'I do believe he's going to wear ship.'

That would be the sensible thing to do, to stay to windward of *Argonaut* and prevent the British frigate breaking through to the north. This Batiste knew his trade and with a gulp Holbrooke realised that he wasn't going to be able to manoeuvre his way past the Frenchman. Well, if he had to fight, it must be short and sharp, otherwise the two to leeward would be upon them. At least with *Argonaut* beating away to the west, the Frenchmen had a more challenging task to combine their forces.

Argonaut was gaining speed now, but so was the Frenchman. Was his ship faster than Batiste's? Perhaps, but not by more than half a knot, and that wasn't sufficient. Batiste would be content with matters until the moment that *Argonaut* appeared to be head-reaching on him, then he would drop down and engage him broadside-to-broadside. It was all too easy for the Frenchman and if nothing was done then Holbrooke knew with a death-like certainty that his first command as a post-captain would be over before the dawn. He'd either be a prisoner or dead. He needed to inject some chaos, to roll the dice and see where they landed.

'Do we have room to tack again, Mister Fairview?'

The master eyed the big frigate to windward. It was closer now, within cannon-shot, but it looked like Batiste was wisely saving his first broadside until his gunners couldn't miss.

'No, sir,' Fairview replied positively. 'If we tack, we'll run him aboard. We can't get across his bow and at the best we'll shave his stern.'

'Then make it so, Mister Fairview. Bring the ship about

Nor'west by North

and keep her coming. We'll cross his stern if we can.'

Fairview opened his mouth to remonstrate but closed it with a snap. He'd served long enough with Holbrooke to trust his judgement, and in any case, he was taken up with the thrill of the moment. It was an insane thing to do, to tack with the moonlit enemy's masts and sails filling the sky to windward, but it was becoming an insane night.

Argonaut's bows shot up into through wind and paid off on the larboard tack. Holbrooke took no interest in the manoeuvre; he was watching the deck of the Frenchman with a ferocious intensity. There! A flurry of activity among the group on the quarterdeck, as though a child had poked a stick into an ant's nest. They weren't expecting *Argonaut* to tack again.

'Ready both batteries, Mister Shorrock. You'll see which one will engage in a moment.'

Holbrooke kept his voice calm and level. He wanted the chaos to be confined to his enemy and not to spread to his own ship. If Batiste was able to assess the new situation dispassionately, he'd come to the conclusion that a collision was in his interests. By the look of the frenetic activity on his quarterdeck, he wasn't being given that opportunity. There were soldiers everywhere, impeding the sea officers on their own quarterdeck. It would be a natural reaction for the Frenchman to tack to match *Argonaut's* movements, anything else almost guaranteed a collision.

'He's tacking!' Fairview shouted.

Argonaut's long bowsprit was pointing directly at the French frigate. Holbrooke could see that Fairview had been correct. If Batiste had held his course a collision couldn't have been avoided. Now he may just be able to cross his enemy's bows.

'Steer to pass to the west of him, Mister Fairview. Don't worry if you luff, just don't let her pay off.'

One chance; that was all he had. He glanced at the quartermaster who was watching the leading edge of the main tops'l, the luff. It was lifting horribly, a cardinal sin under most circumstances, but not now.

There was a dreadful rattle of blocks as the frigate protested, but she was still moving forward, still drawing up on the Frenchman's beam.

Holbrooke blew a single blast on his whistle. There was an agonising pause that in reality couldn't have lasted more than a second, then Shorrock gave his order and the guns of the starboard battery boomed almost in unison. It was a good broadside, and Holbrooke could see the damage being done to the Frenchman.

Holbrooke had time to notice that the starboard battery was being reloaded, then the Frenchman's broadside hit them. Fifteen nine-pounders and two big eighteen-pounders hurled their load of shot at *Argonaut*. In the flash from the guns, Holbrooke saw the main deck as though time had been frozen. The intense activity around the guns, the splinters flying across the deck, the powder smoke, all the blurring action was caught in the frame of a picture, in blacks and greys picked out in contrasting orange and red. Beside him the marines were firing and reloading in silence, apparently oblivious to the two of their number that had been caught in the hail of cast iron shot and now lay in pools of their own blood.

Holbrooke noticed all of that, but none of it mattered. Only the movements of the French flagship had any bearing on his future. Sure enough, the Frenchman was bearing away in a desperate attempt to run his bows into *Argonaut's* stern. In the growing light of the rising moon, he could see a crowd of Frenchmen on the fo'c'sle, and others in the tops ready to bind the two ships together. There was a flash from his own ship's maintop and a man fell from the enemy's yardarm. The swivel guns were in action, but Holbrooke knew that they could hardly stop a determined attempt at boarding. The marines were moving aft now, following the rapidly moving enemy.

Another crash. The French jib boom raked across *Argonaut's* taffrail. It caught briefly in the mizzen, but the clew cringles didn't hold and with a tearing sound a quarter of the mizzen ripped away and the jib boom jerked free. The marines gave one last volley and the French flagship fell away to leeward.

'Can you tack, Mister Fairview?'

The master looked at the wreckage of the mizzen. Under normal circumstances it was vital that the mizzen was properly set to provide the leverage aft to bring the bows into and through the wind, but now it would be of no use. Fairview looked over the side, trying to determine how fast the ship was moving. Without the correct leverage he'd have to rely upon the forward movement of the frigate to tack. Otherwise, they would have to wear, and that would squander too much of the gains they had made to windward.

'I'll bear away first, sir. Two minutes, then we'll have enough way on.'

In the darkness to leeward Holbrooke could just make out the French frigate in the act of tacking. That man Batiste was persistent, and he wasn't giving up on his attempt to bring *Argonaut* to a decisive action. Jackson had a team getting the mizzen under control. They'd brailed it and now an agile bosun's mate was attempting to pass an end of the sheets through the first reefing cringle. That would regain some of the balance of the rig, but Holbrooke could see that the Frenchman would be upon them before the task was complete.

'As soon as you can, Mister Fairview.'

The pale moon's glow offered no points of reference to assess the frigate's speed. Holbrooke gave up trying and left it to the sailing master. He glanced across the main deck; the destruction was worse than he had thought. Three guns had been hit and the starboard gunwale was in a truly shocking state, with great holes where the French balls had smashed their way through at close range. He knew that he must avoid another action at all costs. Over to leeward things were looking grim with the French flagship now beating up towards them and he could see the other two frigates a couple of miles away on the larboard quarter.

'We've passed a mizzen sheet, sir. It's ugly but it will do to get us around and two thirds of the sail will draw.'

'Bring her about, Mister Fairview,' Holbrooke shouted without even acknowledging the bosun's report. That was an exceptional piece of work, but the congratulations would have to wait.

Slowly, so slowly, the frigate's bows came into the wind. At one point Holbrooke thought that they weren't going to make it, that they'd be caught in irons, but then suddenly they were through and bounding north on the larboard tack. Even with their injured mizzen, *Argonaut* was moving faster than the Frenchman. He watched carefully as his pursuer clung doggedly to his heels, until the Frenchman's sense of duty reasserted itself and his bows swung away to the east.

'Keep him in sight, Mister Fairview. We must be in contact at dawn, then perhaps we'll see which way he's going. Mister Jackson, how long to bend on the spare mizzen?'

***

CHAPTER FIVE

Harwich

Tuesday, Twelfth of February 1760.
Argonaut, alongside, The King's Yard, Harwich.

The ebbing tide gurgled noisily under *Argonaut's* forefoot as she moved crabwise across the last few feet towards the floating pontoon at the King's Yard. The heavy warps that hauled her bodily across the stream creaked as they passed around the two capstans on the shore and the breath of the yard labourers hung in clouds in the still, frigid air as they heaved on the bars. It had been two years since Holbrooke had last visited Harwich. He'd been the master and commander of a little ship-rigged sloop that he'd taken from a Dutch pirate in the Caribbean, and he was engaged in the blockade, and ultimately the occupation, of Emden. Much had changed at the King's Yard. The great third rate *Conqueror*, whose massive shape had so dominated the yard, had been finished and accepted into service. Now Harwich was building frigates of the smaller sort and brig-sloops and repairing the damage to King's ships caused by battle and weather. Nevertheless, there was a new energy at the yard and Harwich had its own commissioner, appointed by the navy board. The feeling of a cottage industry was gone.

The master shipwright had estimated three weeks to repair *Argonaut's* damage. With no shot holes below the waterline, there was no need to bring her into a dock, nor to haul her over. All the damage had been done to the ship's upper works and to her mizzen sail, and it could all be repaired while the frigate floated at the pontoon.

Argonaut touched with a creak as the rattan fenders were squeezed between the six hundred tons of the frigate and the solid timbers of the floating platform. There was a flurry of activity as the master rigger made the frigate secure and then suddenly it was all over, and *Argonaut* was in dockyard hands. The master attendant looked visibly relieved when Holbrooke announced his intention to move ashore until his frigate was once more ready for sea. A live-aboard captain in a ship under repair was an intolerable nuisance.

***

Holbrooke, Fairview and Jackson cut comical figures as they all gazed earnestly skywards at the peak of the mizzen yard, which may or may not have splintered in its last yard or so.

'I don't know, sir,' said Jackson as he craned his head from side to side trying to get a better angle, 'maybe it'll do, but I'll ask Chips to have a good look at it.'

'Well, there's no time like the present, Mister Jackson, we can still add it to our defect list. If that yard needs repairing, then let's declare it before the master attendant carries the tally away.'

'I remember,' Fairview started, 'oh it must have been ten years ago, I left a damaged mizzen yard without bringing it down on deck and in a hard sou'westerly blow off…'

'Beg your pardon, sir,' said Shorrock, cutting off the sailing master's story which looked as though it wouldn't be a short one. 'There's a man on shore who says he wants to volunteer; says you may remember him. He looks a likely hand, more of a petty officer than an able seaman, I'd say.'

'I'll come in a moment,' Holbrooke said as he took another look at the offending yard. He really couldn't see…

'Dawson ahoy!' cried Jackson, leaning over the gunwale and waving to a dark-haired man dragging a sea-chest. He turned back to Holbrooke. 'I was wondering what had become of him, sir. But here is, large as life, twice as ugly and apparently wanting to sign the muster list!'

Holbrooke smiled as he saw his old coxswain looking expectantly up at him. He had appointed a seaman to steer his boat when he went ashore or visited other ships, of course, but the man's heart wasn't in it and although he was perfectly capable of managing the crew of a boat, Holbrooke wanted something more. He had an instant recollection of Dawson at Emden, calmly making a stern board away from the jetty as a horde of French infantrymen made a rush at the boat. He remembered the sharp stab of flame as the boat gun, loaded with canister, cut a bloody swathe through their assailants, and he remembered how cool Dawson had been in finding his way back to their ship in the pitch blackness. Yes, Dawson would do. In fact, he was a gift from heaven.

***

'The commodore chose to be jovial,' Holbrooke said in reply to Chalmers' inquiry.

There had been no leisure for Holbrooke since his meeting with the commander-in-chief at the Downs, the day before. During the short passage from the Downs to Harwich, he'd been closeted with the first lieutenant, the bosun and the carpenter assessing the damage and making a list for the yard. They each knew that the list would be ignored and that the yard would make its own assessment of what needed to be done, but there would be trouble from the commissioner if there was no list.

David Chalmers waited in silence for his friend to continue. They had upstairs rooms at the Porto Bello inn on the high street in Harwich, and he could see *Argonaut's* masts over the low dockyard buildings. Already the mizzen had been stripped from its yard and no doubt a horde of sailmakers would be tut-tutting over its appalling condition and estimating how much of the almost-new flaxen canvas could be spirited away to be sold to the merchants to supplement their pay.

Holbrooke and Chalmers had sailed together for four years and knew each other as well as any two men could. Chalmers was an unbeneficed clergyman and had been living on the charity of colleagues while lobbying anyone who had a living in their gift. Rural squires, masters of colleges, minor nobility, they had all been grist to the mill in Chalmers search for a parish, but to no avail. In desperation he'd presented himself to the Bishop of London, who appointed naval chaplains, and had been sent to Minorca before the outbreak of war. The port commissioner at Mahon, having no use for a chaplain had sent him to the frigate *Fury* where Holbrooke was serving as a master's mate. The two had become friends and Chalmers had followed Holbrooke when he in turn had followed Captain Carlisle into the newer frigate *Medina*. When Holbrooke was given his own sloop, Chalmers had naturally stepped across the gunwale with him, and now they had a frigate. Holbrooke's band of followers was of modest numbers and only Chalmers and Jackson had been with him through thick and thin. Fairview could almost be called a follower, but his movements were determined by the navy board and Trinity House, forces that wielded far more power than an unknown sea officer, and it was sheer coincidence that brought him to serve under Holbrooke a second time.

'The commodore found it amusing that I should have damaged my new frigate so soon, but he was pleased to have such prompt notice that Batiste was heading north. I left before he decided who to send to chase the French, but he was speaking of a small squadron of three or four frigates. What an opportunity, and I'm missing it for want of a few yards of oaken gunwale!'

Chalmers took a folded map of the North Atlantic from his coat pocket. It had been his constant companion ever since he'd been embarrassed by expressing the opinion that the entirety of the Scandinavian countries lay to the north of Britain, at once consigning the balmy southern regions of Sweden to a climate more like that of Iceland. He invariably referred to it when questions of geography arose, and now he was smoothing out the deep creases and puzzling over the motivations of this strange French expedition.

'Then does this unknown captain, a commodore himself, perhaps…' he saw Holbrooke's shake of the head, a firm negative, '…does this captain have any realistic chance of finding the French squadron? It's a vast area that he has to cover, and I believe I'm correct in my understanding that King's ships are few and far between to the north of the Thames.'

'You are,' Holbrooke replied. 'The North Sea was the centre of effort in the days of the Dutch wars, but since King William's time, all of Britain's naval power that hasn't been sent abroad is focussed in the Channel. A frigate or two will be patrolling the western approaches and the Bristol Channel, but Monsieur Batiste will find precious little opposition in the whole of the north. Little in the way of soldiers too. There's no formed army north of London, only a few garrisons and some militia regiments. Those fifteen hundred French soldiers will find no substantial force to oppose their pinprick raids.'

Chalmers nodded. He could see the strategic sense in the fleet's disposition, but it did leave the north of England, Scotland and Ireland wide open to whatever injury and insults that the French commodore and his counterpart brigadier-general chose to inflict.

'Pinpricks indeed. But those are the parts of the kingdom that are most loosely bound to the centre. It's only fifteen years since the highlands rebellion and a French landing of that size may find willing collaborators in the west of Scotland.'

'Indeed, and that is why the commodore was so quick to deplete his force by three or four frigates. The real danger of invasion ended when Hawke thrashed the Comte de Conflans at Quiberon Bay last year. I suppose that if news of the defeat had reached Dunkirk in time, the expedition would never have sailed. Now it looks like a privateering expedition on a grand scale, with no real strategic significance. You can be sure that Batiste and the commander of the land forces have firm advice as to where they may find friends in the British Isles.'

'If the strategic aim has been overtaken by events, then perhaps, after all, this Batiste will sail peacefully around Scotland and Ireland and try to make a French port by the back door, as it were.'

Holbrooke pulled a wry face.

'Unlikely. Even if he has heard the news of Conflans' defeat and even if he realises its significance, he still has a useful squadron. He's very much a free agent now, whether he knows it or not, and he'll want to do something to lay claim to a permanent commission in the French navy. Do you know that he simultaneously holds the rank of *lieutenant de frégates*, a sort of commissioned master's mate, and *chef d'escadre*, the equivalent of our commodore? It's a cumbersome system and both of Batiste's ranks are temporary; the good Lord alone knows what rank is listed on his pay docket. All else being equal, the French navy will forget that it ever knew him when this cruise is over. In any case, according to Fairview's friend, he couldn't take on enough victuals in Gothenburg to last him for the whole journey back to France. He'll need to land somewhere that has the capacity to raise enough dry food to last two thousand men – possibly nearer three thousand – for three or four months. That probably means that he'll need to take and hold a substantial town and bleed it dry before a force can be sent to dislodge him. Still, it's none of our business. We'll be sent to the Channel as soon as we're repaired.'

'I'm sorry to hear it. I would have liked to see the northern countries of the kingdom.'

Holbrooke laughed and slapped his friend's shoulder.

'At this season, you surely jest. The channel will be bad enough, but Batiste must pass clear around the north of Scotland, in February or March! I wouldn't wish that upon anyone.'

***

'Now, here's a thing,' said Holbrooke, reaching into the portable desk that his clerk had brought ashore, 'and I'd welcome your opinion.'

The commodore's secretary had handed over a large bag of mail before *Argonaut* had departed for Harwich. There was the usual mass of correspondence from the navy board, a letter from his wife – it still came as a surprise to remember that he was married – and one in an elegant hand that he hadn't immediately recognised.

'This is from Mister Garnier, the owner of Rookesbury House. We met him in the Square at Wickham over Christmas if you remember.'

Chalmers nodded. He'd spent a few days of the festive period at Holbrooke's father's cottage just north of the town. In a different season they'd have been fishing for the brown trout that called the River Meon their home, but in the depths of a frosty winter the trout quite sensibly found refuge under the twisted alder roots and below the drooping bankside grasses and were waiting for the turn of the new year. Then, for a few months, their only interest would be spawning. There was no fishing for them until late March, at the earliest. Yes, he remembered Mister Garnier, a most important person in the small market town of Wickham, it appeared.

Chalmers read the letter slowly. It was a carefully worded invitation for Holbrooke, a speculative offer, hedged around with ambiguity, to consider whether he had a political future in the town. It didn't go so far as to make any promises and no particular position was mentioned. Whether he was considering the market square bailiff or a seat in parliament or something in between remained a mystery. Nevertheless, there it was, a door to a future beyond the navy, being opened by one who held the keys at least to the first step. He read through the letter again and handed it back to Holbrooke with an impassive, inscrutable expression.

The two men sat in silence, but it was Holbrooke who cracked first.

'Well, what do you think?'

Chalmers looked straight at his friend.

'I would urge caution,' he said slowly and deliberately.

'Caution? how so?' Holbrooke replied. 'It's perfectly normal for post-captains to pursue a political career in parallel with their naval business. In fact, it's difficult to see how else I'll fill my time when this war is over and all that's required of me is to collect my half-pay on the quarter.'

Chalmers looked oddly at his friend, the glance that a concerned uncle may bestow on a nephew who didn't quite understand the wickedness of the world. He fumbled in his pocket for a moment and brought out a large bright coin, an inch-and-a-half in diameter, which shone like old, worn gold but didn't have the heft of a precious metal. He placed it on the table between them.

'You've seen one of these, no doubt,' he said.

Holbrooke picked it up and favoured it with a cursory examination before replacing it on the table with a firm click.

'Of course, my father has one, they were a commonplace when I was a youngster. It's a commemorative piece for Vernon's great victory at Port Bello in the year 'thirty-nine. What of it?'

Chalmers picked up the coin and spun it in the light from the window.

'This is, in fact, your father's; he lent it to me. And it's more than just a piece of gilded frippery, it's a cautionary tale for sea officers who venture into politics,' he replied. 'Just look at it with a fresh eye and you'll see its significance.'

Holbrooke picked it up again, but it was evident that he thought the coin not worth discussing.

'These were made hurriedly within weeks of the news of Port Bello's capture reaching England. The presses were urged on by Vernon's friends in parliament, keen to catch the wave of enthusiasm and promote the admiral's interests. They're cheaply made, and they have nothing in the way of artistic merit. This one, I believe, was made by Mister Pinchbeck's company so in a way it's a *genuine* imitation of a gold medal, real pinchbeck! You can see that it's already starting to show the base metal below and it's only twenty years old.'

He used a fruit knife to point out the details of the coin.

'There's the angry admiral himself, in all his pomp, like

some latter-day Caesar, bestriding the narrow world like a colossus. His breeches appear to be chequered, which is a fashion that I doubt very much he would have espoused. He's holding his baton of office; there's a cannon in the foreground and a ship-of-the-line in the background. The inscription lacks any attempt at subtlety or modesty: *THE BRITISH GLORY REVIV'D BY ADMIRAL VERNON*. Indeed so, and the artist has even contrived to set the two Ns in VERNON backwards, such was his haste to beat his rivals to the market.'

Holbrooke smiled at that. He'd never noticed the error, nor had he looked closely at the bas-relief images. It was just a commemorative coin. Cheap, as Chalmers said, and tossed around in the King's Head or the market square with little thought to its paltry value.

'I still don't see…'

'Bear with me if you please. The reverse is just as instructive.'

Chalmers turned over the coin and traced the outlines of the images.

'At least it's a recognisable representation of the siege, if you know what you're looking at. There's the bay with the town of Porto Bello at its head. You can see the two forts that guard the mouth and another smaller fort – San Jeronimo, if I remember correctly – in front of the town. The causeway to the fort has been set to the western shore rather than the eastern, further proof of the indecent haste with which these were struck, but let's not quibble over trifles. There are six ships – men o'-war we are expected to understand – crowding into the bay…'

'Of course there are six ships,' Holbrooke interrupted, 'what other number could there be? Vernon famously only needed six ships.'

'Just so. In fact, the inscription on this side is even less subtle than the obverse. *HE TOOK PORTO BELLO WITH SIX SHIPS ONLY*. The artist is leaving his customers in no doubt as to the monumental significance of Vernon's victory.'

'That's all well known, any schoolboy could tell you as much, and I still don't see where this is leading,' Holbrooke said with a trace of exasperation.

'It's a cautionary tale, my dear George. Hubris and nemesis if you like. Vernon was an intensely political sea officer, a member of parliament for the patriot wing of the Whig party, and he caused Walpole's government no end of trouble in parliament. He was sent to the Caribbean at least partly to remove him from England and to appease the mob, and he did indeed boast that he would take Porto Bello with only six ships. When he did so, true to his word, the country went wild. Every fifth inn in the land was renamed for him – we are sat in one now – and a whole street in London. It's what happened next that is so remarkable.'

Holbrooke was starting to look interested now.

'You mean when he failed to take Cartagena de Indias.'

'Yes. I've even seen the counterpart to this coin, struck in anticipation of a victory that didn't materialise. A dreadful waste of life through dither and delay in the worst season of the year and in the end, Cartagena remained in Spanish hands. The coin is an even worse attempt than this,' he said pointing again to the medal on the table, 'with the poor old Don Blas de Lezo, in all his one-legged, one-armed, one-eyed glory, kneeling in abject surrender, when of course he was really the victor. Now, how many of those inns still bear Vernon's name? The majority were over-painted with the Duke of Cumberland's head after the 'forty-five uprising. This is one of the few Porto Bello inns remaining, there's another near Wickham of course. Even the Royal Duke is in disgrace now and the innkeepers have been emboldened to replace him with the latest heroes, Hawke and Anson and Wolfe.'

'That's just the way of things,' Holbrooke said, disappointed that Chalmers' argument should turn out to be so shallow.

'I agree. Heroes come, and heroes go at the public whim. Innkeepers merely respond to their customers' tastes. Yet there's more to it in Vernon's case. His victory at Porto Bello should have secured his naval future, regardless of the defeat at Cartagena, which could arguably be attributed to factors beyond his control. No, something more sinister was at work against Vernon. What important commands was he given when he returned from the West Indies?'

Holbrooke thought for a moment. Chalmers was right, of course. He could have expected to be given the Channel Fleet, or a place on the Admiralty Board, but instead he was given a squadron in the eastern Channel and then quietly retired. That was surely the malign workings of politics.

'I see. You're warning me of the fragility of a political career.'

'Yes, but I'm warning particularly of naval political careers. A seat in parliament or even a lower provincial office is only obtained through patronage, and if your patron happens to be in opposition to the government – who are your employers after all – it can so easily turn awry. Don't imagine that you will have free rein to determine your own opinions and espouse what you feel is right or even what you hope will further your standing at the Admiralty.'

Holbrooke stared thoughtfully at the wall.

'I have no firm political convictions, in fact I don't even know where Garnier stands, or which faction he supports.'

'Then I doubly urge caution, at least until you know to whom Mister Garnier owes his allegiance. He is not asking for any kind of commitment, so I would keep my powder dry if I were you. Send him a non-committal response in the same tone as his non-committal offer and promise to meet him when you are next at home.'

'He's probably thinking of a county office in any case, not a seat in parliament. I hardly think he has that much interest.'

'Nevertheless, Captain Holbrooke, nevertheless…'

***

CHAPTER SIX

A Revelation

Saturday, Fifteenth of February 1760.
Port Bello Inn, Harwich.

Holbrooke and Ann sat in the large bow window of their rooms at the inn, the firelight and the candlelight their only illumination and the heavy curtains keeping the chill night air at bay. He still couldn't believe his wife was really here, sat beside him in Harwich having made the long and uncomfortable trip from the south coast in the dead of winter. It was made easier by the new post coach that ran from London to Harwich, a necessary communications link for the increased importance of the port, but even so it was an epic journey of two days and a night.

'…so, when your letter arrived, Sophie, bless her heart, announced that we should decamp to Harwich until you have to sail again. Father raised objections of course; the weather, the roads, the distance, but really, I think he was dismayed at being left with the management of the house for a few weeks.'

She looked sharply at Holbrooke.

'Are you attending, George?'

Holbrooke realised that Ann had been talking for some minutes and he struggled to recall what she'd been saying. It wasn't that his wife's talk bored him, quite the contrary, but he was still trying to take in the significance of her arrival. He'd been counting back the days since he'd written to tell her that he'd be in Harwich for three weeks or so. She and her stepmother, Sophie, must have made an almost immediate decision and hurried to Portsmouth to catch the post to London the next morning. They would have had to spend a night in the capital, then up before dawn for the Harwich coach. His mind rebelled at the thought of all the things that could have gone wrong with such a hastily

Nor'west by North

conceived plan. Set aside the normal perils of two coach trips in the dead of winter, they could have had difficulty finding an inn in London. The Harwich coach could have been full, and when they arrived at their final destination, he could have been on his way to London for a call on the navy offices on Tower Hill or the Admiralty at Whitehall. But it appeared that none of these disasters had occurred and only five days after he had sat down to write to his wife, here she was! The only slight difficulty had been in finding a room at the inn for Sophie, but Chalmers had been kind enough to move back into the ship and now Ann's stepmother was recuperating in the adjoining room of their suite.

'Yes, dear. Excuse me if I'm distracted, but I'm just so astonished – and delighted, of course – to see you here.'

'I do assure you that it was the most courageous thing I've ever done,' Ann replied with an attempt at a heroic countenance that made her look even more attractive in the kindly light of the room. 'We barely slept at London; the street noises seemed to go on all night. It's not at all like Wickham, where you could hear a pin drop in the square after the King's Head closes its doors.'

Holbrooke had a vivid mental picture of their shared hometown in southern Hampshire. He'd lived there all his life while Ann's father had only moved the family to Wickham after Holbrooke had joined his first ship. The market square was all a-bustle during the day but the population – mainly rustics engaged in farming or the supporting trades that clustered around agricultural communities – valued their sleep and tended to save on lamp oil and tallow by closely following the setting sun in their paths to their beds. When the King's Head threw down its shutters, it took only minutes for its last customers to make their raucous way towards their homes, and then silence descended on the square like a thick woollen blanket.

'Your father is well, I hope?'

'Yes. He complains right through the winter but he's as hale and hearty as a man of his age has a right to be. His business is thriving, and his customers come from as far afield as Alton and Fareham now that he's started to enrol them in the spring, rather than wait for the harvest as most corn merchants still do. He's seen as a reformer, and I've heard it said that his ideas are all one with the Inclosure Acts. Yet I do wonder at the changes that it's brought to our home. Only last year the remainder of the common land was enclosed – the Hundred Acres, they call it now – and where a family was once their own masters, now they are employed by the great men.'

Holbrooke just nodded at that. Nobody had yet mentioned it aloud, but there was a gathering groundswell of expectation that he'd join his father-in-law's corn merchant business when the war was over, and he was on half-pay without a ship. He hadn't dismissed the idea, but he wasn't prepared to commit himself until he'd walked a few more miles in the boots of a post-captain and considered how well they fit. It would certainly be a social step down to settle into the life of a tradesman in a provincial market town, but then he'd come so far, so fast, that he still feared he would suffer the same fate as Icarus, and the wings that had taken him to these lofty heights would ultimately fail him. Still, he'd amassed enough in prize money to lead the life of a financially independent country gentleman if he didn't fancy the business. He must find the opportunity to discuss it with Ann; after all she could expect to inherit in her own right if he showed no interest. She had no brothers or sisters and the union of the widowed Martin Featherstone and Sophie had failed to produce any other heirs and was unlikely to do so now.

'I called on your father, somewhat in haste, I'm afraid, but he sends his best wishes, and you have the letter that he sent you.'

Holbrooke had read the letter while Ann was washing after her long coach ride. It was a short note, evidently written in the brief few hours before Sophie and Ann left for Portsmouth. The only item of real interest was an account of a conversation with Mister Garnier after a chance meeting in the town square. It was all a bit mysterious, his father had said, but Garnier hoped that George would consider carefully the letter that he'd sent the previous week. Holbrooke knew what that was about even if his father didn't, and he had thought about little else since he'd discussed its contents with Chalmers.

'I left the house in the care of Polly,' Ann continued, 'but Father has promised to keep an eye on affairs while I'm away. I'm not at all certain that Polly can be trusted on her own, with that roving eye of hers.'

Polly was the servant who had previously been attached to the establishment at Bere House, the Featherstone family home close alongside the King's Head in Wickham. Martin Featherstone, at the insistence of his wife Sophie, had released the girl to be the only servant in Holbrooke's small, rented house on the hill leading down from the square to the river. Holbrooke could afford a much better place, but with only a few weeks between the marriage and *Argonaut's* commissioning, it had been decided that they would take a modest cottage close to her father's house until he had a spell ashore and they could think about a more permanent arrangement. Of course, they could live wherever they wanted to. London, perhaps, although Holbrooke struggled to imagine Ann enduring the big city with him away at sea. Given the circumstances, there was a definite advantage to Ann being near the support of her family and friends while George had a ship. In any case, and regardless of the family connections, Wickham was an excellent choice for a sea officer. It was an easy horse or carriage ride into Portsmouth, and Gosport was even closer, from where a hired wherry could take him directly to Spithead or across the harbour to the yard. His own ship's longboat could row right up Fareham creek and meet him at the tidal mill only four miles from Wickham if he knew of the need in advance. If he was called up to town, then the post ran from Portsmouth, or he could avoid the trip into the city by cutting across country to Horndean where the coach always stopped for refreshments after the climb up Portsdown Hill. Yes, Wickham would do until they had the leisure to decide on their long-term abode.

'I met Mister Garnier while I was walking with Sophie. He was most solicitous, more than I deserve, I'm sure. He spoke about the great future that you have in Wickham, should you choose to take it. Do you know what he means, George? I must say that Sophie and I were quite puzzled and if he hadn't been in such a tearing hurry, I'm sure that Sophie would have quizzed him on it, you know how direct she can be. He said that he hoped to talk to Father, and then he was gone, leaving us stranded between a guess and a supposition.'

Three points of contact, Holbrooke thought. Four if Garnier really did approach his father-in-law. Then he must be serious. It was slightly galling, however, that Garnier should be trailing his coat across all Holbrooke's friends and family when he had not had any encouragement at all. But perhaps that was how it had to be when a sea officer was involved, and the country was at war.

'I do believe that Mister Garnier is hoping to sponsor me for a minor position in the county, Ann. A justice of the peace perhaps. I can't believe that he has anything more serious in mind.'

'A justice of the peace? That's the same as a magistrate, isn't it? How grand. Then you'd have to hold petty sessions and quarter sessions and send people to the assizes! Father had to appear as a plaintiff at a quarter session last year when one of his men stole some sacks of barley, and I know that he was worried for days before the event, he was quite overawed by the prospect. But can you be a magistrate while you are at sea?'

Holbrooke shook his head in despair.

'I really don't know, Ann. There are about twenty or so justices in the county, I believe, and I understand that they routinely substitute for each other, so perhaps it's possible.

But I don't even know whether that is what Garnier has in mind, his letter was so guarded. I suppose I should reply soon, but David is pleading with me to be cautious. He's quite right of course, too many naval careers have been destroyed by meddling in politics, and a county magistracy is the first handhold on the greasy pole. Still, let's not talk about such matters on this wonderful evening. Here comes the waiter; I wonder what the soup is today?'

***

Two weeks they had together, two weeks of stolen moments; of windswept walks on the beaches and dunes overlooking the cold, grey, North Sea that beat against the shore before their feet. Sometimes Sophie accompanied them but mostly they preferred their own company and Sophie, with a greater experience of the world and more intuition, left them alone. It was like an extended holiday, and they made up for the time that they had not enjoyed in the immediate aftermath of their marriage, when Holbrooke was concerned with the fitting out of his new ship. Most days there was nothing for him to do. His officers, led by Shorrock, handled the day-to-day work and his clerk, Lister, only intruded when mail had been delivered or when the reports and returns were ready for scrutiny. They both knew that it would be over soon and as the work in the yard progressed, they clung closer and closer to each other, begrudging each minute that the demands of the ship kept them apart.

Soon, all too soon, the time came when the master shipwright announced that they would finish the work in three days' time. The mizzen had already been repaired and bent on and it only required a lick of paint on the gunwales and around the ports for *Argonaut* to be as good as new.

'I asked Lister to make the reservations for your journey,' said Holbrooke, over breakfast.

Ann looked up sharply and Sophie tactfully turned away and feigned an interest in the bustling high street outside the window. Holbrooke knew instantly that he had handled it badly. They had been avoiding talking about her departure although it had been tacitly assumed that George would make the arrangements. He just didn't know a safe way of raising the subject, but he now was aware, to his cost, that blurting it out over the breakfast table in the presence of Ann's stepmother was perhaps the worst possible way. Like a fool he plunged forward.

'You have inside seats on the coach to London on Monday and again on the Portsmouth coach on Tuesday. He's sent a note ahead to arrange rooms for you in London. All that remains is to write to your father so that he can instruct the carrier to meet you at Horndean.'

Ann held back a sob and straightened her shoulders. Her voice sounded harsh and unyielding.

'Will we be able to see you sail?' she asked.

'No, it's better not, we sail on Tuesday, so I'll at least be able to see you on your way.'

Silence. Sophie made her excuses and left clutching a coffee cup and a slice of buttered toast with marmalade. Butter *and* marmalade! Holbrooke's eyes took in the unprecedented indulgence, but his mind didn't register the fact.

When they were alone, Ann turned to him with tearful eyes.

'I have been dreading this day, George, but the one small consolation has been that I could see your ship sail, just as though I was on the Round Tower by Portsmouth Point.'

At that she burst into tears, the first real tears that Holbrooke had seen since they were married. He pushed back his chair and walked around the table to comfort her. Yet he was puzzled; it wasn't like Ann to break down in front of him, and this really was a small matter. It made every sense that she and Sophie should leave before *Argonaut* sailed. It meant that he could spend the last night on board and ensure that all was in order, the innkeeper's account could be settled, and he'd have the reassurance of knowing that the coach had left on time with plenty of daylight left to make it to the capital. Still, he wasn't prepared to spoil their last two days with this contention hanging over them.

'I'm sorry,' he said, 'I didn't know that it meant so much to you. I'll send for Lister and move the arrangements to Wednesday. You'll have to spend two more nights here and I won't be with you for the second of them, but you'll be able to wave from the yard and I'll ask the commissioner for the favour of his carriage to take you to the dunes where you may wave again to your heart's content.'

Ann sniffed and reached for her handkerchief. Holbrooke studied her face out of the corner of his eye, half fearing to see an expression of triumph at having so deftly manipulated her husband, and he was gratified to see no such look. Ann just smiled radiantly, wiped her eyes, and looked over her shoulder to see that they were alone.

'Would you bring your chair to this side of the table, George?'

Holbrooke, still intent on damage limitation, meekly did as he was told and when he sat down again Ann reached out for his hand. They sat for a moment in friendly silence. Holbrooke could hear the sounds of the street outside: the rumble and squeal of iron-clad cartwheels on the cobbled streets, the calls of the early morning venders and, even at this hour, brought to them on the westerly wind, the steady thump, thump, thump of caulking hammers working on the ships in the yard. He could see the hats of passers-by, but not their faces; the room was elevated from the street by a few feet and the bottom of the window cut off all but the tallest of heads. The serving girl had set in front of them everything that they needed and wouldn't appear for another half hour, being wise enough to avoid bringing extra work upon herself by loitering around the dining room. There were no more guests at breakfast today, and they were as private as if they were in their own sitting room.

'I have something to tell you, George,' Ann said, looking straight ahead with a face that – unusually for her – betrayed no emotion.

George stifled an exclamation. Ann had never spoken like this before and he feared the worst, some dreadful illness perhaps.

Ann turned towards him and saw the fear in his eyes. He was little more than a boy, she realised at that moment. He was only just twenty-one and in a moment of empathy she realised the significance of what she already knew of him. His experience of the world was limited by his background. A small provincial town, the boys' school just off the market square, the monastery-like naval academy and then the peculiar womanless life of a sea officer. He barely remembered his mother and probably he'd spoken to few women in his life, almost certainly none other than herself in intimate terms. She reached out and hugged him close, smiling now and at last finding amusement in the situation.

'You look so solemn, George, like a rabbit caught in the light of a lantern, ready to flee at the first hostile movement. Am I really so terrifying?'

George just goggled at that; he could find no words to reply.

'Well, you shouldn't be frightened, George. Perhaps I should be, but not you. You're going to be a father!'

He opened his mouth to speak then closed it again. He made another attempt but the only sound that came out was unintelligible. His mental processes had been shocked into paralysis and he could no more form an opinion on this startling news than he could sprout wings and fly to the rooftop.

'A baby, George. It has precedent you know; many women report a similar phenomenon shortly after being married. Did you not suspect anything?'

At last Holbrooke could speak, although it did little to help the situation.

'A baby? Ours? Oh, my word!' he exclaimed. 'No, I had no idea, how could I?'

Ann looked at him pityingly. Did he really not know?

Nor'west by North

Yes, it was possible and accorded with all that she already knew about him. His innocence was almost beyond comprehension.

'Well, Sophie guessed a week ago. You saw how she so discreetly left us alone? Are you not pleased, George?'

'Pleased? Oh yes, of course,' he replied, his mind still in confusion, 'it's the most wonderful news.' He was trying desperately to find the right words. It really was most unfair, dropping this on a man with no warning.

'You may at least kiss me to show that you still care for me,' said Ann grinning like he had never seen her before.

It's perhaps just as well that neither Sophie, nor the serving girl, nor the landlord came into the room because it hardly accorded with the dignity of a post-captain to be caught in a tender embrace with his wife over breakfast. There was, after all, a time and a place for everything, but luckily only the toast and the bacon and the rapidly cooling pair of kippers were witness to the scene, and they kept their secrets.

***

CHAPTER SEVEN

Sophie Featherstone

Sunday, Second of March 1760.
The Dunes, Harwich.

A cold sou'easterly wind was whipping in off the North Sea, sending tiered ranks of waves surging slantwise up the sandy beach towards the dunes at its back. They looked like cavalry squadrons clad all in grey and white, endlessly rushing at steadfast lines of infantry only to break upon the point of the bayonet.

Holbrooke smiled at the simile. After all, he had more experience of warfare on land than most soldiers. From the bloody beach at Saint-Cast to the forest clearing of La Belle Famille echoing with the cries of the Iroquois warriors; from the night-time charge of the French infantry at Emden to the encirclement of the supposed Moorish corsairs at Saint Honorat, he'd seen it all. On cold days like today he could still feel the wound where the lock of his pistol had been smashed into his ribs by a French musket ball.

The dunes were empty. Normally on a Sunday the townsfolk of Harwich would be taking the air on the beaten path that twisted tortuously between the clumps of marram grass. Today, however, the wind off the sea was just too keen, and it carried a threat of rain. Holbrooke didn't care; he revelled in the wind and snapped his fingers at the lowering, black clouds. He was just pleased to be in the open air and free to walk as fast as he cared without having to slow the pace of his long legs for Ann to keep up. He'd already walked two miles south along the dunes and now he was almost back to the outskirts of the town. He paused to study the Landguard fort through his telescope. The first time he'd walked here he hadn't brought it and had regretted his decision. Now he rarely walked along the seashore without it.

If he had to bring a frigate into the Stour and the Orwell, opposed by that fort – old though it was – how would he do it? He recalled the charts to his mind as he studied the flow of the tide and the position of the sand and mud banks. He was just coming to the conclusion that he would rather not attempt it, when he saw a figure spring into his field of view. It was clearly a woman, and she was coming his way from the town. He hastily adjusted the focus, suspecting – no, hoping – that it would be Ann, rising early from her rest and come to join him. The figure sharpened. It wasn't Ann; he could see that the woman had dark hair under her tied-down bonnet, and she was taller than Ann. Was it Sophie? As the figure came nearer, he became certain; it was Ann's stepmother, alone on the path atop the dune. He closed the telescope and strode forward to meet her. By the time they had reached each other he'd dismissed his initial awful thought that Ann had been taken ill. If that were the case, then Sophie would have stayed with her and sent someone else to find him.

***

'I trust you haven't finished your exercise, George. I was hopeful that we could walk together for a while.'

Sophie was, as always, direct in her manner. Holbrooke remembered that when he had first met her at Rookesbury house two Christmases ago she had positively taken charge of him. It was just as well, though, because in his youthful timidity, he had been on the point of leaving without talking to Ann, and Sophie had all but forced the two of them together. He smiled broadly at the memory, earning a quizzical look from Sophie who mistook it for eagerness to have an excuse to extend his walk.

'I find that I come just in time,' she said before Holbrooke could speak, and she took his arm and turned him around to retrace his steps.

Holbrooke nodded and fell into step with her.

'I'm delighted to find a reason to keep walking,' he said, 'and if Ann's still resting it's better that I don't disturb her.'

He could always have gone to his ship rather than the inn, but that would have disrupted the work. Far better to stay away.

They walked in silence for a while, with Sophie clearly enjoying the keen wind and the salt air that dragged whisps of her black her hair streaming to leeward. She breathed deep and ran her fingers through the tall stems of grass that flanked their way.

'She was still resting when I left her,' she said. 'It's quite normal, you know, for her to need to recuperate during the day. It will pass in a month, or so I'm told.'

Holbrooke inclined his head but said nothing. He wasn't at all sure where this conversation was going. Although he liked his mother-in-law, he was wary of her and still somewhat in awe of her determined, positive manner. She wasn't all that much older than he and Ann, perhaps ten or fifteen years but he really couldn't estimate her age with any accuracy, and he'd never asked.

'However, the reason I sought you out was to talk about the future, without Ann present.'

Sophie saw Holbrooke's frown.

'Oh, there's nothing sinister, George, but let me start by telling you something about myself.'

Sophie tilted her face to the wind, evidently composing her opening lines.

'You know that I have no family of my own? No living parents, no brothers, no sisters, no cousins even. Apart from Martin and Ann, and now you,' she said squeezing his arm slightly, 'I have nobody in the world.'

Holbrooke caught a glimpse of the sadness in her eyes as she stared out at the sea. Was that a tear that the wind carried away from the corner of her eye?

'Well,' she said, composing herself, 'let me not appear pathetic, but the fact is that Ann means the world to me. Now, I know that your ship will keep you away from her for lengthy periods of time and you must be aware by now that Ann has a worrying vein of insecurity in her character. She's not the most suitable person to be left without the support of her husband while she is in her confinement.'

Holbrooke stared straight ahead. Should he object? Was it right that Sophie should be so obviously criticising his conduct, implying a dereliction of his family duty? He was well aware of his wife's character, but he'd known that when he'd married her, and she had entered into the contract knowing full well that he'd be at sea more than he was at home while the war lasted.

'Now don't take this amiss, George,' she said, noticing his rigidity through their linked arms. She tugged at his elbow to slacken his grip.

Really, he thought, she was just like he imagined his own mother must have been.

'After your wedding I spoke at some length to your friend Captain Carlisle, and it was then that I made my resolution. He and Lady Chiara – I hope I've pronounced that correctly – are in an even more difficult situation. At least you can be sure of a certain amount of time in Portsmouth when *Argonaut* needs a refit, and Wickham is very close, after all. Poor Captain Carlisle has to rely upon sympathetic admirals to send him to the Americas. I gather that Chiara is a very confident person and she's quite a lot older than Ann, but even so it must be difficult.'

'Yes,' Holbrooke replied, still unsure of how he felt about this conversation.

He could imagine how his friend would be able to confide in Sophie. They were much the same age and Sophie was very like Chiara in character and, now that he thought about it, they were similar in looks too, although Chiara had the Mediterranean skin tone.

'Edward and Chiara have certainly made life difficult for themselves,' he agreed. 'It was a near-miracle that his ship was in Portsmouth in November, but it was probably asking too much of divine intervention to have Chiara there also. I wonder whether you will ever meet her. I'm sure that both you and Ann would find her charming. He'll be back again soon, after he's delivered his convoy. I do hope he managed to stay at Hampton for a few days to spend some time with Chiara. I wonder what *Dartmouth* will be doing next. Perhaps he'll be sent to the Americas for a lengthy period.'

Sophie looked furtively at Holbrooke's face. She could tell immediately that George came close to hero-worship of both Edward Carlisle and Chiara; it was written in his wistful expression and confirmed by his respectful tones. She marshalled her thoughts again. The last thing that she wanted was for this talk to turn against her. She could see that Holbrooke may soon come to resent her intrusion, her presumption that she had an important role in their marriage.

'What I'm trying to say is that you can rely on my support for Ann while you are at sea, and I'll respect your privacy when you are at home. I have no children, as you know, and I've been so lucky in marrying Martin to have Ann as an outlet for all the love that I would have lavished on a child of my own. She's dearer to me than anything else in the world.'

Holbrooke glanced at her face. He wasn't a naturally empathetic man, he needed to be told people's needs rather than discover them intuitively. Yet in a brief instant of sympathy, he saw how hard it must have been for Sophie to see her stepdaughter married, how much of her own comfort she had to willingly let go to ensure Ann's happiness. He barely knew his own mother; she was just a memory of soft, loving maternal care, and she had faded out of his life far too quickly. Was she really like Sophie? Cold logic told him that it was unlikely, but she surely shared some of the same motivations, the same hopes and fears. Overlaid upon that was Sophie's lack of children of her own, and she had surely cast him in the role of surrogate son.

'I think I understand,' he said, squeezing her arm in return.

'You can be sure of me, George. I'll stand by you and

Nor'west by North

Ann whatever life throws at us. When you are away, you can be certain that I'll be like her guardian angel. She won't want for support whether it's practical or emotional. All you have to do is love her as much as you can when you are at home.'

She stopped dead in her tracks and looked Holbrooke square in the face. Those *were* tears. He could see the salty tracks above her cheek bones where the wind had blown them away.

'There! That's what I wanted to say. Now it's perhaps time that we turned around. Ann will be up and about soon, and I wouldn't want her to misconstrue our both being out and about at the same time.'

She gave Holbrooke a mischievous smile and squeezed his arm as she turned him around for the walk back to Harwich. Holbrooke was strangely comforted. This was the Sophie that he knew so well; the tortured soul that he'd glimpsed over the past few minutes was unfamiliar to him. He felt that order had been restored to their relationship, and they walked back along the dunes chatting happily about inconsequential matters.

***

CHAPTER EIGHT

A Change of Direction

Tuesday, Fourth of March 1760.
Argonaut, at Sea, Off Harwich.

The sun had barely risen in a sparkling March sky when *Argonaut* slipped from the pontoon and dropped downstream on the ebbing tide. Holbrooke paid little attention as Fairview urged on the men to set sail after sail in this prosperous soldier's breeze. Once they had rounded the Landguard Point, a course a little to the north of east would take them clear of the Cork Sands, and then, with a fair offing, they could turn south and reach away to the North Foreland, the first place to look for the commodore.

Holbrooke left the handling of the ship to the sailing master as he levelled his telescope at the dunes that ran down to the beach on the seaward side of the Harwich peninsula. He could see a carriage drawn up, starkly outlined by the low sun, and two figures standing a little distance away. They were certainly women, but that was all he could tell at this distance, although they could hardly be anyone but Ann and Sophie. He thought he could see a flash of a white handkerchief waving, but his eyes were unaccountably blurred.

'Landguard's dipping its colours, sir,' Shorrock reported quietly, not wanting to intrude on his captain's last sight of his wife, possibly for months.

'Very well. Acknowledge.'

Argonaut was flying her largest red ensign, a fantastically expensive affair that his affectionate friends at the navy board expected him to use on only the most important of occasions. A coronation or a royal wedding or a fleet action would have been appropriate, but anything else would certainly be deemed profligate. Luckily, the representative of the navy board at Harwich was a friendly, easy-going character who understood sea officers, having been one himself, and the difficulties they faced in maintaining a family life. Holbrooke hadn't ordered the ensign to be raised and had been surprised to see it flying from the stern of his frigate instead of the smaller, workaday version. However, Shorrock was certain that it was the right way to honour the captain's wife as her husband sailed away to war. The westerly breeze was just sufficient to give the ensign life and its bright colours – red and white and blue – were picked out by the brilliant spring sunshine. Offered as a *fait accompli*, Holbrooke could hardly disapprove of the gesture in the public space of the quarterdeck.

Shorrock had stationed a reliable man at the ensign staff in anticipation of this moment. The old fort had been built to guard the River Stour and the towns of Felixstowe and Harwich against the Dutch and it was here that the marines fought their first land engagement nearly a century ago. The commander of the garrison had a very particular notion of the honours that should be exchanged when men-o'-war passed his fort and *Argonaut's* vast ensign had not gone unnoticed.

'Dip the ensign,' Shorrock called.

The mate of the watch and the messenger hurried aft to assist the seaman. Three men weren't too many for the task of running the enormous ensign down the staff a fathom or two. They waited for twenty seconds then, at a nod from the first lieutenant, they ran it up again. A moment later the Landguard's colours jerked back up to the top of the mast followed by a puff of smoke and the sharp crack of a single gun.

'Landguard's colours are close up again, sir,' Shorrock reported. 'We don't need to reply to the gun.'

The gunner bobbed his head in agreement and pulled a face that looked as though it belonged at some country fair gurning competition. He knew the master gunner at the Landguard and wouldn't be fooled into encouraging that old conceit of firing a gun as the ensign was run back up the mast.

So that was that. They were clear of the King's Yard, a functioning ship of the Downs Squadron again, with ammunition and stores for three months and as yet no certainty of where Commodore Boys would choose to employ them. Holbrooke took another lingering look at the two figures on the shore.

'*Grietje van Dijk*,' said his clerk, half to himself, as he also watched the shore receding. Lister was standing dutifully within hailing range of his captain, in case he was needed, and this strange utterance couldn't help but be heard.

'Did you say something, Mister Lister,' Holbrooke asked without taking his eyes from his wife.

'Oh, I beg your pardon, sir, but it's a phrase in Dutch – my mother is from Amsterdam you know – it's what the sailors say when they take their last departure on a long voyage.

Holbrooke didn't take his eyes from the shore and made no comment. Lister continued, apparently unaware of the shocked and disapproving stares from the sea officers.

'It's a sentimental reference to the last sail that a woman sees as her man sails away. Margriet – Grietje for short – is standing on the dike, just like those dunes, watching the mizzen tops'l dip below the horizon before she turns for home. It's passed into the language of the sea and now *grietje* is the common Dutch name for the highest sail on the mizzen. We always say *Grietje van Dijk* as we take our departure.'

There was a pause, an interval that terrified Lister when he became aware of all eyes upon him as their owners held their collective breath. All eyes except his captain's. Perhaps he'd been too forward with his opinions on the holy quarterdeck. Had he been guilty of pressing unwanted and unrequested information on his captain? This was his first man-o'-war, and he hadn't yet adapted to the social niceties of this strange new world.

'*Grietje van Dijk*,' Holbrooke repeated aloud, trying to

imitate the cadences of the unfamiliar language. 'How appropriate and how very expressive. I had no idea that the Dutch had such poetry in their souls. Thank you, Mister Lister.'

The quarterdeck breathed again, and the young gentlemen could be seen mouthing the words as they attempted to remember just how that phrase was said. Lister would be able to claim a few drinks over the next days, in payment for tuition on the pronunciation of his mother tongue.

***

The fine weather didn't last and before the men of *Argonaut* had digested their dinner the sky had clouded over, and the wind had veered into the nor'west and turned gusty with sharp, cold showers. The sea had lost its colour and the blues and greens and whites had given way to shades of grey: a grey sky, a grey sea and neither land nor horizon to be seen. The best ensign had been struck the minute that it could no longer be seen from the shore and the sailmaker had made himself the most unpopular man in the ship by spreading it to dry from the hammock rings in the forward part of the gundeck.

'We should sight the North Foreland before eight bells,' said Fairview, studying the featureless seascape on the ship's head.

The deteriorating weather had forced a change of plan and instead of cutting straight across the dangerous finger channels that spread out from the estuary of the Thames River, he'd set a course to skirt around the northernmost point of the Long Sand shoal and run down to the North Foreland from the nor'east. That was the blessing of having a sailing master who was also a channel pilot. *Argonaut* didn't need to take a Trinity House pilot with all the inconvenience of embarking and disembarking him, and the expense of paying him when the navy board often challenged such expenditure on principle, even though it was their regulation that demanded that a pilot should be taken.

They were tearing down towards that important landfall, too fast to cast the lead, and Holbrooke was starting to look nervously to the west. He knew that their dead reckoning had placed them clear of the Kentish Knock and now they should be well to the south of those dangerous sands. But he also knew that the tides in this area were fierce and if they had been wrongly calculated, they could be setting his frigate into danger without warning. He walked aft to the taffrail and again forward to the binnacle, trying to imagine the interplay of wind and tidal stream against the ship's course and speed.

'Eight knots and a half, sir,' reported the mate of the watch.

'Very well.'

Surely they'd sight the North Foreland soon. He trusted Fairview's judgement, but the man had the instincts of a fighting officer, not a sailing master, and he was too eager to charge forward when others of his breed would be urging caution. He'd give it another five minutes and if there was no sight of land he'd heave to and cast the lead.

Fairview watched his captain covertly. He could guess what was going through his mind and was as eager as Holbrooke to get a clear sight of land. He knew the North Foreland of old, had seen it from every aspect and in every weather, and if he didn't sight it soon, then something was wrong.

The tension on the quarterdeck was palpable and Holbrooke resisted the temptation to stride nervously back and forth. One more minute…

'Land ho! Land fine on the starboard bow.'

'What can you see?' Fairview shouted, pointing the copper speaking trumpet towards the main topmast head.

The lookout was an old seaman who had spent years in the east coast coal trade. He'd fallen out with the mate of a collier brig and had incautiously walked ashore in Newcastle to find a more convenient berth where he had been promptly snapped up by the impress service. The coal trade qualified for exemptions from pressing, but with no ship his paper was rendered worthless, and he'd been sent south to Portsmouth just in time to make up the numbers in *Argonaut*. Like the master, he knew the east coast as well as other men knew the road from their village to the market town, and he wouldn't be fooled by false sightings.

'It's the North Foreland, sir,' he called. 'Bold as you like.'

The tension on the quarterdeck eased in an instant. In this weather they'd expect to see a headland like that from eight or ten miles, so they were clear of all the estuary shoals and only had to worry about Margate Sands to the west of the Foreland.

Argonaut plunged forward with the wind on her quarter. At this speed, Holbrooke knew, if they didn't sight the commodore soon then they'd have to look elsewhere. With the wind in the west the next place to search would be the Downs, inside the Goodwin Sands, where half the seaborne trade of the empire gathered awaiting convoy down the channel.

'There's just enough daylight left to run into the Downs, sir,' said Fairview, reading his captain's mind.

Holbrooke wasn't so sure. He didn't suffer from a nervous disposition, but the thought of bowling headlong into the space between Deal and the sands with the light fading and the possibility of the commodore's scrutiny didn't appeal to him. He looked over the starboard bow but there was nothing there but a few intrepid double-reefed smacks making their way home after the last haul of the day.

'I think, master, that we'll…'

But Fairview never did know what his captain thought, for at that moment the lookout hailed the deck with the welcome news that there were masts in sight on the starboard bow. As they drew nearer, more information came down from aloft: a two-decker and a frigate, then a cutter came into in sight.

'Looks like they're at anchor, sir,' shouted the lookout, 'and the frigate's missing her main topmast. She looks a right state, sir.'

The two-decker would be the commodore, Holbrooke knew, anchored in the six-fathom patch to the east of Margate Sand. It was a convenient and safe anchorage in anything other than a northerly blow, and with this nor'westerly already showing signs of backing again, it was the best place to exercise command over his widely spread ships. When Holbrooke last saw him, he was flying his pennant in the fifty-gun fourth rate *Preston*. That must be the two-decker that the lookout reported.

'Bear up, Mister Fairview, and shorten sail. We'll heave-to under the commodore's lee. Stand by to anchor if we're ordered.'

'That's *Coventry*, sir,' said Shorrock. 'Francis Burslem has had her since last October. God, what a shambles, it looks like they've had a rare old mauling.'

Francis Burslem. The one thing that Holbrooke knew about Captain Burslem was that his commission as a post-captain dated from just a few days after his own. He felt a sharp thrill that he wasn't the most junior post-captain on the station. With less than six months' seniority, there were already captains of frigates who were junior to him, and in the normal course of events would remain junior for the rest of their careers. Burslem had been commissioned a lieutenant in the last war and had waited through the peace and the first year of this war before being made commander. He must be older by more than a decade, but the fortunes of the times had made him forever subordinate.

'Commodore's signalling, sir. Blue at the fore,' reported the mate of the watch.

There was a puff of smoke that lasted for a second before it was blown away in rags by the keen wind.

'There's the gun sir. Blue at the fore and a single gun. The squadron is to heave-to.'

That was the quickest way for Boys to direct *Argonaut* to come into the anchorage without actually anchoring. The only other ships of the squadron were already riding on the six-fathom patch, so the signal could only be meant for Holbrooke's ship.

Fairview was already issuing orders to bring the ship to. There was no time to lose, with the light starting to fade and this fair wind hurrying them down to the anchorage. Nevertheless, Holbrooke found that he had little to do as *Argonaut*, stripped to tops'ls and jib, approached the anchorage on a good beam reach. He studied *Coventry* through his telescope. Yes, Burslem had lost his main topmast and the jib boom looked like it was jury rigged from the redundant main tops'l yard. As he came closer, he could see that the frigate's starboard side had suffered badly, with a row of three gunports all smashed in so that a great gap appeared in what should have been an ordered row of neat squares. And they were pumping. A steady stream of clear water was spurting from a hose that had been rigged in the space where the three guns had been. Holbrooke had a curious sense that he knew who had inflicted this damage. It could, of course, have been any of the ships of the French navy that still lingered in the eastern part of the channel, Commodore Boys' area of operation. It could even have been a French squadron pushed to the east to surprise the spread-out British navy units that blockaded every port on the channel coast. But Holbrooke thought not. Some sixth sense told him that he was witnessing Batiste's work, and he had a shrewd notion of why he was bidden to heave to rather than anchor as the other ships had done.

'The commodore's got an extra longboat alongside,' said Shorrock. 'That'll be Captain Burslem, sure as anything.'

***

Commodore Boys was a brisk officer who wasted little time on introductions.

'You know Captain Burslem, Holbrooke?' he asked.

'I haven't had that honour, sir,' Holbrooke replied.

Burslem bowed and Holbrooke responded in kind.

'Francis Burslem, sir. *Coventry*.'

That thrill again. An older, more experienced officer

deferring to him. Holbrooke was determined not to take advantage, there was no knowing when he may need Burslem's enthusiastic support.

'I'm delighted to meet you, Captain, a real pleasure.'

Boys sniffed and fidgeted impatiently. When all was said and done, he was only a post-captain himself, although vastly senior to these two newly promoted men. It would be years before the ranks of admirals were sufficiently thinned by the grim reaper for him to hoist a flag, and long before then he'd probably have to strike his pennant and take up his old rank. At one level, this was a meeting between equals, but neither Holbrooke nor Burslem was fooled. Boys had been plucked from the ranks of post-captains and given a pennant and this vital command because he was the best man for the job. It was their Lordships' way of circumventing the archaic system of promotion to flag rank by seniority.

'Captain Burslem has come from the north, Holbrooke,' he said, looking grimly at the younger man.

Then he was right, *Coventry* must have been part of the detachment that Boys had sent to hunt down Batiste. He'd heard that Farlow Chester had been given command of the three frigates that Boys had spared for the task. Chester had *Pegasus* and now he knew that *Coventry* was the second, but he still didn't know which was the third frigate.

'I'll let Captain Burslem tell you the story. Take a seat, gentlemen.'

That was a relief. It couldn't be a discreditable tale, nothing that would lead to a court martial or a reprimand, otherwise Burslem wouldn't have been invited to give his version of events.

Burslem had a quite distinctive conversational style, very much different to Boys' crisp manner, and his narrative was slower and more circumstantial. He took a sip of coffee before he started.

'We sailed north as soon as we had taken on stores and water from the hoys at the Nore,' he said. 'Chester in *Pegasus*,

Coulson in *Fortune* and my own *Coventry*. We got up to Saint Abb's Head then started coasting north, looking for the French squadron. There was rumour of them everywhere and most of the Scottish fishing ports were jammed with boats waiting until they heard of the French passing to the north and west. The coasting trade wasn't moving and only a few Baltic ships were reaching England. It was like one of the plagues of Egypt had swept through,' he said, with an evangelical look in his eye.

Boys was looking impatient and Burslem took the hint.

'Well, to cut a long story short, it appeared that Monsieur Batiste had been indulging in his privateering trade instead of pushing on to land the army. We came up with them at last off the northernmost island of the Orkneys, North Ronaldsay. They'd just taken a pair of herring busses and they were busy taking the catch aboard their own ships. It seemed an unprofitable affair to me, the whole catch could hardly have fed the expedition for more than a day.'

'Chester sent word that he believes that the French are running short of provisions,' Boys interjected, 'take careful note of that Captain Holbrooke.'

Burslem paused for a moment. To Holbrooke it seemed like he was silently signalling his dislike at having the flow of his story interrupted. He may be senior to Burslem, but Holbrooke didn't yet have the confidence to cross his commodore in this way.

'They ran for it when they saw us; they didn't even pause to finish burning the busses. We chased them north and west, out into the Atlantic, and caught them with an hour of daylight left.'

Burslem had a faraway gleam in his eye now, perhaps this was where he came to the damage to his own ship.

'They fought well. The four frigates covered the transports, and we went at it hammer and tongs until it became dark. The biggest of them, a *demi-batterie* with nine and eighteen pounders, I think, ranged alongside *Coventry*. After half a dozen broadsides, we'd lost our main topmast and our jib boom and three of our gun ports were beaten into one. We have four holes between wind and water and without heaving-to my carpenter could only come at two of them. My men have been pumping without pause, but you've seen the damage yourself,'

Holbrooke nodded. 'Many casualties?'

'Six dead and fifteen wounded. Three more died on the passage south.'

Burslem looked as though he was deeply affected by the deaths; perhaps some were friends or relatives. *Argonaut* had been lucky to have got away with a smaller butcher's bill after Holbrooke's own encounter with Batiste.

'When the sun set, a thick blanket of cloud hid the moon, and a rising sea forced us to break off the action. It seemed to me that they were steering for the Faroes. I found that *Coventry* couldn't keep up with *Pegasus* and *Fortune*. Captain Chester came up on my windward side and shouted for me to turn back, and that's the last that I saw of them. That was six days ago on the Wednesday. We had fair winds all the way here, but I didn't dare set too much sail in my ruined condition, and I couldn't anchor or heave to, not until I'd reported to the commodore,' he added, gesturing towards Boys.

Burslem was evidently shattered by the experience of bringing his leaky, battered ship through six hundred miles of stormy waters at the end of a severe winter. He could hardly string his words together anymore, and his story tailed off into mumbling.

'Thank you, Captain Burslem. I'm sure you did your best to bring the news to me.'

Burslem nodded. It may have been in acknowledgement, or it may have been sheer exhaustion.

'Now, Captain Holbrooke, you've probably guessed why I asked Captain Burslem to tell you all this, eh?'

Holbrooke gave a brief bow. His ship was in good condition, it was stored for three months, and he'd already had a brush with Batiste and his expedition. Naturally Boys would send *Argonaut*; he must have appeared as a gift from God when the commodore saw him reaching into the anchorage just hours behind *Coventry*.

'Captain Burslem, you're for Harwich in the morning where I dare say they'll detain you for a month or so. I don't want to see you until your ship is fit to keep the sea. And get some sleep tonight, man, you look like you're fit for the grave! Captain Holbrooke, I'll have your orders made up within ten minutes,' he nodded to his secretary who had been unobtrusively making notes of the meeting.

'You're to make for the Faroes, picking up whatever information you can on the way. If you don't find Captain Chester there, then south through the Minches and make for the Isle of Man, where Batiste has friends, or so it's said. Remember that he could choose to land his soldiers anywhere in Scotland or Ireland or the west coast of England, so don't pass up any chance of gaining intelligence. In the last resort you're to come home west-about and meet me here, at the Downs or at the Nore.'

Boys stared abstractedly out of the great stern windows, then turned back to Holbrooke.

'This man Batiste has been a menace to our trade throughout this war, as he was in the last. He's chosen to head for the northwest of the Kingdom by the northern route, it appears. On his head be it. It's a dangerous path that he'll be following, the bane of the great Armada, no less. Nor'west by north to his doom, it falls well upon the tongue. Let that be his epitaph, Captain Holbrooke.'

In the silence that followed, Holbrooke coughed quietly to bring the commodore back to the point.

'Eh? Of course, you want to be away Holbrooke. I won't see you for a few months at least, so my best wishes to you. If you're quick you can be clear of the Foreland this evening before you lose the light.'

***

CHAPTER NINE

Nor'west by North

Thursday, Thirteenth of March 1760.
Argonaut, at Sea, Linklet Bay, North Ronaldsay, The Orkneys.

Had ever a ship been sent off on such a mission with such flimsy instructions? Holbrooke read his orders for at least the tenth time, hoping to find some nuance that he'd missed, some hint as to how he should conduct himself. They hardly deviated by a word from the verbal brief that Commodore Boys had given him. It could hardly have been otherwise as, true to the commodore's word, the orders had been thrust into his hand ten minutes after the meeting had ended.

He'd made his best speed through the North Sea, but the winds had been obstinately on their head, and he'd paused frequently to speak to passing ships and to look into likely harbours and anchorages. There was no news of either Chester or the French squadron. Holbrooke hadn't been surprised. Burslem had last seen them sailing nor'west between the Shetlands and the Orkneys. Only the Faroes lay in that direction, and beyond the Faroes, Iceland and then Greenland. It was unlikely that Batiste would allow himself to be chased so far north, so far dead to windward, if he had no business in that direction. It was well known that on a previous privateering cruise Batiste had called at the Faroes and had been well received and provided with the food, wood and water that he needed. Probably he was hoping for the same welcome and a respite from the constant gales that were more than likely in March.

The coasting trade and the fishermen had recovered from their fright. They all had to make a living and would have to conclude that a French squadron that hadn't been seen for a week was not worth worrying about anymore. Such a group of ships with so many mouths to feed just could not stay in one place for long, not off a hostile shore and not with the equinoctial gales expected at any time. Holbrooke made enquiries all along the coast from Saint Abb's head, but nobody had seen the French, or the British, for two weeks. This wild and desolate bay was the last place he would touch at and then he'd sail for the Faroes without further delay.

'Mister Shorrock, be sure to ask about *Pegasus* and *Fortune*, as well as the French,' he called down to the longboat. 'Don't take any insult from the locals, they're subjects of King George as much as you or me, even if they pretend to not know it.'

Shorrock waved but his shouted reply was lost on the wind. The longboat pushed away, and the oarsmen bent to the task of pulling the heavy boat the mile or so to the shore, directly into the nor'westerly breeze.

'Can we lie here for a couple of hours, Mister Fairview?'

The master looked up from the notebook that he was consulting. Fairview systematically collected the pilotage advice that he gathered from other sailing masters. He'd never sailed in these waters before, but these private notes gave him some idea of what to expect.

'The stream's setting to the sou'east, sir,' he said. 'We could see the race as we beat into the bay. It appears to be increasing so we should have tide rips to the nor'east as well. We're safe enough here unless the wind veers through the north; we have good shelter and plenty of sea room to leeward. If we get blown to the east, we may find it a little lumpy as we meet the stream.'

Argonaut was lying with her jib backed and her fore tops'l flat against the mast. Each gust of wind that tried to push her head away only increased the leverage of the main tops'l and mizzen and brought her bows back to lie four points from the wind. The frigate was perfectly balanced, and the only problem was the amount of leeway that she would make. Holbrooke looked to the east where two miles away he could see the broken water of the tide race. If Shorrock spent no more than an hour on shore, then he could use the longboat's lugsail to run down to *Argonaut* and be back on board in little more than two hours. *Argonaut* could make sail and beat up to meet him. Meanwhile, his ship was riding comfortably in this sheltered bay, perhaps the last calm water they'd see for a few days if his suspicions were correct, and Chester had chased Batiste to the Faroes.

'Sixty-four leagues to the Faroes, sir, dead to windward,' Fairview said. 'Torshavn is the capital and the most sheltered port. If the French have gone north and west, that's where they'll be.'

Holbrooke and Fairview didn't leave the deck while the longboat was inshore. They could see that Shorrock had arrived at the beach. It was just possible to make out a small group of people standing near three or four fishing boats that had been hauled out. The minutes ticked by, then they saw a flash of white as the longboat's lugsail was set. In half an hour Shorrock was back on deck and the longboat was towing astern.

'Set sail to the sou'east, Mister Fairview. Let's make an offing to get around the tide race.'

It was a shocking sight. The calm water in the lee of North Ronaldsay was abruptly broken three miles to the east by the tumbled confusion that was caused by the fast-moving tidal stream meeting shallower water. *Argonaut* was almost in the race and already Holbrooke could feel the uneasy motion. It wasn't dangerous for a well-found frigate, but on principle it was better to keep his ship out of such confused water, to preserve his spars and rigging. To the sou'east the water was less disturbed but to the south he could see white water again. According to Fairview's notes, there was a clear channel between the two arms of the tidal race that was bisected by the island. Shorrock had returned just in time to allow *Argonaut* to take that channel.

'The islanders were friendly enough, sir, once they realised that we wouldn't harm them. They saw the action off the island two weeks ago, and one of those boats on the shore was burned almost to the waterline by the French. How they got it home without it sinking I will never know. They saw the French and captain Chester sail away to the nor'west and soon after they saw a frigate running south with her sails all astray. That must have been *Coventry*. Since then, they've seen nothing, and they started fishing again yesterday; they only put to sea when the tide is slack.'

Holbrooke gazed at the shore. It was too far now to see any movement but as the tidal stream diminished, he expected that the boats would put off.

'Did you get any sense of their loyalties at all? Did they show any sympathy for the French?'

Shorrock grinned broadly.

'Ah, now that's the interesting part, sir. They were all hiding when we came ashore, they didn't know who to trust any more. Only a few of them speak English, and then in such a thick accent that they're difficult to understand. I had to shout and wave the flag, and even then, they wouldn't approach until we all lay down our swords and pistols and stepped back from them.'

Holbrooke smiled at that. Perhaps his first lieutenant was capable of greater diplomacy than he had given him credit for.

'They're aware in a vague way that their little island is part of Great Britain, but they're so remote and so rarely see anybody with any pretensions to officialdom, that it isn't a subject that they dwell upon. They were certainly disappointed in the way the French treated them. It appears that they've always viewed the French as friends, regardless of any conflict with Britain, and when the fishermen saw the ships, they expected to sell them some of their catch and make some real money, which seems to be scarce in these parts. The possibility of being plundered and burned hadn't occurred to them. I do believe that they won't be quick to trust a French ship again.'

'Thank you, Mister Shorrock, you've done well.'

Shorrock grinned again. Holbrooke had noticed how he

responded to praise.

'I tried to buy some sheep, sir. There was a vast number of them, but they are tiny things, all sorts of colours and the rams have the most horrible horns, they look like so many imps of Satan. Eating seaweed some of them were. However, they wouldn't sell, it being their lambing season, and they had no fish to spare with the boats having stayed ashore this past two weeks.'

Holbrooke stayed on the deck as *Argonaut* threaded between the two tide races and then hauled her wind to the north to start the long beat to windward.

Four days was Fairview's opinion, in the worst case, if the wind stayed in the nor'west. But they both knew that a steady wind was unlikely in March, that month of gales on gales. *Argonaut* would take a short beat north to give the island a wide berth, then make a long tack to the west, hoping that the wind would back and allow them to fetch the Faroes on the next tack.

***

Holbrooke stayed on deck until Fairview's forecast backing wind had become a reality, making a tack to the north essential to avoid being set towards Papa Westray, the most north-westerly island of the Orkneys. Since then, the wind had continued to back until *Argonaut* was hard on the wind on the larboard tack, with her head pointing fairly towards Torshavn, sixty leagues nor'west. With only Norway under their lee, eighty miles to the east, he could at last turn in and take the weight from his aching feet. It seemed like only minutes before he was awakened by a loud knock at the cabin door. It was one of the young gentlemen who had been judged fit to keep a watch along with the more experienced midshipmen.

'Mister Shorrock's compliments, sir. It's seven bells and the wind has increased and backed another point. He begs your permission to call all hands to take a second reef in the tops'ls.'

'Very well, you can tell Mister Shorrock to carry on and

Nor'west by North

I'll be on deck in a moment.'

Holbrooke shook his head to try to clear the sleep. As if by magic, his cabin servant appeared with a bowl of water, and he splashed it over his face and neck before winding a wool comforter round and round below his chin. He had turned in wearing his shirt and breeches and it only required the addition of his coat, cloak and shoes to make him fit to brave the elements on deck. His servant pulled the woollen mittens onto his hands and held the door for him. The blast of frigid air chased away the last of the frowziness, and he was ready to face the deck of his ship.

He could immediately tell that the wind had risen, and a second reef was almost overdue. Shorrock must have held on to give the watch below as much time in their hammocks as possible, but he was close to leaving it too late. It didn't even occur to Holbrooke that his first lieutenant had been more concerned that Holbrooke should get as much sleep as possible, and that the comfort of the watch below was only a secondary concern.

The night was black and the only light on the deck came from the binnacle. There were not even any lights below decks to shine upwards as the hatches were opened; the master-at-arms had ensured that all lanterns were doused as the first watch was set. Not for the first time Holbrooke shuddered at the thought of going aloft onto the swinging yardarm on a night like this. He'd done it himself, of course, as a midshipman and master's mate, but that seemed a long time ago now and he could hardly imagine how he'd found the courage to make that perilous ascent. Nevertheless, it had to be done and reefing the tops'ls in a frigate required the efforts of both watches.

'Carry on, Mister Shorrock.'

There really was nothing more for him to say. Fairview had come on deck to watch over the reefing and Shorrock was eminently competent. The men seemed in good spirits as they climbed the ratlines on the weather side of the mainmast and foremast. There were none of the exuberant daredevil antics that they were prone to in fair weather and in daylight. They all knew that the stakes were higher in this rising gale and in almost total darkness. He listened to the sequence of orders that lowered the yards to allow the sails to be reefed. He heard the calls from above as the earrings were passed and he saw the waisters – the older men and the inexperienced who worked on deck – hauling on their halyards and sheets. In half an hour it was done, and he could feel the frigate riding easier over the waves. With a reduced sail area, *Argonaut* was more upright, and that meant she was carrying less weather helm, so the steersmen's task was eased, and the frigate moved faster through the water, perhaps half a knot faster. He resolved to have a quiet word with Shorrock; nothing like an admonishment, but just to set his expectation that the needs of the ship came first. The comfort of the crew was a consideration, certainly, but that was a decision for the captain, not for the officer of the watch.

'What do you think now, Mister Fairview? If the wind stays westerly, when will we make Torshavn?'

'Sunday morning, sir, but let's not tempt fate by setting a time,' he said touching the binnacle for luck. 'There's a good chance of this wind staying steady for a few days, but if it veers again, we can add a day on to that.'

Holbrooke stayed on deck as Shorrock handed the watch over to the bosun and the men of the middle watch settled in to their four hours on deck. Perhaps a quarter of them had something to do at any one time – lookouts, steersmen, sheet trimmers, messengers – but the remainder soon disappeared under tarpaulins and into the lee of the weather gunwales, to doze until they were called for their trick at the wheel or to make the lonely climb to the main topmast head.

***

Nor'west by North

'This is a bit different to the American wilderness, sir.'

Jackson had been only a few feet from Holbrooke since the change of the watch, but only now, with everything quiet and the ship settled on its course, did he tentatively start a conversation with his captain.

'Aye, it's a little colder here than Lake Ontario in the summer,' Holbrooke replied.

'At least we have a proper ship, sir, and we don't have to rig a tent before we can get our heads down. I wouldn't be a soldier for any money,' he said with a laugh. 'Do you think we'll find these Frenchmen, sir?'

Holbrooke paused. That was just what he had asked himself. If he didn't find Chester at Torshavn or one of the other harbours in the Faroes, then he'd have to turn south and start a possibly fruitless search down the west coast of the British Isles.

'I hope so, Mister Jackson, I do hope so. I can't think where else they would have been heading but it's quite possible that they've been to Torshavn and fled with Captain Chester in hot pursuit. In that case we may be able to discover something of their plans. This Batiste seems to be a talkative fellow and he was quite happy to tell anyone in Gothenburg his business. But all things considered, I expect to find him in two days. He has over two thousand men to feed, and he won't want to start south until he's stored for at least two or three months. We know he didn't get as much as he wanted in Gothenburg, so by fair means or foul he must mulct the citizens of the Faroes.'

'They're Danish aren't they, sir?'

Holbrooke thought for a moment. Where did their loyalties lie?

'Yes, in principle. They're administered from Copenhagen, but they would claim to be Faroese, not native Danes. Denmark is neutral in this war, of course, but the Danes have cause to resent our navigation laws. Their trade has decreased while ours has increased and even in the Faroes they must be feeling the pinch.'

'It's quite a risk for the French then, sir. If they get no stores there, they'll be in an even worse state than when they left Gothenburg. I'd have thought they'd be better to put the soldiers ashore at some small town on the Scottish west coast, or in Ireland and plunder it of everything it has.'

'That would certainly be the obvious thing to do. We have no force worth speaking of in the north and they can come and go more-or-less as they please. I suspect we're seeing the result of jealousies between the land and sea forces. That timber brig told us that there were divisions and that the two sets of officers barely spoke to each other. Putting the army ashore gives its commander, Fouquet, the initiative but as long as they are embarked, Batiste keeps control. Perhaps, just perhaps, he's using the food supply as a way to stay in command of the expedition.'

Jackson was silent for a few moments as he digested this information. He'd watched the politics of command played out in ships since he was a boy, and the season spent as part of the land expedition to take Fort Niagara had shown him how the military mind worked. Holbrooke's explanation seemed most plausible to him.

'Well, in that case, he'll still be in the islands when we get there. Three months of rations for more than two thousand men? He'll have to bleed the population dry to gather that amount of food, and they won't give it willingly, nor sell it even; that's my guess.'

'I hope you are right, Mister Jackson, because *Pegasus* and *Fortune* will have their hands full if Batiste comes out to fight. We may be a very welcome sight for Captain Chester, assuming we arrive in time.'

The muffled bell struck twice and there was a general movement on deck as the half-hour spells of duty were changed around.

'I'll turn in, Mister Jackson. Let me know if the wind veers at all. If we can't make Torshavn on this tack, I'll want to head out to the west again.'

'Aye-aye, sir,' Jackson replied turning back to his duties.

***

Back in his cabin, still in his clothes and wrapped tightly in his blanket, Holbrooke found his mind too active for sleep. At this moment Chester must be wondering whether Boys would send a replacement for *Coventry*. If he had to fight Batiste, he'd be at a sever disadvantage, with two frigates to the Frenchman's four and with less than a quarter of the men. Would he decline to fight and choose to shadow the French expedition? That may well be the prudent course, but it wouldn't be what their Lordships expected. After a difficult start to this war, when Admiral Byng was tried and executed for not doing his utmost against the enemy, the British navy had shown an exemplary fighting spirit. Chester would know that if he chose not to fight and then lost the Frenchmen, which was perfectly possible, likely even, then at the least his reputation would suffer. In the worst case he'd follow the dire path that Byng had trod. Given the circumstances, he expected that Chester would fight the French if he had a chance. Certainly the addition of *Argonaut* to his force would make success far more likely.

And then, of course, it was important to think about Batiste's attitude. He wouldn't want to fight, not with the nearest refitting port a thousand dangerous miles to the south. Whatever else he thought of the British navy, he'd know that even with his overwhelming superiority in numbers, he'd be most unlikely to come out of an engagement unscathed, and then he'd be easy prey for the next squadron to track him down.

Well, there was nothing he could do except make the best speed towards Torshavn and hope that he'd see *Pegasus* and *Fortune* waiting for him. In that case, he could forget about trying to guess Batiste's motives and would no longer have to think about what the French privateer-cum-King's officer would do next. That would be

Chester's responsibility and he'd only have to take his place in the small squadron and follow the motions of its leader. He curled luxuriously into the warmth of the blanket and, his mind clear at last, fell into a deep sleep.

***

CHAPTER TEN

A Meeting

Sunday, Sixteenth of March 1760.
Argonaut, at Sea, off Torshavn, The Faroe Islands.

Argonaut shortened sail in the middle watch and ran downwind for a few hours so that they approached the Faroe Islands from the east with the rising sun nudging over a clear horizon at their stern. The gale had blown through during the previous forenoon, leaving the air crystal clear and the sky an indescribable blue that no painter's pallet could match. Fairview had taken a reliable noon sight only eighteen hours ago and having carefully calculated his dead reckoning, he was confident of the ship's latitude, if not so certain of the longitude. Torshavn was on the bow, but it could be anything between twenty and thirty miles ahead.

'Now, Mister Shorrock, Mister Fairview. If Captain Chester is lying off the harbour – if he ever came here indeed – and if Monsieur Batiste is at Torshavn and not at some other place in the islands, I expect him to be waiting here.'

Holbrooke pointed at the chart, to the eastern end of the wide channel that separated the main group of Northern Isles from the smaller Sandoy Island.

'If the French are at Torshavn, then they'll naturally want to leave to the south,' Fairview agreed. 'I can't see any reason for them trying the northern passage but if they do then in this weather they'll certainly be seen, and Mister Chester can tack around the south of Sandoy and meet them.'

'I can't see why he'd want to escape though,' Shorrock added. 'He'll know that there are only two frigates waiting for him and he has four of his own and three armed transports. He'll like those odds, I would if I were in his shoes. As soon as I'd completed my business I'd come out and take on Captain Chester and be confident of the outcome.'

That possibility had been preying on Holbrooke's mind. Perhaps Chester had already met Batiste at sea, in which case it was quite possible – probable even – that the two British frigates were already prizes of the French or were limping back south to refit. In that case he'd be on his own. But he'd only know that when he reached Torshavn, so it wasn't worth dwelling on.

'You're quite correct gentlemen, but none of that can influence our actions now. We must work on the assumption that Batiste is in Torshavn raking the country for enough supplies to last his passage south. We must hope that when he's filled his holds, he'll come out to fight his way clear, and he's more likely to do that if he believes there are only two frigates waiting for him.'

'Then we must lie off until Mister Chester gives us orders,' said Fairview.

'Just so. I want the best lookouts at the main topmast head until we sight him. When we do – if we do, we'll heave-to and I'll take the longboat in to report. I don't know how long we can remain undetected, probably a fishing boat will carry the news and then we may as well sail boldly up and join the other two. But until that happens, we'll try to keep Batiste in ignorance.'

***

'I hear you plan to go in with the longboat, George,' said Chalmers as they took breakfast together, 'may I come?'

Holbrooke thought for a moment. Chalmers was carried on the ship's books as a chaplain, and it was true that a sixth rate's complement did include a man of the cloth. Nevertheless, it was so unusual for that billet to be filled – there were neither enough chaplains in the fleet, nor enough captains who chose to carry a chaplain – that for a ship like *Argonaut* it would be assumed that the chaplain was a friend of the captain. Probably word of this

Nor'west by North

unusual arrangement had been passed around when *Argonaut* was assigned to join the Downs Squadron back in January. It could do no harm.

'Certainly, David,' Holbrooke replied after only a brief pause. 'In fact, I expect to sight our friends at any moment, so it would be best if we prepare ourselves rather than plunder the cabin stocks any further.'

He carefully folded his napkin and slid it into the silver ring that Ann had given him as a wedding present. Holbrooke was still unused to any kind of luxury at sea, and he treated this trinket with care, handing it to his servant immediately after each meal instead of leaving it at the mercy of the ship's movement. They had no sooner stood up when they heard the lookout's hail floating down through the skylight. A sail! Two sails! Right on the ship's head, just where Holbrooke had expected to find *Pegasus* and *Fortune*.

Argonaut was running towards the two sails at nine knots, so it was only a few minutes before the lookout confirmed that they were frigates, British frigates, and they were lying close to the wind under tops'ls alone, as though they were waiting for something.

'Heave-to, Mister Fairview,' Holbrooke said as the master came down to the cabin to report. 'Bring the longboat alongside as soon as we're steady. Pass the word for my coxswain and boat's crew. There's no need for them to clean into their best rig, this is a working visit.'

The quarterdeck was a haven of peace and quiet now that the frigate was lying quietly. The high land of the Faroes was just visible as an indistinct grey smudge on the horizon, but the two frigates could only be seen from the masthead. The lookout at *Pegasus'* masthead would have seen this strange sail approaching from the east. Perhaps Chester would have guessed that it was a replacement for *Coventry* and perhaps even formed an idea of why it wasn't coming any closer.

'Get underway once we've slipped, Mister Shorrock,

and keep those two in sight. But no closer than you are now. If I'm not back by the end of the afternoon, you are to close them and await orders.'

Holbrooke unobtrusively sniffed the air for any trace of rum on the first lieutenant's breath. Thankfully there was none; in any case, he had found no cause to fault Shorrock's performance, drink or no drink.

Holbrooke and Chalmers were handed down into the waiting longboat. The crew had clearly not complied with the spirit of his orders because although they weren't dressed in the blue and white uniforms that he had provided out of his own pocket, they were in clean jackets and trousers. Those clothes had all come from the same source, the stock of slops carried by the purser, and it gave them a measure of uniformity.

'Shove off forrard,' said Dawson in a gruff undertone.

The longboat drifted quietly away from the frigate as the lugsail was hoisted. Soon the canvas filled, and the easterly wind carried them towards the waiting frigates at a good walking pace.

Holbrooke and Chalmers sat in silence, wrapped in their cloaks and enjoying the sunshine. Probably they wouldn't be back at the ship until past midday. He knew Chester only by reputation, but he hoped he wasn't the sort of officer who felt that no visit was complete without a long, alcoholic dinner. He hoped – he hoped with all his heart – that Chester would see the opportunity to prevent his adversary knowing the size of the force that opposed him.

***

'Captain Holbrooke, you come on the wings of a prayer, sir!'

Chester was a stout man with short legs and a florid face. His stomach filled his long waistcoat, straining against the enclosing fabric and causing a deep horizontal crease to spread to the left and right from each buttonhole. He appeared to be quite old, perhaps fifteen or twenty years senior to Holbrooke, and he evidently enjoyed the good life. *Pegasus'* great cabin had been decorated with care, and the fruits of two lucrative cruises against the enemy trade were evident in the rich damasks and shining silver that showed at every hand.

Holbrooke bowed in reply. He felt out of place in these gorgeously appointed quarters.

'May I present Mister Chalmers, sir? My friend and *Argonaut's* chaplain.'

'Ah, Mister Chalmers, I've heard of you from my cousin – my second cousin, once or twice removed – Eyre Massey of the Forty-Sixth. He wrote to me soon after Fort Niagara fell; told me how you patched him up at La Belle Famille, and how Captain Holbrooke took command of his army when he swooned. Your fame precedes you, sir, and I'm glad to have you in my little squadron.'

Holbrooke tried not to show his relief. He knew of senior captains who would have objected to a chaplain being included in a meeting such as this. But a man who had stood in the line at La Belle Famille could take his place anywhere, it appeared.

'When we have the leisure, I'd welcome your account of the Niagara campaign, Holbrooke. Particularly how you came to give the order for the army to stand and receive the French charge, if my cousin spoke truthfully. I only have his letter and the published reports, but I'm fascinated to know how a sea officer found himself so far from salt water and how you managed to fit into the army's strange ways. Did you and Massey agree?'

'We did indeed, sir. He was my constant friend throughout the campaign…'

'Excellent, then I'm sure we will agree also. Captain Coulson will be with us soon, I hung out a waft for him as soon as I saw your longboat underway. Ah, that sounds like him now.'

The long notes of the bosun's call drifted into the cabin.

'We don't stand on much ceremony,' Chester said, 'and Coulson has been here often enough that he won't be miffed that my first lieutenant is meeting him. Now, you're too late for breakfast and I must not detain you until dinner, but my cook put together a kind of early elevenses when he heard that you were coming.'

Captain Coulson, as long and lean as Chester was short and fat, stooped low to enter the cabin at the same time as a half-dozen servants started bringing out the surprising number of dishes that made up the refreshments for this impromptu meeting. Holbrooke watched in dismay as cold meats, pickled herrings, cheeses of three sorts, an ox tongue and two bottles of wine were placed between the fiddles on the polished sideboard. He'd had a good breakfast in anticipation of a long forenoon, and the thought of food at this hour repelled him. He glanced at Chalmers, but nothing could be gleaned from that inscrutable face.

Chester and Coulson made an almost comical pair, and it wasn't just their physiques. Where Chester was flamboyant, throwing his arms around as he spoke and generously bringing everyone into the conversation, Coulson was austere and reserved, speaking only when he had something to say. Yet they appeared to have a mutual respect and were easy in each other's company. It could have been difficult for Holbrooke to break into this small established group, but both, in their own way, welcomed the new arrivals.

'Now, before we go any further, we must address the sordid subject of prize money,' said Chester. 'Prize money and of course head money and gun money.'

Holbrooke had been expecting this after a note that he received from Burslem of the *Coventry*. The original three ships had come to an agreement to divide the prize money equally between them, regardless of which ship made the capture and whether or not the other two were in sight at the time.

'It's perfectly normal you know, and if you can agree to terms, I can simply substitute you and *Argonaut* for Burslem and *Coventry*. It will mean that I can make dispositions without having to concern myself with the equality of opportunity for you gentlemen. You will have to obtain the agreement of your people, of course,' he added, 'and I hope you can do that quickly.'

Chester laid a single sheet of paper before Holbrooke. There were three signatures appended, one of which had been neatly crossed through and two sets of initials set into the margin.

'Under the terms, *Coventry* ceased to be a party to the agreement when I released Burslem to return south.'

Holbrooke forced back a smile as Chalmers watched his face. Jackson had already spoken to all the ship's company other than the officers, and Holbrooke had canvassed the officers himself. There were a few men who demurred, but that was to be expected among two hundred or so individuals, but Jackson had a paper with well over a hundred-and-fifty signatures, or marks for the handful of illiterate men, and that gave Holbrooke a mandate to make an agreement. It was necessary because the value of a prize – after condemnation by an Admiralty court – belonged legally to every man on the ledger, in due proportion. Holbrooke could find himself liable for recompense, the subject of a suit at law even, if he made an agreement without the majority's approval.

'I already have my people's agreement,' Holbrooke replied, carefully reading the short document.

Chester's clerk offered his pen and Holbrooke signed. Then he produced two more copies which all three men signed. Now it was legally enacted.

'Excellent,' said Chester. 'Now that grubby business is concluded we can get back to stretching our minds to defeat the enemy's schemes. That was clever of you, Holbrooke, to keep *Argonaut* out of sight. Of course, I've been willing Batiste to come out and fight, but it would be a close-run thing without a third frigate to back me up. I can't think what's keeping him in Torshavn unless he's short of supplies, but God knows – I beg your pardon Mister Chalmers –' he apologised for the mild blasphemy, 'how much he'll find there.'

'I can fill in a little, sir,' Holbrooke said. 'I spoke to a timber brig that had been in Gothenburg with him. Batiste had friends there and managed to get some supplies, but it was too little, and he could get no more in the face of the official opposition. The Swedes are reluctant to offend us at sea, even though their army is fighting alongside the French in Pomerania. The master of the brig thought that they had only two or three weeks of food the day he sailed, which was only a couple of days before Batiste got away. Plenty of wood and water though.'

'That would explain why he made for the Faroes then. Didn't fancy the long haul back to France without a full hold. I assume he does plan to make for home west-about?'

'I'm not at all sure, sir…' Holbrooke said.

It took a long time to work through the factors that could affect Batiste's movements. What would Fouquet want to do? Would Batiste's thirst for official recognition persuade him to try something on the shore? Would his privateering instincts send him in search of British merchantmen? Would he double back and try to make Dunkirk through the North Sea, in the face of the Downs Squadron?

Coulson had contributed little to the discussion, and now, when he spoke, his previous silence added weight to his words.

'This conjecture is all very well, sir,' he said, 'but it seems to me that it has precious little bearing on our immediate duty. There's no value in keeping Batiste bottled up in Torshavn. We must persuade him to come out and fight, and the sooner the better before we are blown off station or have to find provisions and water ourselves. From what Captain Holbrooke has told us, Commodore Boys has no spare frigates to relieve us, so time is not on our side. How long before a ship from the east – from Denmark or Norway or Sweden – sees *Argonaut* and reports her presence? With this wind it won't be long, so we should find a way of bringing the French out without delay.'

Chester looked thoughtful.

'He's used to seeing us here. Our tops'ls must be the first thing he sees in the morning and the last that he sees at night. Let's assume that he has stored sufficiently by now and he's just waiting for a good moment to break out.'

Holbrooke and Coulson watched Chester as he gazed thoughtfully at the still heavily laden table.

'I'm sure that he'll sail south when he leaves here, so let's set a trap. We'll persuade him that he has only a single frigate to face. If he sees *Fortune* withdraw, he'll assume that *Pegasus* won't fight on those odds but that I'll just follow him as you did before. Captain Holbrooke, you'll join Captain Coulson to the south, keeping yourself out of sight of the islands as you run down. I'll write out orders for you, Coulson, but essentially, you're to keep *Fortune* and *Argonaut* fifty miles to the south and watch for the French. I hope that I'll be ahead of them, but it depends on the circumstances. In any case, you're to take, burn or sink them wherever you may find them. Now that's a happy thought.'

Coulson and Holbrooke nodded. It was a good plan, but it relied upon Batiste being deceived as to the number of British frigates that he had to face. And waiting out of sight to the south was far better than lurking to the east. Almost all of the traffic for the Faroes came from Denmark, with a little from Sweden and Norway. Only a tiny amount came from the British Isles to the south, so there would be a much better chance of remaining undetected. That much was obvious to them all.

'There's still the fishermen,' said Coulson. 'We've seen them heading south and they range far out of sight of the land. It will only be a matter of time before one of them sees us.'

Chalmers coughed discreetly.

'Can I suggest, sir,' he said, looking at Chester, 'that you detain the first few fishing boats that leave the islands steering to the south? Not long enough to cause an incident, but sufficient time to make them think that they'd be better staying in port until we have left. It's almost legal, with the French being in Torshavn and the Danish suspected of running contraband.'

'It'll certainly make the fishermen think twice about sailing,' Coulson added looking appreciatively at Chalmers, 'and that will stir the Faroese into putting a limit on the length of time that the French can stay in Torshavn. It may have a double benefit in keeping the presence of *Fortune* and *Argonaut* a secret, and in hurrying the French out of the islands.'

***

'What did you think of Captain Chester?' Holbrooke asked as the longboat started its long beat to the sou'east.

'He wears his authority lightly,' Chalmers replied, 'which is a pleasant change from most senior captains that I have met.'

When Holbrooke laughed, every member of the longboat's crew turned to look at him. There was no rowing to do until they were much closer to *Argonaut*, and they'd all gathered in the bows of the longboat, leaving the stern sheets to their captain, the chaplain and the coxswain. Holbrooke and Chalmers had been speaking softly so that only Dawson could hear them. It really wasn't the thing to discuss senior officers in front of a boat's crew, but Dawson had been Holbrooke's coxswain in *Kestrel*, and Holbrooke knew he could trust his discretion.

'He does indeed, but he seems keen enough to bring the French to action and he doesn't mind taking suggestions.'

'He and Captain Coulson seemed to understand each other well enough,' Chalmers added.

Holbrooke looked at the far horizon where *Argonaut's* tops'ls had just become visible from the boat.

'It's so important that we all understand each other,' Holbrooke agreed. 'It's all very well saying that the junior ship should follow the senior's lead, and that works after a fashion for a fleet action, but not so well where a few frigates need to co-ordinate their actions to out-manoeuvre the enemy. For that you have to be in each other's mind. Chester and Coulson, I believe, are well on the way to that understanding, and I fear that I'm not. Still, I at least know how they see the action unfolding; if indeed there is to be an action.'

'Captain, sir. *Argonaut* has filled on the larboard tack. She seems to be aiming to intercept us.'

'Thank you, Dawson.'

Holbrooke looked away to the nor'east where he could indeed see his ship moving steadily to the south.

'You see, Chalmers, that's what I mean. Whether it's Shorrock or Fairview, one of them at least can read my mind. If I had a means of communicating with them, I would have told them to do exactly what they are doing, setting a course to meet us to the south of their destination. You see, if I hadn't wanted them to move, I'd have had Dawson make short tacks to keep between *Argonaut* and the islands. When they saw us standing boldly to the sou'east they guessed what I wanted. Now we'll have a good start on our passage to the south and yet *Argonaut* won't be visible from the islands at all.'

Dawson nodded without taking his eyes from the course. He too knew what was in his captain's mind and his part in the plan was to steal every yard that he could to windward so that Holbrooke could be back on his quarterdeck without delay.

***

CHAPTER ELEVEN

The Snare

Monday, Seventeenth of March 1760.
Argonaut, at Sea, Suduroy Island N by E 16 leagues.

'Mister Jackson's compliments, sir, and he says that the wind is backing to the nor'east.'

The midshipman looked cold and wet and apprehensive. His neck stood starkly pale out of the collar of his coat, giving the impression of a plucked goose waiting for Christmas. Holbrooke opened his mouth to ask why he was so ill-dressed for the conditions when he realised that the young man must have abandoned the enormous wool comforter that Holbrooke had noticed before to appear in a better semblance of uniform when reporting to his captain.

'Very well, you may tell the bosun that I'll come on deck in two minutes, Mister Carew.'

The midshipman stepped backwards through the cabin door, caught his heel on the frame and fell ungracefully into the arms of the marine sentry who gathered him up with the greatest *sang froid*, without even dropping his musket. Holbrooke stifled a laugh. It reminded him of a production of *A Winter's Tale* that he'd seen when he was last up in London. At the point where Shakespeare had written the stage direction (no doubt in a fit of infantile humour) *Exit, pursued by bear*, the enthusiastic extra who had been tightly sewn into what looked like a genuine bearskin had tripped and fallen clean off the stage into the crowd in the pit below. The howls of laughter had set the tone for the rest of the play and whenever an actor left the stage, even with the most solemn demeanour, the audience set up an animal howling and covered their heads.

***

What a difference from the weather of the previous day.

Gone were the blue skies and the fabulous visibility. In their place were lowering clouds, grey-black with the threat of rain and sleet, and a wind that had risen to the point where fishing boats would stay in their harbours without the threat of being boarded by a man-o'-war. *Fortune* was still visible on the weather bow, seen in brief snatches of motion through the scudding low clouds and driving spray. Holbrooke sniffed the wind. It was an unconscious gesture that he'd picked up from the sailing master; it didn't help him at all in forecasting the weather, but more than likely it didn't help the master either.

'I fear we're in for a blow, sir,' said Jackson.

Argonaut had three regular officers of the watch – the first lieutenant, the master and the bosun. They were sometimes supplemented by the two master's mates, when the weather was fair and the enemy far away. Nonetheless, entrusting a ship to inexperienced hands always carried risks, and by age-old tradition the captain held the responsibility for the conduct of the ship even when he wasn't on deck. The smallest ship-of-the-line mustered three lieutenants, which meant that warrant officers didn't generally keep watches, but captains of frigates, with only one lieutenant, had a continual struggle to find suitably qualified candidates. It was widely believed that the Admiralty would soon adjust the complement of frigates to include a second lieutenant, at one stroke employing all those on half pay who were fit to go to sea and opening up a path for promotion for dozens of master's mates and midshipmen. That, however, was for another day and Holbrooke knew he was lucky to have a willing volunteer in Jackson. Yet it was a heavy load along with the bosun's regular duties.

'It does appear so,' Holbrooke agreed as a capful of spray caught him full in the face.

'The wind's shifted four points since the start of the watch,' Jackson said hurriedly to cover the moment.

Holbrooke would have liked to take a reef in the courses

and another reef in the tops'ls but a longer look at *Fortune* showed that his senior officer was still flying along with all plain sail and single reefs aloft. It would never do to shorten sail and find that *Argonaut* could no longer keep station. Jackson evidently had the same understanding of the situation, and he hadn't mentioned reefing. Holbrooke had merely been called on deck in accordance with his standing orders because the wind direction had changed by more than two points.

'Breakfast, sir, if you please.'

Holbrooke nodded to Stitch who had been sent with the message. The boy still looked as though he should be at school, not on the deck of a frigate in imminent danger from enemy action.

The watch below would be called soon, and they'd gulp down their burgoo and biscuit before trooping up from the fetid warmth of the gundeck onto the wet freshness of the upper deck. Not for the first time, Holbrooke blessed his luck that his father – a superannuated sailing master – had found him a place at the naval academy which had led to the quarterdeck at sea. Otherwise, he may well have been hauling a line with the two hundred men under his command.

'I'll be below, Mister Jackson. Watch *Fortune* carefully; he may shorten sail or reef at the change of the watch. If so, call the hands first, and then send for me. I'll hear your shout in any case.'

Jackson was well known for having a voice like a stag in the rut; his bellowing tones could be heard half a mile to windward in a gale and easily carried to the captain's cabin just below his feet.

***

When Holbrooke next came on deck, he could immediately see that conditions had worsened. *Argonaut* was overborne, that was for certain, and a look at *Fortune* told him that Coulson was similarly carrying too much canvas.

'Hand the tops'ls, Mister Fairview,' he said to the sailing

master who had relieved Jackson for the forenoon watch.

'We'll lose sight of *Fortune* in half a glass,' Fairview replied.

'That's for certain, master, but I won't hazard my spars in this weather.'

Holbrooke studied *Fortune* carefully while the watch below poured on deck and hurried to their stations. He turned away for a moment to consult the traverse board.

'*Fortune's* spilling her wind, sir,' the quartermaster reported. 'It looks like they're going to furl their tops'ls.'

Ah, wasn't it so often the case? The weight of circumstances built up in the same inexorable way in any two ships in company, and if they had the same information, their captains would generally come to similar conclusions quite independently. It was unlikely that Coulson had seen *Argonaut* preparing to shorten sail, and now Holbrooke's ship would be just a little faster at doing so than *Fortune*, and consequently add another laurel to his crown. Of course, there was no competition in seamanship; not that anyone would admit to, in any case.

Under easier sail now the two frigates reached away to the west, their quarterdecks soaring upwards as the swell caught them on the quarter and then dropping elegantly into the trough as it passed, like a pair of well-tutored ladies making their curtseys.

Holbrooke stood beside the weather gunwale, thinking himself into the positions of his two senior officers and his enemy. The fishing community of the Faroes had most likely stayed in their harbours at the first sign of this rising wind. Fishing would be impossible in this sea and there was no other purpose in their sailing. Batiste would have seen *Fortune* sail away to the south and no ships had passed by *Argonaut* on their way to the islands. So as far as Batiste was concerned, one of the frigates had been sent away – whether to top up their stores or to report to the commodore hardly mattered – and they were guarded now by just the single frigate. There would never be a better time to escape from the Faroes, except for this blow which started in the dog watches of Sunday. Would Batiste be deterred by the weather? Not on his own account, Holbrooke was sure, but he didn't know how much the experienced seafarer was influenced by the commander of the landing force. Surely Fouquet wouldn't relish setting to sea in this weather, either for his own comfort or that of his men. And yet, all he'd seen so far of Batiste as a King's officer and all he'd heard of the man as a privateer told him that he'd take the bold approach. He'd see this weather as an opportunity, not a threat.

He walked unsteadily to the taffrail and back, keeping one hand on a solid object – the gunwale or the mizzen bits – to avoid slipping on the treacherous deck. One turn told him that it was foolish and that he'd need to anchor himself close to the binnacle.

Yes, all else being equal, these were exactly the conditions that he would expect Batiste to exploit to break free from his British pursuers. In this weather it would be odds-on that after he'd brushed *Pegasus* aside – probably not stopping to take her as a prize – he'd see nothing more of his enemy.

'Pass the word for the first lieutenant.'

Shorrock ran up the companion without a thought to the ship's extravagant motion. Holbrooke envied him his ability to make light of the weather at the same time that he recognised that he'd never be able to match it.

'Ah, Mister Shorrock, I fear that if the French sail in this, we'll get only one chance of action, and we can't afford to miss it. Beat to quarters now, if you please, and when everyone is in their places, lash the guns with their muzzles outboard, leave two men at each gun and set the watch again.'

Holbrooke was pleased to see that Shorrock didn't look perplexed; it was almost as though he'd been anticipating the order. In all truth it was an obvious precaution to take. If there was to be a meeting it wouldn't be an orderly affair with rigid columns of stately ships-of-the-line manoeuvering for position on a calm, sunlit sea. It would be a matter of fleeting violent meetings, a broadside or two, then the enemy would be lost in the smoke and the spray. One chance, and that only if they were lucky.

He heard the rousing tattoo of the drum but otherwise paid no attention to the hurrying men that flooded up through the hatches. He took the first lieutenant's report and saw the men sliding back below out of the weather. Now *Argonaut* was ready for anything with her nine-pounders loaded and lashed tight against the ship's movement and the tompions firmly fitted to keep the powder dry. There were enough men on deck to bring them into action within two minutes of the alarm, and they could fire through the tompions if necessary.

Dinner was a hurried affair for the men, and for Holbrooke it was a matter of ramming down his throat whatever had been offered on his plate; he couldn't afterwards say what it had been. He couldn't bring himself to leave the quarterdeck.

***

The afternoon wore on in an atmosphere of tense expectation. Holbrooke's world had contracted to a circle whose radius was less than a mile. He could see *Fortune* well enough through the flying spray and he could see her maintop where Coulson hung out a blue flag to indicate when he was about to tack, and that *Argonaut* was to follow suit. Other than that, his view was circumscribed by the low cloud that hemmed in the two frigates. If Batiste had sailed from Torshavn, it would take a sequence of miracles for either *Fortune* or *Argonaut* to see his seven ships, and the chances were that they would pass to the south in happy ignorance of the trap that had been so carefully laid for them.

'*Fortune* has hung out the blue flag, sir,'

That was Carew again. He was a promising young man, and he'd been diligently watching the senior ship. This tacking in company was exhausting. It wasn't so bad when the lead ship was ahead, but for half the time she was astern and that meant having an intelligent person looking aft, and the whole business of keeping station became more difficult. On this leg the two frigates were steering to the nor'west, the next leg would take them down to the sou'east.

'Very well, Mister Carew,' Shorrock replied wearily. 'Let me know when he hauls it down.'

He turned to Holbrooke who was also looking astern and had seen the signal at the same time as Carew.

'*Fortune's* preparing to tack, sir,' Shorrock reported. 'I'll call all hands with your permission, sir.'

'If you please, Mister Shorrock.'

Holbrooke knew the extreme discomfort that his people were experiencing. Not only did most of them have to spend four hours at a time on the cold, wet and heaving deck, but in their four hours off watch they were likely to be disturbed by the dreaded call of *all hands*. It was all part and parcel of a life at sea and there was no use complaining because it was no easier in a merchantman and far, far worse in many of the seagoing trades. At a pinch, without the tops'ls set, *Argonaut* could be handled on the watch. That was all well and good when things went smoothly, but in a March gale just a few leagues south of the Faroes, it was as well to take no chances.

'The blue flag's hauled down in *Fortune*, sir.'

Carew knew his business. With everyone else on deck concerned with getting the sail handlers into their correct stations and preparing to come about, somebody needed to do nothing other than watch the lead ship.

Holbrooke swept a glance over the deck. Everything seemed to be in order. Over his shoulder, at the mizzen sheets, he could hear a bosun's mate pushing the last sleepy landsman into position and thrusting a sheet into his hand.

'*Fortune's* luffing, sir.'

There was an urgency now in Carew's voice. Holbrooke glanced astern to see for himself. Sure enough, the leader's sails were starting to shiver as the frigate's head moved into the wind.

'Carry on, Mister Shorrock.'

The first lieutenant opened his mouth to give the order that would bring *Argonaut's* helm a-lee and start the turn into the wind.

'Belay!' Holbrooke shouted and cupped his ear to the wind.

'Did anyone else hear that?' he asked.

'A gun, sir,' said Carew, the first to reply, 'to windward, right on the beam, I would say.' There were cautious nods of agreement from the quarterdeck.

A gun. Chester attempting to bring his squadron together, or Batiste doing the same.

'Hold your course, Mister Shorrock.'

Had Coulson heard the gun? Holbrooke looked astern to see *Fortune's* head passing through the wind. He could see her larboard side now and soon he'd see her stern as she beat away to the sou'west, away from the source of the gunfire. For a few moments Holbrooke was undecided. He could follow *Fortune*, make more sail and hope to come close enough to tell Coulson what he had heard, but that would certainly take some time, at least a half hour, and then only if Coulson realised that his junior officer wanted to speak to him. In that time Batiste would be away to the south and Chester's little squadron would have failed. No, his duty was clear, even at the risk of official censure – for not following Coulson's signalled orders – he must stand on and try to make contact with either *Pegasus* or the French squadron.

'Beat to quarters, Mister Shorrock, and set the main and fore tops'ls double-reefed.'

As the drum sounded its urgent tattoo, Holbrooke looked astern at the rapidly disappearing frigate. They were opening from each other at a combined speed of eight knots or so, and they'd be out of sight in five minutes in this visibility. Even now the details of *Fortune* were indistinct as she started to merge into the background greyness.

Holbrooke rubbed his eyes, looked again, and she was gone.

'I've lost sight of *Fortune*, sir,' Carew reported.

What would Coulson do now, Holbrooke asked himself. He didn't look like a man given to profanities, but in this case, he could be allowed a bitter curse or two. Perhaps he'd spill some wind to give *Argonaut* a chance to catch up, then he'd heave to and wait for a while. In any case it would be at least half an hour before he decided to tack and bring his frigate's head back to the nor'west in search of his errant consort. Holbrooke had to stop thinking about Coulson; if he hadn't heard the gun, *Fortune* was out of the game.

The drum had stopped and now in the relative silence, Holbrooke heard another gun.

'Was that further forward of the beam?'

Fairview shook his head, he couldn't tell.

Carew was almost hopping from foot to foot beside him.

'If you please, sir. I heard a second gun while the drum was beating for quarters, and I heard this one, sir. The sound is moving forrard, it was almost on the beam this last time.'

Holbrooke looked at the blank faces of his officers. They had all been bound up in the management of the ship, and their ears weren't as sharp as this young man's. He glanced at Carew. His sincerity showed in his face, in his hesitation in speaking in front of his betters. There was always a danger, particularly in his young gentlemen, that they'd say whatever they thought their captain wanted to hear.

If the sound was moving ahead of the beam, then the best thing they could do was stay on this tack and try to get a few more knots of speed without endangering the masts.

'The ship's at quarters, sir. The guns are loaded and run out. Mister Fairview has the deck.'

Shorrock looked eager, like a man who relished the prospect of action, even in these appalling conditions.

'Another gun, sir.'

'Mister Shorrock, a gun from the starboard battery and repeat it every two minutes.'

He should have thought of that before, the minute that

he heard *Coventry's* gun; that would have alerted Coulson. Perhaps he would still hear *Argonaut's* guns and realise something was amiss, but it became less likely as each minute passed and the ships drew further apart. Even if he didn't hear the guns, at some point Coulson would grasp that *Argonaut* wasn't following and then, surely, he'd tack back to the west to investigate.

Boom!

Holbrooke heard this one clearly without Carew's report. It was decidedly forward of the beam and that meant that *Pegasus* – if that was who was firing the guns – was moving in a direction that would cross *Argonaut's* bow. *Fortune*, far astern by now, was decisively out of the battle, unless Batiste could be brought to stand and fight, which was unlikely.

'Hold your course, Mister Fairview, full and by.'

That was a holding order, to give him time to think. Where would Chester be in relation to the seven French ships? Astern was the safest place, he'd be to windward with all the options of attack and flight that it offered, and he'd have the French squadron in plain sight and have plenty of time to react to their movements. Yet Chester didn't just want to tamely follow the French, he wanted to bring his squadron into action. Despite the disparity in force, this was Chester's great chance to make a name for himself. He walked over to the binnacle and looked keenly up at the tops'ls, straining at their reefing points.

Boom!

Another gun, nearer this time and still moving forward of the beam. He tapped the binnacle for luck.

'Bear away three points, Mister Fairview. Take careful note of the bearing of that gun; I plan to intercept whichever ship is firing.'

Privately he was now certain that it was *Pegasus*, but he didn't want to make a prediction that may not come true, not in such a public place.

***

CHAPTER TWELVE

A Running Fight

Monday, Seventeenth of March 1760.
Argonaut, at Sea, Suduroy Island N by E 16 leagues.

'Eight knots and a half, sir,' the mate of the watch reported.

Argonaut was rushing at breakneck speed towards whatever was waiting for them.

Boom!

That sounded close now, fine on the starboard bow. On this course the ship that was firing should reveal itself at any moment.

'Sing out the instant you see anything,' Holbrooke said to the quarterdeck at large.

A dozen faces turned towards the starboard bow, straining to be the first to spot a sail emerging from the thick, thick weather. With an irritable sweep of his hand, Holbrooke swept away the moisture that had collected on his eyebrows.

'There!' shouted Carew, losing any sense of decorum in the excitement of the moment. 'Three points on the starboard bow, a frigate, sir.'

Holbrooke saw it an instant later. *Pegasus*, for sure, a mile away or perhaps a little more. She was sailing easy under reefed tops'ls with her main and foresails furled, as though Chester was preparing for battle. Then where were the French?

'Bring us under his lee at shouting distance, Mister Fairview. You'll need to brail up the main and foresail.'

That was an interesting exercise in relative motion. With *Pegasus* steering south, *Argonaut* would have to cross her wake and then put her own stern through the wind. Fairview would need all the speed advantage that the big fore and main courses gave him, but he'd have to slow down rapidly as soon as he was abeam.

'Sail ho! Sail on the starboard beam. Two sails. No, three.'

The lookout at the masthead had seen the French before they became visible from the quarterdeck. Ah, there they were, Holbrooke could just see their spectral shapes looming out of the low cloud and thick spray. Just where they should be, a mile astern of *Pegasus*. Three ships. One of them was a frigate and the other two transports, that much was clear. No doubt the other three frigates and the transport would be still lost in the banks of cloud.

What would Batiste do now? Holbrooke stared fixedly to windward trying get inside the French privateer's mind. He'd see that he'd been led into a trap. Probably he'd recognise *Argonaut* from the Skagerrak, and he'd assume that *Fortune* was close by, still hidden by the low clouds, and he wouldn't know how many other enemies lurked out of sight. He could be facing a sizeable detachment of the Downs Squadron, a two-decker and half a dozen frigates, just to settle the matter quickly. He could turn his squadron back to the north and sail back to the Faroes, but it would be a long, hard beat to windward and at some point, he must know, the British would come up with the slower transports and force a fight on their own terms. He had no friends but the Faroese in these waters. Sweden was too far away and everything to the south was at least nominally subject to King George. It was no business of Batiste's to enter into battle with a British squadron, but he must be feeling ever more forced into it.

'I'm going to shave his tail, sir,' Fairview said.

Holbrooke nodded his assent. Shave *Pegasus*' tail indeed. Without a fixed point of reference, it had been difficult to appreciate just how fast *Argonaut* was sailing. Now, with *Pegasus* looming huge and dangerous on her bow, her speed became evident. Holbrooke gulped involuntarily at the spectacle of the frigate right ahead of them. At first sight it looked as though a collision was inevitable, but a practiced eye could see that *Pegasus*' bearing was drawing to the left and that *Argonaut* would pass close – awfully close – astern. There was a moment of consternation on Chester's quarterdeck, until they realised what Holbrooke planned.

'I'll brail the courses as soon as we've worn around, sir.'

'Do you think that'll be enough?' Holbrooke asked.

'Yes, sir. We'll lose a little speed in wearing. I'll back the fore tops'l if we look like shooting ahead.'

***

Closer and closer, then suddenly everything happened fast.

'Helm a-weather!' shouted Fairview, followed by the sequence of orders to wear ship.

Argonaut bucked and tossed as she crossed *Pegasus*' wake. Then, before she had fairly passed into the clearer water on *Pegasus*' quarter, she started to turn in response to the helm. Holbrooke was aware of the mizzen yard as it swung across the quarterdeck, and he heard in the background the orders to swing the tops'l yards across and haul the tacks and sheets but his whole attention was taken up by the massive shape of *Pegasus* now close – almost too close – on his larboard side.

He felt Dawson passing a length of cordage around his waist and making it fast to the mizzen shrouds. Now he could lean far out to speak to Chester.

'Where's *Fortune*?' Chester shouted.

Holbrooke pointed away to the east. 'He didn't hear your guns, sir,' he shouted back at the top of his voice.

It was easier for Chester, he was shouting downwind, but Holbrooke had to make his voice carry to windward over fifty yards of gale-whipped sea. Holbrooke saw Chester smash his fist onto the gunwale, but he couldn't hear the stream of disappointed oaths that he directed at his first lieutenant.

'Can't wait… We'll try to pick off the smaller frigates even if Batiste and the transports get away… Deal with them later… Follow my movements.'

Chester had a weak voice and Holbrooke heard his

orders in truncated snatches. His meaning was clear, however. *Argonaut* was to stay close to *Pegasus*. He wondered at the wisdom of attacking the frigates. This French squadron existed only to put its force of soldiers ashore and the bulk of them and their military supplies would be in the transports. If he lost just one of them, Batiste's squadron would become impotent, unable to muster sufficient force to attack even a small British town. With half the landing force gone, Batiste's squadron would look very much like a petty privateering enterprise, and that posed little threat to Britain. Or did it? How did Anson view this expedition? Perhaps he didn't care if a northern town or two was sacked. Quite possibly he was more worried about the effect on the city's confidence of four French frigates let loose on Britain's trade.

With a wave of his hand Chester turned back to give his orders.

'He's bearing up,' said Fairview.

'Follow on his leeward quarter, Master.'

Fairview watched carefully as *Pegasus* turned to larboard. Further and further the frigate turned until she was close on the wind, with the luffs of her tops'ls bar taut.

'Down helm,' Fairview ordered.

Argonaut turned fast into *Pegasus'* wake, jumping and corkscrewing as her bows fought with the thrashing water under the leading frigate's stern.

Holbrooke could guess what Chester was doing. Rather than merely let the French ships come down upon the two British frigates, he was stretching away to the east and would soon tack and break into the enemy squadron at speed. In all probability, the transports at least would panic at the sight of two men-o'-war beating up towards them and then Chester would have a chance to get between them and the frigates.

'Furl the main and foresails, sir?' Fairview asked.

'No, leave them brailed,' Holbrooke replied, 'we may need them.'

The Frenchmen were on *Argonaut*'s larboard quarter now. All seven of them were in sight. Batiste's heavy frigate in the lead, a smaller frigate on each flank, the three transports huddled in the centre and a frigate bringing up the rear. Holbrooke frowned. If it were him in charge of that squadron, he'd have the three smaller frigates well astern and to windward where they could wait and see the shape of the attack and respond accordingly.

'*Pegasus* is preparing to come about, sir,' said Fairview.

'Put the ship about as soon as you see him raising his tacks, Mister Fairview. I want to be on his larboard beam when he's settled.'

Fairview gave Holbrooke an appreciative glance. He had wondered why he hadn't ordered *Argonaut* into the leader's wake, and now he knew. By sitting off *Pegasus'* quarter, he was in a perfect position to form an attack line with the two frigates abreast of each other.

***

'Mister Shorrock!'

The first lieutenant was at his post at the quarterdeck rail, where he could see most of his guns and where he could best exercise command of *Argonaut*'s broadsides.

'Sir!' Shorrock responded with a great smile.

'I believe *Pegasus* intends to engage that frigate from the windward. If that's the case, we'll engage from leeward. Stand by the starboard battery, and I believe you may remove the tompions.'

The conditions were shocking for a sea fight. There was no chance of lying alongside the enemy in this wind, and in this sea, and they would be lucky to achieve two broadsides before they were forced to move away. And there was no hope of boarding; it would be as dangerous for the predator as for the prey.

'About our size, sir,' said Fairview. 'Nine pounders or perhaps those eights that the French seem to love so much. Either way, it makes little difference.'

The sailing master shrugged his shoulders and turned

back to his task of handling the ship.

The French frigate was close now and its captain must see his fate bearing down upon him. He was certainly prepared with his guns run out on both sides. Over on the western side of the group, the other flanking frigate had just realised his friend's peril and was bearing away to join the fight. He'd be too late for the opening broadsides.

Holbrooke had a brief glimpse of the upper deck before the ship handling claimed his attention. All along the starboard side the gun crews were crouched in readiness. Even in this freezing weather many of them were stripped to the waist and they all had a look of intense, ferocious concentration. The gun captains were peering over the gunwale, looking for the enemy and keeping their linstocks alight. The midshipmen were walking between their divisions of guns exchanging a few words with the crews and trying to look brave.

'He's bearing up, sir.'

Holbrooke nodded. That was the correct move for the Frenchman. Otherwise, he'd have been raked fore and aft, and probably be out of the fight without firing a broadside of his own.

'Come up a point, Mister Fairview. I want to be closer to him as we pass.'

Argonaut turned quickly to starboard. The closest of the transports was right on the bow now, beyond the frigate. And beyond the transport the westerly frigate was coming up fast. Batiste's ship was a mile away on the larboard bow, leading the three transports south out of the fight. Batiste may be a privateer, but he was thinking like a King's officer with a mission to be accomplished. He could fulfil that mission with one or two or three frigates, but without the transports it was all over.

'Hold your fire until all the guns bear, Mister Shorrock.'

Bang! *Pegasus* opened fire. A little too soon for Holbrooke's taste, the French frigate was still on his bow.

Shorrock looked questioningly at Holbrooke who

slowly and deliberately shook his head.

Bang! The French starboard battery opened fire. Holbrooke saw a spray of splinters sweep across *Pegasus*' deck. The Frenchman had waited just a minute longer than Chester and had created mayhem on the British ship's deck. Now Holbrooke could see the French crews rushing from starboard to larboard. He'd counted on that, not even a regular frigate could efficiently man both batteries and he knew from Fairview's friend on the timber brig that Batiste's frigates were short of trained gunners.

Holbrooke raised his whistle to his lips and blew a single clear note. There was a pause and then *Argonaut* staggered to the recoil of the fourteen guns of the starboard battery. The effect on the enemy ship was extraordinary. The broadside had caught the gun crews in the act of crossing the deck. Some had made it to the starboard side as the single gun that answered *Argonaut* proved, but most were caught without the cover that the gunwales provide, and they were cut down in droves by the splinters that flew across the deck. It was a scene of devastation and confusion, and that single gun was the only one to be fired at *Argonaut*.

'Reload!' shouted Shorrock, 'Give 'em another one, men. Fire when you're ready.'

The men were sweating already, even in this howling gale, and it took a superhuman effort to hold the guns inboard against the rolling of the ship with the wind on its beam.

Bang! The first gun to reload send its ball hurtling into the French ship. The second followed almost immediately and the remainder in ones and twos as the slower crews were ready.

There was no time now to see the effects of his ship's gunnery. Holbrooke was concentrating on the frigate that was hurtling towards them from the far wing of the French squadron. He saw it pass close astern of the nearest transport.

'Which way will he turn?'

It was a private question from Fairview, spoken aloud in the heat of the action. He hadn't meant it to be heard, more less replied to.

'Starboard,' Holbrooke replied. 'He's coming to us. Stand by the larboard battery, Mister Shorrock.'

The first frigate was astern of them now, left behind by *Argonaut*'s superior speed. He could vaguely see that *Pegasus* was shortening sail, Chester was setting his teeth into his Frenchman.

'Bear up, Mister Fairview, don't mind about that fellow on our quarter. If we take away his jib boom, so much the better.'

Fairview looked quickly astern before ordering the turn to starboard. He'd clear the Frenchman, but not by much.

Holbrooke could hear the marines behind him firing over the taffrail at the French ship they had just passed, but it was the enemy ahead that demanded his attention. He desperately wanted to get up to windward so that he could dictate how the engagement would be fought. The Frenchman was hard on the wind now, trying for the windward position himself. It would be a close-run thing but there was one factor that preyed on Holbrooke's mind; a collision now would probably see the end of one or both ships and all the men on board. The weather gauge was certainly desirable, but not at that price!

'Can you get across his bows?'

Fairview took a long hard look.

'No, sir. If he doesn't alter course, he'll come on board of us.'

'Then bear away now, Mister Fairview. Pass down his leeward side.'

Shorrock had been watching his captain, waiting to see what he'd do. He'd obeyed the last order and readied the larboard battery, but he'd kept enough men back to reload the starboard battery. He held up his hand to the quarterdeck and pointed to starboard: guns ready!

Holbrooke felt a wave of pride, in his ship and in his men and in his first lieutenant. There was none of the fatal confusion that he'd seen on the deck of the first Frenchman that they'd engaged, and the trained efficiency of *Argonaut*'s gun crews gave him more tactical options than his French counterparts had.

'Stand by the starboard battery!'

Shorrock replied by lifting his hat. A gust of wind caught it and whipped it away to leeward where it fetched up in the larboard scuppers to be scooped up by a delighted Joseph Stitch.

The two frigates were closing fast on opposite tacks, each sailing a few points free and heeling far over to leeward. Holbrooke could see the gun captains smashing the quoins in to depress the guns far enough to point at the enemy frigate. His opponent had the opposite problem, and his gun captains would be kicking the quoins aside and elevating their guns to their maximum. She carried her guns high, Holbrooke noted, so there was no danger of their being swamped by the sea coming through the ports.

'Brail the mizzen, Mister Fairview. Let fly the fore tops'l.'

Those orders could be quickly obeyed from the deck without stripping the crews from the guns and Holbrooke immediately felt the difference as *Argonaut* came more upright. Shorrock waved again from his station beside the mainmast. The guns could depress far enough now.

Again, Holbrooke raised his silver whistle and made sure that Shorrock had seen it.

'Stand by!'

It was all happening quickly now. At one moment the French frigate was a distant object, its details lost in the thick atmosphere. Now, suddenly, it was upon them, and the enemy's bowsprit was passing across his own. He waited for the span of half a dozen rapid heartbeats as the ships rushed closer together, then he blew a single blast on

Nor'west by North

the whistle.

Argonaut fired her broadside at almost the exactly the same instant as the Frenchman fired his. The noise was tremendous, overwhelming, and Holbrooke felt the twin shocks of his own guns' recoil and the impact of the French shot. He felt the howling wind of round shot screaming at head-height across the quarterdeck even over the gale's blast.

'The wheel doesn't answer,' shouted the quartermaster.

Holbrooke could hear Fairview issuing the orders for the tiller to take over the steering, but it was too late to prevent *Argonaut*'s bows from swinging to windward. His standing orders insisted that at quarters an able seaman was stationed at the tiller, on the gun deck below. It was clear that a single man was insufficient to haul on the tackles that controlled the tiller, and a petty officer and two others were detailed to join him if it was necessary to use the tiller. A further three men relayed orders from the quarterdeck. It all took time and precious seconds flew away as the operation was put into place. Holbrooke watched impotently as the frigate that he'd just engaged ignored *Argonaut* and continued on his way to assist the other Frenchman that he could see was hard-pressed by *Pegasus*.

'How long, Mister Fairview,' Holbrooke demanded.

'Just a few more moments, sir.'

Holbrooke could see the man stood by the hatch, the first link in the chain of communication that would allow *Argonaut* to be a living, steerable ship again.

The seconds passed. Holbrooke could hear the cannonade from the east. The three ships were half a mile away now and the transports and Batiste's frigate had disappeared to the south, lost in the murk and the gale. He glared impatiently at the sailing master then looked forward to the guns where Shorrock was urging the crews to reload the starboard battery. There were no casualties on the deck, as far as he could see. Those shot that had passed over the quarterdeck must have been the only ones that had elevated far enough to strike the frigate's upper works.

'Beg pardon, sir,'

That was one of the carpenter's mates.

'Chips says that he's stopping up three shot holes above the waterline. There are none below, sir, and if you can stay on the starboard tack for another fifteen minutes, he'll have those all secure.'

'Tell Chips…' Holbrooke thought for a moment about how to phrase the reply. In fifteen minutes, he'd have lost sight of *Pegasus* and the two French frigates and in this weather, he may never find them again. In thirty minutes, Chester may be forced to strike unless *Argonaut* came to his rescue.

'The tiller tackles are shot through, sir!'

The seaman at the hatch looked shocked at the news he had to relay to the quarterdeck. Holbrooke thought rapidly as he saw Jackson and one of his mates dropping down the hatch. Even with the bosun rigging new tackles, it would be ten minutes before *Argonaut* could manoeuvre.

'Tell chips he has ten minutes,' Holbrooke snapped, 'and then I'll be coming about.'

***

It was the longest ten minutes of Holbrooke's life. *Argonaut* lay with her head three points off the wind, unable to steer and unable to join the action that was raging away half a mile to the east. There was no hope of moving the tiller by brute force. In this gale of wind, the men who attempted that would be thrown off their feet at every gust and at every uncontrollable lurch of the frigate. Tiller tackles first, then he could bring the ship about and join the fray, then wheel tackles and he'd be fully under command again.

'Tiller tackles are rigged, sir and the ship's answering the helm.'

'Then bring her about, Mister Fairview.'

Nor'west by North

The master pulled a long face, 'We'll have to bear away first, sir and get some way on before she'll stay. I'd rather wear if you please.'

Holbrooke cursed himself, he should have thought of that. *Argonaut* couldn't be tacked unless she was moving through the water with some speed, and that was doubly so in this gale. Wearing would take time, and every moment was precious.

'Very well, wear ship,' he snapped in reply.

Holbrooke looked quickly around the horizon. There wasn't a ship in sight now, but he could hear a steady cannonade to the east where Chester must be wondering whether he'd been abandoned by Holbrooke.

With agonising sluggishness, the frigate's head swung around to larboard. Further and further until *Argonaut*'s bows were heading sou'-sou-west. Then the mizzen swing across over Holbrooke's head and the rate of turn increased. At last, they were starting to move towards the sound of the guns.

'The firing's stopped,' said Shorrock, with his ear cupped to the ship's head.

Holbrooke paced nervously. Had *Pegasus* been taken? It seemed unlikely in that short a space of time. It could take hours for a surrender to be made effective in this weather. No boat could live for long in these seas and surely no captain would be mad enough to attempt a boarding.

Holbrooke strained to see through the low cloud and flying spray.

'Sail ho! Sail on the starboard bow. It looks like one of those Frenchmen, sir.'

Damn. There must be better visibility up there.

'Up you go!' Holbrooke shouted against the gale and the master's mate ran up the mainmast ratlines, nimble as an ape and just as quick. His report came in just a few seconds.

'It's the two French frigates, sir, running to the south under tops'ls and courses. They'll be out of sight in a few seconds. I can see *Pegasus* two points on the larboard bow. She's lost her fore topmast but she's making way to the south also.'

'Hold your course, Mister Fairview. When you see *Pegasus* come under her lee.'

It had only taken Holbrooke a moment to decide that he should speak to Chester rather than pursue the two Frenchmen. It was clear that they were satisfied with losing their British pursuers and now Batiste could escape to the south, to make his way back to France or to fulfil his mission by landing somewhere in Scotland, Ireland or England. Holbrooke felt a sense of defeat. This was the second time that he'd brushed with Batiste's squadron without any decisive result.

***

CHAPTER THIRTEEN

The Challenge

Wednesday, Nineteenth of March 1760.
Argonaut, at Anchor, Stornoway, Isle of Lewis.

The gale blew itself out the day after the fight, and the westerly wind brought clear air and calmer seas with a persistent northerly swell. *Fortune* found *Pegasus* and *Argonaut* at the midpoint between the Faroes and the Butt of Lewis as Chester's ship lay hove-to sending up a jury-rigged fore tops'l. The French were long gone and when *Pegasus* had something to set a tops'l on, they reached away to the south. Now the little squadron lay at anchor off Stornoway's harbour in twelve fathoms with a good sandy bottom.

'I'll send back word as soon as I know how long we're staying, Mister Shorrock. If we're here for at least the rest of the day then I expect Chester will allow us to send a party ashore for wood and water, so have the boats ready.'

'Aye-aye, sir,' Shorrock replied. He managed to look both concerned and respectful at the same time, like a father with a son who had risen far in the world. His concern was justified; Chester may well take the view that *Argonaut* had deliberately shied away from the action, that Holbrooke didn't care to expose his ship to the enemy guns any more than he had already. He may even have the same opinion of *Fortune*, although Captain Coulson could make a convincing case that he knew nothing of the action at all. Holbrooke was the junior of the three and if there were to be any recriminations it was only natural that he would bear the brunt. Shorrock had a cynical view of how senior officers apportioned blame.

Holbrooke was acutely aware of the situation, and he sat bolt upright in the stern sheets of the longboat, looking neither to larboard nor to starboard, as a mute Dawson steered him towards *Pegasus*.

It was unfortunate that Holbrooke couldn't appreciate the scene. The strong gale that had allowed Batiste's squadron to escape had been gone a day or more, and the clean, dry air that replaced it had brought the first hint of spring to the Hebridean Islands. The light blue of the sky matched the deep, intense blue of the sea – almost a Prussian blue – and the hills, still brown with hardly a hint of green, stood stark and bare above the bay. The light westerly wind hardly ruffled the surface of the water and the longboat's oarsmen raised nothing more than the tiniest of ripples as they rowed dry and steady across the bay.

Holbrooke's mind was working fast, and none of his thoughts were congenial. He'd noticed that Coulson hadn't yet been summoned and he assumed that Chester wanted to hear the story independently from the two captains. Holbrooke first because his sin – if indeed there was a sin – was greater than Coulson's. He climbed up the side of *Pegasus* as the pipes played their long call, to be met by the first lieutenant who wordlessly conducted him to the great cabin. Chester didn't rise when he came in and out of the corner of his eye, Holbrooke saw the captain's secretary sitting at a small portable desk in the corner of the cabin, his quill poised to record the meeting and a sombre look on his face. It was hardly a warm welcome.

Chester forced a wintry smile and with slow deliberation moved his rump a foot or so above his chair; that was all that he would concede by way of greeting. No refreshments were offered.

'Captain Holbrooke, I would like to be able to say that I'm pleased to see you, but perhaps not under these circumstances,' he motioned briefly towards the secretary.

Holbrooke was appalled. This was much worse than he'd imagined. He'd entered the cabin with some trepidation but was sure that he could adequately explain himself. This, however, looked far too formal and it appeared that Chester had pre-judged his conduct. His initial concern had manifested itself in a look of meek submission, but it rapidly turned to anger. How dare this man jump to conclusions about his behaviour before ever he had heard the facts? His ship had suffered two well-directed broadsides, it wasn't at all unlikely that he had suffered damage that prevented him re-joining the fight. Holbrooke was aware that he was starting to look defiant, disrespectful even, but he didn't care. There was a chair set a little aside and he reached for it, pulled it into the centre of the cabin, and with a wide sweep of his coat tails he sat down, shocking himself with his confidence. That took Chester by surprise.

'May I assume, sir, that you wish to be informed of *Argonaut*'s motions on Monday afternoon?'

'Indeed I do, Captain Holbrooke,' Chester replied, his own colour rising at the impertinence of this young captain. 'I wish to know why you chose to stand aside while *Pegasus* was assailed by two French frigates,' he held up his hand to prevent Holbrooke responding, 'and you may wish to know that I suffered six dead and twenty wounded in the engagement, one of whom was a cousin and at least four of whom are unlikely to recover.' He paused, glaring angrily at Holbrooke. 'Start, if you please, from when you parted company from Captain Coulson.'

Holbrooke took a deep breath to control his temper. The stark facts, no emotion, that was what he needed now. The ship was unnaturally quiet, and he was aware of the scratch of the clerk's pen coming from the corner.

'I was keeping station five cables to the west of *Fortune*, sir, on a westerly course, when Captain Coulson signalled a tack to the east. At that moment I heard a gun to the nor'west and assumed – correctly as it transpired – that it was you signalling for *Fortune* and *Argonaut* to join you. Captain Coulson, being half a mile further east, couldn't have heard the gun and he continued to the east and was quickly out of sight. I held my course to the west to join you and fired a gun and continued to do so every two minutes until you were in sight. I hoped to draw Captain

Coulson's attention to my leaving him.'

'Did you do nothing else to communicate with Captain Coulson?'

'There was nothing else I could do, sir. I could hear your guns drawing to the south and calculated that if I delayed, you'd be far away before I could tell Captain Coulson what I'd heard. I concluded that one frigate would be more use to you than none, sir.'

Holbrooke tried unsuccessfully to keep the sarcasm from his voice.

'You believe that Captain Coulson couldn't have heard my guns?' Chester asked with an arched eyebrow.

'That is correct sir, he was half a mile further away from you than I was, and I only heard your gun faintly.'

'But you fired guns to inform him. Wouldn't he have heard them?'

Holbrooke realised in a flash that this first part of the interrogation was aimed more at Coulson's conduct than at his own. He would have to be careful, nonetheless.

'By the time I'd cleared away a gun and fired, *Fortune* would have been more than a mile to the east, sir. Consider; he had tacked and was heading east while I had held my course to the west. It's possible that he could have heard my first gun, but equally it could have been lost in the noise of tending to the tacks and sheets after coming about. He would almost certainly have missed my later guns unless he had tacked again in very short order.'

Chester grimaced and looked sideways to confirm that his clerk was still writing; that his nib hadn't broken, or his ink spilled onto the deck.

'Very well. Now we can pass over your engagement of the first frigate, please proceed from the moment you broke off to engage the second.'

Holbrooke noticed that Chester's attitude was softening. It was hardly perceptible in his face which still looked like thunder, but his speech was less harsh and formal, more conversational.

Nor'west by North

'I exchanged broadsides with the second frigate, starboard to starboard. I had then intended to tack under his stern and engage from windward, but my wheel ropes and my tiller tackles were shot through, and my ship was unable to steer. It took ten minutes to recover some steerage and by then you were out of sight in the mist, although I could hear the gunfire to the east. I made haste to join the fight again, just in time to see the two French frigates running to the south and to see *Pegasus* heaving to with a wounded foremast. I judged it better at that point to offer you my assistance rather than chase an enemy in that poor visibility, with the near certainty of quickly losing sight of them.'

Chester looked hesitantly at Holbrooke. There was a knock at the door, and he glanced up irritably to see his first lieutenant beckoning to him.

Holbrooke sat in silence, not choosing to acknowledge the presence of the clerk, as he waited for Chester to return. After two or three minutes the door opened, and Chester walked back into the cabin. He had a strange rigid look on his face. Was that embarrassment? Certainly, Chester's whole attitude had changed.

'I owe you an apology Captain Holbrooke. News of your steering damage has found its way across the water already. Your bosun begged the loan of some spare gear to replace yours that was shot through.'

Chester paused, apparently to mentally rehearse a prepared speech before proceeding.

'I hope you will accept my apology, sir, but I will understand if you find that impossible. I will, of course, receive any friend of yours that chooses to call upon me.'

Good God, Holbrooke thought, did Chester really believe this would lead to a challenge? To a duel? It was possible, certainly. They held the same naval rank even though Chester had been posted many years before Holbrooke. There would be nothing unusual or scandalous about it.

'In any case, I wish it to be recorded that I am perfectly happy with your conduct. Be sure that you write just that,' he said to the clerk.

Holbrooke was speechless. He'd never fought a duel and had never contemplated challenging another man. Of course, Chester's suspicion had been intolerable and not to be borne lightly, but it was, in a way, an understandable human reaction to what had been a very trying day. He smiled with all the warmth that he could muster and bowed as low as the circumstances warranted. In a moment of clarity, not unlike the feeling when he manoeuvred his ship in battle, he knew what to say.

'I'm sure no slight on my character was intended, sir. I trust we can consider the matter closed.'

***

Perhaps it was a gesture of appreciation, of trust, Holbrooke would never know, but he wasn't invited to leave the cabin when Coulson was summoned. It was a quite different interview which started with Chester acknowledging that Holbrooke had already explained how *Fortune* came to miss the engagement with the French frigates. Coulson glanced sideways at Holbrooke, but his face remained immobile. Then Coulson too had been concerned about how his absence from the engagement had been interpreted.

'Well, gentlemen, it appears that Monsieur Batiste has given us the slip. Now, I'll give our ships a day to take on wood and water and then we must be after him. I know, I know,' he said raising his hand as Coulson started to speak, 'I have no better idea than you about where he is going or what he intends. All we know is that he was heading south when we last saw him. Smith, bring me that chart if you please.'

The clerk brought a rolled chart and spread it out on the dining table, holding it down with an ink well, a candlestick and two books.

'Now, coffee.' He looked quickly at his guests, 'but

perhaps something stronger is needed, ask the purser to knock up one of his famous punches, would you, Smith? I'm sure Captain Coulson and Captain Holbrooke are in need of refreshment after an anxious few days.'

Chester smiled broadly. His was not a vindictive nature and his suspicions had their genesis in his own insecurity. He was coming to the top of the captain's list, and he could ill-afford a blot on his record that might prejudice the chances of hoisting his flag. This pursuit of Batiste could make or break him; it could be the difference between blue at the mizzen and the yellow squadron. For himself, he hardly cared and would in fact welcome the opportunity to retire into genteel obscurity, as far from the sea as could be contrived, but Mrs Chester would hear none of it and yearned for the social distinction that came with a husband who was an admiral on the active list.

The chart showed the whole of the British Isles on one sheet. It had no value in pilotage, being of far too small a scale, but it was excellent for this purpose, to attempt to see into the mind of the commander of a French expedition to the northwest of the British Isles.

'The Minches I believe. I would swear that he wasn't steering to the west of the Outer Hebrides. In any case, when the wind turned westerly, he'd have had the devil's own job to beat to the west. So can we agree that he passed this way, as a working assumption, as a point of departure for our deliberations, as it were?'

'I regret that I didn't see the Frenchmen at sea,' Coulson said, 'so I must defer to you, sir and to Captain Holbrooke.'

Was Coulson still worried about his handling of the engagement? Holbrooke knew that he'd described Coulson's actions in the best possible light and that there were other much less sympathetic explanations for *Fortune* missing the fight. Yes, if he were Coulson, he'd keep quiet until he was sure that he was safe.

'Holbrooke, what's your opinion?'

What indeed was his opinion? It was notoriously difficult to estimate the course of a group of ships at sea, particularly after no more than a fleeting glimpse in thick weather. South-by-east, he would have said and that's what he had written in his log. However, it could just as easily have been south-by-west, but no more westerly than that. The wind held the clue, as was normally the case at sea. At this time of year, a north easterly gale could be expected to give way to westerlies within a day or two, so if Batiste had wanted to weather the Isle of Lewis, he would have been steering further west, out into the Atlantic. Holbrooke was merely rehearsing this argument in the second or so that Chester watched him; he had already formed an opinion.

'The Minches, sir, I'm sure of it.'

Chester looked thoughtfully at the chart.

'Then that narrows our search. There's nothing for Batiste on this whole coast until he gets past Tiree and Coll,' he said, pointing to the islands that guarded the southern end of the Hebridean Sea. 'It stretches my credulity to imagine that seven ships of that size could pass through the whole of that… what? Forty-five leagues or so, without being seen. Someone will have word of them, don't you think?'

Holbrooke and Coulson nodded cautiously. There was one critical factor that none of the three men would openly acknowledge, a topic that no English gentlemen would raise without being certain of the family allegiances of those that could hear them. The Jacobite rebellion of 'forty-five was still a recent memory and they were sailing past feudal holdings that had largely declared for Charles Stuart, the youngest of the dynasty of pretenders to the crown. It was only forty miles or so to the spot where Charles had landed and where he had first raised his standard. It wasn't a matter of religion; many staunchly Protestant Tories supported a Stuart succession and there were plenty of Catholics who were loyal to the Hanoverian kings. It was more nuanced than that and allegiances were governed by a complex mixture of family, politics, religion and friendships and, of course, naked self-interest. Holbrooke knew that it was not at all unlikely that one or other of his two colleagues was a secret supporter of Charles Stuart's bid for power. That apart, it was a certainty that there would be plenty of fishermen and masters of coasting ships in the Western Isles that yearned for a return of the Stuart kings. French ships may well find themselves more welcome in these waters than those belonging to King George.

***

CHAPTER FOURTEEN

The Hunt

Saturday, Twenty-Second of March 1760.
Argonaut, at Sea, Island of Rum East Northeast Three Leagues.

Holbrooke paced backwards and forwards on the windward side of his quarterdeck as *Argonaut* ran cautiously in towards the islands under tops'ls, jib and stays'ls. The meeting at Stornoway three days before had ended congenially, with Chester doing his utmost to mend his relationship with his two subordinate captains. The rum punch had been excellent, with the kick of a nine-pounder, and Holbrooke, relieved at having saved his reputation, had drunk a little more than was his custom. He was grateful that Chester decided to stay at Stornoway overnight as it gave him the chance to clear his head before he embarked on the tricky navigation of the Minches and the islands that bordered that long channel.

Chester had come up with a plan for searching the Minches. It was essential – he said – to confirm that the French hadn't landed anywhere in the Western Isles before steering south for Ireland and the south-west of Scotland. After all, if they intended more than a mere raid – the temporary capture and sacking of a coastal town or two – they would need to raise a larger army than the fifteen hundred that Batiste had. What better place than the Jacobite Highlands and Islands? Chester had taken the mainland from Cape Wrath to Skye. Coulson had been given the eastern coast of the Hebrides and Holbrooke had the mainland from Skye down to Tiree and Coll. They were monstrous great areas and if the French had landed it would take a miracle for them to be found in that tangle of lochs, peninsulas and islands. It needed information and that could best be obtained by speaking to every vessel they encountered. In fair weather there was a constant traffic of small vessels supplying the islands and taking cattle and crops to market. However, in late March it was mainly fishermen that ventured out beyond the shelter of the islands, and they tended to run into harbour at the first sight of a man-o'-war. Holbrooke had managed to speak to only two of them since passing Skye, and both had confirmed his fears; the fishermen wanted nothing to do with King's ships, they refused to speak English and Holbrooke had to rely upon the pilot that he'd taken on at Stornoway, a native of Harris in the Outer Hebrides, who spoke Gaelic. Neither of the fishermen had seen a French squadron and Holbrooke could see the way they glared at his interpreter, evidently seeing him as a traitor to his land and his clan.

Backwards and forwards he strode as *Argonaut* crept slowly into the claustrophobic corner of the Hebridean Sea that was bounded by the strangely named islands of Canna, Rum, Eigg and Muck, with the Ardnamurchan peninsula to the southeast and Coll and Tiree to the south.

'You're safe enough here, Master,' the pilot said. 'You've another two leagues before you have to worry about the depth. You can almost put your frigate alongside Rum without touching bottom.'

Fairview said nothing. He didn't trust the pilot and he didn't like not being in control. These were new waters to him and the notes and observations from other sailing masters only went so far; he knew that he must rely upon the pilot's local knowledge. The squadron had taken the only three pilots that were available in Stornoway. Fairview had a strong suspicion that there were more but that they didn't care to be employed by a King's ship. These three had been lured by the solid promise of hard cash that came with a note drawn on the navy board., but it was clear that they offered their services reluctantly.

'A cast of the lead, if you please, Mister Petersen.'

The pilot gave a short derisive laugh and turned his back on the sailing master. Holbrooke was determined not to interfere, not until he had to, but he wholeheartedly agreed with Fairview's caution. It wasn't unknown for pilots to put ships aground. Very often they mistook the draught of King's ships and having been used to navigating much smaller vessels hadn't bothered to inform themselves of the real depth over reefs and sandbars.

They were standing into these dangerous waters with a set purpose. There was a small sloop ahead of them; it had evidently come through the passage between Canna and Rum and looked as though it was heading to pass inside Coll on its way south. It looked entirely unlike the few local vessels that Holbrooke had seen in the harbours and lochs that they had passed, and there was a possibility that it was an English trader on his way home. If it was then there was at least a possibility of gaining some intelligence on the French squadron. Regardless of their sympathies, for the men hereabouts the memory of 'forty-five was all too raw and Holbrooke was becoming convinced that nobody in the whole of the Western Isles wished to be known as an informer. It didn't help that the first person the fishermen saw when they came aboard was the pilot. If they didn't already know him, his Gaelic greeting made it clear that he came from these parts and he could see by their expressions that the fishermen were instantly on their guard. A call through the ship hadn't turned up a single Gaelic speaker in the crew, and it was impossible to know what the pilot said to them, but Holbrooke could make a fair guess. He had resolved that the next fisherman or master of a coaster that he interviewed wouldn't set eyes on the pilot.

'Looks like one of those sloops that run out of Whitehaven or those parts, sir,' said Fairview. 'They trade all along this coast; coal and hay and cattle and anything they can get a penny or two for.'

'Isn't it a bit early in the season to be this far from home?'

'Not for those little sloops. They keep inside the islands and only venture to cross the Minches when they're sure of their weather. There's a thousand lochs along this coast where they can lie overnight or sit out a gale without paying a groat in harbour dues.'

Holbrooke nodded. He'd studied the charts of this area and he could see how a small sloop, with perhaps two men and a boy, could be safe enough so long as they knew the tides and the reefs and watched the weather before they ventured to round a headland. It would be a good business too, with few overheads and decent profits. There was nothing on a fifteen-ton sloop that couldn't be kept working by a few men with a financial incentive and there was no duty to be paid on goods passing back and forth within England, Scotland and Wales.

The sloop was only a mile away now. It showed no signs of having seen the great frigate running down towards them. Surely those lofty masts and billowing tops'ls would have elicited some kind of reaction, either flight or greeting. He'd have expected that either the sloop would have turned on its heels and run closer into shore to round the southern point of Rum, or that it would have heaved-to and waited for *Argonaut* coming down.

'There's a man at the tiller, sir,' said Shorrock who had come on deck after a hasty breakfast and trained his telescope on the sloop. 'Well, I say a man, but a mighty small man, no more than a boy, I would guess.'

The sloop sailed steadily on with the wind on her starboard quarter, a mile offshore and in perfectly safe water. Shorrock laughed aloud and lowered his telescope.

'He's asleep! I can see his head nodding as the sloop's stern rises.'

Holbrooke picked up his telescope to look. Sure enough, the boy – for it was certainly not a grown man – was dozing with his left arm over the tiller. It was hardly surprising, with his boat on a comfortable broad reach and the warming sun now well above the horizon. As Holbrooke watched a head appeared through the hatch and the figure of a man rushed aft and cuffed the sleeping figure. There was a brief flurry of activity – Holbrooke could imagine what was passing between the two – and then the man stood up and looked around. It was hard to resist laughing when his gaze fell on the tall frigate now only five cables or so to windward. Even at that range Holbrooke could see the initial concern slowly change to relief. *Argonaut* didn't usually carry any flags at sea unless there was some good reason, but today he was flying a modest red ensign from the stern, and the flash of colour must have been reassuring to the master of the sloop. With a word to the boy and a few quick movements, the tiller was put down to leeward and the bows eased through the wind to be balanced by the backed jib and staysail. The sloop lay quietly, rising and falling on the light swell that came from the west.

'The tides setting to the sou'east, sir. We've an hour or so before we should think about beating out of these islands.'

Holbrooke had a mental picture of their situation. They were close to the southern tip of Rum and the vast bulk of the island dominated the view to the east. To the sou'east, no more than four miles away, lay Eigg and Muck, and further to the south he could clearly see Coll. In a gale this would be a trap for a ship the size of *Argonaut*, but today with a light westerly breeze and a cloudless sky to windward he could pass through any of the gaps between the islands if he needed to. Nevertheless, the master's advice was timely and if he was to make his rendezvous with *Pegasus* this evening, he couldn't afford to be fooling around among the islands. He needed to get what information he could and be on his way.

'Mister Shorrock. Bring the longboat alongside and call away my coxswain and boat's crew. I'll go over to the sloop. Pass the word for Mister Chalmers, he may wish to join me.'

***

'You should have seen the look that blasted pilot gave me,' said Holbrooke as they sped across the short distance to the sloop. 'I've a mind to refuse to sign his chit when we land him. Whether he's an active Jacobite sympathiser or whether he just resents being set aside, he was clearly unhappy that he wasn't able to give the master of this sloop the evil eye the way he did to the fishermen yesterday. Not that it would do any good, I'm sure the sloop's English.'

'It's hardly surprising,' Chalmers said. 'He married a MacDonald you know, and the memory of Glencoe runs deep. It's doubtful whether he has any allegiance except to his family and clan, and more than likely his attempts to frustrate you are no more than an instinctive reaction against anyone in authority. I doubt whether he's what we would call a Jacobite.'

Holbrooke would have asked his friend whether he knew anything more about the pilot but at that moment Dawson pushed the helm over, the oars were tossed, and the bows of the longboat met the sloop's gunwale in the softest of kisses.

'Lie off, Dawson, I won't be long.'

The sloop was indeed from Whitehaven. It was flush-decked, and Holbrooke took one look into the tiny, low cabin – all the rest of the space below decks was devoted to cargo – and decided to speak to the master on the open deck. He was a young man, not yet in his thirties, and he was sailing with only a boy who appeared to be his nephew.

'I'd prefer to have a mate,' he explained, 'but I can't get anyone to sail with me at this time of year, not at the rate that I can pay, leastwise.'

Holbrooke looked the man up and down. He was just the sort of seaman that he yearned to have in *Argonaut*. He would certainly be rated able after Jackson had seen him, and he'd be a petty officer within six months. But he looked supremely happy in command of his own little trading sloop and as the master and owner he had an exemption that no impress officer would dare to ignore.

'We've been all the way up to Ullapool, carrying whatever we can pick up and now we have a cargo of last year's wool that I'll take up the river to Carlisle, then we're home to Whitehaven for a few weeks.'

The man was confident and didn't appear to have anything to hide from a King's officer. He was talkative and Holbrooke let him chatter away while he looked around him at the small deck. The single mast looked sound and there was a skim of slush over its lower parts to help the mainsail hoops move easily. The sails were patched in places, but it had been done with care, and the shrouds, the sheets and halyards were all in good condition. It looked like a boat that its owner intended to be his livelihood for years to come.

'We had a cargo of barrel staves from Oban which brought in a tidy sum and since then it's been hay, mostly, and whatever else is needed at the islands.'

He paused for a moment and gave Holbrooke a strange look.

'Is there something afoot, sir?' he asked, 'only I saw some other men-o'-war a few days ago.'

Holbrooke's ears pricked up.

'I didn't get close enough of course, but I imagine they must have been King's ships.'

'When would that have been?' Holbrooke asked casually, not wishing to frighten the man by giving the impression that this was valuable information; not yet.

'Now, let me see. Today's Saturday I believe.'

He was counting back the days on his fingers.

'Tuesday it must have been. Tuesday evening off the top end of Skye. They were coming boldly inside those islands that lie a couple of miles offshore.'

It was to be expected that the master of a little trading sloop wouldn't know the names of many of the places in this sea. It was unlikely that he owned a chart of any kind and his knowledge of the rocks and shoals, the headlands and islands, would have been gleaned from his trips as a boy and a mate before he accumulated enough capital to own his own vessel.

'How many, Master?'

Nor'west by North

'Oh, there were three like yours,' he gestured towards *Argonaut*, 'and two smaller, but they didn't look quite the same, more like merchantmen with guns. I was close enough to see that they all had their sides pierced.'

Holbrooke thought quickly. This man had honesty printed all over his browned, homely face. But he clearly knew little of men-of-war, which wasn't surprising in a man who traded in the northwest of the British Isles. It was quite possible that he'd never seen a King's ship before.

'The three like mine,' he said gesturing again to *Argonaut*, 'were they the same or was one larger?'

'Oh, one of them had taller masts than the others and it looked like she carried two guns lower down. I only saw their larboard side, though. They were in a tearing hurry, with tops'ls and t'gallants and they didn't spare a moment for me.'

'Well, I congratulate you, Master, because those were French ships, and they would undoubtedly have taken you if they weren't in so much haste. Your sloop would be flying the lilies of France now, or she'd be a burned hulk at the bottom of the sea.'

The man looked shocked.

'French ships? In these waters? Is it an invasion?' he asked.

'I think not, but they may choose to pause to pillage a town or two. Is there anything else you can tell me?'

He thought for a moment, then came to some sort of internal decision.

'There's one thing, sir. I didn't want to say anything in case I was imagining it, but I thought I saw two sails heading east, perhaps towards Loch Torridon or thereabouts. It was a little hazy before this fine weather set in and it could have been nothing, but the tops'l of one of them looked just like the other ships, like yours, in fact,' and he pointed towards *Argonaut*. 'The other may have been a brig, she was certainly smaller. It was probably nothing but…'

Holbrooke exchanged glances with Chalmers. If only five ships had passed Skye into the Little Minch, then what the sloop's master saw or didn't see deserved investigation. It may well have been nothing, but there was a French frigate and a transport unaccounted for and that added weight to master's word.

'If that's all you can tell me then I wish you a good voyage, Master.' He brought a shilling from his pocket and handed it to the man. 'This is for your trouble and for your good eyes,'

The master flipped the coin in the air. It wasn't a fortune, but it certainly made the delay worthwhile.

'And here's a penny for the lad. You may give it to him if he stays awake through a whole watch.'

***

'We'll have something to tell Captain Chester when we meet him this evening,' Holbrooke said.

He had invited Shorrock, Fairview and Chalmers to dinner in the great cabin. *Argonaut* was safe in Jackson's care, and the bosun was last seen enjoying the officers' favourite sport of provoking the pilot who had taken to sulking at the taffrail. That way he was still on the quarterdeck and couldn't be accused of shirking his duty, while at the same time offering only the bare minimum of advice on the pilotage of these waters. The ship was hard on the wind, beating out to the rendezvous to the west of Tiree.

'You don't think we should go north and look in behind Skye?' Shorrock asked, 'just in case the master of the sloop did see the third frigate heading in that way.'

'I did consider it,' Holbrooke replied, 'but if he's gone into Loch Torridon or one of those places, he'll take days to beat out again, and that's after he's done whatever he's been sent there for. There's plenty of time to deal with him. Anyway, I've disobeyed orders once already and I don't want the ship to get a reputation for waywardness.'

They all smiled at that. The rumour of that awful interview at Stornoway had spread from Chester's officers to *Argonaut*'s wardroom. Even the details of the avoided duel were well known. *Argonaut's* officers thoroughly agreed with Holbrooke's desire to be seen to obey orders.

'No, we'll meet *Pegasus* and *Fortune* tomorrow morning and there'll be plenty of time for Captain Chester to decide what should be done.'

There was a short silence as his guests processed this information. As always, it was Fairview who pushed the point; he had little sense of his own place in dealing with his superiors.

'What would you do, sir, if you had command of these three frigates?'

Holbrooke paused for a moment. He'd thought of little else since he'd stepped off the deck of the sloop. It was an example of a classic naval and military problem: whether to split a force and cover all the enemy's movements, or to keep the force concentrated to deal with the main body.

'I'd ignore the frigate and the brig to the north. They can cause only minor embarrassment, unless they have Charles Stuart on board, of course.'

That raised a laugh. Batiste was certainly not escorting the pretender's son when he called at Gothenburg. No, it was impossible.

'In fact, and this is between us alone, gentlemen, I would never have split our forces at Stornoway. There was a good reason at Torshavn, to fool Batiste into thinking he had superior numbers, but after that we should have stayed together. I imagine Captain Chester now thinks the same.'

'But a frigate action, ship against ship,' Shorrock said wistfully, 'the chance comes but rarely.'

Holbrooke smiled along with Fairview and Chalmers. They all knew that a successful single ship action was a well-trodden path for promotion for a first lieutenant, quite possibly the only route for friendless Shorrock who had neither family nor political influence. Holbrooke sympathised; but from the lofty position of post-captain, he could harden his heart.

'No, ignore the single frigate and the brig, they can be dealt with later. In this case it's only the ship-rigged transports that really matter. The frigates are just an escort and although they can take prizes – and there'll be more opportunity for that as they move south – it's the expedition's ability to make a landing that must concern us. Concentrate our three frigates and I'll warrant that we're a match on any day for the three that Monsieur Batiste's has remaining!'

'Hear him, hear him,' they all shouted and banged their fists on the table, making a racket that brought a smile to the bosun's face and a sour grimace to the pilot's when the sound drifted up to the quarterdeck.

***

CHAPTER FIFTEEN

Fool's Errand

Sunday, Twenty-Third of March 1760.
Argonaut, at Sea, Tiree Northeast six leagues.

True to their rendezvous, the three ships converged as the sun peeped above the low, bare hills of Tiree. It was never going to be a leisurely affair but when Holbrooke brought his news, Chester was impatient to be away in pursuit of Batiste. Coulson had heard and seen nothing; it was as though the French squadron had never passed through the Minches. Chester had heard rumours; a fisherman had word from another boat that some big ships had been seen in the distance. No numbers, no description, not enough to inform any decisions. It was only Holbrooke's news that was credible.

The French were six days ahead of them and if they hadn't remained in Scottish waters, they could already be off the English or Irish coasts. Chester barely paused for thought. He dismissed the solo frigate and brig with much the same argument as Holbrooke had used and gave rapid orders for the squadron to steer south. Holbrooke agreed; there was nothing to detain Batiste in the Western Isles or the mainland coast adjoining them. Once past Tiree, Scotland could be discounted as a target. It must be Ireland or the north of England.

'You've landed your pilots, gentlemen? Good, then we'll form a line abreast,' Chester said. 'I'll be in the centre, *Fortune* to the east, *Argonaut* to the west. The weather's set fair for the day so we'll have a good reach to the south. Stay in sight and if anyone sees anything send up a red flag to the main t'gallant head and fire a gun. We'll close up again at six o'clock and I'll give you your orders for the night.'

He reached for the chart that he'd used before to plan the squadron's dispositions.

'If he'd been planning a descent anywhere from Donegal to Kerry,' he swept his hand across the wild Atlantic shoreline of Ireland, 'he'd likely have taken his squadron outside the Hebrides. However, I we can't entirely discount the west coast, not yet. We'll steer for here, Tory Island. It's a natural departure for the east or the west coasts. If there's no word of Batiste there, we'll abandon the Atlantic side and turn back to follow the coast around.'

Holbrooke said nothing. The logic was sound, but he was still concerned that they didn't know what mission the fourth frigate had been given. Could Batiste have been obliged to steer through the Minches to set some subsidiary plan in train? In that case, having detached a frigate and brig, he could easily have steered for the west coast of Ireland. Nevertheless, with three ships Chester couldn't hope to cover both coasts of Ireland, and most likely he had chosen correctly. A day or so to eliminate the west of Ireland then concentrate on the east.

'We'll look into these places as we move east from Tory Island.'

Chester moved his finger to the two pronounced inlets to the east of Tory Island. Lough Swilly and the deep inlet of Lough Foyle with the old city of Londonderry astride the river at its head.

Holbrooke knew nothing of Ireland and all he knew about Londonderry was that its walls had resisted sieges for centuries and had never been breached.

Coulson shuffled self-consciously. He was a few months senior to Holbrooke and a couple of years older. Holbrooke had always thought of himself as a reticent person and he often had to make a conscious effort to take part in discussions, but Coulson was a few notches further along the scale of self-effacement.

'I've been to Londonderry, sir,' he said, looking sideways at Chester.

In a flash of intuition Holbrooke realised that Coulson was still worried about his action – or lack of action – in the engagement a week before. Both *Pegasus* and *Argonaut* had been damaged, but *Fortune* hadn't even seen the enemy. Even though Chester had exonerated him, the report would look bad. A captain who couldn't bring his ship into action – whether or not it was his fault – was of no use to Anson and it was well known that the First Lord kept himself informed of the doings of even the lowliest ships in the fleet.

'My mother is from those parts,' he explained, 'and I spent much of my youth there. Londonderry has a garrison and as far as I'm aware the walls and the castle are kept in good repair. It's impossible to surprise the city by a descent from the sea. Any attacking squadron would have to work its way up the lough and would be seen long before it could land a force. In any case, Batiste's fifteen hundred are too few for the task.'

Chester looked startled at this intelligence. He was in a difficult position because he'd been sent on this mission without any preparation. Until he'd been detached, he'd been part of Boys' squadron that was watching the French channel ports and escorting convoys from the Downs. It was a far cry from the north coast of Ireland, a country that was largely beyond his knowledge.

'He has an artillery train though, isn't that right, Holbrooke? I believe you heard a report of them at Gothenburg.'

'He has, sir. A number of field guns – six-pounders, I understand – and a few eighteens or twenty-fours, the reports varied. The heavy artillery will only be of any use if he settles down to a long siege, and that sounds too dangerous for him.'

'Yet it must be a tempting target,' Chester mused, 'the chief city in the northwest of the country.'

'Londonderry's certainly a big city, sir,' Coulson said, 'and it's true that Batiste can find provisions and plunder there to keep him at sea for months. But it can't be taken in a day, nor in a week, and by that time he'll have a British and Irish army marching against him and his ships will be blockaded in the lough.'

Coulson was finding his voice now, gaining confidence as he expounded on a topic that he knew well. Chester looked thoughtfully at the map.

'Nevertheless, we can't ignore such a place. We must at least assure ourselves that Batiste isn't there, causing mischief.'

***

The squadron cruised slowly south from Tiree. This was a bleak and little-travelled corner of the ocean and they saw nothing at all, not a single vessel passed inbound from the wide Atlantic, nor anything outbound from the Scottish mainland. Holbrooke didn't envy Chester. The squadron had a huge area to cover, and it was so early in the year that most of the coastal traffic had not yet started. Fishing boats rarely came this far before the weather improved and larger ships in the Atlantic trade would come close around Tory Island, or if they were destined for ports further to the north they would steer for the southern tip of the Hebrides. That left some twenty leagues that they had to cross with little chance of discovering anything new. By the time the squadron came to the wind to receive Chester's orders for the night, they were still twenty miles north northeast of Tory Island. They spent the night beating to windward, out into the cold, grey Atlantic. Four hours before dawn the pre-arranged signal – a blue light from *Pegasus* – brought them off the wind and they reached down towards the island.

Holbrooke looked in horror at Tory Island. Even in this moderate weather the Atlantic waves beat upon its rocky shore sending spray far into the air. It was hard to imagine a bleaker spot, and yet it had a small population that must find some sort of a living. It was well known to seamen as one of the great landfalls of the Atlantic world, a place that provided a departure for ships heading west and a recognisable landfall for those heading east towards the northern parts of Britain. There was no sign of Batiste's squadron, but Holbrooke hadn't expected any.

Nor'west by North

Inside Tory Island they spoke to a brig that was coming around from Sligo, bound for Greenock. The master, an Ulsterman born and bred, had seen no men-o'-war, French or otherwise; the coast of Donegal to the west was quiet.

With that reassurance, the squadron ran east along the coast, looking into each substantial bay and cove. Sheep Haven, Tranarossan Bay, Mulroy Bay, Ballyhiernan Bay, all were innocent of a French invasion. With the last of the light, *Argonaut* nosed into Lough Swilly until Holbrooke could see as far as Inch Island. Nothing; the northern shore of Ireland was basking in its last spell of tranquillity before the seaborne trade came to life after the winter.

Tuesday was much the same. The squadron passed inside Inishtrahull and with the wind on its starboard quarter ran down towards Lough Foyle. Here Chester sent a boat into the signal station at Magilligan to save a day working into the lough and back out to sea, but no French squadron had passed that way. They pressed on to the North Channel, sighting Rathlin Island at the end of the afternoon watch. *Pegasus* and *Fortune* took the seaward route, but Chester signalled for *Argonaut* to pass inside the island.

***

'Slack water in an hour, I believe, sir,' said Fairview, staring through his telescope at the blackened line on the shore that marked the limit of the high tide. The sea was just a yard or so below the high-water mark, surging up and down to the scend of the weakening Atlantic swell. 'We should be through before the ebb sets in.'

Fairview's chart showed tidal rips inside the island and his private notes recommended that the passage only be attempted at slack water. Holbrooke wasn't too concerned. He knew these notes that sailing masters exchanged among themselves; they loved to make each other's flesh creep with greater and greater exaggerations of the force of a tidal stream, of the poor holding ground, of whirlpools that rivalled Scylla and Charybdis. The reality was usually on a different scale, and a well-found frigate, if handled with caution, could dare most passages around the British Isles. Nevertheless, it would be as well to get into the North Channel before the stream set them back into the Atlantic. The wind that had picked up overnight dropped in the afternoon and now *Argonaut* was making a bare three knots through the water.

Holbrooke waited for the change of the watch and spoke briefly to Shorrock when he had relieved Jackson. He noticed that Fairview had no intention of leaving the deck during this interesting passage and he was busy with quadrant and compass, chart and telescope as he directed volleys of comments to a harassed looking midshipman who was losing the battle to write on the slate as fast as the master was talking.

'I'll be in my cabin, Mister Shorrock. Keep us off the rocks, if you please, and let me know if you sight anything larger than a fisherman.'

'Aye-aye, sir,' Shorrock replied with a grin. There was a holiday atmosphere in the ship with *Pegasus* out of sight the other side of the island. Shorrock took the admonition to keep *Argonaut* safe in the spirit in which it was given.

'Oh, and pass the word for Mister Chalmers, would you. I would be pleased to see him in the cabin if he is at leisure.'

Holbrooke's cabin servant had been on the quarterdeck about to offer his captain a refreshment, but he heard the call for Chalmers and knowing the chaplain's thirst for coffee, he hurried below to prepare a pot. It was one of Holbrooke's few indulgences and with coffee beans costing nearly a ha'penny for enough to make a pot for two people, it was an expensive luxury. Gin or rum or brandy were far cheaper, but in an age when alcohol was the accepted lubricant of social intercourse, Holbrooke was one among a very few sea officers who were careful of their intake.

'Shall we have a pot of coffee, David?' Holbrooke asked when his friend came into the cabin.

'With the greatest of pleasure,' Chalmers replied. He rarely used Holbrooke's Christian name on board, it somehow seemed out of place and smacked of disrespect or, even worse, the politics of the Levellers that were gaining ground in some parts.

They smelled the coffee before it was brought in on its silver tray. Holbrooke would have been just as happy for the pot and the cups to be placed directly on the table between the fiddles, but his servant quietly resisted all attempts at such a lowering of his standards. He'd been in service to a baronet before that unfortunate man had been forced by injudicious dealings in the exchange to reduce his establishment, and he had fixed ideas about how to serve a gentleman.

'May I?' Chalmers asked, and without waiting for an answer he poured from the pot into the two cups. Chalmers wasn't poor by any means, not anymore. His service at sea during this war under the fortunate leadership of first Captain Carlisle and now his friend Holbrooke, had brought him a modest wealth in prize money. Nevertheless, the only time that he had good coffee was when he was invited into the great cabin. The wardroom steward had no skill in grinding and brewing coffee and despite a lavish expenditure on the finest beans from the East and the West Indies the coffee in the wardroom never failed to disappoint.

They said nothing for a few minutes as they gratefully sipped the scalding hot beverage. After he'd finished the first cup, Holbrooke turned to his friend.

'What do you think of our quest, David? As frankly as you can?'

Chalmers hesitated, holding his cup clear of the table as the frigate's stern lifted, and wedging it between the fiddles when it dropped. He took another sip before answering.

'I'll say it plainly then. I believe Mister Chester is doing himself a disfavour. With the French squadron more than a week ahead of us, they will have time for all sorts of mischief. Yes, they may have gone to the west of Ireland, but I think we agree that it was always unlikely and now, at last, it can be discounted. If Batiste is to achieve anything and then have a hope of bringing his squadron home, it must be done south of here. By delaying in the north and again in the west – oh, for all the most honourable reasons – Chester is leaving Batiste free to make his descent on a British or Irish town. All he'll have left for his report is an explanation of how he covered all of Batiste's possible courses of action. It's a perfect example of how a systematic approach to the problem guarantees nothing but mediocrity. At every point since we left the Faroes he's drifted deeper into the trap.'

Holbrooke looked surprised. He'd broadly agreed with Chester's plan, had contributed to its formulation in fact, and he still thought that it best met Commodore Boys' directive.

'You think he should have plunged south on Batiste's tail immediately after the action south of the Faroes? And what if Batiste had been bound for a landing in Scotland, or the northwest of Ireland. We'd have been far away, chasing a chimera in the Irish Sea.'

'Indeed, and to an inquiry of rational minds Chester's plan would sound correct. It's the best possible compromise, given all the factors. But that's not the point. It won't be a jury of rational minds that scrutinises the whys and wherefores of Batiste's escape. It will be a politically motivated witch hunt, looking for a scapegoat, and a senior post-captain will be an ideal candidate.'

Holbrooke's surprise turned to shock. He hadn't looked at it that way.

'Now, I wouldn't presume to lecture you on the arts of war at sea, but I think we knew as soon as Batiste fled to the south that he was bound through the North Channel. Yes, there was a chance that he had other ideas, but it was only a chance. By dawdling along, looking into every fisherman's creek along the way, Chester has put himself in a position where he is certain to fail, albeit with a good story to tell.'

Holbrooke was looking out of the big stern windows

where the flat sea reflected the light of the setting sun. It had two hours to go yet, but it was slanting low towards the horizon already.

'What would you have suggested,' Holbrooke asked quietly.

Chalmers looked at his friend seeing the horror on his face. He was part of this debacle after all.

'I would have urged Chester to focus on Batiste's most likely course of action. We know he's been ordered to make a descent, to draw an army from the south to expel him, and as far as we know he hasn't yet heard that his mission is futile. In fact, it looks like he hasn't heard about Quiberon Bay at all, or if he has, he doesn't understand its significance. Why else would he persist in coming down the west side of Britain? If we agree that he's still looking for a suitable place to land his soldiers, then all the likely opportunities are in the north of England or the east of Ireland, not in Scotland. I would have urged that we made the best speed through the Minches and through the North Channel. We may even have caught Batiste before he passed this way, but in any case, the trail would have been fresh. Now we are floundering as though we are trapped in an endless game of blind man's bluff.'

Holbrooke looked solemn as he worked through these fresh ideas. He had huge respect for Chalmers' intellect and now that his blood was thoroughly laced with salt water, he knew that on matters of naval strategy his friend was rarely in error.

Chalmers watched him. One thing he knew about Holbrooke was that when he saw the facts stack up against him, he was quick to change his mind, and he could see that happening now.

'Then it's a want of boldness, a lack of initiative.'

'Just so,' Chalmers replied. 'I hope that I'm wrong, but it seems highly likely that some benighted town in England or Ireland is paying a ransom as we speak, in the hope that these French corsairs will be on their way without putting it to the torch.'

'And now, given the facts as they are, what would you do?'

Chalmers thought for a moment.

'It's futile to rush from place to place looking for Batiste. However, I believe we can expect much more seagoing traffic in these waters and it's likely to be more loyal to the Crown. I would steer for the North Channel between Ireland and the Mull of Kintyre as fast as I could, pausing only to ask one question of passing vessels: *have you seen the French*? As you have often told me, naval affairs are frequently settled in such choke points. Reason has kept the squadron in the north, now instinct should take over and drive us to the south.'

Holbrooke stood and walked to the stern windows. Fair Head with its curious vertical columns – like organ pipes – rose high above the masthead, its grandeur enhanced by the shadows that the low sun cast, emphasising the divisions between the pipes. Astern and to larboard he could just see the start of the ebbing tide, a ripple on the water as the wind blew against the gathering current. He turned to reply, when a loud hail from the masthead broke into his thoughts.

'Sail ho! Sail on the starboard bow, just around the point, sir. It's a brig on the larboard tack.'

Holbrooke heard the flurry of activity on the quarterdeck above his head. He glanced meaningfully at Chalmers who smiled back and inclined his head in acknowledgement. Holbrooke had no truck with superstition, and he didn't believe in divine intervention, but something about this just sounded right. He grabbed his hat, tapped the table three times for luck and rushed on deck, leaving Chalmers to plunder the remains of the coffee pot.

***

CHAPTER SIXTEEN

News of the French

Wednesday, Twenty-Sixth of March 1760.
Argonaut, at Sea, off Fair Head.

'Where away, Mister Shorrock?'

'Starboard bow, sir, about three miles. He must be just off the next headland.'

'That's Torr Head, sir,' Fairview added, looking at the chart.

Holbrooke could see it clearly now. South of Fair Head the land trended downwards but at Torr Head it suddenly rose into a little hill on a peninsula. It looked like a nose, a clown's bulbous nose at a travelling fair. And just off the clown's nose was a brig, perhaps a hundred tons, Holbrooke estimated. It was sailing close under the land, which was unusual in this westerly wind, and it was making hard going of it. Perhaps its master hoped to catch the ebb around Fair Head. If so, he would have to make better speed before the tide turned again and made the whole thing impossible. That piqued Holbrooke's interest. It wasn't like a trading brig to be so careless of his passage speed. There were no harbours here and no road that would hold an anchor in these tidal rips. What on earth was he doing?

'Let me see that chart, Mister Fairview. Now, what's the extent of the tidal rips where that brig is?'

'The worst of it's close into the coast, sir. Maybe out to a mile offshore. You can see the white water clearly now.'

The brig was in shadow as the sun slanted relentlessly towards the green hills of Antrim, but half a mile offshore the orange rays caught the short, steep waves that the tide was kicking up. From three miles away on the deck of a stout frigate, the sea didn't look particularly rough, but Holbrooke knew that a small brig would be pitching and rolling like a mad thing.

'He's bearing away, sir,' Shorrock called excitedly. 'Now he's wearing. God, what a shambles. That mizzen boom came close to taking the mast by the board.'

'Call all hands to make sail, Mister Shorrock. I'll leave it to you, Mister Fairview, but I want to be alongside that brig before we lose the light. Hoist that red flag at the main t'gallant head.'

'*Pegasus* won't see it yet, sir. They're both out of sight behind the island.'

Holbrooke glanced towards the island. There was no sign of the two frigates.

'Never mind, hoist it anyway and fire a gun to leeward; a gun every two minutes.'

Everyone on deck could see that the brig was in a panic, and they were all taken up with the thrill of the chase. T'gallants were set at record speed and soon the stuns'l booms slid out through their irons, closely followed by the stuns'ls themselves that flashed in the dying light of the day. *Argonaut* picked up speed with the wind broad on her starboard beam, casting a wide bow wave that reflected the dying light of the sun in a glory of orange and red and grey and white.

'Nine knots and a half, sir,' Shorrock reported after a cast of the log, 'and we're gaining on him.'

Holbrooke didn't reply, his whole attention was on the chase. The unfortunate brig was caught in the rough-and-tumble waters of the tidal rip and couldn't escape out into deeper water. *Argonaut*, further out to sea and free of the rip, would trap the brig against the land in only half an hour, by Holbrooke's estimate.

'Bring the longboat alongside,' he shouted. 'I'll go over with my crew. A pistol or cutlass for each man and a file of marines. Mister Murray, join me in the boat, if you please.'

Holbrooke was aware of Chalmers standing beside him, smelling of coffee and looking pleased with himself. He looked questioningly at Holbrooke and at the weapons being handed down into the longboat.

'It may be just a guilty conscience, some contraband or a natural reluctance to meet a King's ship. His people don't care to be pressed, perhaps, but I think it's more than that. He positively panicked when he saw us, so much so that he's come close to putting the brig in danger. It could be one of Mister Batiste's prizes, so I want a show of force. And of course, it'll be choppy getting across, and I don't want to be drowned today, or any other day. The longboat it must be.'

'As you've taken such elaborate precautions for the safety of your passengers, may I join you?' Chalmers asked. 'Perhaps he thinks you are French as you're not showing your colours.'

Holbrooke stared at him and slapped the rail in exasperation.

'Are we flying an ensign, Mister Shorrock? No? Then please do so. What are you all thinking of, boarding a merchantman without showing our colours? Hoist it anywhere that can be seen by the brig.'

'*Pegasus* is in sight, sir, and *Fortune's* just coming clear of the island.'

Bang! Holbrooke jumped as a gun fired a few yards from him.

'Yes, Mister Chalmers, you may certainly join me, but let the marines get on the brig's deck before you.'

'Ha! He's almost stopped now,' Shorrock exclaimed, entirely unabashed by Holbrooke's mild admonishment. He'd suffered far, far worse in previous ships. 'Look at that tide rip.'

Holbrooke was glad it was the longboat and not the yawl that would take him over. The smaller boat would have been distinctly unsafe in the anarchic sea that the flooding tide had kicked up. He could have sent Shorrock, but he so desperately wanted to hear the news, and everything about this brig told him that he was scared of something. It could be entirely unconnected, but Holbrooke was becoming increasingly hopeful that the brig had encountered the French squadron.

'He's wearing again, sir. Now he's heaving to. We have him.'

Shorrock was as excited as though he'd just been in a fleet action, or as though a rich prize was in prospect. The men on the upper deck raised a short cheer.

***

Not a guilty conscience after all, far from it. The master of the brig was in terror for his life and his livelihood, and he was pathetically grateful to see a King's officer. His crew, without an exemption certificate between them and the press, took a different attitude to being boarded by a navy longboat and they were nowhere to be seen. The master and the mate may have been the sole crew of that brig for all the life that was visible on deck.

'Thank God, sir, I thought it was those cursed French pirates again,' he exclaimed before Holbrooke had put his legs over the gunwale. He looked a little alarmed as Lieutenant Murray and his three marines followed close behind but was reassured by Holbrooke's evidently English voice.

'I won't detain you long then, Captain. No, let's stay on deck,' he added as the master showed signs of conducting him below.

'You're right of course, sir. If you're after the French, then there's no time to lose. They chased me three days ago. That would have been Sunday, and I've been looking out for them ever since.'

'Where was this?' Holbrooke demanded.

'Off the Calf of Man. Three frigates there were, and two ship-rigged merchantmen, or that's what they looked like, stuffed with soldiers. Transports maybe. They'd already taken three prizes; I could see them just around the other side of the Calf. The three frigates chased me north until after sunset, then I lost them by bearing away into Luce Bay.'

Holbrooke was almost hopping with impatience to be away. He could see the crew of the brig coming cautiously

Nor'west by North

on deck. Naturally, they had hidden themselves when they saw a King's ship, but now that it was clear that they wouldn't be pressed, they all wanted to hear what was happening.

'Anything more? Is that the last you saw of them?'

'Oh, no, sir. On the Monday – two days ago – I plucked up my courage…'

'He may have your honour,' said an anonymous voice from the crew who were clustered in the waist by now, listening shamelessly, 'but we was signed on to the good ship *Brown Trousers* by then, if you know what I mean.'

Holbrooke had to smile along with the crew's laughter.

'As I was saying, sir,' the master continued primly, like a maiden aunt interrupted by a boisterous, irreverent nephew, 'I plucked up my courage, hoping that they were gone, and started to beat up the North Channel, when who should I see but the whole lot of them coming up to leeward of me.'

'Three frigates, two ships and three prizes?'

'Well, yes, sir, but now there were four prizes. I knew one of them, *Fair Lydia* from Liverpool. It's a crying shame what with Bill's wife expecting and all…'

Holbrooke had the feeling that he'd talk for hours about poor Bill's woes and at any moment they'd get onto the scandalous price of sails and cordage, not to mention seamen's wages. He tapped his toe impatiently.

'The frigates, Master, where did the go?'

'Oh yes, sir. Now where was I? I thought they were chasing me. I thought perhaps they'd layed up overnight to wait for me to come out, but I was wrong. Just when I knew my goose was cooked, I tried one last tack over towards Stranraer and lo and behold, they held their luff and stood in towards Belfast Lough. Well, when I couldn't see them anymore, I tacked again and dived into a little anchorage I know just eight miles south of here. We didn't dare venture out all day Tuesday, and when we did today what should we see but…'

He would have gone on, Holbrooke knew, telling the

tale of their escape from the French, but he had heard enough, and he could see *Pegasus* and *Fortune* standing in to see what was happening, and in half an hour they'd be in darkness.

It was quite dark by the time *Pegasus* and *Fortune* came to in *Argonaut*'s lee. The lanterns were twinkling on the three ships' taffrails as they rode easily with their heads to the nor'-nor'west, dipping their bows into the light Atlantic swell that had turned and weakened in its passage around Rathlin Island. The longboat rowed directly from the brig over to *Pegasus*.

***

'Belfast Lough, you say? He's a bold man, this Batiste, to attempt such a great city. Well, if he's still there we have him. He can't escape from the lough without a fight, and he surely can't stay long in Belfast. It won't take half a week to muster enough of an army to clear a thousand Frenchmen out of the city. And we'll be waiting for him.'

Chester rubbed his hands in glee. This was the opportunity he had hoped for. His three frigates against the three French frigates. Even though they had two armed transports and three or four prizes that they could also have armed, the odds looked good.

The wail of the pipes came down from the deck and a few moments later Coulson, tall and shy, stepped into the cabin.

'They're at Belfast, Captain Coulson,' Chester announced before greeting the new arrival.

Coulson nodded cautiously. He wasn't a man to jump to conclusions, nor to give an opinion without being asked.

'Well, you could at least look pleased, man,' Chester exclaimed. 'We have them now!'

Holbrooke moved his finger across the chart that Chester had laid out on the table.

'I beg your pardon, sir. The master of the brig said that they stood in towards Belfast Lough, not that they were steering all the way up to Belfast itself. As you say, attacking

Nor'west by North

Belfast would be a bold move and it carries the risk of failure on land; it's a big walled city with a garrison. And of course, they could find themselves trapped in the lough, particularly if the wind turns easterly. I wonder whether one of the smaller towns closer to the mouth of the lough would be more likely. There's Carrickfergus on the Antrim shore and Bangor on southern side. Either of those would offer an easier assault and a better chance of escape.'

Chester looked again at the chart and stepped off some distances with his outstretched fingers.

'Well, that's as may be,' he said grudgingly, 'but it hardly changes what we must do next. The lough's less than six miles across where it meets the sea, and we can certainly cover that area. What's the distance from here? Ten leagues? Then we should get underway now and be in position before dawn. We'll be able to see them wherever they are in the lough. If these westerly wind holds, then I'll beat into the lough as soon as there's light enough to see both the northern and southern shores. Captain Coulson, you'll be in the centre and Captain Holbrooke, you'll bring up the rear. A red flag at the main t'gallant head if you sight the enemy, then follow my movements.'

***

CHAPTER SEVENTEEN

A Missed Opportunity

Thursday, Twenty-Seventh of March 1760.
Argonaut, at Sea, off Black Head, County Antrim.

'Good morning, Mister Chalmers, it's not often we see you on deck this early.'

Chalmers looked around at the shadowy figures on the quarterdeck and saw Holbrooke's tall shape standing to windward of the wheel.

'Good morning, sir,' he replied, 'if indeed it is the morning. The bells woke me, and I remembered that in a fit of enthusiasm yesterday, I had resolved to be among the first to see this new day, which holds such promise for success.'

'Morning? Not yet, Mister Chalmers, those were only seven bells, and the middle watch still has half a glass to run. In fifteen minutes, you may call it the morning. Nevertheless, our friend the sun is already making his presence felt.'

Holbrooke motioned towards the larboard quarter where the faintest loom of the sun was lightening the sky over the vague, shadowy shape of the Rhins of Galloway, more to be imagined than seen.

Chalmers' eyes were becoming accustomed to the light, and he could see Fairview gazing ahead where *Fortune's* stern light showed through the tangle of *Argonaut*'s rigging. The quartermaster stood like a statue beside the wheel, watching the luff and the leach of the main tops'l and occasionally muttering an order to the steersman.

'The wind has veered a few degrees overnight,' Holbrooke said, 'it's almost nor'west now and it's dropped to little more than faint zephyrs. Black Head is a mile or so on our starboard beam, or so Mister Fairview assures me, and we're coasting in towards Carrickfergus on the Antrim shore.'

'Then can I assume that Captain Chester believes Carrickfergus is the most likely place to find the enemy?'

Holbrooke barked a short laugh.

'Not necessarily. With the wind as it is, if we were to reach across to Bangor first, we'd have to beat back up to Carrickfergus and then beat up to Belfast. This way we keep up to windward. One way or another, unless we sight something soon, we're condemned to beat up the lough until we find some evidence of Monsieur Batiste. At least we are starting early and taking advantage of the first of the light, but even so, it could be a long day.'

The massive shape of the first lieutenant appeared, striding aft from the waist.

'The guns are all ready, sir. I've taken the liberty of ordering the drummer on deck, to save time when you want the men at quarters.'

Holbrooke could see the marine drummer huddled among the bits of the mainmast. He looked cold and his hands were buried deep into the canvas cover that saved his drumskin from the falling dews.

Eight bells, and the watch changed.

'Mister Jackson has the deck, sir,' Fairview reported. 'With your permission I'll go below and snatch a bite before I'm needed again.'

'Very wise, Mister Fairview. Would you ask my servant to bring me a pot of coffee and some biscuit?'

***

Holbrooke and Chalmers stood together in companionable silence, seeing *Fortune's* shape materialise around her stern light, watching the hills to the west and the south take shape, and waiting for the miracle of dawn.

'What will Mister Chester do if he doesn't find the French here,' he asked, 'if they have been and gone, or if they merely looked into here three days ago and went about their peaceable business?'

Holbrooke didn't answer for a moment, giving himself

time to phrase his answer. He'd spent the whole night on deck considering what the dawn would show and how he would react. To a certain extent it was a mere academic exercise, as he admitted to himself. He was the junior of the three captains and Chester had made it quite clear that he and Coulson were to stay in line and not go off adventuring on their own. He had seen enough of his captains taking affairs into their own hands and was determined to keep his force together so that he could have the decisive squadron engagement that he knew would bring him closer to hoisting his flag, and pacifying Mrs Chester. Holbrooke knew very well that it wasn't only about Chester's personal ambition. Without a doubt he had a keen sense of his duty and the best way to destroy this French expedition was to defeat the three frigates then deal with the transports out of hand. The chances of the transports or the prizes making a French port without their naval escort were slim, close to nothingness, in fact. Duty and self-interest: the two coincided today, and Holbrooke couldn't fault the squadron's disposition. He could just have wished that they had made all sail during the night to be off the mouth of the lough a couple of hours earlier. He felt he knew Batiste now, and the Frenchman didn't seem like the sort of person to stay at anchor off an enemy port any longer than was necessary.

Say, for sake of argument, that Batiste had put his army ashore on Monday at Bangor or perhaps Carrickfergus. Both of those towns were lightly garrisoned, and it seemed unlikely that the militia units could hold out more than a few hours against determined French line regiments. How long would the French stay? Two days, perhaps three? In any case, they'd stay only long enough to gather in all the supplies that they needed and to ransom the town against the threat of putting it to the torch. In that case, they could have been underway on Wednesday evening and may now be steering south towards the St. George's Channel, then around the Scillies and across the Chops of the Channel to Brest or Saint-Malo. Of course, if Batiste had chosen to attack Belfast, then he'd probably be there longer than two or three days. It was for that reason that Holbrooke privately discounted Belfast; there was far too great a risk for Batiste of finding himself blockaded by sea and besieged by land. Why, oh why had Chester not been bolder? True, the waxing, gibbous moon had hidden obstinately behind the high layer of clouds, but the navigation wasn't difficult. Holbrooke had the distinct feeling that the enemy had stolen a march while Chester's squadron dithered.

'The wind's heading us, sir,' Jackson reported. 'I can't see *Pegasus*, but *Fortune* has fallen off a point.'

'Follow in her wake, Mister Jackson.'

Argonaut luffed slightly to come up astern of *Fortune*, then bore away a point to fetch her wake. The minutes passed slowly as the promise of a new day spread the faintest of shadows across the frigate's deck.

Holbrooke gradually became aware that the light was not just the loom of the sun, which was still far away over the Galloway hills; the moon had broken through the clouds and was shedding its illumination across the sea. Suddenly Holbrooke could see both frigates ahead of him, and the outline of the land beyond. He turned and looked over the starboard side and sure enough, there was the Antrim shore illuminated by the silver glow of the setting moon.

'Sail ho! Sail three points abaft the larboard beam. It's a ship under t'gallants, standing out towards those islands, sir.'

Peterson was already running for the main shrouds, telescope slung across his shoulders.

'You know what you're looking for, Mister Peterson.' Holbrooke shouted to the climbing figure.

'Aye-aye, sir,' came the gasping reply as the master's mate scurried slantwise up the futtock shrouds.

'You think this may be the French,' Chalmers asked.

'I fear it, Mister Chalmers, I fear it. This is exceedingly early for honest men to be so close to the Copeland Islands and t'gallants mean a man-o'-war, unless it's an Indiaman which is even more unlikely.'

'Red flag, sir?' asked Jackson.

'No, let's wait to hear what Peterson has to say.'

Holbrooke could see that the midshipman in the waist had bent on the square red flag and was shaking the halyard, looking aloft to check that it wasn't fouled, waiting for the order.

'Captain, sir. It's one of the French frigates, I'm almost certain, steering east to round the Copelands, and I believe I can see at least one sail beyond him.'

'Red flag at the main, and a gun to windward, Mister Jackson,' Holbrooke snapped. 'Beat to quarters.'

The quarterdeck was filling up as the word of a sail was passed around the cabins. Shorrock took charge of the signal gun and in a few moments, Fairview reported that he'd taken over the watch, leaving Jackson free to carry out the bosun's duties.

'Captain Chester won't have seen them, sir,' said Fairview, breaking in on Holbrooke's chain of thought.

'No,' Holbrooke replied distractedly.

The Frenchmen – for Holbrooke was certain that the lookout had sighted Batiste's squadron – were only three miles away and every passing second took them further from the British squadron.

Bang! *Argonaut*'s first gun fired.

It was just possible that *Fortune* could see them, but *Pegasus*, two miles ahead, almost certainly not. True, in less than an hour the sun would be above the hills, but by then the French would be even further away, probably just beyond Chester's range of vision in this pre-dawn mist and they'd remain so until they were below the horizon.

Holbrooke looked aloft to see the red flag flying free. Probably it was too dark for Chester to see it, but he would have heard the gun, for certain. He strode to the taffrail and back to the binnacle, torn by indecision. His every instinct said that he should bear away and run down towards the enemy, keeping them in sight until *Pegasus* and *Fortune* should be able to join him. And yet, a cold analysis said he should stay in station. If Batiste was to be defeated, it would take all three British frigates to achieve it, and unless the Frenchman abandoned his transports and prizes – and both his King's commission and his privateering instinct agreed that he should abandon neither – then Chester's squadron should be able to come up with him before he'd gone far south. He could see that Shorrock, Fairview and the quartermaster were all looking at him expectantly. Let 'em, he thought.

Boom. The muffled sound of a distant gun came down on the wind. There had been no flash from *Fortune* and no smoke, it must have been *Pegasus* acknowledging *Argonaut's* gun. Now, what would Chester do? Would he trust his junior captain's judgement and run down to hear the news?'

Now the moon was dipping towards the Antrim hills and soon the light would fade for a half hour until the sun rose.

'*Pegasus* is coming down, sir,' said Fairview, 'I can just see him on *Fortune's* bow.'

Holbrooke breathed out, a mighty sigh of relief.

'Put the ship before the wind when *Pegasus* is abeam of *Fortune*, Mister Fairview, then spill your wind and let him come down to us.'

That would destroy the squadron's line, leaving *Fortune* in the rear, but it was certainly the best way for Holbrooke to speak to Chester. He took a quick look to the east. Sure enough, the French had disappeared. Holbrooke rubbed his eyes. Had he dreamed it? Could a squadron appear and disappear so rapidly?

'It's that mist on the water, sir,' Fairview said, seeing Holbrooke looking concerned. 'They must be about five miles to the east now and I wouldn't expect to see them. The sun will burn it off but not for an hour or more and they'll be past the Copelands by then, steering south, I shouldn't doubt.'

'Thank you, Mister Fairview.'

The master was right, of course; *Argonaut* had been

lucky. If the French were just half a mile further away, if they'd sailed just a few minutes earlier from whatever port they'd sacked, then he wouldn't have seen them at all. In all probability, by the time the squadron had heard news of the French activities in Belfast Lough, they would have gained an entire day in the race for home.

***

The light was growing every moment and now *Pegasus* could be seen clearly in all her details as Chester brought her down on the wind, close to *Argonaut*'s starboard side. Holbrooke noticed that Chester hadn't set his t'gallants nor started to run out stuns'ls as he would have done if he was anticipating a chase to the east and south. He was evidently keeping his options open to beat back into Belfast Lough.

'Where's the enemy?' Chester shouted as soon as his voice would carry across the narrowing gap.

'To the sou'east, sir,' Holbrooke replied, standing in the mizzen chains and holding a shroud as he leaned far out towards *Pegasus*. 'We saw a frigate just before it was lost in the mist, and some other sails beyond. Off the Copelands heading east.'

'Well done, Mister Holbrooke, and well done, *Argonaut*. Is that all you saw.'

'That's all. I'm sure of it though, a frigate for certain and some others beyond.'

'Did they see you?'

Holbrooke hesitated. Could that French frigate have seen them? He caught Fairview out of the corner of his eye. He was shaking his head emphatically. Of course not, he could see the Frenchman in the moonlight against the background of the sea, but *Argonaut* had the Antrim hills behind her, and would have been invisible.

'No sir,' he replied emphatically.

'Then take station to larboard at two miles, Mister Holbrooke,' Chester shouted, '*Fortune* can come up to starboard. We'll sweep south.'

As *Pegasus* surged ahead to the shouted orders for setting

the t'gallants and rigging the stuns'l booms, a ragged cheer broke out from *Argonaut*'s deck, which Chester acknowledged with a wave of his hat. Perhaps he'd do well after all, Holbrooke thought. It might be that his apathy was being blown away by the prospect of imminent action.

***

The squadron hurried east. A shouted exchange with an eager passing fishing vessel confirmed what they had thought. Carrickfergus, the fishermen said. The God-forsaken French pirates had been there for three days looting and pillaging. His boat had escaped by the skin of its teeth because it had put out to sea before dawn on the day that the French had arrived. The fishing had been hard this year and honest men needed to be at sea early…

The rest was lost as the squadron swept on in pursuit.

'Methinks he doth protest too much,' said Fairview, noting the eagerness with which the Irishman justified his being at sea overnight.

'Smugglers, for sure,' Shorrock said with a grin. 'They'll have been looking for a ship from the Americas, putting out before dawn for a fortnight if necessary, waiting for one to pass. Rum and sugar and tobacco, all untaxed. It would only take an hour to load up that old fishing boat and everyone wins, everyone except the King, of course.'

'They could just be brave men or men desperate to earn an honest living,' Chalmers replied, wearing his parson's every-man-has-good-in-him face.

Fairview gave him an old-fashioned look and Shorrock just laughed.

***

By the time they wheeled south past the Copeland Islands, the wind had risen to a fine tops'l breeze on the starboard quarter, and they ate up the smooth miles of the Irish Sea. As Fairview had predicted, the mist was quickly consumed by the rising sun and by the time the forenoon watch came on deck they could see the hills of Galloway to the east and County Down to the west. Yet there wasn't a sail to be seen. That in itself suggested that something unusual was afoot for although the trading season had not reached anything like its peak, in this fine weather there should have been fishermen and local traders and even a few ships embarking on ocean passages. Yet the sea was innocent of sails from shore to shore.

'The news of the French has been passed around,' said Fairview. 'It's hardly surprising. They must have been taking ships here for two weeks now. Word will have got back to the south and we can expect some unwanted help from the Channel Fleet, I should imagine.'

Holbrooke smiled, thrilled by the chase and the hoped-for action.

'I think not, Mister Fairview. Unless something has changed, we three are all that can be spared to deal with Monsieur Batiste.'

'He'll be heading for the Calf of Man, no doubt,' said Chalmers.

Holbrooke and Fairview looked at the chaplain sharply.

'Well, we know that he has friends on Man, and we know that he's been there recently. You keep telling me that he won't have delayed in Carrickfergus, so he'll need somewhere to anchor and distribute the spoils of war and with a handful of prizes and an army hastily re-embarked, he'll have to move men around before his passage south.'

Holbrooke smiled broadly.

'I do believe you are right, Mister Chalmers. And it looks like Mister Chester agrees with you. Look, he's turning further south, steering to the west of Man. Keep station on him, Mister Fairview.'

***

Holbrooke was in his cabin studying his chart of the Irish Sea. The more he looked at it, the more certain he was of Batiste's movements. He'd made his raid, and he would consider that part of his orders fulfilled. Now he would make haste back to France with his prizes at his tail. He'd pick up more prizes along the way if he could do so without much delay, otherwise he would hasten past Dublin, past the coast of Wales, across the Bristol Channel, through the gap between Land's End and the Scillies and then to whatever French port he could find that wasn't guarded by a British squadron. However, Chalmers was correct, and he would want a day at anchor to re-organise and to spread his spoils among his ships, so that the loss of one wouldn't mean a dead loss for the voyage. A glance at the map told him how ideal the Isle of Man was for Batiste's purposes. Having friends on the island and being sure of a welcome only added to the attraction. Ramsay Bay or Douglas Bay would be attractive being sheltered from a westerly wind, but it would take the French squadron out of its way, and it was set about by dangerous shoal ground. Peel harbour was well-placed for a squadron on passage south, but it was too public for Batiste. He may have had sympathisers on the island, but they wouldn't want to be too open in their support for the enemies of the Crown. One of the bays to the east of the Calf of Man would be perfect, secluded and sheltered and only an hour or so out of the way.

'Mister Fairview's respect's sir, and he begs to inform you that the Isle of Man is in sight on the larboard bow.'

The midshipman was in high spirits and only just able to keep a solemn countenance.

'My compliments, and I'll be on deck in five minutes.'

He took another look at the chart. What if he was wrong? What if Batiste was bold enough to put into Peel? Well, speculation wouldn't help now. He was under orders and Chester could think himself into Batiste's skin as well as he could. Perhaps he wouldn't have to. It was quite likely that they would sight the French squadron at sea before they reached the Isle of Man.

***

The sun was as high as it would be and for March, the weather was superb. The westerly appeared to be set in for the day and *Argonaut* was flying every stitch of fair-weather canvas that she possessed. Over on the starboard beam

Pegasus was similarly dressed and further away still *Fortune* was showing a brave suit of canvas.

'The hills in the centre of the island are showing,' said Fairview, offering him a telescope.

Holbrooke focused on the faint smudge that he could see on the horizon. He could deduce nothing from it, in fact as far as he could tell it could have been a dark cloud in the southeast. He trained the telescope further round onto the larboard beam. Nothing. Not a sail to break the purity of the horizon.

'How far do you think you can see, Mister Fairview? At sea level, that is,' Holbrooke asked.

'Oh, perhaps six miles, sir. The mist has gone but the air's still a bit thick near the surface. Those hills must be all of thirty miles, but we won't see a sail at eight, I reckon.'

Holbrooke grimaced and trained the telescope back towards the bow, leaving the hills to the left of his field of view. Was that something almost on the bow? He lowered the telescope, gave the lens a wipe with his handkerchief and looked again. A vague shape swam into view then abruptly disappeared. He looked around the quarterdeck expecting that someone else had seen it, but the officers appeared blithely unaware. He glanced up to the mainmast head. The lookout seemed attentive, but he'd evidently seen nothing.

'Mister Petersen, take a look at our bow, will you? I just thought I may have seen something in the distance.'

Petersen took up the telescope that was kept on deck for the use of the officer of the watch. Fairview had heard the exchange of words and took up his own telescope. There was a pause while everyone stared earnestly ahead.

'Maybe, sir,' said Petersen, 'There could be…'

'Sail ho! Sail right on the bow, sir.'

The masthead lookout's hail dispelled any doubt.

'Red flag, Mister Fairview. No gun. *Pegasus* will see it easily enough and we don't want to alert our friends over there.'

***

CHAPTER EIGHTEEN

Line of Battle

Thursday, Twenty-Seventh of March 1760.
Argonaut, at Sea, Peel Harbour SE by S 10nm.

'They're running in for Peel,' said Fairview. 'My God, that man Batiste has some nerve.'

'Can we take action on the Isle of Man?' Shorrock asked. 'It's not part of Great Britain, as I understand it.'

'I generally defer to Mister Chalmers' knowledge in matters such as this, Mister Shorrock.'

For a few seconds nobody spoke as Chalmers marshalled his thoughts. He gazed abstractedly at the land ahead that was becoming clearer as every minute passed.

'Don't imagine for a moment that I'm an expert on the constitutional relationship between the Isle of Man and Britain. I doubt whether many men can claim that. I do, however, know that it owes its allegiance to the person of King George, or at least to the institution of the Crown, but on the other hand it's not a part of our country in a legal sense. It has its own parliament and its own laws, and I know that it jealously guards its independence. Does that autonomy go as far as the right to harbour its sovereign's enemies? I doubt it.'

'I agree with Mister Chalmers, and I'd be astonished if Captain Chester takes a contrary view. If the French seek refuge in Peel or anywhere else on the island, I'm sure we'll take, sink, burn or otherwise destroy them without reference to anyone. How many ships do you see now, Mister Petersen?'

'Three men-o'-war and six others, sir. They're all still running for Peel.'

'Signal from *Pegasus*, sir.'

That was the youngster that Holbrooke had appointed as the signal midshipman. He'd come along astonishingly since January, and he had a good eye.

'Form line of battle to windward.'

Holbrooke gave a sharp intake of breath and looked to starboard. Sure enough, there was the union flag at the main and fore. Chester hadn't over-burdened his little squadron with signals, but this was one of the few that he had insisted upon.

'Blast it,' he exclaimed and stamped his foot on the deck, 'the rear of the line! Mister Fairview, wait until *Fortune* is in station on *Pegasus*, then take our station astern of her, five cables.'

'What's he doing?' the first lieutenant asked of nobody in particular. 'The French won't be able to form a line, not with those transports and prizes to protect.'

'He's keeping us in check, Mister Shorrock.'

Shorrock nodded. It was true; not only did the line of battle keep the squadron's force concentrated, but it also imposed a legal duty on the captains of the ships to stay in the line until they were released. It was all very well to go wandering off and engaging whatever ship took a captain's fancy, but once the line of battle had been ordered, it turned a more-or-less free choice into a serious matter that could lead to a court martial, and the dark shadow of Byng's execution only three years ago still hung over every sea officer. Aye, and the Matthews Lestock affair in the last war.

'Captain, sir,' Petersen reported, removing his hat in a formal gesture, perhaps to soften the blow as he contradicted the assembled wisdom of the senior officers. 'The enemy frigates are hauling their wind; it looks like they're forming a line.'

'Well, we all live and learn,' Shorrock said as he exchanged a rueful glance with his captain.

'The others are turning to run along the coast, sir,' Petersen continued.

Holbrooke could see it for himself. Batiste was gambling everything on a battle between his three frigates and Chester's three, while the transports and prizes escaped to the south. It was a good plan, Holbrooke conceded. Batiste had more guns and more men than Chester and in stark mathematical terms they had at least an even chance of winning the day. If they did, then they could overtake their charges and escort them back to France. If they failed, then Batiste would be hoping that he'd at least delay the British squadron long enough to give those of the small French army who were in the transports and their four prizes a chance of escaping. He was thinking like a King's officer, not a privateer.

Holbrooke heard the canvas chattering above his head. Fairview was spilling wind to let *Pegasus* move ahead.

'*Fortune's* almost in her station, sir,' the master reported.

'Very well, take our place astern of her.'

It was neatly done. Fairview brought *Argonaut* off the wind until the frigate was on the point of wearing. He watched *Fortune* carefully, taking bearings with the binnacle compass as the line moved away on their starboard quarter. At the critical point, he ordered the helm put down to bring *Argonaut* hard on the wind and with the minimum of fuss the frigate slid into its allotted station at the rear of the line.

Shorrock gave Holbrooke a meaningful look and inclined his head towards the sailing master. It was the neatest manoeuvre that Holbrooke had ever seen, and it was done without either tacking or wearing. A quick look at Fairview revealed that the sailing master was unaware that he'd done anything special; he was busying himself in checking that the master's mate was recording the changes of course on the traverse log.

***

Holbrooke was well positioned to watch the events unfold. He had nothing particular to do; his ship was at quarters, Shorrock was commanding the guns and Fairview was keeping station on *Fortune*. He could see that Jackson had rigged the splinter nets and boarding nets and chained and puddened the lower yards. This was why he had pushed his crew so hard for the three months that the ship had been in commission, so that when they went into battle, the preparations and the drills would be second nature.

'You see how the French are coming on,' he said to Chalmers. 'They're in line ahead, as we are, with their heaviest frigate in the lead. That's Batiste's ship, and she has a *demi batterie*, like the old *Fury* but with more guns.'

'Ah yes, I remember those four guns on the lower deck. They've rather gone out of fashion now, I believe.'

'Yes, they were never a good idea and neither we nor the French are building *demi-batteries* any longer. Batiste's frigate must be old. Perhaps a cast-off from King Louie's fleet. In fact, they're all old ships compared with ours.'

'You're confident about this battle, I gather.'

'Confident? I wouldn't exactly say that. There are too many things that can happen by chance in a fight at sea, and I don't know what's in Mister Chester's mind. But it seems to me that we hold the initiative, and we can fight without worrying about protecting an army and a valuable set of prizes. Nor will we be concerned about French reinforcements, for there are none, but Batiste will be fighting with one eye on the horizon. And every hour that he spends with us is another hour for the word to spread south and for every ship of the Channel Squadron to be alerted and on the lookout for him. It will be praying on his mind when all Mister Chester has to do is fight his battle.'

'Still, they're a formidable force, are they not?'

'Aye, formidable, and Batiste has proved that he's no newcomer to a sea fight. I fear your services may be required below before the day is out.'

'Yes, the surgeon knows that I'll be there before the first gun.'

'That's good of you, Mister Chalmers, and I do believe the men appreciate being tended by a man of the cloth.'

Chalmers glanced at Holbrooke and what he saw convinced him of his friend's sincerity. Of course, Holbrooke had never been on the orlop in the heat of a battle when the casualties were being brought down. A sailor facing the surgeon's saw and knife didn't care whether the assistant was a clergyman, a peer of the realm or the captain of the heads; his mind was wholly taken up with his injuries.

Holbrooke leaned out to larboard and trained his telescope ahead.

'They're closing fast now. Do you see how *Pegasus* is steering to pass their line out of cannon shot?'

'I was wondering about that,' Chalmers replied. 'Surely Captain Chester isn't declining a battle.'

Holbrooke laughed.

'Nothing of the sort. It's no good the two lines passing close to each other on opposite tacks. That will achieve nothing and it's dangerous for Batiste because after we've passed and sent a few ineffectual balls at each other – at that speed there'll be few hits – we'll be between him and his transports. He needs to force an engagement, so Captain Chester is deliberately leaving space for Batiste to tack and parallel our course. That way we'll be heading for the transports and prizes and the French will have had the distraction of working their ships before the engagement. Their sail handlers will have to rush to the guns after they've tacked. We hold the aces, you see. Batiste is constrained by his useless charges while all we have to do is bring him to a decisive engagement.'

Holbrooke and Chalmers watched the French ships approaching. That Batiste and his captains knew their business was without doubt. The French ships were five cables apart, just like the British and they were coming on boldly, without the slightest sign of hesitation, and leaving enough space to tack in succession to bring them alongside their enemy. It was disappointing in a way, Holbrooke thought. He would have expected something more imaginative from such a famous privateer, a rush at the head of the British line, perhaps, to overwhelm *Pegasus* and force a melee. How far were Batiste's manoeuvres influenced by the King's commission that he now had in his pocket?

The transports and prizes were moving slowly away along the coast of Man, which was now clearly visible in all its detail. How many valuable seamen had Batiste lost by manning the four prizes? He would have plenty of soldiers to guard the prisoners, but soldiers couldn't take an unfamiliar ship all the way back to France with a near-certainty of harsh weather at some time during the passage. Would his need to man the prizes leave him short of seamen in his frigates?

Fairview was taking bearings of the lead enemy, squinting across the binnacle compass.

'They should be tacking any moment now... Ah, there they go!'

Batiste's ship turned smoothly into the wind and shifted its tacks in a most proficient manner. No lack of seamen there, Holbrooke thought. In a moment it was on a broad reach, somewhat ahead of *Pegasus* and slanting down towards the British line. The second and third in the line tacked in the leader's wake. Holbrooke shivered involuntarily. They looked thoroughly professional, like a squadron of the Channel Fleet at its drills, and not at all like an ungovernable parcel of privateers.

Holbrooke trained his telescope at the French frigate opposite his own. He recognised it from their two previous encounters, it was a ship of much the same size as his own. Its sides were pierced for two more cannon on each side, but they were probably eight-pounders rather than *Argonaut*'s nines. Suddenly the impending battle became personal. He could see his opponent, could identify the officers on the quarterdeck and could see the individual guns thrusting towards him through the gunwales. There were marksmen in the tops, giving themselves away with a glint of sunlight reflected from the barrels of their muskets. Personal indeed. He knew that he was the prime target for those Frenchmen, and he could do nothing but stand tall on his own quarterdeck. He looked up at *Argonaut*'s maintop. There were marksmen there too, as well as in the fore and mizzen tops, and he could see a petty officer in the maintop elevating and training the wicked looking swivel gun. He'd rather be on his own quarterdeck than the Frenchman's.

Closer and closer, the two lines were converging fast and now they were in range of each other. Soon they'd be close enough for that all-important first broadside with its carefully loaded guns and calm crews. That would be Chester's decision though, not his own, and unless he could see that something was wrong in the British vanguard, he must wait for *Pegasus* to open the engagement. In fact, his own opponent was rather further from him than Batiste's ship was from *Pegasus* because he appeared to be following his leader's wake pedantically rather than steering a little further in towards the British line so that his ship should arrive in its fighting station at the same time as his leader.

'Too far yet, sir,' said Shorrock.

'Yes, indeed, we may have to hold our fire a little longer than *Pegasus*. Pass the word to the men to stay low behind the gunwales.'

Holbrooke could see the word being passed along the deck. Midshipmen were calling to their gun captains who were waving their crews down. He looked forward just in time to see Batiste's ship fire the first broadside. It was interesting to watch from this angle when his own ship had not yet been engaged. Batiste was perhaps just a little further away from *Pegasus* than Holbrooke would have thought ideal. Then *Pegasus* replied.

'Any moment now…' said Fairview, moving purposely into the dubious cover behind the binnacle, as though he was preparing to take another bearing.

'He should hold his fire for another minute or two yet…'

The Frenchman's side exploded in orange flame and grey smoke. Holbrooke was aware of the sound and concussion from a ball that narrowly missed him and ploughed into the weather gunwale. Stray ropes and blocks bounced over his head as they fell into the splinter nets and a shower of oak splinters flew across the waist after a hit on the larboard gunwale. He looked around, nobody was injured on the quarterdeck, but he could see one man writhing on the deck just abaft the foremast and another staring in dumb astonishment at the blood pouring from a wounded arm.

'Too soon,' he said under his breath. 'Mister Fairview, bear away two points, let's get closer to this gentleman before he can reload. Mister Shorrock, stand by.'

The French marksmen were firing, and Holbrooke could hear the patter of musket balls on the quarterdeck. They should have waited, now they would have no time to reload before his swivel guns cut into them. He looked quickly along the deck. The guns were all manned and the gun captains were shifting their aim as the ships came closer together. The spongers were blowing on the slow match twisted around the linstocks, keeping them alight and ready to hand them to the gun captains. There was a solid block of red all along the quarterdeck gunwale where the marines were lined up, their muskets pointing at the enemy, and in between the cannon the deadly little swivel guns pointed at the enemy's decks.

Holbrooke raised his whistle to his lips and blew.

'Fire!' shouted Shorrock.

Argonaut reeled as every gun of the broadside fired simultaneously. He didn't hear the swivel guns, but he saw their destructive effect on the Frenchman's quarterdeck, and he saw the marines firing and reloading. He was aware of all of this but had no time to consider the implications because the second French broadside hit his ship only moments later. That was fast reloading; the French gun crews must have been well-practiced.

The French were firing high. It took real training and discipline to counteract the effect of firing to windward, as the French ships were forced to do. As each gun was reloaded it lost the careful pointing that it was given at the first broadside and few gun captains thought to ram the quoin home to bring the elevation back down to counteract the ship's heel. Also, the leeward line suffered from the smoke of the windward line blowing down onto them. It was far more difficult to command a battery under those circumstances, as Holbrooke knew from past experience.

'That's close enough, Mister Fairview,' he shouted. 'Bring her two points to starboard.'

The sound of gunfire was continuous and although the smoke was being blown clear of *Argonaut*'s deck, there was still enough to make it difficult to see what was going on. What he could see told Holbrooke that his ship was suffering; there were wounded men being carried below, perhaps some of them were dead, it was difficult to say. It wasn't a continuous stream, but there were enough of them to keep the surgeon and his mates, and Chalmers, busy.

There was a crash and a rush of wind from the mizzen mast. Something brushed against Holbrooke's face. He felt no pain, but when he brought his hand away it was covered in blood. A splinter had opened his left check just at the hinge of his jaw. He pulled up his neckerchief to staunch the flow.

How many broadsides was that? Four, or was it five? It was difficult to count now that the rhythm had been lost. He could see that Shorrock had abandoned whole broadsides and now, hatless, he was striding from division to division, urging the men on to hasten the reloading and confirming that the guns were elevated enough to reach the enemy's sides.

Another crash, above him this time, and Holbrooke looked up to see a large chunk of wood, presumably from the maintop, rolling across the splinter netting.

'*Fortune's* luffing, sir,' shouted Fairview.

Holbrooke rushed to the windward side of the quarterdeck. Sure enough, there was Coulson's ship turning its bows away from the enemy. At first, he couldn't see what was wrong. Then, as *Fortune* turned further to windward, he saw that the jib boom had been shot through and the jib was streaming away to windward.

'Hold your course, Mister Fairview. If *Fortune* doesn't get back into line, make more sail to take her place.'

Fortune's bow continued its turn to starboard. Holbrooke watched anxiously as his own ship surged ahead. It would be a close thing, but he could see that he'd clear Coulson's quarterdeck. A quick look told him that *Fortune's* headsails wouldn't be in order quickly.

'Set the foresail, Mister Fairview.'

They'd been fighting under tops'ls to avoid the main and fore courses obstructing the view from the quarterdeck, but now Holbrooke needed to take Coulson's position in the line. *Argonaut* surged forward, still trading blows with the frigate at the rear of the French line.

'Mister Shorrock!'

The first lieutenant heard him and raised his hand.

'As soon as your guns bear on the ship ahead, drop that one,' he pointed at the rear ship of the French line that was rapidly being left astern, 'and concentrate on the next ahead.'

Shorrock's reply was lost in the thunder of the guns, but it was certain that he understood.

'Stand back, if you please, sir.'

Holbrooke realised that he'd strayed too close behind the forward of the quarterdeck three-pounders and was in danger from the recoil. The gun captain turned back to his charge. Holbrooke saw him slewing the gun hard against the side of the gunport. That was a measure of how fast *Argonaut* had surged ahead, the guns could barely train far enough astern to point at the frigate that they'd been fighting. With a final squint along the barrel, the gun captain shouted at the crew to stand clear, and he grabbed the linstock that the sponger held for him and thrust it hard down against the touchhole. Only the quarterdeck guns could fire now, and the deck was strangely silent. So silent that Holbrooke heard the fizz of the priming and then an instant later heard the sharp crack of the gun firing. It was elevated too much, Holbrooke saw that immediately, and the ball must have gone far into the French ship's rigging. A wasted shot, he thought, the crews needed more practice in elevation of the guns. He turned back to look at the frigate ahead of him.

'There goes his fore topmast!' shouted Petersen.

Holbrooke swung on his heels in time to see the Frenchman's plight acted out. That three-pounder ball must have hit the fore topmast squarely somewhere above the top. Had it been a ship-of-the-line, no three-pounder could have smashed its way through that spar, but frigates were much lighter of build and before his eyes the whole elaborate arrangement of masts, yards, rigging and sails that sat above the foretop swayed to larboard. A roll of the ship brought it back to the vertical, but the next wave raised the frigates stern and dipped its bows, so that the fore topmast and everything above it came crashing down to leeward. Immediately the Frenchman's bows swung to starboard, into the wind. Both lines were now fragmented, each sailing on to the sou'east leaving two crippled ships to fight it out among themselves.

'Mister Shorrock. Broadsides when all your guns bear!'

Argonaut was coming up quickly on her new adversary's quarter. He looked keenly at his guns. His twelve nine-pounders were all manned and loaded, their crews gasping for breath in this lull in the action. Beside him the two quarterdeck three-pounders were nearly reloaded.

Shorrock was peering through the number six gunport, the third from forward on the larboard side. That was good, the number two and four guns could probably point at the next frigate already, but they had the advantage of the turn of the bows and could point further forward than the remainder. Holbrooke wanted his first attack against his new adversary to be delivered as one devastating broadside. He could see that *Fortune* had wounded the enemy. There were gaps in the gunwale where shot had smashed straight through, and one port was empty, its gun presumably disabled.

'Good God, look at *Pegasus*,' Fairview exclaimed.

Chester's ship had been wreathed in the smoke of its continuous gunfire. Now an errant gust of wind tore a hole in the smoke and revealed the whole of the ship above the gunports. Its sails were in tatters and the lower part of the mizzen yard had been shot away. Holbrooke could see a party of men cutting away the useless tangle forward of the mast while two others hauled at the vangs to get the sail under control. Nevertheless, *Pegasus* was still firing, apparently with all her guns, and a quick look told Holbrooke that Batiste's ship was faring at least as badly.

'Linstocks!' shouted Shorrock.

It was like a tableau, as the gun crews stood like statues waiting for the first lieutenant's order.

'Fire!

Argonaut staggered as the whole broadside fired as one. Holbrooke saw the impact on the enemy ship, saw his balls smashing into the gunwale and the planking below. He thought he could hear the screams of the Frenchmen caught in the hail of solid shot and splinters.

'Damn my eyes. That was a good broadside, boys,' Shorrock shouted as the gun crews jumped to the tackles to bring the guns inboard for worming, sponging and reloading. 'Let's give him another!'

'Trice up the foresail, Mister Fairview, we're almost in our station.'

Fairview looked ahead at *Pegasus*' quarterdeck which appeared awfully close now. He nodded at Holbrooke and shouted a few commands that sent the sail trimmers rushing forward.

'The Frenchman's closed up on the lead ship, sir,' Fairview said.

'Yes, and we must close up too. Stay on his beam.'

Fairview nodded again. He'd have to watch *Argonaut*'s speed with care to avoid running into Chester's stern.

***

CHAPTER NINETEEN

General Chase

Thursday, Twenty-Seventh of March 1760.
Argonaut, at Sea, off Peel Harbour.

'How long now, Mister Lister?'

The clerk looked at his pocket watch.

'Forty-five minutes since the first gun, sir.'

Holbrooke looked at him suspiciously. Could it have been only that long? It seemed like the guns had been roaring for hours. He looked away to the west and saw that the sun had barely moved since he last looked at it.

'I fancy her fire's slackening, sir,' said Fairview.

Holbrooke stood still; only his lips moved as he counted the enemy's guns, estimating the rate of fire. Now that his attention was drawn to it, he could hear a greater interval between guns from the Frenchman, and more of the shots were flying harmlessly overhead. He looked aloft to see Jackson and his mates busy cutting away damaged rigging and knotting in replacements as fast as they could.

'I do believe you are right,' he said.

'She's luffing, sir!'

It only took a single glance to tell Holbrooke what was happening. His opponent was bearing up to run aboard *Argonaut*. Probably the French captain had concluded that he couldn't win a gunnery contest against this British frigate, and he'd decided to play his trump card, to run his opponent aboard and to let loose the soldiers that he would certainly be carrying above his normal complement. Yes, there were the white uniforms moving towards the bows. Holbrooke could see the glint of the bayonets, and there were seamen in the tops, ready to rush out onto the yards and grapple his ship.

'Grapeshot, Mister Shorrock,' he shouted. 'Cannister for the quarterdeck guns. Hold her there, Mister Fairview.'

He saw the Frenchman's bows swinging slowly towards him. It was a difficult manoeuvre, a desperate one even. If the French captain put his helm down hard and steered too close to the wind, he'd pass astern of *Argonaut* and receive a deadly blast of grapeshot onto his bows for his troubles. If he steered in more gradually, he'd suffer two or three broadsides before he came alongside. Holbrooke could see that his adversary was in a hurry and had luffed too sharply. Soon he'd realise his mistake and come off the wind. In the meantime, what was left of his broadside guns would be thoroughly disrupted.

Well, if the Frenchman was playing his trump card, then Holbrooke would lay down a higher trump. There was no sailing master alive that could handle a frigate in action like Fairview could.

'Don't let her come alongside, Mister Fairview, but keep our broadsides pointing.'

Fairview nodded briefly, his mind already working through this new problem. It required careful use of the sails and the helm, and a good dose of luck.

Shorrock was out of sight under the fo'c'sle, pointing out the mass of soldiers in the enemy's bows. The swivel gunners on the quarterdeck and fo'c'sle, mostly the gun captains from the starboard battery, were sensibly holding their fire for the critical moment.

'I do believe her captain's down, sir,' said Fairview. 'That's a different officer beside the wheel now. Ah, he's seen the error, he's bearing away again.'

Shorrock's head popped out from under the fo'c'sle, looking expectantly up at Holbrooke, who shook his head in reply.

Too soon: Holbrooke could sense the French lieutenant's uncertainty, his desperation when he found himself in command of this increasingly stricken ship. Boarding was his only hope but getting alongside the enemy from the leeward position was fraught with difficulty. Another minute: let his desperation grow and let his crew become uneasy. The soldiers already looked uncertain, they'd expected to board quickly and now they felt exposed on the unprotected deck.

Holbrooke brought the whistle to his lips and blew a single blast.

Argonaut surged sideways as the guns fired. This time they were all aimed at the same point and with the Frenchman so close and the natural spread of the grapeshot, every gun hit its target. The hail of grape and cannister tore great gaps in the fo'c'sle gunwales and knocked down whole files of soldiers who were too tightly packed to stoop and gain even the questionable cover of the gunwales. The swivel guns followed, more carefully aimed at groups of soldiers still standing. The French frigate put up her helm and sheered away, back into the line.

***

'Round shot!' shouted Holbrooke. 'Pound away at him, Mister Shorrock.'

The threat of boarding was over for now. Would he try again? It was quite possible, but Holbrooke was getting a feeling for this replacement for the disabled French captain. He was unsure of himself, unwilling to press home an attack.

'He's slanting away to leeward, sir,' said Fairview.

'Very well. Hold your position in the line.'

The marines had stopped firing and the swivel guns were swinging idly; it was obvious to all that they were out of range.

Bang! The nine-pounders fired. It was longer range now and Shorrock was firing whole broadsides again ensuring that every gun captain pointed his weapon before firing. Even then, more than half of the balls missed their target. And still the Frenchman moved away to leeward. Only the occasional shot came in reply to *Argonaut*'s broadsides.

Holbrooke leaned over the gunwale to look forward at *Pegasus*. Her sails were shot through and there was obvious damage to her upperworks, but she was keeping up a regular bombardment of Batiste's ship. As he watched, he saw Chester himself leaning over the taffrail and waving. Holbrooke waved in reply and ran forward, along the starboard gangway and onto the fo'c'sle. There was no chance of hearing Chester, but he could at least acknowledge hand signals.

As Holbrooke reached the headrail, Chester waved vigorously to leeward and pointed at the second frigate in the French line. A white swallowtail flag broke out at the peak of his mizzen.

Holbrooke waved in reply and ran back towards his own quarterdeck.

'General Chase, sir,' the signal midshipman reported, 'white swallowtail at the peak of the mizzen yard.'

'Very well, hoist the same flag in case *Fortune* didn't see it.'

He looked over at the French ship that was now so far to leeward that Shorrock's guns could barely be certain of a single hit in each broadside.

'Bear away, Mister Fairview. Keep the broadside arcs open. Let's finish this.'

The sweating gunners in the waist, the only ones with an unobstructed view of what was happening, raised a cheer as they saw the frigate's bows turn steadily to larboard. The cheer was taken up by the forward guns under the fo'c'sle, then the aft guns under the quarterdeck. Soon every man on *Argonaut*'s decks was shouting like a madman. If the French could hear that, Holbrooke thought, they would know that it was the end for them.

Shorrock ran up the quarterdeck ladder.

'I can give the lead frigate a broadside from the starboard guns as we pass, sir, he's just in range.'

Holbrooke looked at the *demi-batterie* frigate as the Frenchman's stern crossed *Argonaut*'s bows.

'Certainly, Mister Shorrock…'

But Shorrock was gone, swinging down to the waist and shouting to his gun crews to man the starboard battery.

Nor'west by North

Holbrooke had a moment to look around him. *Pegasus* was firing well, but it was still unclear whether Chester was winning the battle against Batiste's ship. In any case, they were running away towards Peel still and soon they would be none of Holbrooke's business. *Fortune* was astern, closely engaged with the third French frigate and it appeared that Coulson was having the worst of the fight. His main topmast was down, and his guns were firing raggedly, with long gaps between discharges. Holbrooke considered disobeying Chester and beating up to help *Fortune* but thought better of it. Coulson would just have to look after himself. If his ship was taken, it would take a miracle for the French frigate to carry it back to France.

His own adversary had slanted away so far that he was running free with the westerly wind driving him away towards Jurby Point. If he wanted to round the Point of Ayre at the northerly tip of Man, he'd have to wear ship. There was something psychological about that. While he was on the same tack as his commodore, he could still be said to be in the battle. Wearing ship onto the larboard tack would make it clear that he was abandoning the fight, forsaking the transports and the prizes, and making his own way to safety.

Bang!

The starboard battery fired its first shots of the battle. It was long range but perhaps three or four balls had reached their target. Holbrooke saw the impact on Batiste's ship's stern then he turned away to concentrate on running down his own opponent.

'There goes her mizzen!' shouted Petersen in excitement.

Holbrooke turned back in time to see Batiste's mizzen mast sway to leeward, swing around to the stern, then, with the last of the weather shrouds parting at the chains, go overboard with a drawn-out crash that could be heard on *Argonaut*'s deck.

Another cheer from the deck.

'That's our contribution,' said Fairview, grinning broadly.

Holbrooke nodded, but he wasn't so sure. Probably it had been a shot from *Pegasus* that had brought down the mast, and nothing to do with his own guns. Nevertheless, at a stroke the balance of this battle had swung decisively in favour of the British. Batiste could fight on, but he'd be lucky to avoid becoming a prize before the hour was out. Only *Fortune* appeared to be in difficulty, but Holbrooke was confident that he and Chester could save Coulson when they'd finished their own actions.

***

'He's wearing, sir,' said Fairview, looking forward across the strangely quiet deck. There were no enemies in range of *Argonaut*'s guns, all the casualties had been taken below and the gun crews were lying or sitting, recruiting their strength for the next engagement.

'I'll follow him if I may, sir.'

'Certainly, Mister Fairview, I'll leave it to you to make sail to overhaul him as quickly as possible.'

Shorrock climbed up the quarterdeck ladder. He looked weary but elated, and with good cause. In a frigate-on-frigate action his gun crews had pounded the enemy so hard that he'd been forced to withdraw – to abandon the line – and leave his colleagues to fend for themselves.

'All guns are ready, sir. I've had word from below that we have two dead – Davies and Parsons from the number four gun – and five injured. I'd like to try a few shots from the chase ports, if I may.'

Shorrock was being diplomatic, Holbrooke knew. He should have thought of the chase ports himself. He'd never served in a ship that was so fitted and it had entirely slipped his mind. Shorrock would have to take the number one and two guns – the forward nine-pounders of each battery – and haul them into the otherwise empty ports under the headrails.

'Very well, Mister Shorrock, carry on.'

Nor'west by North

Out of the corner of his eye. Holbrooke saw the gunner come blinking onto the waist. He'd heard rumour that the chase guns may come into action and that required fine pointing of the weapons. It was a quite different matter to engaging with broadsides. Accuracy was important there, of course, but they were generally firing at close range and against the enemy's side. Nothing but his own death would keep him in the magazine when the chase guns were to come into action, and even then Shorrock passionately believed that the gunner's ghostly form would appear, offering advice and criticism, and a tap on the quoin.

Soon, Holbrooke could hear the rumble of the trucks as the guns were hauled into position. He could see nothing of the skilled labour that was required, it was all hidden under the fo'c'sle, but it had been well practiced and he expected a report that the gun was ready in only a few minutes.

'This won't take long, sir,' said Fairview, 'we're walking up to her.'

Holbrooke realised that he hadn't looked at the chase for some minutes, and in that time the situation had changed for the better. *Argonaut* was fairly flying along under all plain sail and stuns'ls and indeed, as the master said, was overhauling the Frenchman at a steady pace, even though every sail was shot through and through. The range was about four cables, not easy for two nine-pounders on a heaving deck, but not impossible. What he dearly wanted was to bring down a mast, then surely the Frenchman would be forced to strike his colours without the need for further bloodshed.

'Mister Steel,' he shouted.

The gunner, having seen the guns hauled into place, had left the securing of the tackles and breeching to come onto the fo'c'sle to test the wind.

'Mister Steel. A bottle of brandy for every man of the crew that brings down a mast.'

'Aye-aye, sir,' he shouted back, 'we'll do our best.'

'You may open fire when you're ready, Master Gunner.'

With that the gunner disappeared under the fo'c'sle and two minutes later Holbrooke heard the first of the chase guns fire, the starboard gun. A spout of white water appeared and quickly disappeared, short and to the left, but not bad for the opening shot.

The larboard gun fired. The sound was muffled, coming from so far forward and under the fo'c'sle. That was well pitched up but to the left again.

Now the guns were firing regularly, with less than three minutes between shots for each gun. He could imagine the scene at the chase ports and dearly wanted to be there himself, but he knew that Shorrock and Steel could handle this kind of fine gunnery better than he could. He looked up at the sails. They were all drawing well despite the shot holes and *Argonaut* was sailing as fast as she could in the circumstances.

'He's pumping, sir,' said Fairview, pointing ahead and offering his telescope.

Holbrooke focussed carefully on the ship ahead of him. There was a steady jet of water pouring from each side. Then he must have been holed below the waterline. As the frigate's stern dropped in a trough, he had a brief glimpse of the quarterdeck. It was filled with figures in white uniform with barely a sea officer to be seen among the crowd. It looked like a vigorous discussion. It must be most uncomfortable in that ship, being fired upon without being able to reply unless they changed course. Probably the soldiers were at odds with the sea officers, one faction advocating continued retreat while the other pressed for the ship to turn at bay and fight it out. There was, of course, another possibility that Holbrooke hardly hoped for. One of the sides may have recognised the futility of fleeing through enemy seas with a damaged ship and was urging surrender.

He kept the telescope trained on the French frigate's stern, hoping for another view of the quarterdeck. He looked away to rest his eye and when he looked again the whole scene had changed. A lucky shot that must have been fired as the bow lifted to a wave had smashed the mizzen yard and the upper half had already fallen across the quarterdeck.

Fairview grimaced. 'That will hardly slow him with the wind almost dead astern' he said. 'I'd considered furling ours in any case.'

Holbrooke smiled at that. His sailing master was missing the point. Regardless of whether that frigate could still float and move and fight, this was another item to add to the lengthening list of her woes. Holed below the waterline, her guns mauled, and her boarding party decimated and parted from the rest of her squadron, it would be a determined captain that stood up to the mark again. It was only a matter of time now...

'She's struck, sir!' shouted Petersen, 'and she's heaving to.'

***

CHAPTER TWENTY

Captures

Thursday, Twenty-Seventh of March 1760.
Argonaut, at Sea, off Jurby Point.

'Will they honour their parole, do you think,' Chalmers asked when he had heard Holbrooke's account of the French frigate's surrender. They were alone for a few moments in a lull in the activity which was sure to heat up again soon.

'Oh, yes, I'm sure they will, the personal consequences of breaking their word are too terrible to contemplate. If they had any chance of carrying their ship to a friendly port, I would have thought twice, but they have no such hope. If they take the ship from Murray and Peterson – and they'll find that difficult – they know that they will certainly be retaken before they leave the Irish Sea. There would be no second chance, not for parole-breakers, not even *verbal* parole breakers. And if anyone were hurt or, God forbid, killed in the process, there would be a charge of murder to be answered, under the shadow of the hangman's noose.'

'Yes, of course, parole is one of the mechanisms that make war – how can I put it? – less uncivilised than it might otherwise be. For the officers at least.'

'It suits us, of course. If they hadn't given their parole, we would have had to herd them all below and put a much heavier guard on them. This way, we have managed to wrap the whole business up in two hours and we can catch up with them in Peel. There's still time for us to sort out whatever lies ahead before we lose the light.'

'And what does lie ahead, I wonder,' Chalmers mused.

***

'What do you think, Mister Shorrock?'

Shorrock looked a fright. Every inch of his clothes and skin was covered in powder smoke, except where he'd rubbed some water on his face and left the impression of untidy stripes. There were scorch marks on his sleeves and his waistcoat and a trickle of dried blood that had started in his scalp had wended its way down his cheek and behind his stock, ending in a dry, dark stain on the front of his shirt.

'It looks like *Pegasus* has won her match,' he said looking to windward over the starboard bow. 'I can't see any colours on the Frenchman and the guns have all stopped.'

Holbrooke looked carefully at the two ships dead to windward. Having secured his prize his first thought was to rally to his leader's ship, but now it was starting to look unnecessary. They were both lying quietly a short distance apart and as he watched he saw the first boat pushing away from *Pegasus*.

'Yes, it does look like *Pegasus* is taking possession. What will that last Frenchman do?'

Holbrooke and Shorrock both trained their telescopes on the pair of ships that lay some two miles north of *Pegasus*. There was no doubt that they were still engaged; they were wreathed in smoke and the sound of a steady cannonade drifted down on the breeze.

'Mister Fairview, can we fetch them if we come about now?'

The sailing master took a hasty bearing and looked at the dogvane that streamed away to the larboard side of the quarterdeck.

'I'd like to give it five minutes, sir,' he replied. 'It won't help to have to put in a short tack before we arrive.'

'Very well, bring us about when you see fit.'

Argonaut plunged on into the setting sun. Holbrooke looked critically at the deck, at the men. All his guns were ready, and he'd lost mercifully few of his valuable seamen. The crew were still at quarters and under the urgings of the petty officers were arranging all the accoutrements of war into their proper positions. The worms, the sponges, the hand spikes, the buckets and all the other equipment that a gun needed were being made ready for a fresh engagement.

They looked tired but cheerful and under the relaxed discipline that came after a successful action, they threw jests at each other and spoke to their officers with a freedom that they wouldn't normally use. The carpenter and his crew were busy on a gunport that had suffered more than the others, and Jackson was directing bands of men in repairing the rigging.

'Mister Lister, run down to the purser and tell him, with my compliments, that he's to serve supper to the men at their quarters. He has half an hour before we'll be engaged again.'

The clerk ran below. He knew as well as Holbrooke did that the purser would have already thought of feeding the crew; it was in Holbrooke's standing orders when the men were detained at quarters over a normal mealtime.

'Captain, sir.'

That was Carew, covering for Petersen while he was away with the prize crew. He had removed his hat to address his captain in a fitting manner after the informality of the battle.

'The French frigate is breaking away, sir.'

So it was. *Fortune* was still firing albeit slowly and unevenly, but the Frenchman had evidently seen *Argonaut* beating up and had decided to cut and run in the hope of keeping away from the British frigate for the two hours of daylight that was left.

'He's running for the Calf of Man,' said Fairview, looking at the frigate keenly, 'and he's cleared away the wreckage of his fore topmast. Look, he's sending up a jury rig, he must have carried a spare topmast. Now that's seamanship for you.'

'Hold your luff, Mister Fairview. Now, can you cut him off before sunset?'

The sailing master took another bearing and again looked at the dogvane. He grimaced and made a very French gesture with his palm downwards, rocking from side to side.

'It'll be close, sir, and we'll want to come off the wind.'

Nor'west by North

'Very well. If we end up in a stern chase, we can call on the gunner again to bring him to his senses.'

***

The two ships raced south as the sun crept inexorably towards the unseen hills of County Down. The wind was dropping with the sun, weakening and veering so that both ships were soon on a broad reach a mile and a half apart, with the Frenchman keeping somewhat ahead despite the loss of her fore topmast. Holbrooke had a moment to look around again. *Fortune* was almost out of sight, as was *Argonaut*'s prize, but they were both steering south to join *Pegasus* and her prize. The battle was over, and it was just the loose ends to be gathered in, the transports, the prizes that Batiste had taken in his rampage through the Irish Sea and this, the last of the French fighting ships left.

'May I try a shot or two, sir?' Shorrock asked.

Holbrooke looked at the range. The two ships were closing on each other, but slowly. It looked like the French captain was reluctant to come any further to the west. Perhaps he realised that he had to make ground to the south at some point and that his best chance was to keep ahead of his pursuer rather than take the apparently easy way out that would leave him with the same problem, just a few hours delayed. But there would be a moon tonight, the same old gibbous moon, and it wouldn't set until well into the morning watch. Holbrooke tried to put himself in the Frenchman's position. If he made it back to a French port, the only survivor of the expedition, what would be his welcome? Not good, Holbrooke decided, so what could he do to improve his standing? Of course, he was hoping to pick up the transports and escort them home! It could be done. Probably there was a rendezvous against just this situation, but the transports wouldn't wait, not with three known British frigates searching for them. This unknown captain must have a rendezvous tonight, and he showed every sign of a profound determination to keep it.

'Eh, what was that Mister Shorrock?'

Holbrooke had been deafened by the battle and like everyone else on *Argonaut's* deck, he was talking unnaturally loudly.

'I'd like to try the range, sir. We may be able to slow him down.'

'Very well, but aimed shots, and get Mister Steel up here.'

'Mess cooks! Mess cooks to the mainmast,' shouted Carew.

He looked tentatively at his captain who nodded his approval.

That young man will do quite well, Holbrooke thought. He'd heard me order supper brought up, saw that I was talking to the first lieutenant and decided to call the cooks on his own initiative.

'Thank you, Mister Carew.'

Carew removed his hat and bowed.

Bang!

Number one gun was still at the chase port, so Shorrock had started with number three gun. The gunner scurried out from under the fo'c'sle and squinted along the barrel of number five gun.

Bang!

Holbrooke knew that there was little chance of a hit at this range. Both ships were rising and falling on the long swell that was running down from the north and crossing the short, choppy sea that was being kicked up by the westerly wind. The tide was setting northerly further confusing the pattern of waves and it would have taken extraordinary luck to time the shot accurately. Holbrooke had heard that the navy board was experimenting with flintlocks for the great guns, which would make the exact time of firing more predictable. Now that would be an innovation worth having.

Bang!

Another gun and no sign of a hit. The French frigate was sailing faster than *Argonaut* and it was evident to Holbrooke that he wouldn't bring it to action before it disappeared into the blackness.

Bang!

The guns fired monotonously as Fairview tried everything he knew, every trick that he'd accumulated over a lifetime at sea, to wring an extra knot of speed out of his ship.

'Eight knots, sir,' said a midshipman, still grasping the dripping log.

'He must be making nine then,' said Fairview, evidently impressed by the Frenchman's turn of speed.

Holbrooke said nothing but strode to the taffrail and back to get his tired mind working. It appeared hopeless. The sun had set nearly an hour ago behind a thick bank of cloud. In ten minutes, they would lose sight of the Frenchman. What then?

'Mister Lister, my compliments to Mister Chalmers and if he's at leisure I would be pleased to see him in my cabin. Mister Shorrock, keep firing until you no longer have a mark. Steady as you go, Mister Fairview. Call me if the wind veers any further.'

***

'I didn't disturb you, David?'

'No, not at all, I was merely helping the doctor with some dressings. He can manage perfectly well with his mates.'

'I need a fresh eye on this problem,' he said, 'I've run out of ideas. Now here's a chart…'

He outlined the situation to Chalmers who listened in silence.

'Now, where would you have arranged to meet in the event of your cruise home being interrupted by the enemy? It must be far to the south so that the prizes and transports can keep making ground towards home and aren't kept waiting on the men-o'-war. Somewhere on the Wicklow coast, or Anglesey? Perhaps St. David's.'

Chalmers looked briefly at the chart and dismissed it with a wave of his hand.

'We came upon them unawares, I understand, as they were heading for refuge in Peel, is that correct?'

Holbrooke nodded cautiously.

'Then I disagree with you, utterly. I believe the rendezvous must be one that they agreed back in Carrickfergus, when they imagined that they would have at least one more meeting before moving into waters more often visited by King George's ships. It's likely to be a familiar one, sheltered from the wind – westerly isn't it – and above all, close.'

Holbrooke looked sceptical and moved his hand restlessly towards St. George's Channel and further south. He was reluctant to give up his theory.

'No, no, he can't possibly plan to meet down there. You have asked my opinion and I've given it in general terms. Now I'll be more specific. You'd be unwise, sir, to pass south of the Calf of Man without looking into these bays and coves to the east of it.'

Chalmers thrust his finger at the enticing coastline to the east of the Calf.

'There, there and there. That's where they met before, that's where they organised their prizes and that's where I would look for them first.'

Chalmers' certainty was infectious. Holbrooke looked carefully at the chart, moving his finger from sounding to sounding, a look of concentration creasing his brows.

'Very well. If they are not there in the morning, then I fear I must find *Pegasus* and report that I've lost them. It will be a hollow victory for Captain Chester to have taken two old frigates and let the best part of a French army and four valuable prizes slip through his fingers. But so be it. The die is cast.'

***

The night was bible-black and neither the moon nor the stars showed through the thick, enveloping blanket of cloud. The wind – such as it was, a mere light breeze that barely ruffled the water's surface – had shifted into the sou'west and showed signs of backing further. The ship should have been silent by now with the watch below catching its three or four hours sleep before being called on deck, but not tonight. *Argonaut* was alive with parties of men working under the bosun and the carpenter, repairing the damage from the day's battle.

'Six miles west-nor'west of Peel,' said Fairview when he saw the tall shape of Holbrooke coming up the quarterdeck ladder, 'although there's not a light to be seen now. I reckon the visibility is less than three miles.'

The wind was certainly light, but the swell coming down from the North Channel was causing an uncomfortable corkscrew motion. Holbrooke leaned against the capstan drumhead to steady himself. He felt something give and pulled his arm away with a jerk. Fairview smiled in the darkness.

'Bosun's easing the capstan around, sir. That ball that came through number nineteen port took away one of the cheeks off the lower capstan. Chips has replaced it, but Mister Jackson wants to be sure that it hasn't knocked the mechanism off.'

Holbrooke slapped his thigh in exasperation. He'd walked right past the lower capstan on his way from the cabin to the quarterdeck. He'd seen the two bars that had been shipped and he'd exchanged a few words with Jackson and his mates, but he hadn't connected it with the movement of the twin mechanism on the quarterdeck.

'I keep forgetting that we have a double-banked capstan. It's a far cry from the old *Kestrel*, isn't it?'

'That it is, sir,' Fairview replied turning away to hide his smile. 'We've come up in the world, from a windlass to a double-banked capstan. Whatever next?'

Whatever next indeed, Holbrooke pondered. He was perfectly happy with his frigate but if the war lasted much longer, he knew very well that he'd have to move up to a fourth rate, or perhaps to the indescribable heights of a third rate.

'We'll be off the Calf just after midnight if the wind doesn't die out altogether. It will be twilight by five o'clock. We should give the Calf a good two miles clearance, there's a tide race there and I'm not certain when it runs.'

'Tide races. Haven't we had enough of them?'

'We need a commission in the Med, sir. No tide races there.'

Holbrooke noticed the almost pedantic use of *we*, rather than *you*. Fairview would be a hard man to shake off when Holbrooke's time in *Argonaut* was over.

'Very well. Then unless anything else happens, aim to be three miles sou'east of the Calf at the end of the middle watch.'

'You believe they will be there, sir?'

'Perhaps, but I don't have any better ideas and Captain Chester will start to wonder if we stray many more leagues to the south without definite word of them.'

'If this wind shifts any further into the south, they'll have the devil's own job working their way out of there.'

'They will, Mister Fairview, but they're no fools and I expect they'll stand off and on until the morning rather than anchor. What the transports and prizes will make of that French frigate joining them out of the dark, I cannot tell.'

'I expect they have a night signal, sir, otherwise there'll be chaos.'

'There'll be chaos for sure when they see us blocking their escape at dawn, if they're there at all.'

Fairview seemed to consider this for a moment. Holbrooke had always found it difficult to guess what his sailing master was thinking. Did he believe this was a fool's errand? Was he secretly laughing at his young captain?

'Three miles sou'east at four o'clock it is then, sir,' said Fairview touching his hat.

***

CHAPTER TWENTY-ONE

Housekeeping

Friday, Twenty-Eighth of March 1760.
Argonaut, at Sea, off the Calf of Man.

The capricious wind had veered again during the night and just before twilight a fine breeze from the nor'west blew away the clouds. There was a brief display of stars before the first loom of the sun appeared in the east, casting its pale, fragile, pre-dawn light over the ocean. Gradually the dark bulk of the Isle of Man appeared, shutting in the northern horizon.

Holbrooke was pacing the quarterdeck, his hands clasped behind his back with his fingers tightly entwined to prevent them fidgeting. Forward and aft he paced, from the quarterdeck rail that looked down onto the waist to the taffrail with its flag lockers, its single lantern bracket, and the socket for the ensign staff. He had the luxury of nearly half the length of the ship to himself, as all his officers stayed carefully out of his way.

He heard the masthead lookout relieved with the cry of, 'nothing in sight, sir, no sail nor no light.'

If he was wrong, if the French had fled south, then he'd have to report back to Chester without any success to mitigate his sailing away without a word. That would be a difficult meeting, he was sure. He knew that Chester was still smarting from his captains' earlier displays of independence. Difficult, but it was not a matter that Chester would press when they returned to the Downs Squadron. He had two fine prizes and he'd broken up the French expedition's attempt to set Ireland and the north of the Kingdom aflame. What had the French achieved? They had sacked Carrickfergus and taken four prizes, which they would have the greatest difficulty in bringing home. By any standards Chester's mission had been a success. No, it wasn't Chester's opinion that he was concerned about, it was his own opinion of himself. He'd fought one French frigate into submission, and he wouldn't rest easy while another calmly carried its prizes and the French army home. He scanned the horizon, willing the French to appear to windward of him, waiting for the dawn to continue their withdrawal to the south.

'The ship's at quarters, sir,' said Shorrock, removing his hat which had by some miracle survived yesterday's battle. 'The damage to the guns has been repaired and you have them all at your disposal.'

Holbrooke saw him smiling in the gathering light. At least he'd cleaned himself up since the day before. Now he looked like the second-in-command of a King's ship again.

'We'll soon know,' said Shorrock, sensing his captain's unease. He pointed north to where the outline of the hills was becoming more distinct. 'Any minute now,' he added.

Holbrooke realised that the whole ship had caught his mood. It wasn't surprising; he was like a sort of feudal landlord with the power of praise or punishment, and his visible nervousness set the tone for all his people. It was something that even now, after a couple of years in command, he easily forgot.

'If they're not there then we've done our best and we can report back to *Pegasus* with a clear conscience,' Holbrooke replied in as breezy a tone as he could manage.

'Yet it will set the crown on the cruise, sir, if we can clean up all the Frenchmen.'

Holbrooke nodded silently and turned to continue his pacing.

***

Slowly, slowly, the loom of the sun spread over the sea. Now the Calf of Man could be distinguished as a separate block of land to the main island. Still no sign of the French. In ten minutes, Holbrooke estimated, if there was nothing to see there would be no hope left. He allowed himself another turn to the taffrail.

'Deck ho, I think I see something moving, away past the land on the larboard bow.'

Holbrooke walked as calmly as he could to the larboard main chains and rested his telescope against the shrouds. It was a good telescope, optimistically advertised by the makers as a night-glass, with a wide lens that captured even the faintest of light. It was of no use in the dead of night but at twilight it showed its worth.

He worked his way steadily from the silhouetted point of land around to the ship's head. The first sweep revealed nothing but on the second he caught something in the corner of the lens. An indistinct square of grey that was lighter than the shades all around it. Then another, and another. They weren't where he'd hoped to see them, embayed in the six-mile complex of inlets between the Calf of Man and Langness Point, but there was certainly something there, and it looked like a group of ships creeping eastward out of the bay.

'Deck there! Seven sails. I can see 'em all now, a point on the larboard bow.'

That confirmed it. In this early twilight the masthead lookout always had a better view than all the expensive telescopes on the quarterdeck.

'Make sail, Mister Fairview.' He glanced at the binnacle and looked up at the sails. 'East by south if you please.'

By the time that *Argonaut* had set her stuns'ls the rising sun had revealed the French fugitives in all the stark glory of a crisp March morning. The frigate had evidently made straight for the rendezvous – just as Chalmers had guessed – and realising the imminent danger had gathered up his charges and run to the east, despite the darkness, in the hope of evading his pursuers. Another hour, Holbrooke realised, and there would have been no sign of them when he sailed around the Calf. It would still have been odds-on that they were found before they weathered Anglesey, but for the French, where there was life there was hope, and every day that they could keep clear of Chester's squadron gave them that much greater chance of a safe return to France. He could only imagine the dismay when the lookout reported a frigate – and it could only be British – making sail and running down to them.

Shorrock was rubbing his hands in anticipation, a smile of pure joy on his face.

'You'll deal with the frigate first, sir?' he asked.

Holbrooke didn't reply and kept watching the French. Shorrock made it sound so easy, and yet this frigate's captain was the only one of the French who had fought his opponent to a standstill. If *Pegasus* and *Argonaut* hadn't intervened, then he'd have won a famous victory against an evenly matched opponent. And it had taken real seamanship to rig a jury fore topmast after the battle. He was a dangerous man, Holbrooke knew, and airy talk of *dealing* with him understated the difficulty and danger of the task.

'He'll turn at bay as soon as he's clear of that land,' Shorrock added, not discouraged by Holbrooke's silence. He gestured at Langness Point, the southwestern tip of the Isle of Man.

The devil was on Holbrooke's shoulder whispering in his ear. He didn't have to fight this frigate, he'd done his duty by finding the remains of the French expedition and now he could beat back around the Calf, find Chester and bring the whole squadron south and east to cut off the French escape. That was the classic role of a frigate although usually it brought a squadron of ships-of-the-line into action, rather than two battle-worn sixth rates. Nevertheless, throwing his ship straight into the fray without a thought for the consequences was what his peers would expect of him. Anything else would be viewed with suspicion and he'd have to suffer from it for the rest of his career.

Then an unwanted image flashed across his mind. Ann, his wife of less than four months, smiling shyly as she walked up the aisle of the church in Wickham holding a posy of flowers from his father's garden. The quarterdeck of a frigate was a desperately dangerous place in action. It had none of the protection that a poop deck afforded to ships-of-the-line and the lists of past sea officers were littered with men who had fallen on their own deck in action with the enemy. He could avoid that peril; he could turn away now.

Unless…unless *Pegasus* and *Fortune* hadn't moved south overnight. They may have been detained by their prizes or by their own battle damage. Quite possibly Chester believed that he'd done enough and was determined to consolidate his gains rather than risk it all on another engagement. He could be anchoring off Peel harbour right now.

Holbrooke looked around the deck. The signs of yesterday's fight were evident everywhere, the stark white wounds where cannon balls had ploughed through gunwales and across decks, the knots and splices in sheets and halyards and the powder stains where his own guns had fired and fired again until they were so hot that they'd jumped clear of the deck with each discharge. *Argonaut* had fought the good fight and now she carried the scars. Then he looked at the faces of his officers. They looked hastily away but it was evident that they'd been watching him, eager to know what he would do, even if only vaguely aware of the dilemma. He took a few paces forward from the binnacle and looked down into the waist. The gun's crews didn't have the same sense of propriety as his officers and they all looked back at him, a sea of faces turned towards the quarterdeck. They looked tough and competent, powerful of limb and sinew to an extent that Holbrooke knew he would never achieve. They hefted the ponderous weight of worms and sponges, hand spikes and rammers with as much insouciance as the sailing master held his quadrant. He'd known most of the faces for no more than a few months, but over there, at the number eight gun, was a man that had served with him in *Fury* in the long-ago days in the Mediterranean. Scarrow, that was his name; he'd volunteered at Mahon when he'd had a disagreement with the master of a Liverpool barque. Scarrow was conscious of Holbrooke's scrutiny and smiled broadly, as from one old shipmate to another.

'Three cheers for Captain Holbrooke,' Scarrow shouted, and waved his Monmouth cap in the air.

The ship echoed to the wild yells of the crew. Holbrooke waved his hat once in reply and turned away so that they wouldn't see his face. He knew that he was committed now.

'Yes, Mister Shorrock, I do believe we must fight that frigate first, the rest can wait their turn.'

***

'He's reducing sail, sir,' said Fairview, 'he's hauling his wind. Well, he's game enough.'

'Steady as you are, Mister Fairview, we'll reduce to fighting sail when we're closer.'

'Steady as she goes, sir,' Fairview replied.

Chalmers was watching the Frenchman through narrowed eyes, against the sun that was just starting to peep over the horizon.

'I admire him,' he said reflectively. 'He could abandon all those ships and run to the south and it's a safe bet that alone, without the transports and prizes, he'd make it. The expedition is over and whatever had been its purpose has failed. It's unlikely that anyone would criticise him in France, even if they notice his return.'

'True,' Holbrooke replied, 'and by one reading of the situation it could be said that this fight is unnecessary, futile even.'

Chalmers walked with Holbrooke to the taffrail, the only place in a ship at quarters and cleared for action that private conversation was possible.

'You are troubled, George.'

Chalmers had never used Holbrooke's Christian name on deck. Its use now startled Holbrooke.

'I am, David. I feel I'm being hustled into this fight without being able to judge it rationally. Men will die today, probably some of those on the quarterdeck now, and all perhaps for nothing. We've already won and if any of those Frenchmen make it home, they'll be the lucky few.'

Chalmers listened in silence.

'I thought of Ann just now. For myself I care nothing, but I can't abide the thought of Ann as a widow so soon.'

'Then you are in the wrong profession, brother,' Chalmers replied brutally. 'Now listen. For better or for worse, you've taken the King's shilling. You have the trappings and privileges of a commissioned officer but with that comes a responsibility to act only in the King's interest. Think of Byng! Was something alike going through his mind when he retired to Gibraltar and left the Minorca garrison to face certain defeat?'

Holbrooke flinched at that. Chalmers saw that he was looking horrified but continued remorselessly.

'It's a question of duty, and Ann understands that as well as you or I do. Ask yourself this: can you return to Wickham knowing that you did not do your utmost?'

Holbrooke stopped dead and stared back at Chalmers. Did his friend realise that he'd used the wording from the twelfth article of war *'...or shall not do his utmost,'* the article that had condemned Byng to death by a firing squad? Probably so, there was not much that Chalmers said accidentally.

'You're right, of course,' he said, his mind now clearer.

Then he'd fight this Frenchman and if he were spared, he'd hunt down every last one of the transports and prizes. That is what he held a commission for, and that is what he must do.

'But remember, George, there's always another way to do your duty, the straight path is not always the most direct.'

***

'Let's get the stuns'ls in now,' said Holbrooke. 'This doesn't look like it will turn into a chase,' he added nodding towards the French frigate that was now moving slowly east, waiting for them.

There was a rush of men to the fore and main yardarms and in a flash the stuns'ls were furled and the booms were slid back inboard through the irons.

'T'gallants,' said Holbrooke simply and the same band of seamen climbed further aloft to take in the upper sails.

'Brail up the courses, Mister Fairview, I want to have them ready to set in an instant.'

Argonaut's speed fell off as the sails disappeared.

'Two knots and a half, sir,' Peterson reported.

'Very well, that will do, he shows no sign of running,' he replied gesturing towards the French frigate.

Both ships had reduced to their fighting sails: jib, stays'l, fore tops'l, main tops'l and mizzen. That gave them the maximum manoeuvrability without having to take men away from the guns to handle the sails. It was the clearest possible statement of intent; both ships would fight to the death. Holbrooke could see that the Frenchman had been mauled in the action against *Fortune* the day before and like *Argonaut*, her splinter nets and boarding nets still had great gaps in them. He counted the guns, fifteen each side, two more than *Argonaut*, and they were all run out.

'The transports aren't standing on ceremony,' Shorrock observed, 'they're even leaving the prizes astern. Look at them stretching away to the sou'east. They'll be out of sight soon.'

Of course, the thousand or so soldiers in those transports were more valuable than the prizes. Undoubtedly, they'd be faster and if they could make a French port, even alone, then their masters in Versailles would judge that something had been salvaged from this disaster.

'Take your station if you please, Mister Shorrock.'

Holbrooke wanted time to think without his first lieutenant's commentary. This would be like no other battle he'd fought. Previously he'd always been able to manoeuvre in the hope of gaining an advantage, he'd become adept at using speed and guile to win the day. This morning, under this bright spring sun and gentle breeze and with an alert and bloody-minded enemy, there was no such option. He'd have to slug it out toe-to-toe. Still, it was worth a try to start the engagement under his terms.

'He's hauled his wind, sir,' said Fairview. 'He's beating up towards us. By God, what a fighting cock.'

Quite right, Holbrooke thought. The French captain knew that he must keep the engagement as far from the valuable and vulnerable transports as possible. He was giving them the best chance of escape in case he should be taken.

He started to pace to the taffrail again, partly to get away from Fairview's remarks and partly because he always thought better when he was moving. He took one step then froze with one leg outstretched and the other almost lifting from the deck behind him. He looked absurd, he knew, but he didn't care, he must capture the thought that had just sprung to his mind. Perhaps there was a way to achieve his objective without engaging in a stand-up fight with an equal foe. In an instant he knew that he'd been mesmerised by this obstinate Frenchman who apparently knew no better than to make a fight to the end. There was *always* another way, as Chalmers had said.

'Mister Shorrock, Mister Shorrock. On the quarterdeck if you please. Master, Bosun, a moment of your time.'

Fairview and Jackson exchanged glances as they gathered around their captain. This was better, this was the old Holbrooke, untroubled by self-doubt as they fondly imagined. It sounded like he had a plan.

'Can you spare enough men from the guns to man the upper yards, Mister Shorrock? Belay that. Whether you can spare them or not, I want them stationed in the tops immediately, I'll accept that the guns may not be so well served.'

Shorrock nodded cautiously. 'I can take a man from each gun, sir. You'll hardly notice it for the first few broadsides then the crews will start getting tired and slower.'

'Very well, so be it. Now, you have time to draw your shot, I want both broadsides loaded with chain. Here's what I plan to do…'

***

Argonaut crept towards her opponent across a sea that was barely ruffled by the light breeze and sheltered from the northerly swell. It was almost glass-smooth, and the two ships had the barest minimum of speed for steerage way. He watched the French frigate carefully. *Argonaut* had the weather gauge and although his opponent probably discounted that advantage, it was vital for Holbrooke's plan.

'Steer as though you aim to cross his stern, Mister Fairview.'

That would be an obvious opening manoeuvre, a prelude to the two ships lying alongside each other at pistol-shot range where their great guns could hardly miss and where even the relatively light eight and nine-pounders could do the maximum damage. That is what Holbrooke had decided to do before he'd had his epiphany.

The Frenchman's head was to the south, waiting for *Argonaut* to come down to him; the challenge was unmistakable. Would he tamely accept being raked from astern? Holbrooke watched him carefully, his telescope trained on the frigate's rudder as being the first true sign of his intent. But Fairview saw it first.

'He's turning to larboard, sir. Could he be intending to wear?'

To larboard. That would do. The Frenchman was slowing down deliberately to let *Argonaut* come up on his beam while not offering a free shot at his stern.

'Stand by the starboard battery,' Holbrooke shouted. 'Lay me alongside his larboard side, Mister Fairview.'

Holbrooke trained his telescope at the figures on the quarterdeck. As with the other frigate that he'd taken yesterday, there was a good sprinkling of soldiers among the sea officers. It certainly wouldn't do to let himself be boarded, not with Murray and most of his marines away with the prize crew.

'Keep her well off, Master.'

Fairview nodded. He'd seen the white uniforms on the deck.

That French captain must have convinced himself that his opponent would fall in with his plan for the battle. His own bullheadedness had blinded him to the possibility of independent thought, or so Holbrooke hoped.

'Do your guns bear, Mister Shorrock?'

Shorrock shouted something unintelligible and waved his hat.

Holbrooke blew his whistle. The familiar lurch as the frigate took up the guns' recoil, the same flash and smoke, but with chain shot the sound was different. Even on the firing ship it couldn't be mistaken for round shot, and on the receiving ship its sound was utterly distinctive, an ululating howl that induced terror disproportionately to its effectiveness.

Crash! The French broadside smashed into *Argonaut*. No chain shot this, but the genuine eight-pound cast iron shot that shattered stout oak and fragile flesh. A gun was over in the waist and Holbrooke heard a great metallic clang below his feet that suggested another gun had been hit. There were wounded on his waist, some of them would be dead in all probability before the day was over. The French captain had held his nerve and had fired at the best possible moment, and the fruit of his patience was strewn in bloody tatters across *Argonaut*'s deck.

'Set the t'gallants and mizzen tops'l, Mister Fairview. Let fall the courses. Stuns'ls when you are ready.'

If his opponent had any imagination at all, he'd know that the chain shot meant that *Argonaut* had no intention of standing to fight. If he still had any doubt, the sudden blossoming of canvas in the British frigate would confirm it. The shattering of a plan, the end of any chance that he could save the rest of the French army that waited impotently in the transports.

Argonaut picked up speed and dashed past the Frenchman with a swiftness that made it look like the other ship was dead in the water.

Bang! Another broadside. It was a little slow because chain was always more difficult to load, and now there were only twelve guns firing on the starboard side.

Crash! The Frenchman fired. Ball again. Holbrooke saw Fairview give him a queer look, almost of admiration, but he had no time to appreciate it. This was a more ragged broadside and not so well pointed, he could almost feel the orders and counter-orders swirling around his opponent's deck, the fatal confusion that spread from his wanton destruction of the French captain's plan.

'He's bearing up,' shouted Holbrooke.

Fairview nodded. He'd seen the danger. The Frenchman, unable to set his sails fast enough, was gambling everything on the oldest of all tactics, he was attempting to board.

'Helm a-lee, two points to larboard,' he said calmly to the quartermaster, waving his hand to windward to make sure there was no misunderstanding.

'He'll fall astern sir,' said Fairview calmly.

Sure enough, the Frenchman's gamble failed. His head came up and his jib boom thrust alarmingly towards *Argonaut*'s taffrail, but with only tops'ls set he was falling rapidly astern.

Holbrooke heard the quarterdeck six-pounders fire. They'd been loaded with cannister and should have been deadly for the close-packed ranks of soldiers, but a lucky swell caught the French frigate and lifted its bows at the crucial second. The load of musket balls was spent harmlessly on the headrails.

Another broadside of chain shot from *Argonaut*. That would be the last as the guns would no longer bear. The last, but it did its work. Slowly and with a stately grace that rapidly transformed into a squalid rush of broken spars and torn canvas, the frigate's jib and stays'l came down over the jib boom. There was a moment of equilibrium before the whole of the foremast, jury rigged topmast and all, dropped over lee side.

'Cease firing, Mister Shorrock. He won't get that sorted out in a hurry. Now, let's get after those transports.'

***

CHAPTER TWENTY-TWO

Prizes Galore

Friday, Twenty-Eighth of March 1760.
Argonaut, at Sea, the Irish Sea.

Were it not for the agreement that Holbrooke had signed off Torshavn, he and his crew would have been made rich men in the few hours following *Argonaut*'s engagement with the last of the French frigates. After a short chase, they overhauled first the four British prizes and then the two transports. The prizes and one of the transports hauled down their colours after a single gun across each of their bows, but the second transport sped on southwards, ignoring the polite warning. Holbrooke could see the disagreement on the chase's quarterdeck, a disagreement so profound that he saw the flash of a sword being drawn. It wasn't clear whether the soldiers were demanding that the master hold his course in the hope of escaping, or whether they favoured instant surrender. In either case, the transport had to be stopped and Holbrooke favoured a bloodless end to the affair.

'Mister Shorrock! A fully shotted broadside if you please, with all the quoins hammered home. I'd prefer not to harm anyone, but they'll have to take their chances with the ricochets.'

'Aye-aye, sir!'

It took a few minutes to be certain that all the guns were pointing as far downwards as their carriages would allow. He saw Shorrock judging the movement of the ship and when it had just started its roll towards the enemy, he gave the order to fire.

Holbrooke ineffectually fanned the smoke away but still couldn't see the result of the broadside. He couldn't see any damage to the transport, but he saw another scuffle break out on the quarterdeck. He heard a single pistol shot, and the scuffle ended. The white of France came fluttering down from the peak of the mizzen yard and without further ado the transport backed its tops'ls and soon lay rising and falling to the gentle swell.

'Mister Shorrock. The men are to stay at quarters and the ship is to remain cleared for action. Take the longboat, if you please, and put a prize crew under a master's mate aboard that obstinate fellow over there. He's to have a corporal and two files of marines. All the commissioned land officers and the ship's master are to be brought back here. All of them, mark you, and demand to see the muster roll. Batten the remaining soldiers below decks and don't take any nonsense from them. Make it clear that I'll hang the whole lot of them for piracy if they offer violence to the prize crew.'

'Aye-aye, sir,' Shorrock replied, looking shocked at Holbrooke's brutality. 'I expect the other transport will lie there peacefully until we can turn our attention to him.'

'Just so, Mister Shorrock. Make haste, though, because that gentleman whom we left behind may feel that it's not yet over.'

He pointed to where the frigate could be seen getting underway to the south with no foremast. She moved with an ungainly, jerking motion, with her head seeking the wind despite the best efforts of the steersman.

'Now, Mister Jackson. Take the yawl over to those merchantmen, release the British prisoners and remind them that as it's been over twenty-four hours since they were captured by the French, they are now legal prizes of *Argonaut*. Leave one petty officer in each of them just in case they should have difficulty understanding. If their masters have been sent to the French ships, we can arrange their return at leisure. They are to lie under our lee and follow us until they are told otherwise. If all else fails, they are to rendezvous in the lee of the Calf of Man. Bring the French prize crews back here.'

Jackson hurried off to pick four reliable petty officers, shouting orders for the yawl to be swung over the side.

***

'Well, that was easy,' said Chalmers as the French frigate hauled down its colours. 'Seven prizes in as many hours and barely a casualty to speak of. Although,' he added thoughtfully, 'young Adams is in no position to agree.'

Holbrooke looked dead tired. He'd quite forgotten that a young topman had lost his life in the first engagement of the day, and two others were still in the surgeon's hands. It was all he could do to form a coherent reply.

'We were lucky,' he replied. 'The four British ships were easy, all we had to do was bring the French prize crews back here and the only risk was that their original crew would feel themselves free to continue their interrupted voyage. The petty officers will bring them to their senses; those are their prizes as well, after all. In any case, they'll all be insured so at this point it matters little to the masters, they'll just be pleased to be avoiding a French prison.'

'It will be marvellous to watch the insurance rates after this,' said Chalmers. 'I heard that they had reached unprecedented heights when Batiste left Dunkirk. Now they'll plumet, I expect. It would be interesting to take a coffee at Lloyds when this news reaches the city.'

Holbrooke nodded wearily. Was that what they were fighting for? Was that why Adams had to die? It was depressing to think that in the end he worked for the merchants and the crafty speculators and underwriters who daily gathered at Lloyds coffee house in Lombard Street.

'I heard that the insurance men are planning to set up a more formal organisation and base it at Lloyds. *The Society for the Registration of Shipping*, or something of that nature.'

'Yes, Hammond wrote to tell me. He seems to believe that it's a prize agent's job to advise me on investments.'

'Are you tempted?'

'Not I. I'm no speculator.'

Holbrooke glanced out of the window at the string of prizes. He was no speculator, for sure, but he was becoming increasingly aware – he was being advised from all sides – that his money wasn't working hard enough lying in the vault of Campbell & Coutts on the Strand. He would have to address that issue when he next had some time ashore. Investments, a house perhaps, a share in a business; whenever he thought about it, he realised how little he knew, and he had no close friends with the knowledge to advise him. It was all very puzzling, and along with his marriage and impending parenthood, it distracted him from the serious business of commanding a King's ship. He almost yearned for the old days when he had no money to worry about and no ties ashore that demanded his attention.

'The transports won't cause any problems now that the troops have lost all their officers. I must admit I was expecting more difficulty with the captain of that third frigate – he had an obstinate look about him – but *Pegasus* and *Fortune* came around the Calf just in time. He was caught, he had nowhere to go and was already disabled and his crew didn't appear to relish rigging another jury mast. It would have been foolish, immoral and verging on criminal, to have resisted after that one broadside. Now we have the whole squadron here and the wind's coming southerly, we'll be able to anchor off Douglas and sort ourselves out.'

The wind had indeed shifted and was now coming in mild gusts from the south southeast. It wouldn't last, or so Fairview assured them, and within the day it would shift into the west again.

'Douglas is sheltered from the west, and it has shipyards, or so I'm told, and we'll be able to refit before the whole fleet – if I may call it that – heads south.'

'How long will we be there, do you think?'

'Oh a few days, a week or two at most. The three French frigates have all been badly mauled, and *Pegasus* and *Fortune* both fared worse than us. However, if I'm asked, I'll have to admit that we are fit to sail immediately, and I wouldn't be surprised if Captain Chester has plans for us.'

***

Douglas Bay offered a wide, sweeping, sheltered road with a firm, sandy bottom. It could have happily taken the Channel Squadron at anchor, but even Chester's more modest gathering filled the bay with more ships than it had seen in many a year: six frigates, two fat transports and four British merchantmen. Each of the prizes – British and French – flew a red ensign over the Bourbon white, to make their ownership clear and it lent a holiday atmosphere to the town. Every coastal community loved a prize, even when it wasn't their own, and here were three British frigates that between them owned the condemned value of nine vessels. The shipyard owners, the chandlers, the victuallers, the tavern owners and the prostitutes all rubbed their hands while the men of law and government calculated how long they could decently detain all those men-o'-war and prizes for repairs. They all knew that a proportion of that flood of money must come to them by hook or by crook, it was only fair, and they settled down to a long game of obstruction and obfuscation.

However, Holbrooke and his men saw none of this. Chester was eager to send news of the victory to the Admiralty, and *Argonaut* was the least damaged of his three frigates. A day after arriving at Douglas and minutes after the last of his marines and sailors returned from their prize crew duties, *Argonaut* weighed anchor and took advantage of the renewed westerlies to sail for Liverpool with Chester's dispatches. After a day of receptions and dinners – the merchants of Liverpool were entirely aware of the danger that Batiste's squadron had posed to their commerce – *Argonaut* was away again.

***

'You know that Batiste is dead?' Holbrooke asked Chalmers when at last he had a moment to sit quietly in the great cabin. 'Cut in half by a nine-pound ball. I would like to have met him; he must have been an extraordinary man. Fouquet survived, however, although he may rue the day. He'll have to explain the loss of the whole expedition without Batiste to shoulder the blame.'

'I had heard it,' Chalmers replied taking a sip of wine. 'I also heard that his ship was so burdened with plunder that they couldn't come at the eighteen-pounders to bring them into action.'

'It seems extraordinary that a man like Batiste should allow that to happen. He must have known that he wouldn't see France again without a fight. And yet the man was audacious! He must have been to even attempt to circumnavigate Britain in winter.'

'Yes,' Chalmers replied, 'an extraordinary man indeed, and it appears that there was no meeting of minds between the sea officers and the soldiers, and no clear command structure. There was tension from the moment they left Dunkirk, and when the news of Quiberon Bay eventually made its way to them, there was open dispute as to whether the expedition should be abandoned.'

Holbrooke nodded. He was half asleep.

'In the end it was little more than a privateering affair on a grand scale. Henry Morgan would have recognised the sacking of Carrickfergus, and the disagreements between officers holding the French King's commission were worthy of the buccaneers of old.'

Chalmers stared at the lamp that swung from the deck head.

'What I don't understand is why Captain Chester is so unconcerned about the frigate and the brig that appear to be still on the loose. I was fully expecting that *Argonaut* would be sent out to find them.'

'Well,' Holbrooke said, his speech slurred through drowsiness, 'I wondered about that too, but Chester wasn't interested. *It's not of any importance*, he said, *let them find their way home or fall into the hands of the Channel squadron, or hurl themselves onto the Scillies.* He just didn't care, and I can see what he means. This is his victory, it's enough for his purposes and he doesn't want to risk spoiling it. After all, if we came across the last French frigate, it would be an even match and we could be taken ourselves. If we prevailed, he wouldn't share the laurels. I just wonder whether their Lordships will see it that way.'

***

CHAPTER TWENTY-THREE

The Port Admiral

Monday, Seventh of April 1760.
Argonaut, at anchor, Spithead.

South around Land's End, butting their way into the persistent sou'westerlies, then a day of calms before the wind turned easterly just in time to head them as they rounded the Longships and broke into the Channel. Days and days of contrary winds and it took all of Fairview's skill, working the ebb tide as well as the flood, to bring them eventually to the Isle of Wight and so into the sheltered waters of the Solent.

Holbrooke breathed a mighty sigh of relief when the cable smoked through the hawse and sank into the deep sand of Spithead. Within minutes the longboat was rowing into a keen wind to take Holbrooke to report to the port admiral for orders.

***

'Captain Holbrooke, welcome, although it's taken you the devil of a time to get here.'

Holbrooke was ready for his reception. He remembered that Vice Admiral Holburne had a disconcerting way of dominating conversations, of putting people off their stride. He'd almost done for Holbrooke two years before when he interrogated him over bringing his damaged sloop *Kestrel* back to Portsmouth without the leave of Commodore Howe, under whose command *Kestrel* had been providing a screen to the raids on the coast of Brittany.

'I missed the last of the westerlies as I rounded Land's End and had to tide up the channel, sir,' he replied. 'I carry copies of Captain Chester's dispatches.'

Even a land-locked admiral watched the weather, it was vital for determining when his ships could sail and when he could expect returning ships to arrive. Yet if he sympathised with Holbrooke's week-long battle against the contrary winds, he gave no sign of it.

'Oh, don't worry about those. The news reached here days ago, overland from Liverpool. All London's been agog with it, and I know the content of those letters better than you do.'

Holburne waved dismissively at the precious bundles that Holbrooke had brought south and east in the face of all the unpleasantness that an early spring passage in the western seas could offer.

'I should congratulate you, nevertheless, Captain Holbrooke,' he continued in a more conciliatory manner, 'it was a well-managed affair and it's done wonders for confidence in the city. Now, what's the state of your ship?'

Holbrooke had at least been prepared for this. He listed the damage that his own bosun and carpenter and gunner had been unable to repair, and the stores that his purser insisted they needed desperately. It was important not to exaggerate for fear of being again accused of preferring to languish in port rather than keep the sea. Nevertheless, it was a lengthy list that would occupy the yard for a few weeks, at least, and Holbrooke steeled himself for the onslaught of downright suspicion that he was sure would follow, perhaps even with the humiliation of having his report scrutinised by the master attendant, as had happened the previous time. He knew the dynamics of the royal dockyards by now, the interplay of the King's business and self-interest, of the divergent motivations of sea officers and the navy board's resident officers. The master attendant would exaggerate the work and the time needed in order to keep his men in employment. The resident commissioner – it was still Sir Richard Hughes – would provide a moderating brake on the master attendant's estimate, and then the port admiral would halve it, *and damn your eyes, sir, if it's a day longer*.

Admiral Holburne sat in thought for a moment and consulted a private paper that he had kept hidden under a book on his desk. Holbrooke guessed that it was a list of ships waiting for repair and docking, a lengthy list it seemed.

'Well, Mister Holbrooke. You appear to have kept your ship in good order considering the number of engagements. Commodore Boys doesn't want you until you're properly refitted and stored, and the yard is already running at full capacity. I'll send this list over to Sir Richard and no doubt he'll declare that you need a year and a day in dock.'

He laughed, an unpleasant and strangely humourless sound.

'You'll be out in two weeks, mark my words.'

Holbrooke was about to ask the question that most preyed on his mind, but Holburne, as though he were a mind reader, pre-empted him.

'However, *Argonaut* won't be brought in for a day or two and while you're at Spithead you're to remain on board or in the yard. When the yard has taken your ship, I won't confine you to Portsmouth. I know you'll be wanted in London, but and I also know that you're recently married,' he added, his face expressionless, 'so make the most of your time and don't let your men straggle.'

'Thank you, sir,' was all Holbrooke could manage. It was far more generous than he had hoped, having previously suffered under Holburne's restrictions.

'And you'll come to dinner, Holbrooke, and bring that new wife of yours. Frances will be pleased to meet her, and you can tell me all about your battles. Shall we say Wednesday at half past two?'

It wasn't a question that needed much consideration, not coming from a vice admiral.

'Ann and I will be delighted, sir.'

***

CHAPTER TWENTY-FOUR

Carriage For Hire

Tuesday, Eighth of April 1760.
Wickham, Hampshire.

'And you absolutely could not come home yesterday?'

Ann was looking pale, and her demeanour was, to put it politely, waspish. The news of *Argonaut's* arrival at Spithead had been all over Wickham within hours, and long before the King's Head had shut its doors for the night, it had become a subject of general gossip. The next morning Ann had suffered the well-meaning but insensitive questions of her friends, her acquaintances and just about anybody in the town who thought it was their business: *has Captain Holbrooke not come ashore yet? Does he not know your condition? How can men – naval men – be so insensitive?* and much else in the same vein. Ann knew enough about the navy to be aware that her husband had done well to escape from his ship only a day after anchoring at Spithead, but the importunate questions had worn away at her resilience, and she struggled hard to offer George the welcome that deep within she knew he should have.

For his part, Holbrooke was concerned at how his wife had altered in the month since he'd seen her in Harwich. He'd been prepared for the changes to her figure, slight though they were at this early stage, but her pallor and the fragility of her nerves came as a shock to him. He tried to say the right words but found that he was stammering incoherently.

It was fortunate that Ann had been at their new, rented home when Holbrooke arrived, rather than at Bere House where she had been spending an increasing amount of time with her stepmother. It gave them time to get used to each other's company without any intrusions. Ann's servant Polly had established an advance picket outside the front door and the callers – there were many of them – were turned away before they had even reached the brass door knocker. Squire or farmhand, family member or casual acquaintance, it made no difference to Polly. Since she had moved out of Bere House and away from the stifling influence of the longstanding housekeeper, she had blossomed – if that was the right word – into an indefatigable harridan. Even Sophie, Polly's erstwhile employer and Ann's stepmother, kept her distance for those first few hours.

Slowly, Ann's face softened, the colour came back to her cheeks, and she started to smile. The effect on Holbrooke was remarkable. The frightened, cringing wreck who had first faced her bitter, unjust reproaches recovered quickly. It was as though he could know no happiness in Ann's presence unless she was happy too, a universal truth that seasoned husbands took for granted but that he was just starting to recognise.

'Then you are well, Ann? I was so concerned when I first saw you.'

'It was nothing,' she replied, 'just a passing feeling of faintness, and I'm sorry, but I can be a bit sharp when that comes over me. And your poor face! Does it hurt?' she asked, tracing the line of the scar on his jaw with her finger.

Holbrooke steeled himself to avoid wincing.

'Not at all,' he replied, 'I rather hope that it will give me a dangerous look.'

Ann smiled at that, the first real smile since he returned.

'Not dangerous, but perhaps romantic,' she said. 'I shall have to keep a close eye on you from now on.'

'I suppose my return was a surprise?'

'Oh no, not really. The newspapers were full of your battle – or *action* as they all call it. I prefer *battle*, it sounds grander – and it was well known that you were coming home around Wales and Cornwall. It's just that everyone said you would be here by last Saturday, and when you didn't come, I felt so disappointed. Then they all said that *Argonaut* was at Spithead yesterday, and I expected to see you immediately, although your father warned me that the port admiral – a terrible person, or so I've heard – wouldn't let you come home for days, perhaps not at all.'

'Well, I'm here now and you'll get the chance to decide for yourself how terrible Admiral Holburne can be. We are bidden to dinner tomorrow.'

Ann appeared not to have heard him.

'And then all those horrible people in the town kept asking the most tactless questions. I fled indoors but they pursued me even here until I gave Polly orders to send everyone away. Do you know, I peeped out of the window an hour before you arrived to see her sending Father packing! I could hardly believe her temerity, and he positively apologised to her!'

Holbrooke looked at her and smiled.

'Perhaps I spoke too softly, dear. Dinner, tomorrow, with Vice Admiral Holburne. Of course, if you don't feel able, I can offer your apologies. Perhaps he'll let me off the hook too.'

'Dinner with an admiral? Oh, of course we must go. I have the blue silk brocade from our wedding, you remember, George, don't you?'

Thankfully, Ann didn't wait for a reply, but plunged straight on, leaving Holbrooke to search through his memory for the colour that his bride wore at their happy day. It could have been blue, he decided, but then again…

'Oh, I should have said sooner. Mister Garnier called as soon as he heard about the battle and about your likely return. He said in a most meaningful manner that you should come to dinner at Rookesbury House. How romantic, I told him, that is where we first met. He hadn't remembered until I mentioned it, and I do believe that when he said *you* should come to dinner, he meant you alone. But he did admit that it was a most auspicious venue for us, and he gave me a significant look again.'

'Ah, I've been so busy recently that he entirely slipped my mind. You know that he wants to talk to me about some sort of future in the town, we spoke of it in Harwich, didn't we? I expect that's what all the meaningful looks were about.'

'Well, in any case, I feel perfectly well and ready for dinner with any number of admirals, however ferocious their reputations may be. And if Garnier should want my presence at dinner, I'll condescend to grace his poor home.'

***

It was late in the afternoon when Captain and Mrs Holbrooke stepped out of the door of their small, rented house to take the air. Although it was a pleasant home for two people and a servant, it was really little more than a cottage of the better sort. It was in the centre of a row of similar dwellings on Bridge Street, all nestled cheek-by-jowl, close to the road on a steep hill that led from the market square down towards the dip hole on the river where the people of Wickham drew their water, and to the bridge that carried the Alton road. By leaning out of the upper windows of the cottage and looking to the right the old stone bridge could be seen and beyond that the squat shape of the church of Saint Nicholas, planted atop a small hill on the eastern bank. The cottage was two hundred yards from Bere House where Martin Featherstone lived in some greater style, and half a mile from William Holbrooke's modest cottage that nestled in a wooded bend of the river Meon. All of Ann's friends lived within a mile of their new home and the location suited her admirably.

Holbrooke instinctively looked aloft at the hurrying clouds. The wind was still easterly, but a change was in the air. The rain had stopped and although it was still a brisk, keen breeze, it didn't have the sharpness of a few hours before. To Holbrooke, after the Faroes and the north countries, it seemed positively balmy, but Ann pulled her cloak close to her chest and buried her chin in the fur muffler that Polly had wrapped around her.

'You are sure you are prepared for this, Ann?' Holbrooke asked. 'You look better now but I was worried when I first saw you.'

Ann turned towards George and laughed.

'Are you sure *you* are prepared, husband? I've grown accustomed to your saintly status in the town, but it's reached a fever pitch since the news of you battle with this Frenchman, Batiste, isn't it?

'Yes, Captain or Commodore or Lieutenant Batiste, or just plain Monsieur, depending on which of his commissions you read. His soldiers insisted that he was no more than a lieutenant perhaps a captain at best while his sailors insisted that he was a commodore.'

They turned left into the square and Ann clutched George's arm more tightly. It wasn't a market day, which was perhaps just as well, but the butcher and the baker were doing a thriving trade from their shop fronts that faced the square. Right in the middle of the square, in defiance of a statute enacted by King John five hundred years before, a farmer was selling winter vegetables from the tail of his cart, his horse still harnessed, calmly watching the world go by despite the cold wind. There was a steady stream of people moving from place to place, the women looking in the window of the haberdashery and the men casting anxious glances between the clock and the still-closed doors of the King's Head. Ann smiled mischievously at her husband.

'What do you sailors say? Stand by?'

Wickham's inhabitants were, by and large, a respectable lot and not given to public displays of emotion. Yet one by one, as each person became aware that their neighbour was looking towards the north end of the square, they stopped in their tracks and craned their necks to see the famous post-captain and his lady taking their afternoon stroll. There were whispered explanations for those too dull to recognise Wickham's man of the hour and his wife, and significant smiles as each acquaintance hoped to be recognised.

Holbrooke was appalled. He had only wanted a walk and perhaps the opportunity to step into the haberdashers to buy some new mittens for Ann. He felt as though he was on public display and perhaps should do something remarkable to please the crowd. Ann saw that he was on the point of turning around and fleeing back to the cottage. She tugged at his arm and guided him deeper into the square.

'Don't worry, George, you're not expected to make a speech, but we could at least greet our friends. Look, there's Mary talking to Sophie.'

Ann waved to her friend and her stepmother, and Holbrooke was carried along on a wave of cheerful talk. It was curious though. He'd been hailed as a notable man when he'd come back with news of the first victory of the war at Cape François, and again when he'd returned from Emden in command of his sloop *Kestrel*, but there had been a different feeling to his welcome. Then, he was greeted as a young man who'd made good in a modest way, but not really to be taken seriously. Now, as a post-captain with a famous victory behind him, and a string of valuable prizes, he attracted a deeper level of respect. The crowd was more subdued in his presence, aware that he had become a man who wasn't to be trifled with, one who may resent an outpouring of public adulation.

Sophie attached herself to them as they passed from group to group, shaking hands, exchanging how-d'ye-dos and utterly failing to break away towards the haberdashers. Holbrooke was aware that Ann loved every moment of their progress around the square, and that Sophie was delighted to take some share in the fame. He looked across at Bere House to see his father-in-law hurrying in through the door, anxious to avoid being caught up in the affair, and yet in a few moments his face appeared at the upper floor bow window, looking out at the scene with evident pleasure.

There were people pressing to speak to Holbrooke too, although most hung back, too shy to accost to the great man in public. Holbrooke had been born and brought up here and he knew a great many people, although it had been a number of years since he had lived in Wickham for any length of time. His eye caught a familiar face that he couldn't quite place. A man of his own age, neither rich nor poor, jostled his way forward.

'You may not remember me, your honour. Billy Stiles, we used to play cricket when we were youngsters, over in the meadow behind the church.'

Holbrooke looked puzzled for a moment then it started to come together. It wasn't that he'd forgotten his childhood friends, it was just that he hadn't often thought of them since he left home for the naval academy in Portsmouth, and that was nearly a decade ago. All those who had remained in Wickham saw each other frequently, and their names came easily to each other, but Holbrooke's life had involved fresh faces and unfamiliar places at regular intervals. It was no surprise that he hadn't remembered the name.

'Yes, forgive me, Billy, it's been a long time. How do you do?'

'Very well, thank you, sir. I've a part share in a two-horse chaise that we keep at the inn out on the Fareham road. You remember the old Porto Bello?'

'I certainly do,' Holbrooke replied.

Admiral Vernon's great victory had been much on his mind lately, ever since Chalmers had used it as a metaphor for the fragility of political careers. The Porto Bello inn was about a mile south of Wickham and it was one of the few that had stayed loyal to the memory of the embittered old admiral. How strange that he and Ann had stayed at an inn of the same name in Harwich. Holbrooke felt that he was the victim of curious coincidences.

'You'll be needing a carriage, I don't doubt sir. My rates are good, and I can deliver you and your lady anywhere in the finest of style. Ask anyone around here.'

Holbrooke looked towards Ann, but she was lost in a crowd of her friends and wasn't paying attention to her husband. He was constantly amazed at how many people Ann knew even though she'd only lived in Wickham a few years. She had a far wider set of acquaintances than he had.

Nor'west by North

It appeared that Billy had done well. Holbrooke remembered him as coming from a poor family that his father barely managed to keep together by picking up labouring jobs. It was only through the democracy of youth and the free-and-easy life in a provincial market town that he ever came into contact with a boy such as the young Stiles. If he'd ever thought of it, he'd have imagined that Billy would have followed his father into itinerant, low paid occasional employment, to be a constant drain on the town's poor chest. It was a salutary reminder that he wasn't the only one to have moved up in the world. Billy's rise from near-starving poverty to part-ownership of a chaise was no less a feat – perhaps it was even greater – than his own progress from the son of a sailing master to post-captain.

***

They stayed in the square for half an hour, until Holbrooke and Sophie persuaded Ann that she really should come indoors out of the chill. He had been constantly engaged, meeting and greeting, yet a part of his mind kept returning to his encounter with Billy. It was true that he would need a carriage and he could certainly afford to pay any reasonable rates. In fact, he needed one at his disposal for the next few weeks, while *Argonaut* was in the yard. It would be an intolerable nuisance to be forever engaging carriages at need, and Wickham wasn't London where they were available for hire on every street corner. Nor was Portsmouth much better. He'd been content to hire carriages at need up to now and, as a commander, it attracted no notice. As a post-captain, however, and as one with a large amount in prize money lodged at his bank in London, whether he liked it or not there was a certain dignity of rank to be maintained. He spotted Billy walking towards the King's Head with clear intent.

'Would you mind if I leave you for a moment, dear?' Holbrooke asked. 'Perhaps Sophie would walk home with you.'

'Oh, did you not hear me? Sophie has invited us for tea,

we're bound for Bere House.'

'In which case I'll be only a few minutes behind you.'

Holbrooke strode across the square and hailed Billy just before he disappeared into the King's Head.

'I've been thinking about your proposal, Mister Stiles,' Holbrooke said, dropping the Christian name as this was business. 'I would like to view the chaise and then, if it meets my needs, we can discuss terms.'

Billy looked ruefully at the door of the inn, torn between his thirst and his livelihood. But his instinct for business, his need for customers in these dog days before the weather warmed and people started travelling again, had the better of the argument.

'I'll fetch it immediately, your honour, within the hour, before it grows dark. I know where you live.'

'Better to bring it to Bere House,' Holbrooke said, pointing at the Featherstone home just a few steps from the inn. 'I believe we will be there for some time.'

***

Billy was as true as his word and within the hour, measured by the clock in the square that regulated Wickham's daily life, he swung a little two-horse, two-door covered chaise to a halt in front of Bere House. As Holbrooke came out of the door, he was still officiously dusting it down.

'I beg your pardon, your honour, but I wasn't expecting to show it today and hadn't had time to shine it up.'

Holbrooke walked around the vehicle. It would be unremarkable in Portsmouth but for a town like Wickham it was almost pretentious. He wondered how Billy and his unknown partner found enough clients to maintain their business.

'It's sprung fore and aft,' said Billy, hoping that a smattering of sea language would ease the deal.

Holbrooke smiled. *Fore and aft* was fine but *Sprung* in naval terms referred to a cracked mast. However, he knew what Billy meant, the body of the carriage was suspended on stout leather straps that would ease the shock of the holes and bumps in the road.

'How long will you need it for, your honour?' Billy asked, seeing a growing approval in Holbrooke's manner.

'A week at a time,' Holbrooke replied, inspecting the interior. It had two doors and a hard roof and was furnished in dressed leather with velvet curtains. It would be comfortable for two passengers and only mildly cramped for four. There was no provision for a footman – for which Holbrooke was privately grateful – and the only crew would be the driver. There was a fold-down step for passengers to board and alight, and Holbrooke tested it to make sure it was safe for Ann. 'I believe I will be home for two weeks, but I cannot be certain. A week at a time if you please.'

Billy was clearly on the point of naming a price when Ann and Sophie came out to join Holbrooke. One thing that Billy knew about dealing with a rich man – and he certainly included Holbrooke in that category – was that if his wife approved of the chaise, then he could safely raise his price by twenty per cent. He could have rubbed his hands at the sight of Ann *and* her stepmother examining the vehicle with obvious approval.

'It'll need it to be available at short notice, Mister Stiles,' Holbrooke said when they were alone again. 'The Porto Bello is too far away, and I would have to send a messenger every time.'

'I can keep it at the King's Head, sir,' he said, 'and I can sleep there as well. You'll have it available at a moment's notice any time of the day or night.'

Billy thought quickly. His normal daily hire rate was eight shillings, but that was based on the coach being used only two or three days a week. If he was guaranteed seven days of hire, then he could afford to do it for four shillings and sixpence a day. But there was the cost of stabling at the King's Head, and he'd need to be presentable as a coachman-cum-footman, so he'd want a bed for himself as well. Say five shillings and sixpence a day, one pound eighteen shillings and sixpence for the week. Would George Holbrooke balk at that? He didn't think so. He opened his mouth to speak then thought again, rapidly adding something for the bargain.

'Two pounds ten shillings for the week, your honour, all found.'

Billy stood still, hardly breathing. It was a bold bid, but it might just work.

Holbrooke thought for a moment. He was unused to this kind of transaction and had little experience to fall back on. Nevertheless, he knew that old friendships notwithstanding, he was an easy mark for tradesmen of all kinds, and Billy would be no exception. Guineas were always a good bargaining tool, both ways.

'I'll give you two guineas a week, starting at noon tomorrow,' he said, 'half at the start and half when the week is over, and I'll expect the same rate if I need another week.'

Billy pretended to think it over. He muttered a few words including something about his partner and the cost of fodder. Then, after a decent interval to impress upon Holbrooke that he had a good deal, he brightened.

'Then I'll be here at twelve o'clock, your honour,' he said, and smiled broadly.

***

CHAPTER TWENTY-FIVE

Perilous Politics

Wednesday, Ninth of April 1760.
Wickham, Hampshire.

Carriages were not a familiar sight on Bridge Street unless they were passing through. It was largely because the houses were not of the sort to attract people wealthy enough to either own or hire one, but also because the street was too steep for vehicles to stop. Holbrooke had agreed with Billy that the chaise would wait at the top where it joined the square. There were two substantial houses on the corner and the second of them had a wide cobbled public way in front. It was an altogether more likely place to find a privately hired carriage and it was only a walk of a hundred yards from the house on Bridge Street.

They'd been bidden to the port admiral's residence for dinner at the newly fashionable time of half past two o'clock. The admiral's residence was close alongside the wall of the yard at Portsmouth, and it was twelve miles from Wickham along reasonably well-maintained roads.

'I've always thought that was a pleasant house,' said Holbrooke, waving his arm to his left as they stepped up into the coach. 'It's on the square but set back far enough to avoid most of the bustle of market days and it must have all the amenities, judging by its size.'

Ann looked at the house without much interest. She'd known it ever since her father bought the corn merchant's business in Wickham, and she could see it from her old bedroom window in Bere House. It was a brick-built house on three stories in the style that was popular when Queen Anne was on the throne. The style was still a firm favourite during the previous George's reign, but it was starting to look a little dated. The lower windows had brick arches with moulded stone impost bands and the copings higher up were also of moulded stone. *A desirable gentleman's residence that has matured with age*, an agent for the sale of such a property would no doubt say.

'Do you know who owns it now?' he asked. 'When I was a child, it used to be an old, old man who lived alone but he must have passed on by now.'

Ann didn't answer, she was smiling and waving out of the window at friends and acquaintances. Wednesday was market day in in Wickham and the square was crowded with people buying and selling, and others just enjoying the bustle.

'Beg your pardon, sir,' said Billy, 'but I couldn't help hearing you. Mister Strapp lived there alone for as long as I can remember, but he passed on two years ago. There was some problem with the probate, a disagreement between nephews somewhere to the north, they say, but it will soon be up for sale or rent.'

'Thank you, Billy,' Holbrooke replied, not attaching any importance to the answer.

There was a pause while Ann made herself comfortable and Holbrooke tucked a blanket around her legs. He rapped twice on the roof and with a theatrical crack of the whip the coach started moving. There was only one way that the coach could go towards Portsmouth, and despite the crowds, that way led through the crowded square. The space between the tightly packed market stalls and carts and the houses at the east side of the square was only just wide enough for the chaise, and the shoppers were forced aside to make a passage. It could have led to an ugly incident, but Wickham was not yet sated with the novelty of its own naval hero, and the chaise rolled out of the square followed by a swell of good-hearted cheer.

***

Nor'west by North

Dinner with the port admiral passed off well. He had recently shifted his flag ashore and his wife had determined that he would start to live like a normal human being instead of entertaining on board in an all-male environment. She had insisted that he invite only married officers – three on this occasion – and those with their wives close to hand. Being Portsmouth, that category covered fully half of the navy.

Under the moderating influence of his wife, Holburne was positively mellow. There were no barbed comments about captains choosing to consult their ease ashore, no suspicious interrogations about stores or damage. Ann had taken it all in her stride and the admiral's wife, full of solicitude for a young lady in her first pregnancy, left the gentlemen before the third remove and carried Ann and the wives of the two other officers away on waves of good-natured fellowship along with large helpings of pudding.

'Well, that went rather well,' Holburne said after the men were alone. 'I dreaded asking Frances to leave us to it, but it seems that your lovely wife has reawakened a sort of motherly instinct in her. I raise my glass to the better participants in our marriages!'

'Now, Captain Holbrooke, perhaps you can be persuaded to give us an account of Batiste's demise?'

Holbrooke cleared his throat. He knew very well that this was coming but it was always a trial to have to recount a battle in which he had been engaged. There was a fine line to be navigated between bold bragging and simpering modesty. In this case, the action off the Isle of Man, it was difficult to find anything to say that didn't reflect well on him, or on Chester, and although *Fortune* hadn't been so lucky, he didn't feel it was right to highlight Coulson's failings. Yet he had a good audience. Admiral Holburne had invited two other post-captains to the dinner, Gratton of *Audacious* and Franks of *Naiad*, and they could read between the lines of the narrative as well as anyone. And the story was worth telling. So far, he was the only participant to reach a naval port. The other two captains, as far as he knew, were still at Douglas refitting and repairing the prizes before embarking on the long voyage home. They asked questions about *Pegasus* and *Argonaut* but were too polite to quiz Holbrooke about *Fortune*. Not so Admiral Holburne who dug into each part of the battle, into each of the separate actions, until he knew everything he wanted to know. Holburne made no mention of Coulson by name, but it was clear to the three captains that his card had been marked, perhaps only with a question mark, but still…

'Well, we can expect to see Chester nominated for a seat in parliament before the year's out,' said Gratton, laughing.

Holburne glared at him disapprovingly.

'That's no laughing matter,' he said. 'Juggling a naval and a political career demands making choices that are not for the faint-hearted. I would advise any sea officer to think twice and then think again.'

There was silence for a moment. They all knew that Holburne was moving heaven and earth to be nominated for a safe seat, but none chose to mention it.

'We all have to make difficult decisions in the service. Good God, I was on Byng's court martial board, after all, but those decisions are made doubly, trebly more difficult if you're looking over your shoulder for the political consequences.'

Was that an allusion to Holburne's well known – infamous even – insistence on Byng's guilt and his determination that the board should not be relieved of their oaths of silence in order to plead for a mitigation of the punishment? Although he'd been at the fatal battle of Minorca, Holbrooke was still undecided whether Byng had been justly tried and legally executed or whether he had been the victim of a political conspiracy to save the government of the day.

'And yet sea officers still clamour for seats,' said Franks. 'You must have thought of it, Holbrooke, after the service you have done for your country.'

Holbrooke came close to jumping out of his seat. Yes, he'd thought about it but only because so many people around him raised the subject. He still thought it was a chimera, a will-o'-the-wisp, a fantasy that could never become a reality. He knew nobody who had a seat in their pocket, had no political friends, and there were legions of men far older and with far better claims than he who were daily manoeuvering to find a way through the invisible wall that surrounded the selection of candidates.

'Me? No, I assure you, gentlemen...'

Holbrooke realised that he was stammering but he hoped that at least he sounded sincere. He didn't want to be tagged with the label of a parliamentary hopeful, not when so many other matters were demanding his attention and, in all probability, he would never want it.

The admiral gave Holbrooke an appraising stare.

'Well, tread carefully all ye who pass this way, I say.'

***

'Did you speak of anything important, dear, after we left?'

The chaise was rattling its way back towards Wickham and they had just passed through the Hilsea Lines. The army had cut a good road between the chalk escarpment and the top of Portsmouth Harbour all the way to Fareham, and they would make good time on that stretch. It was the road from Fareham to Wickham that would delay them, but at least they would pass it before dusk.

'Oh, just service matters,' Holbrooke lied, not wishing to reveal the talk of a political career before he had determined his own mind on the subject, 'who's getting which ship, who's going on half pay, what Pitt and Anson will do next to force the French to sue for terms.'

'Do you think the French will be brought to terms,' she asked. 'I do hope so, then you'll be able to come home.'

'Oh, I dare say they are thinking of it although they've already lost the greater part of their overseas territory. You could say that they have little left to lose by continuing the war. In any case, while they have a hope of recruiting Spain to their cause, I believe they will keep fighting.'

He was replying carelessly, the admiral's wine having dulled his senses, otherwise he would have saved his wife's feelings. He didn't see the sudden change, how quiet and withdrawn she had become.

'What did you talk about?' he asked.

Before Ann replied he knew that he had been manoeuvred into asking that question. That had been the point of Ann's question, to force him to reciprocate.

'Oh, women's things,' she replied innocently.

Holbrooke nodded, satisfied with the answer, and gazed out of the window at the upper reaches of Portsmouth Harbour.

'And then the subject came on to homes. I was forced to describe our rented cottage and Frances – isn't that strange that the admiral and his wife have such similar names – was shocked! It hadn't occurred to me that Bridge Street was so far below your station. You must think me so naïve, and she didn't say so, not in so many words, but it was clear that she thought it too small a place to bring up our child. What do you think, George? Is it too small, too lowly?'

Holbrooke was shaken out of his torpor. He hadn't really thought about it other than a vague plan that when he was without a ship, when the war ended or when he fell out of favour at the Admiralty, they would find a larger place to live.

'You must have considered it, George, otherwise you wouldn't have so deliberately mentioned the house on the square.'

'Oh, I meant nothing by that other than to point out how handsome a building it is and how well located. It's too big for us. But I tend to agree, the cottage will feel small when there are three of us and Polly. The lease is up next month, would you like to think of a larger place?'

'I don't know, George, I really don't know. A larger

house will mean more servants and they'll need to be managed. The thought of it makes me tired. Can we think about it, later?'

They sped on past Portchester with its Norman castle built upon Roman foundations, and on to the tidal mill at the head of the Fareham Creek where they turned off the military road, north towards Wickham. The leaves were starting to burst out now and the slanting late afternoon sun cast a green iridescent halo over every tree that they passed. Holbrooke was happy, pleased to be in Hampshire in the spring and delighted to be sharing a carriage ride with his wife, in the certain knowledge that tomorrow, within five minutes, they could call on this same chaise to take them anywhere they wanted to go. Life was good, he decided.

'I don't even know what sort of house we can afford,' Ann said, in denial of her plea to think about it later, 'we never seem to have the time to discuss those matters.'

Holbrooke turned and smiled. In the bag of mail that had been waiting for him at Portsmouth was a letter from Campbell & Coutts, his London banker. It had included a statement of his account and the figure at the bottom right corner of the page was inexplicably greater than he could possibly have imagined. The second letter that he opened was from his prize agent on Bond Street, Hawkins & Hammond, which solved the mystery; he had been awarded a share of the prize money from Howe's raids on the Brittany coast two years before. The same letter pointed out that the prizes taken during the Niagara campaign of 'fifty-nine were before the Admiralty court and he could expect them to be condemned in the present session. He had been amused by a short informal note on the turned-back corner of the letter: *The town is aflame with rumours of the capture of Batiste's expedition, in which I understand you took a part. My congratulations, sir.* The word *capture* had been underlined for emphasis and it was initialled *H*. Clearly his stock was high on both The Strand and Bond Street.

'There are few houses in Wickham that we can't afford,

dear. Rookesbury is out of our range of course, but the houses on the square, I imagine, are all attainable.'

If he only knew what thoughts and ideas he had started with that simple confession.

***

Ann was tired after her long day; the travelling had worn her out and she took an early supper and retired. Holbrooke paced for a while, his mind now full of new possibilities as he methodically dissected the conversation at the admiral's residence and in the coach on the way home. The talk of politics was nonsense, of course, but a house of his own? That was much more sensible. He was forcibly reminded of the cramped quarters here at Bridge Street as he stooped to pass through each door and the furthest that he could walk in one direction was a mere five short strides. He could have gone outside into the yard, of course, but that was no larger and the damp had started to set in, making the moss-grown flagstones slippery. He didn't want to retire yet and he knew that he'd disturb his wife if he came to bed so soon. With a start he realised that he had not yet visited his father, who was only half a mile away. Chalmers was there too; he and his father had formed a friendship that had started with a mutual passion for angling and now Chalmers invariably stayed at the Holbrooke cottage when he was in Portsmouth.

He looked out of the window. It was still not fully dark; he could walk there and then borrow a lantern to walk back when it would surely be fully dark. Resolved, he pulled on his boots, and started to reach for his cloak.

'Are you going out, sir?'

Polly heard his movements. Even if he had wanted to leave quietly, he knew it was impossible.

'I'll be stepping over to the cottage,' he said. 'I expect I'll be back before midnight.'

'Wait a moment, sir, and I'll run over to the King's Head and fetch your chaise.'

Polly started to turn away to fetch her own outdoor

shoes and cloak.

'That won't be necessary, Polly, I can perfectly well walk it.'

Polly turned sharply and placed her hands on her hips in a confrontational pose.

'What would Mrs Holbrooke say, sir? It's getting dark, there's rain in the air and you've paid good money for a chaise. There was talk of poachers on the Rookesbury estate and you don't want to get tangled up in that. Now you sit down, and I'll have Billy Stiles here in a jiffy.'

Holbrooke opened his mouth to dismiss Polly's impertinence, then realised that she was probably right. The days when he could wander the roads alone at night were gone. They had faded with his commission as a lieutenant, tended towards absurdity when he was promoted to commander and vanished entirely with his posting; he just hadn't yet come to terms with the fact. Ann would agree whole-heartedly with Polly, there was no doubt of it. He also knew that Polly's cup was overflowing with delight at being the only servant in a house that had its own carriage, however temporary it may be. The opportunity to march boldly into the King's Head and demand that Billy Stiles put down his tankard and attend to his patron was almost more joy than she could bear.

Was he in danger of becoming a martyr to an overbearing servant? Probably, he decided, but it would do no good to impose his will on the household and then disappear to sea again for God-knew how long. He would just have to live with it.

***

Holbrooke knew that it was only sensible, but as he sat in the chaise trundling the half mile to his father's cottage, he felt ludicrous. He would have been there half an hour earlier if he hadn't had to wait for Billy to dress in his coachman's attire, harness the horses and bring them across the square to the corner of Bridge Street. To make matters worse, the coach had to pass downhill in front of the rented house, with the brake squealing enough to wake the dead; he was sure that it would have disturbed Ann. And what would his father think? He was a retired sailing master and had never had any airs and graces. Holbrooke was afraid that he may look as though he was showing off.

The road was in deep shadow by the time the chaise crossed the bridge by the dip hole and turned cautiously onto the Alton road. It was that time of day when objects became indistinct, but lanterns were of no help. As they passed the church, he could see the verger lighting the porch but otherwise the road was empty as they departed the town. On their left side the trees spread upwards from the unseen river while on their right the tenant fields of the Rookesbury estate crowded close to the road. The cottage came upon him suddenly. He remembered that its light couldn't be seen from the road until a traveller was almost upon it. Billy knew that, of course, and the chaise edged carefully off the road and onto the tiny gravel frontage. Holbrooke was relieved to see that there were lanterns shining through the windows. It would have been an embarrassing end to the day if his father and Chalmers were not at home.

***

CHAPTER TWENTY-SIX

Local Boy

Wednesday, Ninth of April 1760.
The Holbrooke Cottage, Wickham.

Father and son eyed each other appraisingly. For his part, George Holbrooke became forcefully aware of how much his father had aged in the few months since he had last seen him. He'd given up his teaching position at the naval academy in Portsmouth. It was to take advantage of the spring fishing, he said, but really at his age he must have become an anomaly, and the recent advances in navigation must surely have challenged him.

William Holbrooke, meanwhile, tried to keep the surprise from showing in his face. He'd noticed a change in his son when he was posted and given a new frigate to command, and that was only natural, a post-captain's commission was a serious matter. Yet there was a more fundamental change. George was not yet twenty-two, still a boy as far as William was concerned, but his demeanour, his poise, was that of a much more mature man. William had become a father late in life and his wife Mary had died when George was still young, so he could be excused for taking a sentimental view of his only child. He was impressed, but not at all sure that he was comfortable with the man that his son had become.

David Chalmers, the ever-vigilant observer of the human condition, watched the two with interest. He was attached to both of them. In fact, it could be said that he had no other friends in the world, except Jackson the bosun who had followed Holbrooke from ship to ship, much as Chalmers himself had. His residence at the cottage was a settled affair by now, and he had moved his few possessions into George's old room and offered his services at the church, *pro bono*. If he could be said to reside anywhere, it was in Wickham and if he could be said to have a patron then it was certainly George Holbrooke, to whose rising star he was immovably attached.

'I'd given up hope of seeing you,' said William, shaking his son's hand, 'and you have a coach, I hear,' he added looking out of the door at the two horses stamping and snorting.

'Just for the week, Father, and perhaps a few days more if *Argonaut* is delayed in the yard. That reminds me. I must tell Mister Stiles when I need him again. May I assume my welcome extends to the next two hours?' he asked, smiling.

Holbrooke ducked under the low lintel of the door and stepped outside to give his orders.

'Is that young Billy Stiles? How d'ye do, Billy?' William asked. He'd known Billy since he'd been a young tearaway, stealing apples and pears from the trees in the cottage garden.

'Very well, Mister Holbrooke,' he replied with a proud sweep of his hand to indicate the fine carriage that he owned in part, 'and I hope you are in good health, sir.'

'Couldn't be better, Billy, couldn't be better. I would offer you an apple but it's not the season.'

Billy's grin was caught in the lamplight. It was tacitly agreed that youthful indiscretions could be forgiven with the passage of time, even if they weren't forgotten.

They watched as Billy turned the coach in the road. It was a tricky manoeuvre, executed with skill, but William still quietly moved a clay plant pot to preserve it from the coach's wheels.

***

George Holbrooke walked quietly around the parlour, looking to see what had changed, as everyone does in returning to their childhood home. William was deeply attached to the memory of his wife, even after so many years, and George could find little that he didn't recognise from his earliest memories. Mary Holbrooke's benign ghost was everywhere, comforting and protective. Holbrooke loved the peace of this room, just as he had as a young boy when he'd run in sobbing from a scraped knee. The girl that came daily to help William knew that nothing was to be moved, nothing added, and nothing taken away. It was a place out of time, and he wondered how Chalmers felt as a stranger in such a hallowed, venerated room. Perhaps he didn't notice it, but then his other profession, as a man of the cloth, presumably made the atmosphere of the cottage quite familiar.

Supper was a simple affair of bread and cheese and ham, with small beer. It came as a relief to George, who was still feeling the effects of the admiral's dinner table. They talked as they ate, but it was unsatisfactory, in a way. George struggled for things to say to his father who already knew all about *Argonaut*'s doings from Chalmers, and for his part he found that the gossip of a small town didn't much interest him.

'You missed Edward Carlisle, you know,' William said. 'He brought *Dartmouth* in after he'd delivered his convoy from the Americas, and he was good enough to call on me. He had a quick scrape of her bottom and a few fathoms of caulking then he sailed again for the Mediterranean with Admiral Saunders.'

'I had a letter from him, waiting for me at the port admiral's office. He seems to be thriving although he's yearning for some time at his home in Williamsburg.'

'Do you think he's settled there?' William asked. 'It's a strange place for a post-captain to put down his roots. Even stranger for that foreign wife of his, I expect.'

'As far as I can tell, Lady Chiara loves the place. What do you think, David?'

Chalmers was never quick to answer, he preferred to consider carefully before committing himself.

'You haven't met her, have you, William?'

'Not I,' he replied, shaking his head, 'although I'm told she's a rare beauty.'

Chalmers looked as though he was choosing his next

words carefully.

'Lady Chiara – it's an honorary title you know – is one of the world's rootless people, and to understand her you need to know her history. She grew up in a Genoese enclave in North Africa and when that fell to the Dey of Algeria she and her father fled step by step to Nice, part of Sardinia by that time. She has no concept of her nationality, not as we know it, and unless I'm mistaken the house of Angelini has no place for her. Virginia absorbs people like that; to a certain extent you can be whoever you want to be, and she finds that fascinating. My opinion – and it's only mine – is that she will never willingly live in either Sardinia or England. She has a forceful personality, you know, and whether he likes it or not, Edward Carlisle is destined to return to the place of his birth.'

George nodded slowly.

'Bravo, David, I believe you have captured the situation exactly.'

'Then he'll find it difficult to progress further in his career when the war is over,' William said, 'but it sounds like he doesn't much care.'

'I pity him, really,' David added.

The two Holbrooke's looked at him in surprise.

'Do you know that there are no brown trout in Virginia? Oh, they have something similar, I'm told. Brook trout, they call them, and their spots are lighter than the body colour. On their backs, their spots merge to form patterns of lines. It goes against nature, and they're nothing like the true Meon browns.'

'Which we will be angling for tomorrow, without a doubt,' William added.

***

'So, you survived a dinner with Admiral Holburne,' his father asked when the conversation was in danger of lapsing into silence. 'That's more than many a young officer can say. He has a fearsome reputation.'

'Oh, we are old protagonists. I've come to understand

his methods,' George replied. 'You see, he wants to start by weakening you, then when he's stripped your defences bare and has seen you as nature intended, if he's satisfied, he eases off. Then you can have a sensible discussion with him.'

'You're becoming a philosopher,' Chalmers laughed.

'I've learned from the best,' George replied with a mock bow.

'And what is it that occupies the port admiral's mind today,' William asked, 'apart from his perennial tussle with the dark forces arrayed behind the officers of the King's Yard.'

Holbrooke smiled again. That was something that all sea officers could agree upon. From the master attendant down, the motivations of the management and workers in the yard were quite different to those of the sea officers who in the end were their customers. Continuity of employment and a smooth flow of work were everything to them, and the end result, a ship ready to be taken to sea to fight the King's enemies, was barely considered. At least, that was how it looked from a sea officer's perspective.

'He wanted to know all about Batiste, of course, and he pressed me hard on the conduct of my fellow captains.'

William looked up swiftly, he hoped his son wasn't becoming the sort of sharp-elbowed, ambitious officer that climbed through the service upon the shattered remains of his colleagues. He'd known enough of them in his career.

'Oh, I was very circumspect, but he's a wily old bird, you know, and Coulson didn't cover himself in glory. The fact is that he was beaten, and if *Pegasus* and *Argonaut* hadn't been there, *Fortune* would be flying the white of France by now.'

William looked down at his plate. To him, loyalty was everything and even if it came to outright lying, he would cover his brother officers' failings.

'Then we talked broadly about politics and how it's a perilous path for a serving officer to take.'

'Pah! That's rich, coming from Holburne,' William said, 'I trust you're not tempted…'

The elder Holbrooke stopped uneasily. He realised that he may be taking his son's attitude for granted. He didn't know him anymore, not as he used to. It would only cause friction if he were too absolute in his condemnation of political officers when it was gradually dawning upon him that George could be one himself, in the fulness of time.

George smiled and patted his father's arm, a curiously comforting gesture for the older man.

'I have far too much on my plate to worry about politics,' he said. 'And in any case, I know nobody and am known by nobody. The whole thing is just a fantasy.'

'I spoke to Mister Garnier the other day. He said that he hoped you would dine with him. Now there's a man to watch, he has fingers in every pie in the borough.'

'Yes, I'm dining at Rookesbury House tomorrow.'

'Ann will be with you?'

'No, Garnier hasn't invited Ann, and in any case, she's looking forward to a quiet day after our visit to Portsmouth. You know, she really stepped up to the mark at the admiral's residence.'

'No women invited? Then you can be sure that Garnier is going to talk politics. Rumour has it that he's looking for a candidate in Wickham to put forward for county magistrate.'

'Then he can think again, Father. I've too much to occupy my mind without thoughts of being a justice of the peace. This war has some years to go yet, and I must make the most of it. There'll be plenty of time to consider my future when I'm cast ashore. David and I have discussed this before, he knows my mind.'

Chalmers inclined his head and smiled, keeping his thoughts to himself. *Do I know your mind? Do you know it yourself? I very much doubt it.*

'That may be so, George, but do remember, he who sups with the devil should have a long spoon.'

***

Nor'west by North

Billy arrived punctually and Holbrooke took his leave. It was wholly dark by now and the riverside trees seemed to squeeze the road, their branches overhanging and waving towards the fields and low hedges on the other side. He clutched the slim book that Chalmers had pressed on him while William Holbrooke was occupied in the kitchen, a loan from the parson, he'd said. For some reason he felt that his father shouldn't know about it and had quickly slipped it into his pocket.

By the dim light of the chaise's lantern, he could just spell out the title on the cheap card cover: 'The Magistracy of England: Its History and its Ancient Obligations.'

Well. He couldn't fault his friend for trying to protect him. If he were to be in a position to make a defensive case tomorrow, he should at least know what he was talking about.

The chaise swung onto the bridge and Billy whipped up the horses to make the climb up Bridge Street and the left turn into the square.

'Half past one tomorrow, Billy, unless you hear from me earlier, and I hope you have a peaceful night. I'm afraid the tap at the King's Head will be closed by now.'

'Right you are, sir,' Billy replied, touching his whip to his hat.

Billy swung the chaise diagonally across the square and through the gate that led to the livery at the back of the inn. He'd already heard rumours that connected Holbrooke and a soon-to-be-vacant magistracy. It mattered not at all to him, so long as the justices left the old ways alone, and his next stop was a good example of that. As soon as he'd seen to the horses and covered his driving seat against the anticipated rain, he walked boldly into the back room of the King's Head. The dim light of a shaded lantern struggled to pierce the fug of tobacco smoke but what light it did offer revealed a surprisingly large number of men sitting around the tables or standing against the walls. The click of dice could be heard from one corner while in another the bowed heads and silence showed that a serious game of cards was under way. This was a nightly democratic gathering of the high and the low of Wickham society, with a smattering of farmers from outlying hamlets, and it had been going on since time immemorial, law or no law.

***

Holbrooke was let in by Polly who looked as tired as he felt. Nevertheless, he asked for a candle and refused any refreshment. He sent Polly back to bed and sat himself beside the fireplace where the embers still had some heat. He took the book from his pocket. It was indeed a slim volume, perhaps no more than thirty pages with well-spaced type, and it had been produced as cheaply as was possible. It was the sort of book that was thrust upon a thrifty reader, purporting to tell the whole story but really only scratching the surface. He noticed a price inked on the inside cover: sixpence. That was about the rock-bottom price for a book of any kind; he wondered whether it had any value at all. A quick skim showed that it at least attempted to do what it said on the cover. There was a brief history of the magistracy, for context, he assumed. The next three chapters covered the appointment of magistrates, their duties and their *modus operandi*.

This was a world of which Holbrooke knew nothing. He'd heard of magistrates and justices of the peace, but the fact that they were two names for the same office had entirely eluded him. He knew that they dispensed justice at petty sessions and quarter sessions, and he was vaguely aware that they could refer complicated cases or capital offences to a higher court, but the detail that lay behind those bare assumptions was lost to him. As he read, he realised just how little he knew. Roads, public buildings, lunatic asylums, the poor laws, gaols, licensing of public houses, the militia, the police, county taxation, all of those were administered by the magistracy. Minor theft and larceny, assault, drunkenness, bastardy examinations and arbitration were among the judicial matters that came under their authority. It was a fascinating world that he had never given much thought to.

Holbrooke read right through the book and closed its covers as the candle started to gutter. He sat in the dark for a few minutes, the moon shining through the curtains affording him a meagre light. Did he want this in his future? He really couldn't tell, but of one thing he was certain, he would bring a very long spoon to dinner at Rookesbury.

***

CHAPTER TWENTY-SEVEN

Sea-Change

Thursday, Tenth of April 1760.
Wickham.

The chaise was waiting in front of the intriguing house at the corner of the square, with the horses stamping and fretting, eager to be moving. Holbrooke was starting to get used to having his own transport, available at his merest whim. He was becoming inured to the stares of the townsfolk as he strode towards the carriage, his cane in hand in lieu of his sword. The blustery wind set the harnesses jingling and blew Billy's coat around as he hurried to settle his passenger. They started rolling down Bridge Street and Holbrooke barely noticed the children that ran alongside risking life and limb under the iron-shod wheels.

Billy knew the way to Rookesbury house; who didn't? It was the largest place locally and the Rookesbury estate sprawled away to the northeast of the town. The house was clearly visible from both the Alton road and the Southwick road. It could be viewed beyond the noble English scenery of tall elms, majestic oaks and sheep-nibbled parkland that lay between the house and the two major highways. In fact, Holbrooke could be said to have grown up on the Rookesbury estate. His father's cottage was a freehold enclave within the estate and the stretch of river that the cottage's fishing rights pertained to ran entirely through Rookesbury land. The last time he had come here, he remembered, had been at Christmas two years before, and there he had met Ann for the first time. Rookesbury was implanted firmly and irrevocably in his personal history.

The chaise crossed the bridge and turned onto the Southwick road. Past the church that sat on its small hill and then sharp left into the drive leading up to the big house. Holbrooke couldn't help but be impressed, and that led to him wondering whether he could ever be a master of a house and estate such as this. It had been done before, and it had been entirely funded by prize money in many cases. Dreams, dreams, this would never do. He pinched himself and sat upright preparing himself for meeting the men of consequence in this part of rural Hampshire.

***

George Garnier was the owner of the copyhold of the Rookesbury Estate. His grandfather had fled France a hundred years ago, along with thousands of other Protestants whose lives and liberty were threatened by the revocation of the Edict of Nantes. The refugee's son had married a rich heiress who brought with her the copyhold of the house and land. For a man of consequence, Garnier carried his dignity and his post as physician to the Duke of Cumberland and apothecary-general of the army lightly. He was genial and approachable, but he clearly held in his hands most of the strings that controlled Wickham and the outlying villages and hamlets. For all his medical knowledge he didn't look well at all. How old would he be? In his late fifties, perhaps, although his hollow cheeks, his stoop and his dry skin made him look much older.

There were two other men at dinner: Parker, who was a county magistrate with the girth of a dedicated gourmand yet the exquisite manners of a nobleman, and Watkins, tall, lean, and with his own hair tied in a queue for all the world like a common seaman. Watkins owned a large estate further along the road towards Southwick and to judge by the way that Garnier deferred to him, it was a more substantial property than Rookesbury. Holbrooke wondered whether it was Watkins who owned the freehold of Rookesbury estate; that would account for the deference. He was vaguely aware of the different forms of land ownership in England, but the detail eluded him, and he had no idea how it might impact upon the relative status of the holders.

It was a gruelling dinner for Holbrooke. He was evidently being sounded out, his suitability for a magistracy or some other county position was being assessed. There were no direct offers and no clear indication of when a position may become available or even what that position might be. Was this how things were done? He wasn't at all sure that he liked or approved of it. However, there it was, an opportunity, perhaps, should he wish to take it. Parker had spoken earnestly –yet without commitment – about the need for a magistrate who would be in place for the long term, rather than one who saw it merely as a steppingstone to greater things. He wasn't concerned about periods when the candidate may not be available in the county, and the prospect of having to wait a few years for the right man wasn't a block to appointment to the office. There never had been a time when all the justices had been in residence simultaneously, and the excuse of being required abroad on the King's business was always acceptable. The important thing was to be committed to the county and to the town, and to have sound political views. What those views should be was not made clear.

At the end, Holbrooke was still unsure whether he'd passed muster and even less sure whether he would take the post if an offer were made. He left feeling dissatisfied both with the three men who had subjected him to such a hard grilling, and with himself for not demanding clear answers to his own questions. He was keenly aware that every inquiry had been met with hints and evasions. At one time Parker had even winked knowingly at him, although what he was supposed to know, Holbrooke couldn't tell. To cap it all, he had the suspicion that he'd been patronised and wasn't at all sure that he'd behaved with the lofty dignity that his new rank demanded. The short drive back to Wickham was barely long enough for him to regain his humour.

***

George and Ann walked the few short steps up Bridge Street to the square. The wind had turned into the west and the grey overcast sky promised rain showers, again. Polly had anxiously adjusted Ann's cloak and bonnet and mittens so that no drop of water should penetrate to her skin. Polly, Ann was starting to realise, was becoming a dedicated fusspot and she suspected that it would only get worse as her pregnancy progressed.

'What is the name of this gentleman we are to meet?' Ann asked as they turned the corner.

'Ferrers, he's a solicitor. As soon as I asked a question about the house Garnier sent his man to Fareham with a note that I didn't see. I immediately regretted asking the question, but before dinner had ended, his man had returned with an assurance that we'd be met here at six o'clock. He must have ridden like the wind. I'm afraid I rather landed us in this.'

Ann didn't regret it at all. She didn't want to burden her husband but the burning shame of having to describe the rented cottage to the admiral's wife was still with her. Probably this would come to nothing, but at least, in future, she would be able to say with truth that they were *looking around* for something more suitable.

'What a strange time to do business,' Ann said, glancing at the clock as it chimed the hour. 'Do you think that's him?'

Ann didn't point, she would never have made such a vulgar gesture in public, but the subject of her question was obvious. A man dressed largely in brown – even his stockings were a light dun colour – with an overcoat so vast that it would have gladdened Polly's heart, was standing outside the house that Holbrooke had admired just the day before. Between the tricorn hat and the upturned collar of the overcoat were a pair of astonishingly blue eyes that twinkled out of the shadows like gaudy glass jewels.

'Captain Holbrooke, sir?' he asked, sweeping his brown hat low to the ground to reveal a short wig. 'We have not been introduced, I regret, but our mutual friend Mister Garnier asked me to meet you. Samuel Ferrers of Carter and Ferrers, solicitors on the High Street in Fareham. Perhaps you know of us, sir?'

Holbrooke bowed in reply, just a little less deeply than

Ferrers; he was learning the dignity of his rank, slowly and painfully.

'Sadly not, Mister Ferrers. May I introduce Mrs Holbrooke?

Ann made a short bob in reply to Ferrers' even deeper obeisance. She also was learning the dignity of her husband's rank.

'I'm delighted to meet you, Mrs Holbrooke. I know your father – he nodded towards the other side of the square – we often act for him in his business.'

Holbrooke could have kicked himself. It hadn't occurred to him to talk to his father-in-law before this meeting. Of course they would be acquainted. Martin Featherstone did business as far south as Fareham, further even, and a solicitor in Fareham must naturally have connections in Wickham. Holbrooke looked keenly at Ferrers. If his family circumstances had allowed him to continue his education, this was probably where he would be now: a country solicitor, brokering purchases of land and estate, preparing contracts and indentures and generally being a man of business. He'd had a lucky escape, he knew, although without a good deal of luck in his naval service, he'd only be a lieutenant now and perhaps enjoying a similar social rank to Ferrers. And there was something familiar about Ferrers. Could they have been at school together? No, not school. He couldn't quite place it, but he did have the feeling that he already quite liked Ferrers.

'Now, sir, I understand you would like to view Mulberry House.'

He swept his hat to his right and as if by some mechanical contrivance the pair of doors that faced the street opened inward. Holbrooke peered into the darkness and saw an immensely old man, and a woman who could not have been much younger, standing either side of the entrance. They must have been watching through a spyhole, waiting for Ferrers to make a move.

'After you, Ma'am,' Ferrers said with another flourish of

his hat.

They stepped into the hallway. It had an air of disuse although it was scrupulously clean. The unblemished tiled floor shone redly where the rays of the setting sun reached it, but all beyond was in shadow. The smell of beeswax infused the air with its heady scent.

'The gentleman who lived here passed away two years ago but there have been certain difficulties in clearing probate. Competing claims on the estate, you understand, that I have been attempting to clear. We have chosen to retain two of the staff to keep the place in good order. This is Mister and Mrs Jenkins,' he said as the two servants bowed as low as their stiff old bones would allow.

'Happily, that process is nearing its end,' Ferrers continued, 'and I hope that we will be able to advertise the property in, let us say, three months or so. That is, unless we receive an offer that is acceptable to the beneficiaries before that time.' He looked keenly at Holbrooke to gauge his reaction.

Holbrooke disappointed him by not reacting at all. He nodded at the two servants. Ann smiled at the old lady whom she had seen at the market for years, occasionally exchanging a word or two, although she had never connected her with this house.

'So, perhaps we can look around? If you have any questions, please don't hesitate to ask. I've been so involved with this house that I feel I know it better than my own,' and he let out a low chuckle.

That was it! Holbrooke looked keenly at Ferrers. No, they hadn't met before, but his resemblance to Major Hans Albach of the Austrian Artillery was uncanny. The same build, the same gait and posture and that same laugh. Even their clothing was similar, the Austrian artillery's uniform being predominantly brown. He was prepared to like Ferrers very much. After all, Albach had saved his life on that beach at Saint-Cast and despite being at least nominally on different sides in this war, they had become fast friends.

Ferrer's saw Holbrooke's grin and Ann's answering smile and his heart lightened, he almost skipped. A client who smiled was half won, as any man of business knows.

***

They toured the ground floor of the house, looking in every room and every cupboard, with Ferrers carrying a lighted candle to illuminate the corners.

'How on earth do Mister and Mrs Jenkins keep the place so clean,' Ann asked.

Wasn't that just like her to remember the servants' names, Holbrooke thought. He'd forgotten them as soon as the words were out of the solicitor's mouth.

'Ah, yes, they are a little old. Well, the secret is that I send two people up from Fareham every week to do the heavy cleaning. The Jenkins merely do some light dusting and polishing. You see, as executors of the deceased's will, we can spend as much as is required to maintain the value of the property. You often see places go to rack and ruin between the death of the owner and the clearance of probate, and again while the beneficiaries wait for a buyer. And that, ma'am, is false economy. The buyer of this property will find that it has been kept warm and aired all through the winter and that it is ready for occupancy.'

'What will happen to Mister and Mrs Jenkins?' Ann asked. 'They won't be thrown onto the parish, will they?'

Ferrers glanced at Ann to try to detect why she was asking. Was it out of compassion or out of a reluctance to be encumbered with decrepit tenured servants? What he saw seemed to satisfy him.

'Now that is one of the more morally uplifting aspects of the will. These last two servants – the others were all more-or-less itinerate – have been at the house for nearly half a century. Just imagine, they were here when Queen Anne was on the throne! The deceased gentleman made provision for them in his will, in a way that can't be challenged by the principal beneficiaries.' He smiled conspiratorially, as if to say that the beneficiaries had already attempted to question the matter. 'There is a cottage and a pension allotted to them. However, like the nephews and nieces they must wait for probate.'

Ann nodded happily. She also was starting to like Ferrers.

'Now, shall we assay the upper floors?' He looked questioningly at Ann. How he had spotted it through Polly's generous layers of outer clothing was unclear, but he had evidently noticed her condition. Or perhaps he had already known from his contact with Martin Featherstone.

'I believe I will stay here, Mister Ferrers,' she replied, casting a questioning glance at Holbrooke, who nodded in reply. 'I have a very slight acquaintance with Mrs Jenkins, although I didn't know she was in service here, and I'm sure we'll find something to talk about.'

Ferrers turned to fetch Mrs Jenkins while Ann sat at a little chair beside a gleaming mahogany and green baize card table.

'Ah, here she is, and she's brought tea!' Ferrers exclaimed.

Holbrooke was starting to understand the ties that bound these three strange bedfellows. The Jenkins' knew very well that Ferrers held their future in the palm of his hand, he could always find a fault in the will – despite his assurances to the contrary – if he chose to, and then they could be begging from the parish poor-chest. And that was a matter for the justices, as he now knew. For his part, Ferrers knew that a good part of the sale price of the house was in the gift of this old couple, and as the executor his fee was a percentage of the value of the estate when all the assets had been realised. Probably he hadn't asked for tea, but Mrs Jenkins was eager to please. She and Ann settled down at the table with the pot between them.

***

Holbrooke and Ferrers inspected the first floor and the second floor, the attic rooms and the basement. They saw bedrooms and storerooms, water closets and dressing rooms. Then they returned to the ground floor where they examined the kitchens and sculleries, and they paced the gardens, admired the eponymous mulberry bush in its solitary splendour and rummaged the stables. Everywhere was fresh polish and sparkling glass windowpanes and clean draperies. He had been ready to dismiss the place, but despite himself, Holbrooke was impressed. Yes, it was too big for he and Ann, even after the baby was born, and it would take a staff of at least five to keep it up. And it had to be said that it was just a little old-fashioned and some of the facilities would need to be brought up to date. But perhaps he should be looking to the longer game, making an investment in his family's future. And after all, the price – only as a guide you understand, Ferrers insisted – was within the budget of a successful prize-taking post-captain.

'I expect to have reconciled the warring parties and be able to clear probate by the end of the quarter year, by midsummer day, which I do assure you is very rapid progress indeed, given the obstinacy of the beneficiaries. It wouldn't be inappropriate for a prospective buyer to enter negotiations, let us say, a month from now. Of course,' he added, 'there are other properties of this size in the area, although none so fine and so imminently available as this.'

Holbrooke was struck by the oddly old-fashioned and formal way that Ferrers spoke. Perhaps that was how country solicitors became, mimicking what they imagined were the manners of their grander colleagues in the great cities.

'I understand, Mister Ferrers. As you can imagine Mrs Holbrooke and I must think this over. I'll have to return to my ship in a week or two and I cannot tell when I will be back in Wickham. In the meantime, if anything arises, if the beneficiaries should change their instructions, for example, may I ask that you speak to Mister Featherstone, my father-in-law?'

Ferrers bowed and continued in confidential tones.

'Between you and I, sir, I have never known such enmity

between blood cousins. You would think from the way they contest every issue that a half of them were English and the other half French,' he said, 'although you'd know more about that than I do.'

Holbrooke nodded and smiled.

'Undoubtedly, but in the navy, we have a robust way of solving our differences with the French,' he replied, 'a way that perhaps you couldn't reconcile with your profession.'

'Just so, sir. Just so. Now, may I ask your general impression of the property?'

***

'What did you think?' Ann asked as soon as they were back in the parlour of their rented home.

Holbrooke looked around at the closeness of the walls, at the height of the ceilings and at the overall *cottagey* feel of it. He'd had some salutary lessons over the past few days. He'd learned that there was more to the rank of post-captain than standing tall on his quarter deck as the shot ploughed up the oak planks around him and brought the yards and sails down around his ears. Professionally, a post-captain was further above a commander than a commander was above a lieutenant, and he had willy-nilly moved into a far higher strata of society. Even his father-in-law treated him with a new respect and his own father's surprise had not gone unnoticed. People that he'd known for years expected to be treated with a loft condescension. Take Billy Stiles, for example. They *had* met since they were children, although Billy pretended that he didn't remember. Holbrooke had been a lieutenant then, just after his return from the Mediterranean, and Billy had affected a familiarity that was at odds with his present display of respect. He understood now that he would be approached with business and political proposals, and he had better get used to it. Ann had likewise had her expectations re-moulded; he could tell from the way she also looked around the parlour. Three months ago – no, three days ago – she would have been perfectly happy with the cottage perhaps with the prospect of moving up to a double-front on the square in a couple of years. He had a pang of regret for his lost innocence; they had both suffered a sea-change. He stared out of the window at the old mill opposite. Unbidden, Shakespeare's perceptive lines came to his mind, and before he could stop himself, he was reciting them aloud.

'Full fathom five thy father lies;
Of his bones are coral made;
Those are pearls that were his eyes:
Nothing of him that doth fade
But doth suffer a sea-change
Into something rich and strange.'

Ann looked startled, then nodded her head slowly in understanding. She too had seen a performance of The Tempest and had read the script.

'We still have our fathers dear,' she said, 'so the quote is not strictly apt, but we are losing something, a part of our youth perhaps,' she said thoughtfully. 'A sea-change; that exactly captures my feeling of uncertainty. Six months ago, I had nothing but a vague hope that we could be together. Now I have a handsome post-captain for a husband, who is being wooed by great men, a child on the way and the prospect of a house that far eclipses my old home. I hope I'm not flying too close to the sun.'

Holbrooke stood and held his wife's hand.

'Then we must face this together, you and I, and make a place for ourselves in this rich and strange world.'

***

CHAPTER TWENTY-EIGHT

Unfinished Business

Tuesday, Twenty-Ninth of April 1760.
Argonaut, at Sea, the Seven Stones SSW 6 leagues.

Argonaut swooped and dipped as she ran before the strong sou'westerly gale. It had been blowing hard ever since the frigate left Portsmouth and except for one blessed day of a sou'easterly, the wind had been constantly foul for their passage to the Scilly Isles. A whole week it had taken them, seven days of beating to windward with the cold, cold spray driving into the faces of the men on deck. There had been constant sail changes as Fairview set and furled, reefed and then shook out the reefs from the tops'ls and t'gallants in an effort to claw a few more yards to windward. It was a relief when they lay in relative shelter off St. Mary's for a few hours while Holbrooke was rowed ashore, then they were away to the north and east with the fresh wind at their stern and the promise of spring in the air.

'Mister Shorrock, Mister Fairview, Mister Jackson, can you leave the deck to Petersen? Then join me in my cabin, if you please, and pass the word for Mister Chalmers.'

It was quiet in the great cabin. They could still hear the wind in the rigging as it was transmitted through the shrouds, through the deadeyes and lanyards, to the chains and into the very fabric of the ship, but it was muted compared with the continual howling of a ship fighting its way to windward. The motion was easier too. There was none of the stomach-dropping pitching and the loud slamming of the bows as they hit each wave. The rhythmic lift of the stern, the corkscrew motion as the wave passed forward and the slow descent before the next wave were positively pleasant by comparison. Nevertheless, the fiddles were necessary to keep the coffee cups in place on the table, and the chairs had been lashed to ringbolts.

'You may have been wondering why we turned west after we cleared Portsmouth, rather than east to meet Commodore Boys,' Holbrooke said, watching the faces of the four men. Shorrock and Fairview and Jackson certainly had, but Chalmers' face was inscrutable as ever. He could have been pondering upon the existential meaning of life or the difference between east and west, there was no way of knowing.

'Well, now that we've cleared the Scillies, I feel that I can reveal the contents of my orders. Admiral Holburne was most specific that they should remain a secret until *Argonaut* passed around Land's End. I believe we can be said to have done so now, is that correct Mister Fairview?'

'Aye, sir, we can,' the sailing master replied, 'we *could* beat back to the south from here, but we'd have a hard time of it. I would say that we've rounded Land's End.'

Holbrooke knew his ship's position very well, but he wanted his officers to know that he'd taken the first legally permissible opportunity to reveal the ship's mission. He'd always made it a point to bring his officers into his confidence, but on this occasion the secrecy of the orders had prevented him doing so, until now. He paused a moment, consciously creating a dramatic effect.

'We're to hunt down the fourth frigate and the brig.'

Holbrooke saw the knowing glance that Shorrock threw at Fairview and Jackson. They'd been speculating, certainly, but there were half a dozen good reasons to send a valuable new frigate hurrying westward to the Scillies. Nevertheless, the fate of the last two hulls of Batiste's squadron had been discussed ever since the battle off Jurby Point that had dealt the deathblow to the remainder of the French expedition. It would be unusual if they hadn't considered it. Quite probably there was a wager involved, and from Fairview's wry expression and Shorrock's discreet scratching of his palm, it looked as though his first lieutenant had won.

'Well, it appears that it's not so much of a surprise, nor a secret,' Holbrooke said smiling. 'However that may be, the admiral was concerned that word of our mission might spread and come to the French captain, wherever he's hiding. Our orders are necessarily brief. We've completed the first part, to touch at the Scillies for intelligence. I'll tell you what I learned in a moment, but if I had heard news of the Frenchmen passing that way, southbound, we were to turn east and join Commodore Boys at the Downs or the Nore. As I heard no such thing, we are to proceed to hunt down this frigate and transport brig until we have definite word that they've escaped back to France.'

Fairview pulled a long face.

'When we last heard of them, sir, they were running in to Loch Torridon, and that was more than five weeks ago. They could be anywhere by now, snugged down in Saint-Malo, I don't doubt.'

'Indeed, Mister Fairview. However, the admiral had more current information. It appears that this frigate – *Les Jeux*, is her name – had a separate, subsidiary mission: to stir up trouble among what remains of the Jacobites in the highlands. She did indeed go to Loch Torridon, taking the brig with her, and she stayed there for some days or perhaps even two weeks. Anyhow, her mission appears to have been a failure. The local people gladly accepted the muskets and ammunition that were offered then politely declined to rise against King George. There's a regiment on its way now to round up the weapons, and I don't doubt that the French will have done more harm than good to the people that took them.'

'At least it's not Butcher Cumberland they have to deal with,' Chalmers said. 'There'd be widows aplenty by now if he were still commanding in the north of the country.'

Holbrooke moved on quickly. There was nobody to hear them in the cabin, but it was best not to criticise the royal duke's brutal tactics after Culloden. It was fourteen years ago, but memories were long, and the scars of the battle's aftermath hadn't yet healed.

'As an interesting footnote, it appears that we were at

least partly correct in our assessment of Batiste's aims. A landing in Scotland was never contemplated, in fact it was specifically forbidden. From the perspective of Versailles, the highlanders are seen as sympathetic but not of any value as allies, and it was clear that wherever Batiste's force landed they would need to victual their ships whether they were invited to or not. King Louis chose not to alienate the only friends that he has in Britain.'

'I wish that it was out of compassion,' Chalmers said, 'but I fear that King Louis cares little for his allies, potential or otherwise, and if he saw any value in raising a storm on the west coast, he wouldn't hesitate to do so. These muskets, I take it, were a sort of token gesture, to remind the remaining Jacobites that they still have a King over the water? I hope it won't be a bloody reminder.'

'Well, that's not our business,' Holbrooke said, to close that line of discussion. 'Our sole concern is *Les Jeux*. Like you,' he said looking at Fairview, 'I had imagined that we would be shutting the stable door after the horse had bolted, but I did hear something at St. Mary's.'

A pause: he had their interest now. He was learning that drama and rhetoric had a place in the command of a King's ship.

'A Portuguese wine ship homeward bound from Bristol called at the Scillies for shelter two days ago, and the master, in the course of his normal business, told what appeared then to be an everyday tale of ships sighted. In fact, the harbour master had almost forgotten about it until I asked about sightings of men-o'-war. It turns out now to be an interesting, possibly vital, story. The gales had forced the Portuguese to make a long board to the north and off St. Govan's Head he'd seen a frigate and brig reaching down to the southeast. The frigate had lost a topmast, but from which mast he didn't say. The harbour master didn't have any further details, but it must have been a week ago, at least. The Portuguese could hardly have made the Scillies in less than a week in these gales.'

Nor'west by North

'I beg your pardon,' said Chalmers, 'but where is this headland you speak of?'

Shorrock laughed. 'You really should look at a chart occasionally,' he said. 'We passed St. Govan's after we left the Isle of Man a month ago. It's the southerly tip of Pembroke, in Wales.'

'Don't be too hard on the chaplain,' Fairview said. 'The closest we came to Pembroke was St. David's Head and I'm sure Mister Chalmers remembers that.' He looked at the chaplain. 'After all, it's named after you, so to speak.'

'Ah yes, I remember. Then St. Govan's is to the south of St. David's, I gather.'

'Yes, to the south and east. It's an important mark for anyone steering for Carmarthen Bay.'

Chalmers nodded, apparently not the least put out by Shorrock's mild chafing. Holbrooke realised with a pang of regret that his officers had formed a tight, friendly community that necessarily excluded him. Even Chalmers, his closest acquaintance, had a circle of friendship that he could not join. Well, a life of solitude was just one of the prices that had to be paid for the splendour of his rank.

'And that is all that we have to go on for now,' Holbrooke said.

'Was this master certain that it was a French frigate?' Jackson asked.

'Far from it, Mister Jackson. He made no mention of the nationality. In fact, the harbour master who told me this assumed that it was one of the frigates that look after the Bristol trade, and that's why I didn't ask about French frigates; I kept my enquiry broader than that. No, he *thought* it was a British frigate, only we know better. You see, the admiral told me that both Bristol frigates are off station. One is meeting a homeward-bound convoy off Cape Finisterre while the other is being docked in Portsmouth. He hasn't told the Bristol merchants that the channel is unguarded; they would certainly raise some dust in Whitehall, as they pay in cash for the privilege of their own private navy.'

'But why are they standing into the Bristol Channel?' Fairview asked, unrolling the chart that he'd brought, just in case. 'There's no sympathy for the French in Wales or Cornwall or Devon, and it's the devil of a place to beat out of in any westerly wind.'

Fairview moved his hand across the wide mouth of the Bristol Channel and showed where it narrowed rapidly past Carmarthen Bay.

'Reaching down to the sou'east, you said, sir. There's nothing down there except the Devon coast. There's no chance at all of refitting without being seen, if that is their aim.'

'If you please, Mister Fairview,' Holbrooke said as he moved the master's hands away from the chart. 'I agree, a French frigate and brig would be reported immediately they anchored anywhere on the Devon coast, or indeed on the Welsh coast. I thought about the islands, but they are all so close to the shore that the masts of a frigate would be easily seen.'

He paused, again for effect.

'All that is except this one.'

Holbrooke's hand moved southeast of St. Govan's head, towards the bold headland of Hartland Point close to the border between Devon and Cornwall. There, eleven miles offshore, the chart showed a long thin island. There were no details, the draftsman who drew the chart clearly attached no importance to it, and even the name was in small, faded letters.

'Lundy Island. Does anyone know anything about it?'

He looked around his officers but found no help among the blank faces.

'I've never been there, sir, nor spoken to anyone who has,' Fairview admitted. 'From this chart I can't tell what sort of island it is, whether it has any anchorages or even whether it's inhabited.'

Shorrock and Jackson shook their heads. It was the sort

of place that King's ships had no business in visiting. The very fact that none of his officers knew anything about it spoke volumes about its status. Apart from the obvious danger that it posed to shipping heading up the Bristol Channel from the south, it appeared that there was no reason any sea officer should be aware of its existence.

'I heard something,' Chalmers said, in the silence that followed Fairview's confession. 'It's not much but there was some sort of scandal about the owner contracting to carry convicts to Virginia – that was why I noticed it – but taking them to Lundy instead and using them as slave labour in the fields there, and to enlarge some caves for smuggling. But he was found out at last, and the convicts were shipped across the Atlantic. I regret that's all I know; it was a short letter in a broadsheet, and I don't imagine many people read it.'

Holbrooke stared at the chart looking for inspiration. He had nothing better to go on, and Lundy must surely be the first place that he should search. At least Chalmers had offered something; if a ship could land convicts on the island, then it suggested that there may be an anchorage.

'Set a course for Lundy, Mister Fairview. If there's an anchorage it must surely be at the eastern side where it's sheltered, and there's just a hint of a little peninsula here at the southern end. There may be a bay there. In any case, we'll approach from the south and lie off that bay – if it exists – as soon as we can see enough to be safe.'

'Twilight about half an hour before the morning watch, sir, sunrise a few minutes after five o'clock.'

'Very well. Quarters and clear for action at six bells in the middle, Mister Shorrock.'

***

Holbrooke had stretched his long frame luxuriously across the lockers that extended right across the cabin under the stern windows. He was re-reading a letter from Samuel Ferrers who, true to his calling, had wasted no time in putting into writing the heads of the matters that they had discussed when viewing Mulberry House. The idea that he might become the owner of such a property was growing upon him, and although he and Ann had taken rides in the chaise far out into the country surrounding Wickham, in ever wider spirals, he had seen no other that so caught Ann's fancy. She was at heart a homebuilder, he knew, and her ideal would be to live close to or within the town where she had spent the past few years of her life. He hadn't mentioned living elsewhere because he had enough intuition to know that Ann was rooted to Wickham and her family that lived there. Strangely, it wasn't so much a desire to be near her father, but her stepmother. They were remarkably good friends, and Holbrooke could see the advantages of Ann being close to family support when he was away at sea.

Yes, Mulberry House was looking more attractive every time he thought of it. Under the previous reclusive owner, it had faded into obscurity behind its rampant growth of ivy. However, Holbrooke could imagine that with a young family and the consequent bustle and industry, and with some renovation, it would soon regain its status as the most notable house on the square. He would reply to Ferrers in encouraging terms, and he'd write to his father-in-law and ask his opinion. It was remarkable how Martin Featherstone's attitude had changed as soon as Holbrooke was promoted to post-captain. He'd spent two years resisting the growing intimacy between the young sea officer and his daughter, but as soon as Holbrooke was posted, all his objections had melted away. Now Holbrooke felt comfortable enough to ask his opinion, particularly on commercial matters of which his own father had no experience.

A knock at the door disturbed Holbrooke's reverie.

'Beg your pardon, sir,' said Jackson, his powerful frame blocking the evening light that would otherwise have streamed into the cabin.

'Not at all, Mister Jackson, please come in.'

'I've found someone who knows Lundy, sir.'

He ushered a short, dark-haired seaman into the cabin. The man was clearly ill-at-ease. It looked as though he'd never before set foot in the great cabin and he looked around himself with evident awe. Holbrooke smiled. His cabin was sparsely decorated when compared with other frigates. There was no carpet, no damask hangings and no silver lamps. It was all rather utilitarian but compared with the gun deck it must look like a palace. Holbrooke thought rapidly, running through the muster list for the man's name, but Jackson spoke before he had found it.

'Lewis, sir, main topman larboard watch. Go on, Lewis, tell Captain Holbrooke what you told me.'

Holbrooke remembered now. Lewis was a new man; he'd come to them from the impress tender at Portsmouth along with half a dozen others to replace the men that he'd lost in the battles against Batiste. He was marked as a volunteer but whether that was merely an artifice to secure his bounty, or whether he had really decided that life in a King's ship was for him, would never be known. He'd certainly learned his trade somewhere, otherwise Jackson would never have recommended that he be rated able seaman and would certainly not have given him the responsibility of the maintop.

Lewis looked uneasy and for a moment appeared tongue-tied, twisting his woollen Monmouth cap between his fingers. When he plucked up the courage to speak it was in the soft lilting tones of a native Welshman.

'Well, sir. I've been to Lundy a few times. I grew up on the Mumbles coast and my da' had a fishing boat that we used to take over to Lundy with supplies and bring back the fleeces. It used to be a regular thing then a new man bought the island and there were some funny goings-on. I haven't been there since.'

Holbrooke considered offering Lewis a chair, but he knew that would make him even more uneasy.

'Can you tell me anything about the anchorage?'

'Oh yes, sir…'

'Wait a moment, Lewis. Mister Jackson, would you pass the word for the master, the first lieutenant and the chaplain?'

They waited in silence. Lewis stood rigidly still, only his eyes swivelled, taking in the unfamiliar sights in the great cabin. Was it wise to bring in all the officers? Would Lewis be intimidated? He'd soon know.

Fairview arrived first, closely followed by Shorrock with Chalmers some two minutes later, still adjusting his stock. Holbrooke wasn't the only one to have been taking an afternoon break.

'Now Lewis. The anchorage first, then we'll go on to the island and its people.'

***

The Welsh seaman knew a surprising amount about the island. It came out hesitantly and he darted anxious glances either side as he spoke, but his confidence soon grew. Holbrooke smiled to himself. It must be a nerve-wracking experience speaking in front of the four officers who had the most power over his mortal body, and the chaplain who took care of his immortal soul.

Yes, there was an anchorage, and it was indeed at the southeast corner of the island as they had guessed. It was sheltered from westerlies and had a holding ground of sand and mud and broken shells in ten fathoms, half a mile from a little stone jetty. There was a castle overlooking the anchorage, but it hadn't been used for centuries, Lewis said, and it was in ruins. Marisco Castle it was called. There were only a handful of houses on the island and perhaps two dozen people, if there were any left there after the goings-on with the convicts.

As Lewis told his tale, Holbrooke became increasingly

convinced that he'd find the French ships were there; in fact it was the only place that was even remotely suitable for refitting a frigate away from prying eyes. Would the captain of *Les Jeux* know about Lundy? Probably Batiste did; he seemed to have known the coast of Britain better than any English sea officer, and he may well have passed that knowledge on to his captains. It could even have been a pre-determined rendezvous where they were all to meet up again.

'Well, thank you, Lewis,' Holbrooke said when his tale was evidently told. 'Is there nothing more that you can think of?'

Lewis shook his head, struck dumb again now that he'd finished.

'If I have any more questions, I'll pass the word. Now, my servant will give you a bottle of brandy for your mess tomorrow. Not tonight, we'll all need clear heads in the morning.'

Lewis grinned and nodded. He'd have preferred the bottle today, but tomorrow would do, or the next day, whenever they'd done what the captain had in mind.

***

'That makes things somewhat clearer,' Holbrooke said, when Lewis had left.

Fairview was positively beaming. With that information he could find his way to a safe anchorage, or he could lie off the bay in safety.

'Now I think of it,' said Chalmers, 'that description of the castle has reminded me of something else I know about Lundy. It was the last place to hold out for the royalists under the first Charles. It must have been a lonely outpost with the rest of the country held by parliament. The castle was old then, so I imagine it's crumbling by now.'

Holbrooke had remembered something too. It was nearly four years ago and at Saint Honorat Island in the Lerins group, off the Mediterranean coast of France. He'd been sent to negotiate with a suspected Moorish corsair, and his knowledge of that island had been no more than his knowledge now of Lundy. That expedition had turned out well; he just hoped this would be as easy.

***

CHAPTER TWENTY-NINE

Fatal Errors

Wednesday, Thirtieth of April 1760.
Argonaut, at Sea, off Lundy Island.

Holbrooke could sense Fairview moving around behind him and he could hear soft snuffling noises. The sailing master was actually sniffing the air, trying by some unfathomable means to determine what the wind would do next.

'It's veering, sir,' he said.

Holbrooke knew that. It had already shifted four points into the west and had dropped to nothing more than a moderate breeze, a profound change from the sou'westerly gales that had driven them here. The question was, would it veer further? A westerly wind would still allow him to come up to the anchorage without tacking. A nor'westerly would be right on the ship's head, a most inconvenient development.

'It'll haul further around yet,' the sailing master continued, remorselessly.

Holbrooke tried not to show his frustration. His plan had been to steal up to the anchorage with the first of the light and – if the Frenchmen were there – to anchor so as to shut them in, and then open negotiations for a surrender. He was heartily sick of the fighting that had already cost him half a dozen good men and he hoped to complete this business without further bloodshed. If he had to beat up to the anchorage, it would give the Frenchmen – he so hoped to find them there – an opportunity to cut and run. Then he'd be into a sea fight against another frigate of equal force.

'The men are at quarters, sir and the ship's cleared for action. I've provided battle lanterns but they're not lit.'

Shorrock had caught the mood of pessimism and he too was speaking in subdued tones.

'Very well, Mister Shorrock. What do you make of this wind?'

Shorrock wetted his finger and held it up to the breeze then he squinted at the binnacle compass.

'It'll veer some more yet, sir,' he said apologetically.

Holbrooke walked to the taffrail and back, scattering the three-pounder gun crews who crowded against the gunwale as he passed. The men were on edge, uneasy in the grey light of the pre-dawn. He saw that Fairview was looking at him questioningly.

'Hold your course, Master, full and by,' he said gruffly, trying to keep the disappointment out of his voice.

He was gambling that the wind would veer as far as the nor'west and no further. That would still allow him to execute his plan – just.

'Run out the larboard battery, Mister Shorrock.'

That would ease everyone's nerves. They would settle down when they heard the music of the gun carriages on the oak deck, when the sweat started to run down their backs.

***

'Land ho! Land two points on the larboard bow.'

Holbrooke didn't pause in his pacing. Fairview had made a perfect landfall again and that in the notorious tidal stream of the Bristol Channel.

'I can see it now,' said Fairview. 'Moderately tall cliffs, just as Lewis described it.'

Holbrooke steadied his telescope against the main shrouds. The land was just emerging from the gloom. Sunrise was still an hour away, but darkness was already in retreat. They would be off the anchorage in half an hour so long as the wind didn't veer more than three points.

'You're loaded with ball, Mister Shorrock?'

That was an unnecessary question and Holbrooke immediately regretted it. It was amazing how the captain's mood transmitted itself to the men and he could see his own edginess was replicated a hundred times in the faces of the gun crews. Shorrock wisely replied with a simple affirmative.

Slowly, with infinite elegance, the light increased, and the details of the island gradually emerged. Tall grey cliffs topped with salt-blasted grass. The sea that the gales had kicked up beat remorselessly on the southern shore, sending spray soaring as high as the main topmast head. The bulk of the southern part of the island was away to larboard and then the lower peninsula that sheltered the anchorage from southerly winds trended away towards their bow, stepping down in height until it ended in sea-washed outlying rocks.

'How close can we pass to those rocks,' Holbrooke asked, keeping the telescope to his eye.

There was no answer.

'Blast it! Get Lewis here.'

There was a commotion around number eight gun as Lewis hurried to the quarterdeck while his mates reorganised themselves to fill the gap that he left.

'How much water is there around those rocks?' Holbrooke asked without preamble.

Lewis knuckled his forehead and answered with a good deal more composure than Holbrooke had managed in his question. Holbrooke shook himself; this tension on the quarterdeck was fatal, and he felt that he'd been shown up by an able seaman.

'That's Rat Island, sir. There's maybe five fathom of water three cables off that furthest rock. But there's a nasty tide rip off that southern end, on the flood and the ebb.'

'Stay here beside the binnacle Lewis and sing out if you see anything you don't like.'

'Can't say that I know what the stream's doing, sir,' said Fairview, 'but it'll be fierce with it being just two days before spring tides.'

He gestured to where the thin silver crescent showed that the new moon was nigh, the new moon whose darkness gave life to the spring tides.

'In any case we'll know soon enough.'

Holbrooke bit back the retort that came close to

escaping his lips. It was unfair to expect the master to know the state of the tide in this forgotten corner of the kingdom. Not for the first time, he thought what an obvious boon to navigation it would be if the times of tides were printed in a table. After all, they were entirely predictable, as inevitable as the waxing and waning of the moon. The Admiralty or Trinity House really should look into that. Well, in a few minutes they'd be able to see the tidal stream against the shoreline and as they came closer, they'd get an idea of its height against the weed on the rocks. Then they'd be able to calculate with some accuracy the times of high and low water and the direction of the stream for as long as they stayed in this area. He took another look through the telescope.

'No closer than six cables off those rocks, Mister Fairview.'

Holbrooke saw the master look askance at Lewis who nodded briefly. The man's composure was impressive now that he was away from the great cabin. He wondered why he'd never noticed him before. Was he witnessing the birth of a future midshipman? He'd have to look more closely into this Welshman.

***

The wind was dropping still and already it had veered another point or two. *Argonaut* was as close hauled as could be, ghosting in around the point. It was obvious that they'd only just be able to make the anchorage without tacking.

Now the island was clearly visible and if there were any watchers on those cliffs, they would surely have seen *Argonaut*.

'You can see the castle, sir,' said Lewis, 'the square bit just atop the high land,' he added pointing across the larboard bow.

Holbrooke shifted his telescope fractionally. If he'd been expecting a ruin barely above ground level, he was sadly disappointed. Those walls looked square and sound. Perhaps it wasn't habitable, but it would be inconvenient if the French had mounted a couple of nine pounders up there.

'By the deep, eighteen.'

Fairview must have ordered the lead to be cast. He could expect steadily decreasing depths from here.

'Tide's flooding,' Fairview reported. 'I can see the race to the south of the island. God, it looks like about two knots! It's not dangerous for us but it will set us away from the anchorage.'

'And a half, fifteen.'

Fifteen fathoms and three feet, and still half a mile off the cliffs.

Holbrooke watched anxiously as Rat Island and its outlying rocks crept closer on the larboard bow. He desperately didn't want to be set up-channel by this flooding tide. If the French were there, this wind would give them an opportunity to slip out to the south and be away downchannel before *Argonaut* could beat back towards them. His mission would end in a hopeless stern chase where the best he could hope for was the capture of the brig, although even that would be in doubt if *Argonaut* were five miles to leeward.

'Deck there. I can see tops'ls over that island now. Looks like a man-o'-war.'

Then they are here! Holbrooke smashed his fist down upon the binnacle. Despite his misgivings this may all turn out well. He could see that the broken topmast had been repaired. The upper spars of the frigate – for that was clearly what she was – were intact.

Boom!

As if by magic a waterspout leapt from the sea half a cable from *Argonaut*'s larboard bow, like a long, white arm reaching from the depths. Excalibur wielded by the Lady of the Lake.

Boom!

A second spout, closer than the first.

'Eighteen pounders!' exclaimed Shorrock, 'or I'm a

Dutchman's uncle.'

'Twenty-fours, I think, Mister Shorrock,' said Fairview calmly. I remember in...'

'Silence on the quarterdeck. Look to your business.'

Holbrooke was in no mood to hear the conflicting opinions of his officers. Nevertheless, that was heavy artillery, presumably fired from the fort. He tended towards the twenty-four-pounder notion. That brig must have carried part of Batiste's siege train and the captain of the frigate was evidently an energetic man, to take the trouble to haul those ponderous weights ashore and up to the castle. Who knew what notions had persuaded Batiste and Fouquet to send a part of their heavy artillery away? Perhaps they realised that wherever they landed it would have to be a quick affair before an army could be sent to dislodge them, no time for landing heavy guns.

Boom, boom!

Closer now. Those were well-aimed shots. Whether Shorrock or Fairview were correct, that was far too heavy metal for the likes of *Argonaut*, and she had no means of replying. Nine pounders fired from close to the sea surface would be lucky to even reach a castle perched on a cliff, much less do any damage.

'Lewis! Can that castle command the whole anchorage?'

He knew the answer before Lewis opened his mouth.

'That it can sir. It's sited to cover the whole of the southeast side of the island.'

That settled it. *Argonaut* was not built to withstand the plunging fire of heavy artillery from fixed positions.

The next shot was followed by an almighty crash. Holbrooke grabbed the binnacle and was only saved from falling by the steady shoulder of Lewis. *Argonaut* staggered to a mighty blow amidships. He looked over into the waist. One gun was over on its side while another had been flung backwards to be brought up by the mainmast. Five or six men were on the deck. It was a frightful scene made worse by the cold, grey light of the still-hidden sun, making all the shapes indistinct and erasing the details. It looked like one of those charcoal-on-paper apocalyptic views of the underworld that had become so popular.

'Bear away, Mister Fairview. Take us out of range to the east as fast as ever you can.'

Holbrooke had time for one last thought: that was Lewis' gun that was down. Probably, if he hadn't been called to the quarterdeck, he'd be lying there with the others, sliding in a pool of his own blood as the frigate turned sharply to the east.

***

The boom of the twenty-four-pounders sounded like the minute guns of a funeral as *Argonaut* hurried east, pursued by the white pillars of water to remind them all that they were still in range, still in danger.

'Heave to, Mister Fairview,' said Holbrooke as five whole minutes passed without a shot from the French.

He needed time to think. His plan was in ruins and if that French captain was as enterprising as he appeared, then the frigate and the store ship were likely to escape entirely.

'Two killed outright, and the doctor has four under his care,' said Chalmers. 'Scottsdale and Gibbons.'

Holbrooke nodded, not trusting himself to make any comment. It was normally the first lieutenant who reported casualties, but a glance over the rail showed that Shorrock was busy supervising the remounting of one gun and replacing the breeching and train tackles on another. At quarters, Chalmers helped the doctor down below on the orlop when there were casualties but clearly that was all under control.

'A bloody business,' Chalmers added.

'Yes, bloody and futile, and it's not over yet,' Holbrooke replied brutally.

'Beg pardon, sir, but we're being set fast to the east by this tide, and the wind seems to have settled in the west at least for now.'

That was a measure of how dislocated things were in his

command. The sailing master never, ever begged his pardon. It was a firm rule that he could break into any conversation without apology when the navigation of the ship was in question.

Holbrooke looked towards the island. The sun had just appeared, and Lundy was revealed in all its glory. He could see the strong tidal rip off the southern tip of the island, a band of white water whipped up by the stream passing over the rocks. The combined influence of the tide and the wind had thankfully taken them away from danger before any more damage could be done, but now they were being set swiftly to the east, away from the island. Every second that he'd spent in self-recriminations, wallowing in his own misery, his ship had been set further and further away from the island. He shook his head to clear away the depressing thoughts.

'Bring her onto the wind, Mister Fairview. Let's beat back towards the island.'

'Aye-aye, sir,' Fairview replied. 'We won't make much westing until the tide turns.'

Holbrooke knew that and was tempted to berate the master for pointing out the obvious, but he knew that he'd indulged his temper too much already this morning. In the back of his mind lurked the thought that if he'd been in a more positive frame of mind, he'd have anticipated all the woes that had befallen his ship. He should have anticipated the French fortifying the anchorage and a proper reading of the wind and tides should have told him that his plan was flawed.

'We'll do the best we can, Mister Fairview.'

Down in the waist he could see that the bosun and the gunner had set up a complicated cat's cradle of tackles and nets to hoist the nine-pounder back onto its carriage, while the other gun was already re-rigged and ready for service. Two men were scrubbing the dark stains from the deck and scattering fresh sand to help the men keep a grip as they hauled at the tackles.

'Deck there! The frigate's weighing anchor and making sail. The brig too.'

Then they'd abandoned the heavy guns and were making a dash for safety. Quite right too. He tried to think himself into his opponent's shoes. He'd seen off one enemy frigate, but when he'd last seen this same British ship, it had two consorts. Perhaps they were close by and would be brought hurrying to the sound of the guns. This was no time for heroics and certainly no time to be caught at anchor, particularly if the wind should shift into the east.

Holbrooke watched as the two vessels rounded Rat Island and hauled their wind on the starboard tack, bucking and plunging as they cut across the vicious tidal stream to the south of the island. They were making for Land's End of course, less than thirty leagues to the south-sou'west. And from Land's End the wind was set fair for France. They could be around the corner and into the Chops of the Channel before dawn tomorrow. Holbrooke could see this mission slipping away from him.

'Wind's stuck in the west, sir. It'll be a long chase,' said Fairview.

Holbrooke looked aloft. They were carrying all the sails that would set for tacking to windward, and still they were losing ground. The Frenchmen would be out of the worst of the tide in half an hour while he would have to battle against it until it turned.

***

A long chase indeed, and *Argonaut* was having the worst of it. By the time Fairview had coaxed the frigate through the Lundy tidal race, the Frenchmen had disappeared into the southwest. The wind had proved fickle and had backed again, a point or so south of west, and it had brought a thin mist with it, so that when the hands were called for dinner, there was no sign of the Frenchmen at all. Even the brig had managed to make more ground than *Argonaut*.

'Well, at least we know where they are going. They must have completed their repairs the day before we arrived off

Lundy and now they have only one thing on their minds, to get home to France.'

Holbrooke was being deliberately optimistic. In his heart he knew that the morning's debacle had been largely caused by his own frame of mind. He'd spent too much time in gloomy introspection and had not paid enough attention to the rapidly changing tactical situation. The shifting wind, the tidal race, the guns on the castle, the enemy's escape; if he hadn't been mired in misery and self-doubt, he would have predicted all of these and changed his plan accordingly. And his officers and the men had detected his mood and themselves been affected by it. How much of that was caused by the other matters on his mind? Family, political career, a house purchase. He needed to focus on the business at hand.

'We'll be off the Longships at dawn if the wind holds,' said Fairview. 'If we're lucky we'll sight them before they can put before the wind'.

That was the danger, Holbrooke knew. Once around the Longships, those perilous islands that lay menacingly to the north and west of Land's End, the frigate and brig would be able to reach across to Brest or run up the channel to any of the Brittany ports. Even a brig could contrive to stay out of a British frigate's reach if they had a few hours head start at the Longships.

'Look to your steering and sail trimming, Mister Fairview. If they're not in sight at dawn, we'll have lost them.'

***

CHAPTER THIRTY

A Bitter Failure

Thursday, First of May 1760.
Argonaut, at Sea, off Land's End.

'Deck there! Nothing in sight, nothing but those fishing boats on the larboard bow.'

The lookout knew that his captain was in the foretop, scanning the horizon through his telescope, and he was being more than usually diligent in reporting everything, to avoid being found at fault. The whole ship knew that it was better not to cross the captain today. He wasn't a flogging man – the cat had been out of the bag only once in the commission – nor did he encourage starting or gagging or any of the other lesser punishments that were customarily used at sea, but nobody was prepared to push him, not after yesterday.

The wind had failed towards the end of the middle watch and now *Argonaut* was struggling to make better than two knots, and that was the bare minimum for steerage way. And the tidal stream was against them. If the French had made it into the Channel before the tide turned, there'd be no catching them.

As the day dawned the outline of the Cornish shore became clear, although Holbrooke couldn't make out any distinguishing features. It was just an iron-bound coast of high cliffs and pounding surf, even in this moderate wind. If the master's reckoning was accurate – and it usually was – they should sight the Longships soon, on the larboard bow. Probably that was what had attracted that cluster of fishing boats; the Longships were famed as a productive, though dangerous, mark.

'Deck there. I can see islands four points – no five points – in the larboard bow.'

Holbrooke shifted his telescope further around to

larboard. Yes, he could see the islands. He'd rounded the Longships once or twice before and somehow these seemed different, and surely he shouldn't be able to see land to the right of them.

'That's the Brisons, sir.' Fairview shouted from the quarterdeck, using the speaking trumpet. 'The Longships will be about five miles ahead.'

Holbrooke was pleased to hear that Fairview sounded a little brighter this morning. He moved his telescope towards the bow, but the visibility was only about three miles, at best.

'You know what you're looking for?' Holbrooke shouted up to the lookout.

'Aye, sir,' he replied from his lofty perch, 'that bloody frigate and the little brig.'

'Then keep a good lookout.'

He folded his telescope and made his careful way back to the deck. He knew he was being watched by everyone whose eyes weren't being used for the ship's business. It was a rare event to see a post-captain aloft and there was a morbid curiosity to see whether he would put a foot wrong and slip on the ratlines. The bosun was poised to run up to his rescue.

However, he made it safely down to the fo'c'sle and walked back along the gangway to the quarterdeck. He passed Lewis who was slapping some paint on the raw scars left by yesterday's twenty-four-pound cannon ball.

'Will we catch 'em today, your honour?' he asked, knuckling his forehead.

Holbrooke was momentarily startled. It wasn't usual for a seaman to address a post-captain without being invited.

'Eh? Oh, I hope so, Lewis, but if they're ten miles ahead of us I'm afraid they may escape.'

'Well, we owe them one, sir,' Lewis replied, 'for my messmates.'

'We certainly do,' Holbrooke replied, 'we certainly do.'

***

Holbrooke had retired to his cabin when a knock at the door heralded the arrival of Chalmers. The chaplain had his usual grave countenance, but he managed a smile for his friend.

'Will we catch them, do you think, George?'

'It's strange, isn't it, David. Only two men on board presume to ask me that question. The chaplain and an able seaman.'

'Everyone else is walking on eggshells around you,' Chalmers replied with a smile. 'I do believe that you are becoming a tartar.'

Holbrooke raised an eyebrow and contrived to smile at the same time. They had often discussed whether it was necessary to be a tyrant to be an effective leader.

'Well, I don't know about that, but I do know that if we don't sight them before we pass around Land's End, then I shall make for Portsmouth. I've been phrasing my report, in my head, you understand, and it won't make pretty reading:

The frigate and brig made sail close-hauled to the southwest and Argonaut, under my command, was unable to come up with them. They are assumed to have rounded the Longships and escaped to a port on the French coast.

'If I'm ever employed again after that it will be a miracle. There's no value in whingeing about the tide race off Lundy, or the changeable wind; a captain who can't even catch a fat old brig, let alone another frigate, is unlikely to meet with their Lordships' pleasure. Admiral Holburne didn't have to send *Argonaut*, you know. I do believe he sent us as a compliment to me, and I've let him down.'

Chalmers nodded in sympathy. Privately he thought that Holbrooke was being pessimistic. He had a string of other successes to his credit that should at least outweigh this failure. And in any case, it wasn't over yet.

***

'Deck there! Sail on the larboard bow, it's that French brig, sir.'

The lookout's hail came floating through the cabin

skylight. Holbrooke was on his feet in an instant, all thought of waiting for a messenger from the quarterdeck was gone in his urgent need to come to grips with the enemy.

Every telescope on the quarterdeck was trained on the larboard bow. A midshipman nudged Fairview to warn him that the captain was hurrying up the ladder.

'He's steering inside the Longships, sir.'

Holbrooke didn't comment but stared hard through his telescope. Yes, that was the French brig and it certainly appeared to be committed to the dangerous passage inside the islands. He scanned the sea forward. Nothing, no sign of the frigate. Had the French captain raced on ahead, intent on saving himself and his ship and leaving the brig to fend for itself? That would not be an unreasonable course of action. The brig, now presumably empty of its muskets and siege artillery, was worth little to King Louis. The frigate, on the other hand, was the last surviving man-o'-war of this misconceived expedition and its survival had a morale effect beyond its intrinsic value.

'Masthead! Any sign of the frigate?'

'Nothing sir, just that old brig and a few fishermen.'

Holbrooke forced himself to stand still when every fibre of his being wanted to pace backwards and forwards to the taffrail while he made his decision. If he chased the brig then the frigate – wherever it was – would almost certainly get away. There was a chance that it may blunder into units of the Channel Squadron, but it was surprising how easily a ship could cross to France without ever being seen. If he ignored the brig and went in search of the frigate, he may never find it, and then he'd have nothing to show for his efforts. The brig it must be. He opened his mouth to give the order that would bring *Argonaut* off the wind to intercept the brig as it left the inside passage.

'Deck ho! Sail! Sail right on the bow. It looks like the frigate, sir.'

Holbrooke moved swiftly to the starboard side of the quarterdeck and steadied his telescope against the main shrouds. He could see nothing, just a blank wall of moist air that hung like a curtain a league ahead of the frigate.

'Mister Petersen. Aloft with you and tell me what you see.'

Petersen ran up the fore shrouds like a topman. In no time at all his report came back strongly.

'It's the French frigate, sir, for sure. He's bearing away towards the sou'east under all sail, just on the edge of the visibility, coming and going.'

Holbrooke took a pace towards the taffrail then stopped dead. Really there was no decision. If King Louis valued his frigates more than a hired brig then so did King George value a prize frigate more than a prize brig. Certainly, the capture of the brig was a near certainty while the frigate had already shown that he wouldn't be easy to catch, but nevertheless, the frigate it must be.

'There's your chase, Mister Fairview,' he said pointing ahead, 'put me alongside him as soon as possible, if you please.'

***

It was a chase, perhaps, but it had none of the drama and excitement that the word conjured up. The brig was quickly lost to sight astern and that underlined the fact that Holbrooke had no more choices to make. *Argonaut* pursued the will-o'-the-wisp that was *Les Jeux* all that day, never sighting it from the quarterdeck. It hovered tantalisingly on the edge of visibility from the masthead, neither gaining nor losing distance.

'He's steering sou'east by east, sir,' Fairview reported. It looks like he's making for Saint-Malo. I expect he doesn't fancy running into the Channel Squadron off Brest.'

True enough, Holbrooke thought, and if anywhere in the Channel, the approaches to Brest would be the place to find British men-o'-war. They'd been blockading the French Atlantic fleet since the start of the war and no doubt would do so to the end.

'Don't forget that he's a privateer, really, and probably

doesn't hold a King's commission, and his ship is only hired by the French navy. Saint-Malo is a privateering port, after all.'

'He won't want too much officialdom around when he has to report that he left the brig behind,' Shorrock added with a grin. 'Saint-Malo won't jump to judgement as quickly as Brest, and he'll hope that the brig makes it home before he's called to account.'

In this weather, with this visibility, Holbrooke thought, it was five to one against the brig being taken. For that matter, it was five to one against the frigate being taken unless *Argonaut* could find some wind, or another British cruiser came onto the scene to cut off the retreat.

'A gun every two minutes to windward, Mister Shorrock, let's see if we can bring down reinforcements.'

On and on they sailed, the guns dolefully marking the passage of time. In the afternoon watch the breeze strengthened slightly but didn't improve the visibility. It was one of those dread Channel days when sea and sky mingled, and the sun just failed to break through. Everything was in shades of the lightest grey.

Sunset, and still they hadn't gained on the *Les Jeux*. They were in mid-channel now and the Frenchman's course hadn't deviated. He was steering for Saint-Malo without a doubt and in this uncertain wind he was relying on the effect of the tidal streams to even out over the passage. *Argonaut* held its course through the night. Holbrooke didn't leave the deck and nor did Fairview. They both paced the quarterdeck through the long dark watches lost in their own thoughts.

***

'Deck there. Nothing on the horizon, nothing all round.'

Sunrise, and the mist had lifted to reveal a cloudless sky and sparkling sea. The wind had shifted back to the sou'west, and it was blowing a moderate breeze, it was the sort of day that sailors prayed for, but of the French frigate, there was nothing to be seen.

Holbrooke ordered a reverse of course in the hope of finding the brig. The wind shift had been their first piece of luck since they left the Scilly Isles. Now they could reach to the nor'west two points free on the larboard tack. The hands were enjoying themselves even if the weather hadn't lifted the gloom from the quarterdeck, and there was smiling and skylarking for all.

'We'll press on until the Lizard's abeam, Mister Fairview.'

If earnest searching was worthy of fortune's favour, then it ignored *Argonaut* all day and at eight bells in the first dog watch Holbrooke reluctantly ordered a course up-channel for Portsmouth. He retreated to his cabin to sup from the cup of bitterness in solitude, but it was not to be. First the purser arrived with his accounts to be signed, then the clerk who wondered whether he was ready to write his report – *come back tomorrow, blast you* – then the first lieutenant to remind him that he should visit the sickbay. It wasn't until the sun had set on that disastrous day that he was at last able to be alone.

He tried again for isolation. He attempted to read a book and for a while he stared abstractedly out of the stern windows, and lastly attempted to formulate the report that he must make to Admiral Holburne. The words wouldn't come, and he found that today, this evening, solitude didn't suit him after all, and he passed the word for Chalmers.

***

'You are not yourself, I find, George,' Chalmers said after he had settled down with a glass of Madeira.

'Well, that's one way of putting it,' Holbrooke replied. 'I was sent to bring in an enemy frigate and a storeship – not a particularly difficult task, you would think – and I must return having done neither, and I've lost some valuable seamen into the bargain, and sustained significant damage to His Majesty's property. I'll find that hard to explain in my report and I don't relish Admiral Holburne's remarks on the subject.'

'Come now,' Chalmers said, 'I find that you sea officers are far too literal in your reports of proceedings. There's always another way to describe a situation. Remember that Admiral Holburne has to report to the Admiralty Board, and he needs ammunition to justify his sending a single frigate on this mission. We must make things easy for the admiral, mustn't we?'

Holbrooke looked at him sceptically.

'Go on.'

'You cleared out the last of a French expedition from British waters, didn't you?'

'Well, yes…'

'And there are two valuable siege guns waiting to be collected from Lundy.'

Holbrooke leaned forward, interested now despite his gloom.

'And if I may be so callous, in this case a few casualties only underline the fact that you didn't shrink for doing your duty. I would say that a well-written report can mitigate most of the evil consequences of this cruise. Would you like me to make a first draft?'

***

HISTORICAL EPILOGUE

Europe in mid-1760

Broken at Lagos Bay and Quiberon Bay in 1759, and after losing a third of its ships trying to maintain New France, the French navy in the middle months of 1760 was in no state to contest the mastery of the oceans and had largely abandoned any plans for an invasion of England. The diversionary raid to the north of Britain had ended in abject failure and the loss of three frigates and two whole regiments that King Louis could ill afford. Versailles now accepted that it was only by diverting its resources to the army in Germany that anything could be salvaged from this ruinous war. Assaulted by large and vigorous French armies, the allied forces could only hold the line in Hanover.

North America in mid-1760

After a fearful winter in Quebec, the British army was defeated at the battle of Sainte-Foy in April 1760, just a short walk from where Wolfe had beaten Montcalm in the previous year. However, the French commander at Sainte-Foy, the Chevalier de Lévis, was unable to follow up his success and when in May a British navy squadron sailed up the Saint Lawrence as the ice melted; it was all over for New France. The promised French squadron failed to materialise after the terrible defeats that the French navy suffered at Lagos Bay and Quiberon Bay, and the supply ships were sunk at the Battle of Restigouche.

Lacking men, provisions and even a clear means of communication with France, and with British armies closing in on three sides, Montreal surrendered in September. The long dream of New France was over.

The Long War

The powerful squadron that Admiral Saunders took into the Mediterranean in 1760 was calculated not only to pin down the French in Toulon, but to make it clear to the King of Spain that only defeat awaited him if he should join the war on France's side. France had already lost substantial possessions in North America, West Africa and India, and only its sugar islands in the Caribbean remained largely intact.

France had nothing to bring to the table in any peace negotiations and fought on in the hope of luring Spain into the conflict to turn the tide. Without Spain, France could not see a way to end the war with its remaining colonies – and its honour – intact, yet Spain couldn't afford to enter the war and was fearful of the consequences if it did. The bloody stalemate had a few years yet to run.

***

FACT MEETS FICTION
François Thurot

Historical novelists face a dilemma each time they set about a new work: when to use real, historical characters and when to invent their own. In general, I prefer to use the real people whenever I can, and particularly when they are well-known to readers of history. Nevertheless, I occasionally have to create my own characters so that I can adjust the timeline without misrepresenting the historical facts.

The character of the commander of the French naval forces in *Nor'west by North* – Philippe Batiste – is just such a case. He is inspired by a real person, François Thurot, whose name was on every Englishman's tongue in 1760. Thurot was a remarkable man whose career included privateering, smuggling, intelligence work, imprisonment in England and, finally, command of an expedition to land an army in the north of Britain. The plan was the brainchild of the French secretary of state for war, the Maréchal de Belle-Isle, and he gave Thurot a temporary commission in the navy to command the ships of the squadron. Thurot's expedition was timed to coincide with the main landing in the south of England which would be accomplished when the French Atlantic and Mediterranean fleets joined forces and won control of the English Channel. That grand strategy was soundly defeated when Hawke caught Conflans' ships at Quiberon Bay and, in a rising storm on a lee shore, utterly destroyed them. That story is told in *Rocks and Shoals*, the eighth in the Carlisle and Holbrooke series.

Unfortunately for Thurot, his squadron sailed from Dunkirk before the news of Quiberon Bay reached him, and he had to take the long way home by circumnavigating Britain. After a brief landing in Carrickfergus, the expedition was caught by a British squadron off the Isle of Man. Thurot died in the fight and all his ships were captured. That set the background to the plot for *Nor'west by North*.

The story is told from the perspective of George Holbrooke because that is the purpose of this series of books. Nevertheless, I hope that I have offered, by imitation, an insight into the genius of that great Frenchman, François Thurot.

If you are inspired to discover more about Thurot, I have noted in the bibliography the details of a book that I found useful.

Nor'west by North is dedicated, with the deepest respect, to the memory of François Thurot.

***

Francis Holburne

Vice Admiral Holburne, on the other hand, really was the port admiral at Portsmouth in 1760. I have portrayed him as a formidable – even frightening – figure, and that does appear to have been his true nature. If you doubt it, take a look at his likeness painted by Joshua Reynolds which you can find on the British National Maritime Museum's website. It's one of the most believable portraits that I know from that time, and Reynolds has made no attempt to flatter him or to soften his character. To me, it shows a hard, uncompromising, thoroughly professional fighting admiral. I wouldn't have liked to be on the wrong end of Holburne's investigation into my conduct.

***

The Porto Bello Coin

Life is full of astonishing chance encounters. I was sitting at my desk puzzling over a way to describe the perils of serving officers dabbling in politics in the eighteenth century, when my wife Lucia suggested a trip to Wickham. Holbrooke's hometown is only ten miles from our home and there, in a glass case in a small antique shop on the square, a dull golden gleam caught my eye. It was a Porto Bello coin, and

I snapped it up for the princely sum of eight pounds. Eight pounds! That's coffee for two and a shared slice of cake, not a vast sum to pay for a genuine two-hundred-and-sixty-year-old artefact. I knew of these coins, I'd seen illustrations in books, but had never handled one, and there in the palm of my hand was the answer to my quest. Admiral Vernon is the perfect illustration of a sea officer brought low by politics, and the coin was acquired within fifty yards of Martin Featherstone's house and just half a mile from Rookesbury House and the Holbrooke cottage. Perhaps it's the very one that belonged to the old sailing master.

The coin is just as David Chalmers described it in chapter five, worn and tarnished but with all its fascinating details still visible. The thing that struck me was how ordinary it is; it clearly wasn't intended for the great and good of society. I can imagine it being slapped down on the table in the King's Head to underscore a political point in an argument between a tenant farmer and a carpenter. Now it sits on my desk as I write, conjuring the eighteenth century into the twenty-first and reminding me of the wonderful coincidences that follow us on this extraordinary journey that we know as life.

***

OTHER BOOKS IN THE SERIES

Book 1: The Colonial Post-Captain

Captain Carlisle of His Britannic Majesty's frigate *Fury* hails from Virginia, a loyal colony of the British Crown. In 1756, as the clouds of war gather in Europe, *Fury* is ordered to Toulon to investigate a French naval and military build-up.

While battling the winter weather, Carlisle must also juggle with delicate diplomatic issues in this period of phoney war and contend with an increasingly belligerent French frigate.

And then there is the beautiful Chiara Angelini, pursued across the Mediterranean by a Tunisian corsair who appears determined to abduct her, yet strangely reluctant to shed blood.

Carlisle and his young master's mate, George Holbrooke, are witnesses to the inconclusive sea-battle that leads to the loss of Minorca. They engage in a thrilling and bloody encounter with the French frigate and a final confrontation with the enigmatic corsair.

Book 2: The Leeward Islands Squadron

In late 1756, as the British government collapses in the aftermath of the loss of Minorca and the country and navy are thrown into political chaos, a small force of ships is sent to the West Indies to reinforce the Leeward Islands Squadron.

Captain Edward Carlisle, a native of Virginia, and his first lieutenant George Holbrooke are fresh from the Mediterranean and their capture of a powerful French man-of-war. Their new frigate *Medina* has orders to join a squadron commanded by a terminally ill commodore. Their mission: a near-suicidal assault on a strong Caribbean island fortress. Carlisle must confront the challenges of higher command as he leads the squadron back into battle to accomplish the Admiralty's orders.

Join Carlisle and Holbrooke as they attack shore fortifications, engage in ship-on-ship duels and deal with mutiny in the West Indies.

Book 3: The Jamaica Station

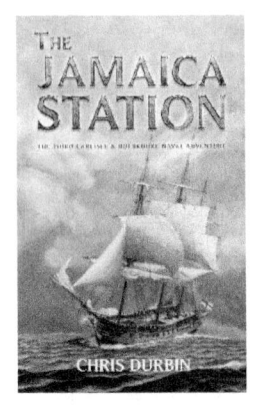

It is 1757, and the British navy is regrouping from a slow start to the seven years war.

A Spanish colonial governor and his family are pursued through the Caribbean by a pair of mysterious ships from the Dutch island of St. Eustatius. The British frigate *Medina* rescues the governor from his hurricane-wrecked ship, leading Captain Edward Carlisle and his first lieutenant George Holbrooke into a web of intrigue and half-truths. Are the Dutchmen operating under a letter of marque or are they pirates, and why are they hunting the Spaniard? Only the diplomatic skills of Carlisle's aristocratic wife, Lady Chiara, can solve the puzzle.

When Carlisle is injured, the young Holbrooke must grow up quickly. Under his leadership, *Medina* takes part in a one-sided battle with the French that will influence a young Horatio Nelson to choose the navy as a career.

Book 4: Holbrooke's Tide

It is 1758, and the Seven Years War is at its height. The Duke of Cumberland's Hanoverian army has been pushed back to the River Elbe while the French are using the medieval fortified city of Emden to resupply their army and to anchor its left flank.

George Holbrooke has recently returned from the Jamaica Station in command of a sloop-of-war. He is under orders to survey and blockade the approaches to Emden in advance of the arrival of a British squadron. The French garrison and their Austrian allies are nervous. With their supply lines cut, they are in danger of being isolated when the French army is forced to retreat in the face of the new Prussian-led army that is gathering on the Elbe. Can the French be bluffed out of Emden? Is this Holbrooke's flood tide that will lead to his next promotion?

Holbrooke's Tide is the fourth of the Carlisle & Holbrooke naval adventures. The series follows the exploits of the two men through the Seven Years War and into the period of turbulent relations between Britain and her American colonies in the 1760s.

Book 5: The Cursed Fortress

The French called it *La Forteresse Maudite*, the Cursed Fortress.

Louisbourg stood at the mouth of the Gulf of Saint Lawrence, massive and impregnable, a permanent provocation to the British colonies. It was Canada's first line of defence, guarding the approaches to Quebec, from where all New France lay open to invasion. It had to fall before a British fleet could be sent up the Saint Lawrence. Otherwise, there would be no resupply and no line of retreat; Canada would become the graveyard of George II's navy.

A failed attempt on Louisbourg in 1757 had only stiffened the government's resolve; the Cursed Fortress must fall in 1758.

Captain Carlisle's frigate joins the blockade of Louisbourg before winter's icy grip has eased. Battling fog, hail, rain, frost and snow, suffering scurvy and fevers, and with a constant worry about the wife he left behind in Virginia, Carlisle will face his greatest test of leadership and character yet.

The Cursed Fortress is the fifth of the Carlisle & Holbrooke naval adventures. The series follows the two men through the Seven Years War and into the period of turbulent relations between Britain and her American colonies in the 1760s.

Book 6: Perilous Shore

Amphibious warfare was in its infancy in the mid-eighteenth century – it was the poor relation of the great fleet actions that the navy so loved.

That all changed in 1758 when the British government demanded a campaign of raids on the French Channel ports. Command arrangements were hastily devised, and a whole new class of vessels was produced at breakneck speed: flatboats, the ancestors of the landing craft that put the allied forces ashore on D-Day.

Commander George Holbrooke's sloop *Kestrel* is in the thick of the action: scouting landing beaches, duelling with shore batteries and battling the French Navy.

In a twist of fate, Holbrooke finds himself unexpectedly committed to this new style of amphibious warfare as he is ordered to lead a division of flatboats onto the beaches of Normandy and Brittany. He meets his greatest test yet when a weary and beaten British army retreats from a second failed attempt at Saint Malo with the French close on their heels.

Perilous Shore is the sixth of the Carlisle & Holbrooke naval adventures. The series follows Holbrooke and his mentor, Captain Carlisle, through the Seven Years War and into the period of turbulent relations between Britain and her American colonies in the 1760s.

Book 7: Rocks and Shoals

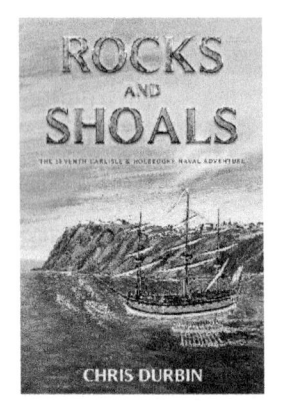

With the fall of Louisbourg in 1758 the French in North America were firmly on the back foot. Pitt's grand strategy for 1759 was to launch a three-pronged attack on Canada. One army would move north from Lake Champlain while another smaller force would strike across the wilderness to Lake Ontario and French-held Fort Niagara. A third, under Admiral Saunders and General Wolfe, would sail up the Saint Lawrence, where no battle fleet had ever been, and capture Quebec.

Captain Edward Carlisle sails ahead of the battle fleet to find a way through the legendary dangers of the Saint Lawrence River. An unknown sailing master assists him; James Cook has a talent for surveying and cartography and will achieve immortality in later years.

There are rocks and shoals aplenty before Carlisle and his frigate *Medina* are caught up in the near-fatal indecision of the summer when General Wolfe tastes the bitterness of early setbacks.

Rocks and Shoals is the seventh of the Carlisle & Holbrooke naval adventures. The series follows Carlisle and his protégé George Holbrooke, through the Seven Years War and into the period of turbulent relations between Britain and her American colonies in the 1760s.

Book 8: Niagara Squadron

Fort Niagara is the key to the American continent. Whoever owns that lonely outpost at the edge of civilisation controls the entire Great Lakes region.

Pitt's grand strategy for 1759 is to launch a three-pronged attack on Canada. One army would move north from Lake Champlain, a second would sail up the Saint Lawrence to capture Quebec, and a third force would strike across the wilderness to Lake Ontario and French-held Fort Niagara.

Commander George Holbrooke is seconded to command the six hundred boats to carry the army through the rivers and across Lake Ontario. That's the easy part; he also must deal with two powerful brigs that guarantee French naval superiority on the lake.

Holbrooke knows time is running out to be posted as captain before the war ends and promotions dry up; his rank is the stumbling block to his marriage to Ann, waiting for him in his hometown of Wickham Hampshire.

Niagara Squadron is the eighth Carlisle and Holbrooke novel. The series follows Carlisle and his protégé Holbrooke through the Seven Years War and into the period of turbulent relations between Britain and her American colonies in the 1760's.

Book 9: Ligurian Mission

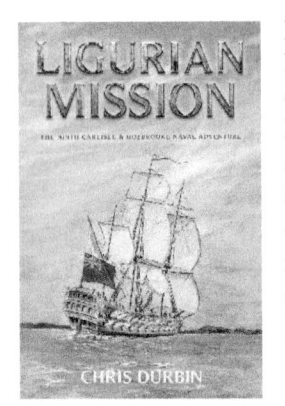

It is the summer of 1760 and the British navy reigns supreme on the oceans of the world; only in the Mediterranean is its mastery still seriously challenged. Admiral Saunders is sent with a squadron of ships-of-the-line to remind those nations that are still neutral of the consequences of siding with the French.

Edward Carlisle's ship Dartmouth is sent to the Ligurian Sea. His mission: to carry the British envoy to the Kingdom of Sardinia back to its capital, Turin, then to investigate the ships being built in Genoa for the French.

He soon finds that the game of diplomacy is played for high stakes, and the countries bordering the Ligurian Sea are hotbeds of intrigue and treachery, where family loyalties count for little.

Carlisle must contend with the arrogance of the envoy, the Angelini family's duplicity and a vastly superior French seventy-four-gun ship whose captain is determined to bring the Genoa ships safely to Toulon.

Ligurian Mission is the ninth Carlisle and Holbrooke novel. The series follows Carlisle and his protégé Holbrooke through the Seven Years War and into the period of turbulent relations between Britain and her American colonies prior to their bid for independence.

BIBLIOGRAPHY

The following is a selection of the many books that I consulted in researching the Carlisle & Holbrooke series:

Definitive Text

Sir Julian Corbett wrote the original, definitive text on the Seven Years War. Most later writers use his work as a steppingstone to launch their own.

Corbett, LLM., Sir Julian Stafford. *England in the Seven Years War – Vol. I: A Study in Combined Strategy*. Normandy Press. Kindle Edition.

Strategy and Naval Operations

Three very accessible modern books cover the strategic context and naval operations of the Seven Years War. Daniel Baugh addresses the whole war on land and sea, while Martin Robson concentrates on maritime activities. Jonathan Dull has produced a very readable account from the French perspective.

Baugh, Daniel. *The Global Seven Years War 1754-1763*. Pearson Education, 2011. Print.
Robson, Martin. *A History of the Royal Navy, The Seven Years War*. I.B. Taurus, 2016. Print.
Dull, Jonathan, R. *The French Navy and the Seven Years' War*. University of Nebraska Press, 2005. Print.

Sea Officers

For an interesting perspective on the life of sea officers of the mid-eighteenth century, I'd read Augustus Hervey's Journal, with the cautionary note that while Hervey was by no means typical of the breed, he's very entertaining and devastatingly honest. For a more balanced view, I'd read British Naval Captains of the Seven Years War.

Erskine, David (editor). *Augustus Hervey's Journal, The Adventures Afloat and Ashore of a Naval Casanova*. Chatham Publishing, 2002. Print.

McLeod, A.B. *British Naval Captains of the Seven Years War, The View from the Quarterdeck*. The Boydell Press, 2012. Print.

Life at Sea

I recommend The Wooden World for an overview of shipboard life and administration during the Seven Years War.

N.A.M Rodger. *The Wooden World, An Anatomy of the Georgian Navy*. Fontana Press, 1986. Print.

François Thurot

The plot of *Nor'west by North* was inspired by the exploits of the famous French privateer and commander of an ill-fated expedition to land an army in the north of Britain. The best text that I found was written in English.

Young, G.V.C. and Foster, Caroline. *Captain Francois Thurot. Privateer, Agent Extraordinaire, Smuggler, Saboteur-Elect and Naval Officer*. Mansk-Svenska Publishing, 1986. Print.

THE AUTHOR

Chris Durbin grew up in the seaside town of Porthcawl in South Wales. His first experience of sailing was as a sea cadet in the treacherous tideway of the Bristol Channel, and at the age of sixteen, he spent a week in a tops'l schooner in the Southwest Approaches. He was a crew member on the Porthcawl lifeboat before joining the navy.

Chris spent twenty-four years as a warfare officer in the Royal Navy, serving in all classes of ships from aircraft carriers through destroyers and frigates to the smallest minesweepers. He took part in operational campaigns in the Falkland Islands, the Middle East and the Adriatic and he spent two years teaching tactics at a US Navy training centre in San Diego.

On his retirement from the Royal Navy, Chris joined a large American company and spent eighteen years in the aerospace, defence and security industry, including two years on the design team for the Queen Elizabeth class aircraft carriers.

Chris is a graduate of the Britannia Royal Naval College at *Dartmouth*, the British Army Command and Staff College, the United States Navy War College (where he gained a postgraduate diploma in national security decision-making) and Cambridge University (where he was awarded an MPhil in International Relations).

With a lifelong interest in naval history and a long-standing ambition to write historical fiction, Chris has completed the first ten novels in the Carlisle & Holbrooke series, which follow the fortunes of a colonial Virginian and a Hampshire man who both command ships of King George's navy during the middle years of the eighteenth century.

The series will follow its principal characters through the Seven Years War and into the period of turbulent relations between Britain and her American Colonies in the 1760s. They'll negotiate some thought-provoking loyalty issues when British policy and colonial restlessness lead inexorably to the American Revolution.

Chris lives on the south coast of England, surrounded by hundreds of years of naval history. His three children are all busy growing their own families and careers while Chris and his wife (US Navy, retired) of thirty-nine years enjoy sailing their Cornish Shrimper 21 on the south coast.

Fun Fact:

Chris shares his garden with a tortoise named Aubrey. If you've read Patrick O'Brian's *HMS Surprise*, or have seen the 2003 film *Master and Commander: The Far Side of the World*, you'll recognise the modest act of homage that Chris has paid to that great writer. Rest assured that Aubrey has not yet grown to the gigantic proportions of *Testudo Aubreii*.

FEEDBACK

If you've enjoyed *Nor'west by North*, please consider leaving a review on Amazon.

This is the latest of a series of books that will follow Carlisle and Holbrooke through the Seven Years War and into the 1760s when relations between Britain and her restless American Colonies are tested to breaking point.

Look out for the eleventh in the Carlisle & Holbrooke series, coming soon.

You can follow my blog at:

www.chris-durbin.com

Printed in Great Britain
by Amazon